Unspoken

Unspoken

a novel

Laurie Lewis

Covenant Communications, Inc.

Cover image © PhotoDisc Blue/Getty Images.

Cover design copyrighted 2004 by Covenant Communications, Inc.

Published by Covenant Communications, Inc.
American Fork, Utah

Printed in Canada
First Printing: April 2004

10 09 08 07 06 05 04   10 9 8 7 6 5 4 3 2 1

ISBN 1-59156-446-8

DEDICATION

To my wonderful family—
To my mom, Bernice, who is my pioneer and gave me
my spiritual roots;
To my dad, Allen, who always gave his family his best;
To my husband, Tom, who gave me the support to grow, the courage
to try, and love to always fall back on; and
To my children, of whom I am so proud, whose love by the tons
makes my life joyous and fun every day.

ACKNOWLEDGEMENTS

First and foremost, I want to thank my husband, Tom. Without his support, in every conceivable way, this book would never have happened. In the face of four impending college educations, he supported my desire to come home from work so I could care for my family and work on this novel. His constant investments of faith and love have been my greatest blessings. I love you, honey.

Unbeknownst to my children, Tommy, Amanda, Adam and Josh, each played in big part in the writing of this book. I would like to thank them each:

Tommy, you believed in me first. What an honor to watch the child exceed the parents in faith and courage. The Lord invested much in you and you have always been the faithful steward. Krista, you are his equal in every way and we are grateful you chose us. Thanks for giving Dad and I the perfect grandson, little Tommy. Tons of love.

Amanda, you are the personification of Proverbs 3:5–6. Your humor and faith molds friends into family wherever you go. Your passion for music, your determination, and your compassion inspired me as I wrote. We love you, Mandy.

Adam, my Brigham Young: Stalwart and true, you have been the North Star to many. When your hard work and dreams were shattered, you picked up the pieces and began again, always keeping God first. Love you, pal.

Joshua, the last of the line, you stood faithful, though alone. Quiet goodness and a gentle, generous heart are your hallmarks. The Lord has blessed you with many talents, so hold your light high. Love you, bud.

My mom was the first person to read the original manuscript in its roughest form. Her glowing review gave me the courage to submit the first draft to Covenant. (I still think she would have praised me equally if I had handed her the bread wrapper and told her I had written it, but after all, isn't that what moms are for?) Thanks, Mom. I love you.

To Brandon Jamison, thanks for the weekly encouragement! Love you, Brando.

To my seminary kids, thanks for helping me start my day in the best of ways.

To Robin Barker—on or off the IU soccer field, retrieving my lost manuscript will go down in my mind as your greatest save! You're a sweetheart.

I cannot forget the N-1 Old Farm girls. Thanks for the encouragement and for always making me feel welcome.

To Dr. Jeff Fillmore, ER doctor, friend and choir buddy, go my thanks for lending me his medical expertise and answering my innumerable questions and e-mails.

I must also thank Covenant and my editor, Angela Colvin. To her go thanks galore. So many times I was ready to throw in the towel, but it was her patient encouragement that nudged me through all the red ink and made this a much better novel.

Lastly, to my friends and extended family, with whom I have laughed and cried—I thank you. I hope you will pour yourselves tall glasses of lemonade and have a good read.

Prologue

Thomas Jefferson Johanson slipped through his family's fingers in the late spring of 1976, following his high school graduation; in reality, he had been slowly slipping away for years. His rebellion had begun so slowly it had been easy for his tentative parents to pass it off as a "phase," but by spring it seemed to have increased exponentially, until Benjamin Johanson could no longer deny that his son was out of control. A bitter confrontation had erupted days before TJ's high school graduation when Ben's fear-driven questions hit an angry nerve in his son. When TJ's initial fury was vented, an acrid ceasefire settled in, filling the house with a tense, angry silence. Then, the day after his graduation, he'd packed his bags for a weeklong graduation trip and hadn't returned all summer.

TJ's departure only compounded the strain that suffocated the Johanson home. Ben's wife, Natalie, openly mourned her son's absence, and as the sun set on each fretful day, Ben felt her reproach and castigated himself. As June's summer weather surrendered to September's fall, he continually prayed for some word regarding his son, and when his prayers were finally answered, peace was again denied as new conflicts appeared with TJ's return.

Ben Johanson saw the derelict 1966 van parked near his barn on that early autumn morning. When he opened the door, his longhaired, unkempt son, TJ, tumbled onto the ground, while TJ's disheveled friend, an unknown to Ben, lay in the corner in a stupefied slumber atop a macramé mat. Any momentary joy Ben initially felt was completely obliterated by what he noticed next. Beer bottles littered the dirty van floor, and misshapen cigarette-looking stubs—from what he assumed was marijuana—floated in a Styrofoam cup, piercing him with sharp disappointment.

The anger and tension that had hovered during graduation returned to the Johanson home and seemed to drive the very oxygen from it. But TJ's return brought an even greater dimension of worry. His errant moral condition, as evidenced by his new lifestyle and choice of companions, seemed to be impacting his impressionable, sixteen-year-old sister Martha. This tomboyish late-bloomer had, to Ben's great alarm, apparently developed some sort of crush on the rootless, pseudo-intellectual sitar player their son had brought home, and this new attraction had instantly catapulted her into the confusing world of teenage fashion, passion, and angst. Worse yet, despite their best efforts at diffusing the situation, Ben and Natalie knew things were coming to a head.

After a month had passed since TJ's return, the family seemed to be sinking deeper and deeper into irreparable despair. On that particular late October morning, Natalie was numbly dusting the living room furniture, contemplating all that had changed so drastically in the past few months with her children—one had already slipped out of her grasp, almost beyond all hope, and the other was possibly beginning that same path herself. Suddenly, she heard Ben shouting at Martha and held her breath as her daughter ran sobbing from the house in the direction of the barn where the boys had been staying, slamming the screen door wildly behind her. Natalie slumped heavily against the mantel, knocking the old photo of her family to the hardwood floor. She stooped to pick it up and her tears fell on the shattered glass. The images, taken seventeen years previous, were of herself—long auburn hair curled to gently frame her beaming face, her figure still trim despite being visibly pregnant with Martha—and a slim, uniformed Ben holding then two-year-old TJ as they stood before their powder blue Rambler sedan.

She smiled wistfully as she recalled the day they were handed the keys to their new car, their first married purchase. It had been their pride and joy. They cruised around in it as a young married couple hopelessly in love. She remembered how many times they had driven past the orchard on their way from Fort Ritchie to downtown Smithsburg, often stopping there to buy a peck of one fruit or another. Ben would always jokingly ask the orchard's owner if he wanted to sell. The man would laugh and reply, "Not today, but ask me tomorrow." Ben would drive on, dreaming about what a wonderful life they could have on a farm like that, filling the old house with lots of beautiful children—and soon Natalie bought the dream as well. During one of their visits some time later, Ben again asked the man if he was ready to sell, but that time his reply was, "Not today, but pretty soon." Ben immediately handed the man his phone number and asked him to call if he ever needed a buyer. They started that very day to add every possible penny to the money Ben's parents had given them, just in case the call ever came.

We were so sure of our dreams back then . . . She gingerly touched the happy faces beneath the fractured glass. It was only a few months after the photo was taken that they brought Martha home. *So many changes so quickly . . .* What had happened to them since that blissful time? She knew the answer, but just as she had for the last sixteen years, she tried to push the pain of the past away and not deal with all the hurt and recriminations buried there. She had drawn wide emotional boundaries around herself and had clearly taught the perimeter to Ben, all the while believing that, in spite of their emotional detachment, she could pour all her love on the children and raise a healthy family. Yet, in spite of all her careful efforts, she watched in unbelief as everything began to unravel before her eyes.

Suddenly, Ben came crashing down the stairs, wailing like a wounded bear, bringing Natalie back to the present. He brushed the wall, knocking their copy of their complimentary Johansons' Orchard 1976 calendar to the floor. The October calendar page lay faceup, featuring Ben standing with a smile before a mountain of bushel baskets filled with crisp Johanson apples. It was difficult to believe that the agonized man ranting before Natalie could ever have been the subject of such a serene moment, when he now stood before her, chest heaving, while his trembling hands shook a letter in her direction.

"Do you know what she wants to do?" he bellowed, his emotions exaggerating his mild Danish lilt. "She wants to run off with that boy, that hippie boy!" He banged his hand on the table. "What is she thinking? What kind of girl has thoughts like this?" he groaned, slumping over an old wooden chair, letting his sorrow rest upon its back. "Not Martha . . . not our Martha . . ." he repeated in a throaty whisper. "She has always been a good girl. It's that boy!"

He began pacing in circles, grabbing large locks of gray-tinged hair with one hand while thumping the letter against his flannel shirt with the other. "I'll not stand for it, Natalie! Mark my words, I'll not stand by silently and lose another child."

Natalie pulled herself together and pushed away from the mantel, rising to her full five-foot, one-inch height. She set her jaw and shot him a preemptive glance, firing with her gray-green eyes, admonishing him not to press things with the children. "You're overexaggerating, Ben," she warned with a calm that mocked his pain.

"Am I?" he countered loudly. "Well, listen to a few of these lines here and tell me if I am overexaggerating." He began to read, emphasizing every word. "'Dear Peter, last night TJ confronted me about us. He was really angry and he told me he is planning to leave on Saturday and he's taking you with him. Is that true? I love you. I'll go with you. I'll be packed and ready and I'll meet you in the barn Friday night. Don't tell TJ. We'll go together, just the two of us. Love, Martha.'"

"'Love, Martha,'" he spat. "What would make her even consider running away? Didn't she see how TJ's leaving nearly tore our hearts out?"

His hanging head shook back and forth. "That longhaired boy's put these notions into her head. I swear, if he's touched her . . ." He sucked in a sudden gasp of air as his fists clenched and unclenched.

"Leave it alone, Ben," Natalie countered firmly. "She's just infatuated." She tried to sound more assured about the situation than she was. Martha's infatuation had caught her mother off guard as well. But the one thing she feared more than Martha's adolescent desires was the devastation that might occur if Ben's old-world values forced their daughter into a corner.

Natalie shot Ben "the look." It was the look that had effectively neutered his role, more particularly in the last few years, warning him when to back off. But today it was Natalie who was left feeling impotent as he turned and glared at her, though his voice, now controlled and soft, belied the angry resolution in his eyes.

"Is that your answer to everything, Natalie?" He shook his head incredulously. "'Leave it alone, Ben. It'll blow over, Ben,'" he said, mocking her false calm. "My son used to adore me, then in the past year he suddenly has no use for me, loathes the farm he once loved, and seemingly hates everything I stand for. I wanted to talk to him then, but you told me to leave it alone and that it would all blow over. Last fall he became angry and secretive. The whole year he threw every family rule in our faces. A thousand times I wanted to confront him, but again you warned me to back off. I didn't want any more distance between us than we already have suffered, so I backed down, and what did it get us?" Ben's voice began to rise. "Four months ago something happened to TJ, something terrible. I know it, and whether you want to admit it or not, Natalie, you know it too. I tried to talk to the boy about it the day he graduated, to clear some of the poisonous air out of this house that's choking our family to death, but as I stood face to face with my son, trying to get to the bottom of it, you took his side—*against me!*" His voice emphasized the last few words in disbelieving sorrow, as if he were still reeling from the memory of that emotional betrayal. "He got his dander up and stormed out of here on the night of his graduation, leaving home for months without a word. We didn't know if he was alive or dead until he showed up here last month—broke, filthy, dragging that hippie boy along with him—and still you forced me to say nothing, to do nothing . . . to 'let it go.' And so I did. 'Give the prodigal son a chance,' I thought, but he hadn't changed. There was no remorse, no apology, no respect. He just came back to refill his supplies and filch money from us. He just walked in here as if we owed *him* an apology, and brought some dirty, bleary-eyed boy along with him who's been up to . . ." He raised his eyes to the ceiling . . . "well only God knows what they've been up to. If that is their choice then I should have tossed them both out weeks ago."

Fire flew from Natalie's green eyes. "Is that always your solution? Bully people into submission because you think your position is right, and if they don't comply, leave them feeling like they're a disappointment?"

Ben knew this wasn't just about TJ anymore, but he tried to stay focused on the issue at hand. "My position? Under the circumstances, Natalie, what other position is there? We may not have taken them to church every Sunday, but we raised them with good Christian values.

They knew right from wrong," he wailed, then slumped into a kitchen chair and stared out the window.

For sixteen years he had been consigned to live within the boundaries of an emotional minefield, tiptoeing to avoid confrontation. Courtesy and kindness had been a grateful improvement after the loathing Natalie had shown him the year following Martha's devastating birth. He had patiently accepted the stilted terms, hoping in time love would come again, but the passion and devotion of their first three years of marriage never returned. There had been brief periods of real happiness, and the desire still burned within him to reclaim what they had squandered. He felt sure he had seen a longing in Natalie to reclaim it as well, but fear always kept his emotions locked inside the minefield. But not today. He'd had enough.

Ben raised his hands as if to shield himself from the chill he knew his next words would evoke from his wife. "I should have faced TJ four months ago, Natalie, and not let you cow me. I don't know if we can save our son, but I will not stand by and lose my daughter as well. Not to that boy TJ dragged in here from off the streets."

Ben headed for the door and Natalie shrieked his name. He turned and saw two emotions play across her porcelain face: utter fear and a return to the coldness that chilled his blood. He nearly backed down again, as he almost always had since that day following Martha's birth, but Ben was engaged in a battle for the survival of his family, and for that prize he was willing to plunge head-on and risk whatever blowup might occur. He stole a final look at his wife, seeing past her anger to the love for her children that anger was meant to protect. He remembered the first time he saw her and how he had admired the feisty spirit that belied the soft gray-green eyes and the girlish features and figure. From that first day he could see that her delicate, physical persona was contrary to her strong personality, and it was so today as well. His head dropped forward and his arms fell limply to his sides as if in apology for what he was about to say.

"I love you Natalie . . . I always have and always will, but I swear, woman, I don't know what you want from me anymore. I feel as though you threaten to veto every display of my authority. At times I've hardly even felt like a man in this house, and I allowed it, thinking it a fair compensation for whatever hurt you feel I've caused you. And what have we built here because of it? A polite little house. You've been a good mother and I've tried to be a good father, but having a good mother and a good father doesn't mean our children have had good parents. We've fallen a tad short of the mark, darling. I don't know all the answers, but I'll not stand around and be a silent partner anymore where the children are concerned." He again turned toward the door, and then placing his hand on the knob he turned and added quietly, "I can't stand by and do nothing. I simply cannot." His eyes pled with her to understand. And then he was gone.

Natalie had watched carefully as his expression changed from determination to that far-away sadness he had come to bear more frequently these past few years. An old memory flashed through her mind that she had been previously been unable to summon. Suddenly it hit her, and the remembrance took her back twenty years to the little base canteen near Fort Ritchie, where she worked after high school graduation. For a moment she saw the lanky, brown-haired, blue-eyed young soldier; a handsome, proud, first-generation American who gave his immigrant parents the ultimate gift of citizenship—a son serving in the U.S. military. To Natalie, who was the unplanned and unwanted child born to embarrassed older parents, Ben's background and outlook had been like a ray of sunshine, and for weeks she would bribe other waitresses to let her work his table. On their first date she asked him what all the different medals and ribbons bedecking his uniform were for, and, with reluctance, he shyly explained them. He had been raised to captain in a field promotion, but when she asked for more details he had grown quiet, and that same expression that he bore today had clouded his face then.

It was only after they were married that he finally spoke of the Korean War, especially of the skirmish that killed his commander and many of his buddies and earned him the field promotion and honors. Although long discharged, those memories still caused him to relive that day, reevaluating his every move to determine if he could have done anything better, saved any more of the men, and, though he was honored as a hero, he still carried the pain. It was the same look of pain that appeared on his face too frequently these last few years.

What had he called the reason for that skirmish? She remembered—*friendly fire.* A jittery young soldier at the border station mistook a backfiring engine for gunfire and sent a volley of bullets toward the enemy. It instantly shattered the fragile, temporary cease-fire that had been established while peace talks were being conducted, and the two groups of enemies, posted yards apart, spent the next eight hours engaged in a bloody struggle. Natalie could relate to the situation. She could understand how a person, however well-intentioned, could innocently miscalculate and catapult people onto dangerous ground. *Isn't that exactly what I did sixteen years ago?*

She walked over to the window that overlooked their beloved tree farm. To the left were the fields of famous Johanson evergreens. Some were occasionally sold for landscaping, but most of them were lovingly planted in anticipation of future Christmases—to bring families joy every winter as they stomped about searching for the perfect Christmas tree. The fields behind the house and those straight ahead and to the right, running toward the main road, were filled with fruit trees—apple, peach, and pear. The sight of them reminded her of all the warm hours she and the children had spent picking and peeling fruit and making delicious pies and tarts.

Natalie scanned the barn, carefully searching for signs of what was transpiring inside, when the small door burst open by the force of Martha's explosive exit. Within seconds, the diminutive but emotionally charged Martha had thrown the kitchen door open, sobbing hysterically as she ran blindly up the stairs clutching a blue piece of pottery. Natalie assumed it was from "him," from TJ's friend. Natalie heard the door to Martha's bedroom slam with a vicious bang. Her mind ran over numerous scenarios as she struggled to know what to do, but once again, her instincts failed her. She had lost confidence in her instincts long ago, because following them had led her down the path that had nearly destroyed her family already.

It was 1958, immediately following TJ's birth, when the doctors dropped the bomb that shattered her perfect, secure world with one simple but devastating revelation—no more babies for Natalie. Armed with catastrophic predictions of complications and possible death for her, her future babies, or both, they encouraged her to speak to Benjamin and sign for immediate sterilization. But for Natalie, a woman reared in a loveless home and married to a man from a large, tight-knit family, the thought of no more children decimated her view of her worth in the marriage. She postponed the surgery, using an upcoming transfer to a new home and base as the reason, and never told Ben. They moved into a little base house sixty miles south on Fort Meade in Maryland, and within two years, she conceived again.

She remembered the radiant joy Ben's face registered when she told him she was pregnant again. He had wrapped his arms around her, enveloping her in so much love that she had dared to believe the doctors had been wrong. Although her second pregnancy became arduous, Natalie clung to the hope that all would be well. Ben never knew about the doctors' concerns over her failing condition until the day he entered the house and found her unconscious in a pool of blood. Within hours, a determined but tiny Martha was born six weeks premature by emergency cesarean section.

When Natalie awoke from the sedation her heart broke. She found a tortured-looking Ben, head hung down, under intense scrutiny by the medical staff that held him accountable for the threat this pregnancy posed to his wife's life. As they bluntly explained how precarious her medical situation was, Ben's face registered confusion, but Natalie knew it would only be moments before he realized she had intentionally deceived him. For the first time in her life, Natalie feared she was losing his devotion.

Ben was holding a clipboard full of forms. Before a word had been spoken, Natalie knew what the forms were, but she was not prepared to face him, to explain the well-intentioned reasons for her deception—let alone to face the reality of her barren future—without first being assured of absolution and unbounded love from a husband whose solemn face she could not read.

When the doctors finally left, Ben stared silently at the floor for what seemed like an eternity. *Talk to me, Ben,* she prayed, but he offered no words of insight into what he was thinking, and when he finally raised his eyes to hers, his expression was vacant and haunted. *What is hidden there?* He touched her arm mechanically, then rose and left the room with no explanation. Natalie had never felt so unwanted.

When he returned, he approached her bedside, stiff and nervous. Tears were in his eyes but his words issued forth in a rigid cadence as he methodically explained that she *must* sign. All she felt was coldness. She hadn't wanted to die. Dying wasn't a possible outcome in her weakened mind. She only knew that she and their dreams of a large, happy family had been everything to Ben, and she couldn't bear being the one responsible for ending that dream. So she dug in her heels and refused to sign, while silently praying that he would say something, anything, to assure her that she was still, and forever would be, fully loved. Then she could consent, then she could have the surgery without fear or recrimination, but like two empty vessels, they both came to the well and they both left empty and dry.

Several days of a silent standoff followed. Natalie awakened from brief periods of rest, hoping to find Ben by her side. And although she caught him peering into her room from time to time, her doubts over his loyalty were compounded each time she saw the chair, placed by her bed especially for him, sitting empty. She felt utterly abandoned, and she closed her heart to her husband. By the end of the second day her fever spiked, prompting her worried nurse to give orders for a volunteer to hurry downstairs to where she knew Ben could be found, keeping a vigil near his tiny daughter in the nursery. He burst into Natalie's room, tearful and panicked, but she hardly acknowledged him.

From that moment on he maintained a constant bedside vigil, sponging cool water over her fevered body and bathing her hands with his kisses as her health continued to decline. Slowly, her thoughts turned to the two motherless children—one barely days old—that she would leave behind, and she began to place a fragile trust in his show of devotion. She was about to relent and agree to sign the authorization when the surgical nurse walked in to prep her for immediate surgery. Astonished, she discovered that that very morning Ben had declared her medically unfit and signed for her. She was amazed that he would do such a thing to her without even asking. Her walls of mistrust went up again and she locked her betrayed heart.

Tiny Martha's strong spirit had beaten the odds, and within three months she was able to come home. Natalie's physical recovery had been steady, though emotionally she remained distant and cold. Still, Ben devoted every effort to her care. Unfortunately, it left his military career in shambles, and he decided to submit his request for a discharge. Though it was not openly acknowledged, his sacrifice did not go unnoticed by his wife.

Ben became frantic to relocate his family. It was winter and their base housing was due to expire in two weeks. And then it happened. One day, as they drove to Washington County to get away from their problems and to see the reported beauty left behind by a strong winter storm, on a whim they drove past the old farm. A "For Sale" sign sat in the snow at the end of the road where the owner was shoveling. Ben rolled the window down and asked his usual question, but this time the man's smile nearly reached beyond his face. He was ready to sell. In fact, he was shoveling snow at that very spot so he could put up the "For Sale" sign. He said it must have been their lucky day since, after having searched and searched for the card with the soldier's name on it, to no avail, he had given up hope of contacting Ben and had finally decided to just place the ad and post the sign.

When Ben heard the man's story, he drew a deep breath, closed his moist, shining eyes, and, in a husky whisper, thanked God. To him, being there at that moment was much more than luck. It was a sign from God that his prayers had been answered. He was devastated when Natalie resisted his efforts to ascribe holy intervention to what she wanted to see as a coincidence, because she no longer had any interest in making a fresh start there. That had once been the house of their child-filled dreams, and the memory of those dreams had since become repugnant to her.

One night after tucking the children in, Natalie searched in vain and couldn't find Ben anywhere. She had stood by the back screen door for several minutes and listened for any sound of him when she heard a faint voice in the darkness. She found him, kneeling under a tree with his head sagging and his shoulders stooped, the visage of an old man, and she knew it was her disinterest that had driven him out there. She was about to approach him when he suddenly drew in a deep, shuddering breath, raised his face to the starry night, and began to plead again with God. Her hardened heart broke and she withdrew as silently as she had approached. She didn't know what he had petitioned God for, but she had a good idea, and she knew if she were right, it was within her ability to grant it.

Ben arrived home the next day to find a contract for the farm waiting for him on the table. Natalie had arranged it, and that gesture had meant everything to him. She had not forgotten his detachment when she desperately needed his compassion, but his warm appreciation of this gift gave her courage, so she redrew her boundaries and moved from a position of cold indifference, to one of courtesy and concern, allowing her and Ben to be colleagues in the rearing of the children. For fifteen years they had muddled pleasantly along through their marriage, neither asking too much of the other, each investing their love entirely in the children. They rounded out their world with good friends and generous service in the community until they become pillars in the county. It wasn't the passion-filled bond of their early marriage, but the buds of basic trust had slowly begun to return.

It was too brief a period of happiness. As she and Ben grew slowly closer, the problems with TJ pushed father and son further and further apart. She could see the widening chasm between them, between cultures and generations, between traditional values and the rebellion of youth. In her efforts to play peacemaker she became a self-appointed buffer between father and son, constantly making it clear to Ben how very delicate the balance was, and silently assuring him that there would be no tolerance for upsetting that balance. Ben had learned the lesson well, knowing not to press too far, but as his role as head of the family was diminished, he became withdrawn and quiet, and Natalie knew she had invited indifference back into her home.

The additional tension began to hover over the dinner table and every time TJ crossed through the doorway. Natalie's and Ben's questions were returned with lies, and the consequences they meted out were met with blatant disregard. Their hearts broke. Natalie hovered more protectively and Ben prayed.

Though it was part of their family plan, they had never managed to agree on a single course of faith, so Ben simply drew upon his own upbringing, teaching his young family to pray and read from the scriptures. Natalie had been ambivalent about it at first, but she could not deny the peace and comfort that seemed to wrap itself around her every time they kneeled together. Little by little the occasions became more scarce until their only family prayers were those offered at the dinner table. Still, Ben prayed. *How many nights have I seen him on his knees?* So many times she had considered kneeling by his side as she once had, but it was too intimate a thing for her to share at that point in their fractured relationship. And then TJ left. Silently, she blamed Ben, and judging from the way he withdrew further from her, she felt sure he held her equally responsible. More walls and boundaries . . . and now Martha and today's disaster.

Suddenly TJ exploded through the door, spouting expletives until he noticed his mother by the window. Immediately his tone changed as he tried to plead his case with her before his father entered the room. She could see what was happening. It was "divide and conquer" time again.

When did he become such a master at this game? Natalie wondered. She scanned her son's suddenly unfamiliar face. He had always been her all-American boy, clean, strong, confident . . . until last spring. No, the changes began earlier than that. It was during football that his appearance began to alter. It was more than the ratty clothes and the longer hair. It was his eyes. Those eyes that once reminded her of black pearls, smoky but soft and warm, were often red-rimmed— reflecting changes in his previous commitment not to drink or smoke. And then Natalie tried to deny an added element, the misery that appeared there in the spring, before he fled. But now, those once-gentle, charming eyes seemed almost ominous, with fury and confusion flashing alternately. His dark hair was long and tangled and sorely needed washing, as did his ragged jeans and T-shirt, his almost daily apparel, and she wondered what had happened to him to effect such a dramatic change from the handsome high school senior who was always so concerned about his appearance. She approached him to pull him to her, to try and calm him down, but he tensed, unwilling to be consoled.

"I was trying to fix things . . ." he rambled. "I told Peter we were going to leave on Friday. It would have been alright but . . ." He struggled to organize his thoughts. "Captain Ahab out there went off on everybody," he continued, making an angry reference to his father. "He has Peter so freaked out the guy's ready to bail without even packing. He just wants to get away from this crazy place." He pounded on the wall, emphasizing his frustration.

"TJ," Natalie said nervously, "what were you trying to fix?"

The question startled TJ and he suddenly clammed up, aware that he had disclosed something he hadn't intended. He quickly exited the conversation. "I should never have come back. Man!" he exclaimed in anger. "What was I thinking? I should have known nothing was going to change here. How could I have been so stupid?"

Natalie firmly grasped her son's arms, and though he towered over her, her touch calmed him. She looked deeply into his eyes, trying to assess what percentage of this fury was hype and what portion was real, but she was unable to read him.

"What are you saying—that if you leave today you're never coming back again?" Her voice trembled, betraying her earlier resolve.

"That's exactly what I'm saying." He pushed away from her, needing to be apart to emphasize his determination. He wasn't aware that his father was standing in the doorway directly behind him, now absorbing every word. "I'm sick of Dad looking at me as if I'm guilty of something all the time. I'm sick of all his questions and stupid rules, and I'm tried of being blamed for everything . . ."

"Who is blaming you, TJ, and for what?" Ben asked as the boy spun around, stopping cold in his tracks. "You and I have barely spoken since you came back."

"How great that our one and only father-son chat happened to be about what's going on between Peter and Martha. I may have brought him here, a decision I regret for his sake, but I am not the one who made them like each other."

"This isn't how we raised you—drinking, smoking, living out of a van. I saw the marijuana. What are you doing with someone like that?" Ben's voice rose and TJ's matched it.

"Someone like what? Peter may look a little rough but at least he doesn't judge people. He accepts everyone."

"It's easy to accept everyone and everything when you live a life without any rules, TJ."

"You think that living on this mountain gives you a perfect view of life? The one and only perfect view of life? Let me tell you, there's a whole other world out there past Johansons' Tree Farm and, frankly, I prefer it."

"No one ever told you you were a prisoner here. Of course we . . .

I hoped you would love the farm as much as I, but you were free to run the farm or not. It was your choice. But is this the best alternative you can find? Is this what you want for Martha?"

"I already told you," he argued defensively. "I hadn't expected Martha to fall for him. I was planning on getting him out of here by the weekend anyway! But don't worry. Since I am soooo evil and because I somehow seem to be responsible for everything bad that ever happens around here, we'll leave today so the Johansons' world can return to its state of perfect bliss."

There was a note of sarcasm in TJ's final rebuttal and it cut Ben deeply. He shrank in exasperation and backed down, addressing his comments as much to Natalie as to TJ. "I am trying to have a serious conversation with you, and you are being ridiculous."

"Am I?" TJ spat back, declining any overtures. "Think about it. Think long and hard. You know it's true. You hold me responsible for everything."

The topic had suddenly shifted and Natalie's heart skipped a beat. TJ was no longer referring to Martha and Peter or anything related to this recent trip home. He was challenging Ben on the same issue from a few months ago, the one that they had danced around, skirted, even suffered over, but about which they had never spoken directly. To most of the residents in rural Washington County, what had happened was a devastating tragedy, but Ben had tried to convince Natalie that it was the horrific and unbelievable result of their son's declining behavior, which had been slowly spiraling downward his entire senior year. And what was more, Ben believed that the memory of this nightmare was still haunting TJ day and night. He could never prove anything, but in his gut he knew TJ had been involved. There was a complete withdrawal in his already rebellious son after that night, and he had always felt unlocking the truth of that tragedy would finally set his son free . . . or push him away forever.

"Tell me what I am blaming you for, TJ," Ben challenged, trying to draw his son out, but TJ didn't answer. "Tell me," he urged a little harder. "You accuse me—now back it up. Tell me what I'm holding you responsible for."

TJ stood frozen, seething silently at his father. The tension level in the room was making Natalie nervous and she started to move from the spot where she had been standing to intervene, but Ben put his hand up, urging her to stay, and he pressed on.

"You imply that I think you are a horrible person or that you are to blame for everything bad that happens. Have I ever said such words to you? No, but why do you feel that way? Because those feelings are coming from inside you, not from me."

TJ never lost eye contact but it was clear his thoughts were elsewhere, considering Ben's comment. Finally he answered defensively, "I've seen it in your eyes. I can tell it's what you think."

Hearing TJ's stinging indictment of his father's opinion of him was a sharp blow, but Ben wasn't willing to serve as his scapegoat anymore. "Tell me something, TJ. You didn't see me for more than four months. How did you feel when you were gone? Better? Happier? I don't think so, or you wouldn't have ended up coming back here filthy and penniless. So think again . . . is it what I think of you that bothers you, or could it be what you're thinking about yourself?"

The question threw TJ off and his face reflected it. Natalie gasped at Ben's insinuation and she began to move to her son's side to comfort him, but Ben again put his hand up demanding her to hold still, never letting his eyes leave his son's. He needed to press TJ to the limit while he still had time. "Because there is something bottled up inside you that's eating away at you," Ben finished.

TJ nervously shifted his weight as he absorbed the statement. He suddenly hated his father, hated him for summoning back all the images and agonizing emotions he fought daily to hold at bay. A boy's eyes kept flashing in TJ's mind and the pungent smell of beer was instantly present. He heard the startled gasp and the nauseating scraping sound as fingers hungrily slid over gravel and earth. And then there was the cartoonlike scream, and then the silence . . .

The memory was like a movie playing out on the screen of TJ's countenance, and Ben could tell they were approaching the climactic moment. TJ's eyes could no longer bear his father's gaze and they suddenly became pained and darted away. Ben wanted to grab his son and cry with him but he knew he couldn't break the moment, not yet. He had to let him wrestle this alone a few more seconds, so he held his place silently and watched and waited. But Natalie noticed his pain also and she would no longer be kept away. She moved to TJ and wrapped her arms around him, showering him with words of praise and love. Ben's heart sank. The spell was broken and TJ's armor was on again.

TJ returned the embrace and buried his face against his mother's head for a brief moment. When his head lifted, Ben could see the shadow of pain still hovering there, but there was relief there too as he had managed to push the demons back once more. He smiled sardonically at his father. "You're good." He laughed sadly, shaking his head. "I'll give you that. You had me going, alright. Who'd have thought? Military hero, tree farmer, psychotherapist! Well, I'll give you one thing, Dad, you are indeed everything your loyal fans say you are. You are a man among men, and since I willingly admit that I will never be your equal, never be the worthy heir of the Johanson crown, I concede the title to you."

He dipped in a mock bow and Ben felt sick. "Stop it, TJ. You're behaving like a fool."

"Well, then, I guess that means it's time for me to make my exit," he sneered.

Natalie clutched him tighter, and Martha suddenly appeared on the lowest step. "No, TJ," Natalie pled. "Everyone is just upset. We can work this out, just please stay." Then to her husband, she begged, "Ben, do something."

Martha began to cry and ran to her brother. It was more than TJ could bear. The tighter they held him the more he wanted to get away. The scene was killing Ben as well. "Look what you're doing to them!" Ben cried. "You can't solve what's bothering you by running away."

"Really, Dad?" he countered smugly. "Well, in case you hadn't noticed, that's what we Johansons do best." And then he added, "All except you, of course."

He was now turning the tables on his father, dishing out to him a little of the hurt he had felt previously, but the only ammo he could use on a good man was to throw his very goodness back in his face. And so TJ aimed and fired.

"Yes, Dad, I run. Heck, I'm making a career of it, it seems. And Martha . . ." He turned, using her to sharpen his point, though her eyes begged him not to. "Well, she'd obviously rather run off with a guy she barely knows than live in this house."

Ben's eyes glanced quickly to look into his daughter's face and caught her quivering lips whispering the words, "It's not true," as she released her hold on TJ and turned instead to her father. "Stop it, TJ!" she suddenly shouted, but her defense hurt Ben as well. This was not what he wanted, a house divided into two loyalties, so he returned his stare to TJ, who, finding his support dwindling, fired again.

"And Mom . . ." Natalie looked into his eyes with fear of what he was about to unleash. "Everyone in town knows she's been running away from you for years!"

Natalie gasped and pulled away abruptly. "That's enough, TJ!" she commanded. She couldn't bring herself to look at Ben, fearing what unspoken indictment might be waiting there.

TJ saw it, and for a moment the hurt he had caused the man he most loved and hated left him empty. But he knew his father was the one man who could expose his secret. He decided to destroy his enemy so he would never have to face or fear him again, and once more, he fired.

" . . . and once we're gone she'll finally be free to leave too, and you'll be left here all alone with your perfect sense of right and wrong. You won't have to be bothered by we mere mortals who feel things and want more than justice and your mercy, people who mess up and dare to believe they're still worth loving in spite of it. So go on and live in your sterile, perfect world. I'd rather live anywhere but here. And—"

Ben didn't hear the last of TJ's words. He had broken free of Martha's grasp and walked out toward the fields of trees. Natalie and Martha faced TJ, astonished at the hurt he had inflicted at their cost. He shrank back, then grabbed his coat and exited the house, slamming the door ferociously so Ben would be sure to hear. Then he and Peter sped away down the lane.

* * *

Natalie and Martha sobbed for hours in their rooms as they struggled to sort out their emotions. Dusk came and Ben had still not returned. Martha had fallen into an exhausted sleep. The relationships with the three men she loved most were each dramatically altered, and she feared the terrifying secret that had prompted her to consider running away with Peter in the first place.

Natalie tucked a quilt around her daughter and wrapped another over her shoulders as she left Martha to search for Ben. She knew exactly where she would find him—by the tree. It had been his place of solace since the day they moved onto the farm.

Years earlier, on their moving day, the previous owner had taken Ben on a long walk to survey the property before turning over the keys. They passed squares and squares of trees planted ten by ten with broad, mulched tractor paths between them. Suddenly a stray sprig caught Ben's attention. Springing up in the crosshairs between two busy tractor paths was a tiny, stray evergreen seedling the owner had never noticed before. It should have been crushed and broken a hundred times by the wide nubby tires that rolled past nearly every day, but nevertheless, there it stood, healthy and firm. "Watched over by the fairies," the old man had mused, but Ben had ascribed a more sacred protection to its existence.

Just as she had years before, Natalie heard his trembling voice before she saw him. The melancholy sound hung like fog in the night's stillness and led her through the dusk to a place where she could stand unnoticed. What she saw stabbed her heart. Ben was lying prostrate on the ground under the evergreen as he sent his petitions up to God. She fell back against a fence post and cried silently. With each of them so badly wounded, how could they ever hope to heal?

Chapter One

Twenty-One Years Later

The heavyset woman in her fifties set a mammoth-sized burrito, complete with nachos on the side, in front of her favorite, bearded civil servant. "There you go, Mr. Johnson. That ought to hold you for a while."

Jeff looked at the ticket and counted the money onto the counter. He felt a vibration from his cell phone, checked the number, and muttered to himself, "I've got to move it or I won't ever get to eat this." And then to the waitress he said with a smile and a flirtatious wink, "I'm one of those bachelors who's not much of a cook, so I count on you to take good care of me, Maggie."

"Anything for you," she said returning the wink and smile. Jeff Johnson and Dennis Martin grabbed their food and ran for the elevator.

Dennis turned to Jeff and made a mock pouting face.

"So what is this look all about?" Jeff asked with rolling eyes.

Dennis replied, "Another woman conquered by the Johnson charm."

"Yeah." Jeff rubbed his closely cropped beard and responded with equally comic sarcasm. "Well, what can I say, my friend. Some of us should have 'lethal weapon' tattooed on our foreheads. Lucky for you my brand of irresistible charm is only effective on women twice my age. It's a Perry Como/Daffy Duck kind of a thing."

"Lucky for me," Dennis responded as he wiped the sweat of pretend relief from his brow. "You've stolen the heart of my burrito lady, but at least you're promising to leave me my wife and children."

Jeff smiled absentmindedly at the remark.

"So what are your plans for the holiday?"

Jeff's face went blank until the realization finally set in. "That's right. Wow. Frankly, I had completely forgotten that this is Labor Day weekend. I guess my mind is preoccupied with all the cases I'm juggling right now. Uh, I really don't have any set plans . . . maybe I'll take in an Orioles game or something."

"An Orioles game? Ooh, now you're tempting me. Do you know that I haven't been to an Orioles game since the night Cal Ripken broke Lou Gehrig's consecutive game streak?"

"You were there?"

"Yep. September sixth, 1995 . . ." His voice lingered on the date, as if savoring a sweet memory.

"How'd you get tickets? They must have set you back plenty. What'd you do, rob your daughter's college fund?"

"Nah. My uncle is an usher at Camden Yards, and some guys with a corporate skybox offered him two tickets as a thank-you for taking care of them all season."

"Swell," Jeff moaned. "If you've got such great connections then why haven't you taken your best friend here to a single game?"

"You know how it is. Whenever I've got a free weekend I feel like I should spend time with Liz and Allie."

Jeff desperately wanted to change the subject before his friend extended an invitation to join his family for the holiday. "Say, Dennis, you wouldn't happen to have some leads on some good community service opportunities in the Washington County area, would you?"

"Hmmm, I don't know, why?"

"I've got a folder on a kid, a girl named Meredith Davenport, who was picked up last weekend. The courts are considering recommending her for the program, and I'm just scoping out the possibilities for placement in case I need to assign some service hours."

"What were her infractions?"

"Drunk and disorderly mostly. She was a passenger in a stolen car some friends of hers took joyriding though, so I think the judge wants to give her a wake-up call."

"If that's the case then she'll probably be assigned some counseling and won't be ready for a placement for six or eight weeks."

"Yeah, that's what I figure. Her infractions are in both Frederick and Washington Counties, but we're going to try to handle her service as close to her home as possible. I don't think she's a bad kid, just pretty angry. I'd like to make this as easy for her to comply with as I can. Right now the juvenile department has her undivided attention, and I think if I keep things real simple she'll be an 'honor student' in the court system. Maybe I'll be able to help salvage her future."

Dennis had been thoughtfully considering every word of his coworker's inquiry. "You should know that area as well as anyone." He offered the comment carefully and waited.

Jeff Johnson visibly tensed as he forgot for a second who it was that had connected him to that area. He slowly relaxed and responded, "I'm not sure what part of the county she's from and I . . . I really haven't kept up my contacts there."

Dennis regretted the awkwardness his comment had caused and he quickly stepped in to take control of the moment. "I can't think of anything off the top of my head, but let me talk to a friend over in Hagerstown. She might know of something."

The elevator doors opened at the fourth floor as the two men hurried out. "Hey, I'll check into that service info for you. If I don't get back to you before you leave today, have a great weekend."

They each turned through the door marked "Juvenile Services," and Dennis turned left into the small room that served as his office, while Jeff turned right into his tiny space. Jeff lay his lunch on his desk and checked his clock. He had ten minutes to eat before his next appointment. He sat down and unwrapped his burrito with his right hand as he riffled through the stack of folders with his left.

First impressions of Jeff Johnson's office would suggest that he was a straightforward, uncomplicated man. The few adornments and personal items were simple and unpretentious, but this exterior simplicity was a carefully engineered façade to allow him the privacy and anonymity he had sought for so long. His life was finally . . . comfortable. That was a word he would have scoffed at twenty years ago, but he was at a point in his life, and more importantly in his life experiences, where "comfortable" meant the attainment of a measure of peace and solidarity—two factors sorely appreciated and painfully attained.

He counted very few close associations. Those who knew him best were those who inquired the least into his life. That's why he was so fond of Dennis. Dennis's friendship was the only relationship in his life that extended more than ten years into his past. He remembered names of former friends and associates, but none were people with whom he currently kept in touch. He had lived a fast life, a selfish life, and now he was finally climbing upward toward something better. As he grabbed for the next rung on the ladder, he left all reminders of his previous world behind.

As for the lack of female companionship in his life, he found that many women were willing to occupy a vacant heart for one night or even for a few, but he no longer had any interest in company of that sort. Such selfish dalliances had cost him the one woman he had ever truly loved. She was a childhood friend, the first person he called with news or to sound out his dreams. She had made him believe he was better than even he believed he was, and by the time he'd realized he loved her, he had already taken all the gifts she had invested in him and squandered them on others. Though years had passed since they had shared their one and only kiss, the sweetness of her memory convinced him he could never again be satisfied with less. He finally understood that the kind of women who were willing to invest a lifetime in a man would settle for nothing less than his whole heart. It was what he longed for, yet he was still unprepared.

One simple step at a time was his motto, and his office reflected that. Aside from his government-issued desk and institutional-gray filing cabinet, the spartanly decorated room had only four embellishments. To the left of his desk sat a cylindrical, metal garbage can painted to look like a can of soda. On the wall beside his desk hung a large bulletin board completely covered in photos of young people—some with families, some alone, and many photographed with Jeff. On the wall behind his desk hung an aerial photograph of a mountain orchard with a pond, farmhouse, and carefully manicured lawns and fences. Next to the small window behind his desk stood the most eye-catching item in the room. A six-foot, perfect evergreen, stunningly trimmed with Christmas regalia. It was growing in a large blue terra-cotta pot. Golden suns, moons, and stars with serene faces were hand-painted in a Renaissance style that covered the entire vessel. The artist who created this magnificent piece signed his initials in long, avant-garde letters that ran along the pot like children holding hands.

Unlike Dennis's office, there were no family photos and no diplomas. There were no obvious hints that would give a visitor any personal insights into who Jeff Johnson was. Each of the four items, however special some of them were to Jeff, served a purpose in his work. The soda-painted garbage can gave the room a relaxed atmosphere that put kids at ease. Likewise, the bulletin board of past clients and their families was a boost to all the participants. To parents it was a sign of hope and comfort. They knew they were not alone, and in seeing the progression of photos of other normal-looking parents with their kids, whose appearances became brighter and healthier from photo to photo, they felt the pall of judgment and despair fade. To the kids, the bulletin board gave Jeff credibility. It told them he knew about kids and that he was okay. The person most served by it, however, was Jeff. On lonely and discouraging days, it cheered him and gave him the courage to open the next file and face the next family.

The faces on that board represented the closest associations in his life these days. They were like family to him, and it was generally with some of these friends that he often celebrated the holidays. Many of them were married, young adults now with children of their own.

His eyes often lingered over one of the photos in particular. It still stunned him. It was a photo of him standing beside the first boy assigned to his care. It was also the earliest photo taken of him since . . . since high school, he mused. The first time he saw it, it had shocked him. Sure, he had stood before a mirror every morning for years, but the changes had, for the most part, been gradual, except for the jagged scar that ran along his jawline. He would always remember that night in vivid detail, so he had grown a closely trimmed beard, as much to blur the event's memories as to conceal the scar. Additionally the photo had chronicled other changes, such as his graying hair and maturing features and form. He was grateful for the regimen of exercise that helped maintain his sanity during the dark days of his past and which now fought the war forbidding his waistline to exceed the ratio of forty inches on his six-foot, three-inch frame. *When did this boy become a man?* he wondered. Yes, each look at that photo summoned a moment of realization that he had indeed squandered his youth.

Yet each time he mused over it, a satisfied smile would finally appear. He was older now, a more steady man than before, with eyes that reflected a relative sense of peace. His life was not at all what he had expected it would be; it was better. Better than anything he could have dreamed about or understood when he was the young, selfish man whose potter friend created the beautiful piece that held his decorated fir tree.

The tree was a great conversation starter. It broke the ice and tended to initiate intimate conversations about home and holidays, opening doors that would have otherwise required months to open. Even the terra-cotta pot served a purpose. Stories of his relationship with his friend, the artist, were lessons he felt would benefit "his kids," and so, from time to time, with certain ones, he would bare this small sliver of his soul. And as for the photo of the orchard—that was purely for Jeff. It centered him and helped him remember what he was fighting for with each of these kids.

It was 7:45 on the lobby clock when Jeff finally left the county office building, laptop and files in tow, and headed down the sidewalk to the employee lot. His green '97 Blazer was one of only three cars remaining in the lot. Just seeing it there made him feel a little better. It was a small compensation for his solitary, often lonely life, but it was beautiful and it was his. Well, it would be his after forty-seven more payments.

He opened the door and filled his lungs with the sweet smell of the luxurious leather upholstery. That smell still brought back satisfying memories of his childhood: Sunday afternoon drives in the family's new car, shoe stores filled with back-to-school shoppers, and baseball mitts at Christmas. It was the sweet, clean essence of normalcy, and it helped to air out the last of the nearly twenty-year stench of his adulthood that still lingered in his life. He gently set his bag on the passenger seat. He mused at how that bag had been the first thing to ever fill that space, and likely the only thing to fill it for some time. He slid in behind the wheel, rolling his hands over the executive-deluxe cushioned steering wheel, and smiled like a little boy. A few years ago, he wouldn't have dared to even dream of owning such a vehicle, and yet here he was. He was successfully digging out of the hole.

He put the car in gear and backed out.

Maybe I'll see that Orioles game tomorrow, he thought contendedly.

Chapter Two

Natalie was scurrying around the huge, airy kitchen preparing supper and humming an oldies tune that was stuck in her head. She kept her voice low, trying hard not to disturb Ben who was in the adjacent room watching the weather forecast with a furrowed brow. Her body instinctively began moving to the music and she almost laughed when she realized her feet were carrying her in waltz form from the fridge to the sink, *1-2-3, 1-2-3*. *How long has it been since we danced?* she wondered. She remembered. It was 1958, almost forty years previous, right after they arrived at Fort Meade. The officers' wives had thrown a party to welcome the new captain, his young wife, and his infant son to the base. Actually, she could recall one dance after that, but it wasn't really a dance. It was more like forced movement across a floor to music. It was the farewell party the same women's group threw when Ben left the military two years later. The crowd had insisted that the handsome couple take a final spin on the Officers' Club dance floor, and Benjamin and Natalie complied. They had been so stiff and ill at ease with one another that when they'd left the floor, an awkward silence hung in the air until a few random hands offered them an anemic round of applause.

There had been many opportunities since then. Dances at the fire hall and the grange, and even a few fancy affairs at the Veterans of Foreign Wars building, but they never danced. Ben would always tell her how nice she looked, and they would each find their friends and chat the evening away, eventually sharing a table and a beverage or two with some group in small talk. From time to time, when friends would ask their spouses to dance, they would invite Natalie and Ben to join them on the floor, but the Johansons would always smile appreciatively and reply that they were too tired, or one or the other of them would use the "two left feet" excuse. On the way home they would share whatever news was circulating that night and then they would turn in. Looking back, those evenings weren't unpleasant, but how she longed to dance!

She continued humming and swaying to the music and her mind moved on to more pleasant things, such as their upcoming trip. Then she suddenly remembered something she wanted to ask Ben.

"Ben? Do you think they'll let me take a cake as a carry-on?" she called, referring to their upcoming flight to Los Angeles to attend their daughter's late October wedding. Well, they weren't going to be attending the actual *wedding*. Martha had met a Mormon doctor at the hospital where she worked in California, and the couple was being wed in a special ceremony in one of the Mormon Church's temples. Martha had nervously approached the topic, taking great pain to delicately explain to her parents that they wouldn't be able to attend the actual ceremony since they were not members of the Church. She rambled on about how a special certification of worthiness was required and that not even all "Latter-day Saints" could enter. At first Natalie had been devastated and even considered not flying out at all, but she remembered the careful thought and prayer Martha and her twenty-year-old son David, had given to their decision to be baptized into The Church of Jesus Christ of Latter-day Saints, and when they had asked Ben and Natalie for their support, they had given it.

They had never met their daughter's fiancé, but Sam had called and spoken with them, and he seemed to be as lovely and personable as Martha had told them he was. More importantly, David adored him as well. *Sweet David*, Natalie mused. The news of Martha's unplanned pregnancy had dropped like a deadly final blow the fall of Martha's junior year of high school. Coming in the wake of the emotional plunge the entire family had taken following TJ's angry departure, it had almost destroyed them. But the child was a healing balm rather than the wound they expected. David had never met his biological father, but Martha had given him one token to hold on to, a colorful blue pot his father had made. From childhood on it had been his treasured whatnot holder.

Natalie had frequently caught herself wistfully staring at the beautiful raven-haired child with the tousled curls, thick dark brows, and deep-set, dark eyes. On more than one occasion while growing up, David asked why he was the only one with such dark looks. She couldn't remember how she responded then, but she knew she had evaded telling him that he resembled his birth father more than his mother. His preoccupation continued, and it became increasingly important to him that he see himself in the images of the family. Then one day, when he was a young teen, he had carefully examined the photos on the mantel and announced that, in spite of the differences in coloring and complexion, he felt he bore a strong resemblance to his Uncle TJ. His mother and grandmother humored him and agreed good-naturedly, but later that day Natalie had made it a point to scrutinize the last photo they took of her missing son and she also saw the resemblance for the first time. The hair and eyes were different, but their slightly upturned noses and strong jaws were similar, and she then began catching herself staring wistfully at her handsome young grandson now and again with new eyes.

She posed her question about the carry-on to the back of her gray-haired husband for the second time, but his attention was so focused on the weather report that he didn't respond. Another thought occurred to her, and it made a chill run down her spine. *What if they expect us to dance at the reception?* Now she wished they weren't going at all. She knew Martha was hiring a DJ and dancing was planned. She certainly didn't want a repeat of their awkward last performance. More than just embarrassing, it had accentuated the emotional abyss between them, and as awful as it had been in front of a room of casual friends and coworkers, it would be horrifyingly unsettling to Martha and David. *What would Sam think? Or his family? What can I do?*

Ben stood up to turn the TV off and grabbed his coat and hat from the hook near the door. "Has the forecast worsened?" she asked.

"The Baltimore station says we should only catch the fringe of the storm, but I want to herd the animals into the corral just in case they need to get to the barn. These city stations rarely get our weather right."

"Is there anything I can do to help?"

A curious smile tugged at his lips. "You don't want to be out here in this wind and cold. You could gather up the kerosene lamps and the oil just in case the power goes down. I'll bring some diesel fuel up for the generator so we can keep the furnace and the well pump going. That's about all we need to do right now, but thank you." He lowered his head, pulled his hat down over his brow, and plunged into the icy wind.

Natalie quickly put her casserole in the oven and lined up the lamps and oil on the counter. She looked out at the barn and could see Ben jostling the animals into the lamp-lit corral. She bit her lip as an idea formulated in her mind and then she grabbed her own hat, coat, and mittens and made her labored way to the barn. Ben was shoveling cans full of grain into feeding troughs, and she could see by the extra bales of straw that he was planning on adding an extra layer to the floors of the stall. He paused for a second and again offered her a curious smile when he saw her standing in the lighted doorway, and it did not fade away as he continued with his work.

"Cold, isn't it?" he offered, attempting to make conversation.

"I laid the lanterns out and then I thought maybe you might need a little help after all."

The offer was so unexpected he again stopped his work for a second and looked at her quizzically. He nodded his head toward a large scoop. "I could use another scoop of oats in the horses' feed boxes."

Natalie moved to the workbench that stood over the oat bin. She saw the old radio Ben kept on the bench and turned it on, fiddling with it until she tuned it to an easy-listening station. *"What's new? How is the world treating you . . ."* began to play, and she started humming. She slowly started swaying to the music as she filled the scoop with oats. She cast a glance toward Ben and saw him looking and smiling. She smiled shyly back and slowly drifted over to the feed boxes. Three times she made the trip, always swaying, always humming. Soon she heard a whistled harmony as Ben turned toward her and playfully exaggerated being a horn player; the surprise pleased her. She offered a modestly playful curtsy, and finding him willing to play along, she continued her dance, shyly moving toward him, hoping she could engage him in a practice turn or two around the barn floor, but as she did she saw his expression change from humor . . . to wonder . . . to ardor. It had been unexpected.

She was an arm's length away from him when his hands instinctively reached for a partner's. Ben held her gingerly in his arms but his hands took hers firmly, holding her in the spot near him. Natalie could feel his heart beating. The steam from his warm breath brushed past her chilled face, warming her own graying hair. She looked up into his face and felt the same giddy rush she felt that first day they'd met, the day at the diner when this handsome Korean war hero strode in and stole her heart. They began to sway together in time to the song, and Natalie felt Ben's arms slowly tightening, drawing her closer. She opened her mouth to speak but couldn't find the words or even the voice to make a sound.

Ben slowly drew her to him tighter and closer until his jaw brushed her temple. His head bent down, his cheek brushing hers, and he softly whispered one word, "Natalie . . ."

He pulled his head back to look admiringly into her face and, holding her left hand, brought his right hand up to run his thumb along her jaw, stopping at her chin and tipping it up slightly until her lips were barely inches from his own. Again he softly uttered her name.

She felt caught in a spell and was transported back forty years, not only to a time and place, but to the shy, self-conscious girl who had been a humiliation to her parents, a burden to her family, and a disappointment to Ben. Awkwardly, she stammered, "I . . . I thought we should practice . . . dancing . . ."

Confusion washed over Ben and he suddenly stopped moving. "What?"

"Martha's reception . . . I thought we might be asked to dance so . . . I thought we should practice . . ."

Ben's hands released hers and his arms went limp as they slid back to his sides. "Is that what this was all about?" he asked in disbelief as he turned his back to her and grabbed his pitchfork, clenching and unclenching the handle as the conversation continued.

"No . . . I . . . I . . . at first I just wanted us to practice . . . We haven't danced in years."

He spun around, the look of rejection apparent. "No . . . we *haven't* danced in years, have we?" He turned around and thrust the fork deep into the bale of straw, angrily tearing the bale apart.

She knew the spell was broken and she couldn't get it back. "It felt nice, Ben. Really. Why don't we try again?"

Ben looked dismissively over his shoulder and offered weakly, "Don't you remember? We have two left feet." He again plunged the pitchfork into the bale of straw, and Natalie turned and left the barn.

Her eyes stung as she fought the wind on her way back to the house. The oven buzzer was sounding and she burned her hand as she pulled the casserole dish from the oven and slammed it down on the table. She ran cold water over the red streak on her hand and then she just let the tears flow. Fearing Ben would come in and see her upset, she grabbed a few ice cubes from the freezer, made a cold compress for her burn, and ran up the stairs to her room.

* * *

Ben busied himself in the barn for over an hour, replaying the scene with Natalie over and over in his mind. He was hurt, even embarrassed, but more than anything he was filled with regret. Again he had missed an opportunity. Again his pride had been wounded and he had pushed the moment away. "She's making me crazy," he muttered, but then he considered how she had offered her help back in the house and how much courage she had shown to come out to the barn after he had told her to stay inside. He thought about how unlike Natalie it was to turn on the radio and flirt as she did. And this time, as he replayed the scene, he reflected on how wonderful it had felt just to see her there, trying to be playful. He paused on the image rather than focusing on what he would have liked the moment to have become. "Our timing is terrible," he moaned. "Maybe we really do have two left feet . . ."

Ben looked up at the light in the bedroom window as he crossed the distance from the barn to the house. He knew Natalie had gone upstairs for the night. He listened at the foot of the stairs for some sign that she might be coming down, but at that very moment the light switch snapped and darkness was his answer. He drifted over to the kitchen table. The casserole was a little overly browned, a consequence of Natalie's impromptu trip to the barn. He scooped up a plate and sunk heavily into his easychair as he considered how he could possibly bridge this new gap in their relationship, and then the first signs of sleet began ringing against the windows.

Ben went back out and moved the cattle from the corral into the barn for the night. By nine he was scouring the different stations for any news of the impending storm. Suddenly the phone rang. It was Sterling Davis. Sterling chose his words carefully, knowing the pain they might dredge up. "Ben, I'm worried about you and Natalie up there all alone on the windward side of the mountain."

Sterling Davis, the Johansons' longtime friend and neighbor, was correct in his concern at what inflamed emotions those words, "all alone," would trigger. Since his son's final exit, Ben Johanson worked twice as hard as any man to keep his farm running smoothly. The mortality rate for family farms was bad enough anywhere, but in this section of the fruit belt, where most of the farms reflected generations of dedication, the loss of an heir to keep the farm going, or the inability of a family to work as a team, almost always signaled an eventual sale. Gossip had flown every season for nearly twenty years as to whether or not this would be the season poor Ben Johanson would call it quits. While it would have delighted him to have TJ carry on the traditions he and Natalie had established between the farm and the community, he never would have required it of his children.

The farm had been his dream, a balm for the aftereffects of the war and a link to his past. But he remembered the fall of 1976 when TJ left home for good. Dozens of well-intentioned offers of help with the harvest and autumn activities poured in, but each one seemed wrapped in the pitiful reminder that he needed the help because his family was falling apart. He supposed it was his pride that made him see it that way, but each offer of help was a stinging reminder that, in addition to losing his son, he was, in every important way, losing his wife as well.

"I've made preparations. We'll be fine," he said as he brushed Sterling's offer aside with curt politeness. But his friend persisted.

"I know you have, Ben. You know how these freakish early ice storms can get. It's just that the sleet is coating everything with ice. Power lines are going down and you've got that steep driveway. Why don't you and Natalie come here and stay the night with us just in case the weathermen are wrong and the temperatures don't rise."

Ben read Sterling the litany on his foul-weather supplies and preparations, politely turned down his offer, and hung up the phone. He took another look out the door to assess the situation and was surprised by how much icier it had become in the last hour. He turned the TV off and fiddled with the radio to pick up a Pennsylvania station sixty miles away in Breezewood. That area's geography and elevation made it notoriously susceptible to inclement weather, and he knew whatever they got was a good indicator of the worst it could get in Washington County.

The signal was weak and the static was so annoying that, after a half hour, he gave up in frustration and grabbed his coat, heading outside toward the barn to make a final check on the animals. True to a habit developed over the last sixteen years, as soon as Ben's eyes crossed the door's threshold and the motion-light came on, his eyes set upon his old friend—the twisted old evergreen he had miraculously found as a sprig and eventually named David's Tree. It had spent its first twenty years in the tractor path where Ben had originally found it. But even though Ben believed Providence placed it there, the spot had been an unsafe one, and the poor little tree took several disabling beatings. It was after the worst of these, when the tree saved his grandson's life and nearly gave its own in the process, that Ben relented and dug up his old friend so it could spend the remainder of the winter of in a half barrel under the protective care of the cattle barn. It was there that Ben grafted and nurtured it back to health. In the spring, Ben selected a prominent site at the crest of the hill where the parking pad began, and there he planted the famed tree that would soon be bedecked in holiday regalia for the crowds of shoppers and friends who came by to select their Christmas trees.

Ben was amazed at how much more ice had built up in the last thirty minutes. He could barely walk from the house to the barnyard, only a hundred feet away. The house was positioned on a broad green knoll. The older orchards rose in steep terraces behind it and the fields of evergreens filled the area below, rolling downward to the bottom where a beautiful pasture surrounded a one-acre pond. Except for a four-foot-wide flower bed that ran the perimeter of the entire home, only a large parking pad—two thousand feet square—filled the space between the kitchen side of the house and the barn and shed. From there the paved driveway fell off sharply down the winding lane, bordered on the left by grassy double-fenced pastures with a row of twenty-five fruit bearers between fences, and on the right by more evergreens.

He reached for the light switch and illuminated the entire paved area. One stray steer was lying on the icy pavement just beyond the paddock, feet splayed in four directions and struggling to get up. Ben was dumbfounded as to how the animal had escaped from the barn, but he brushed the mystery aside. Knowing he couldn't lift the animal alone, he went to get his small tractor, towing chains, and a thick coil of rope, then headed out to save the stranded beast.

Ben eventually worked the rope under and around the wildly flailing animal and tied it off in a strong knot. He then shoved the hook at one end of the tow chain under the rope bellyband and hooked the other end on the tractor. Frightened out of its mind, the steer lurched in a mighty heave, yanking the tractor from its icy spot on the high ground above the two-foot retaining wall to where Ben and the beast struggled below. One of its powerful hooves caught Ben near his right temple, sending Ben sliding across the ice and leaving broad streaks of blood on the frozen ground. When he finally regained his senses, he realized he and the animal were in dire circumstances. During the tractor's fall, the links of the tow chain tangled with the chain guards in the tires. The rotating wheels were now acting like a winch, drawing the bawling steer toward its steel-linked jaws.

Ben saw the horrific fate that awaited the poor, terrified steer. Summoning as much clarity and strength as he could, Ben crawled on his hands and knees behind the tractor to reach the tethered animal. He knelt on a small patch of ice between the churning tires and the flailing steer, pulled his knife out, and began sawing away at the rope band, watching as each fiber broke free. When he cut the last fiber and the counterweight of the steer was gone, the tire spun wildly, tossing the chain in a large, exaggerated circle that caught Ben's jacket on the back swing. Before his startled mind could register what was happening, he began to be drawn into the chewing action of the tires.

As he struggled to unbutton the jacket far enough to slip it over his head, he screamed for Natalie, but his pleas were swallowed up in the icy wind that had started the cursed storm in the first place. Before he was free, he heard the tearing sound as metal links reached the fabric of his pants and then, immediately, he felt the searing pain of tissue and muscle being gouged from his thigh, followed by the strange warmth of his own blood streaming from the wound.

Ben kicked so ferociously against the tire with his other leg that the coat tore free. For a second he felt safe, though he lay there in agony trying to gather his wits. Reality soon flooded him as he considered that, at the rate he was losing blood, he would bleed to death if he didn't get help soon. So again, summoning his faculties to work in concert with his will, he began a slow crawl to cover the twenty-yard distance to the house.

His momentary progress was broken by his awareness of the untethered, panicked steer standing behind him now, on four shaky legs. Too wild-eyed to notice Benjamin sprawled across the ground before it, the animal headed directly toward him, lost its footing, and again went down. His front hooves splayed forward, sending a powerful thrust directly into Ben's ribs. Momentarily senseless and powerless, Ben's body skidded across the pad toward the steep, icy driveway.

The mental battle began again. *Surrender or fight?* Ben knew if he continued to skid, the deep ditch by the side of the road would become his grave, so he desperately dug his fingers into the crusty snow. He was praying for a handhold when his foraging hand brushed the lowest bough of David's Tree. Frantically, he clawed at the little tree and slowly, painfully, he turned his body until it was supported against the tree trunk on the high side of the slope. Finally, for this brief second, he breathed with relief. With his descent under control, his mind now began to consider the next and most critical problem.

The fear and the struggling had caused his heart to race, which had increased the bleeding. He knew it wouldn't be long before he would lose consciousness, and he fought to remain lucid. His dizzy mind worked skittishly over his options.

He looked up through the crystal boughs of David's Tree, focused his eyes on heaven, and prayed. The icy boughs had become solid sheets of ice, and as they caught the glow from the floodlight by the porch, they in turn captured Ben's attention. He raised his aching body upward and stretched his arm toward the thickest branch within his reach. His head was spinning from the effort, but at last he caught hold of a heavy bough near the trunk. With a whispered apology, Ben allowed his body to slump back to the ground until his bearing weight was too much for the limb and it snapped with a sharp crack. He laid the icy bough across the gash in his leg and piled on snow to add weight, then pressed down to slow the bleeding. At some point he saw more lights and then the blackness took over.

* * *

Within minutes, Sterling's headlights gingerly ascended the hill. When he pulled up near the house he felt he had entered a war zone as he stared at the blood, upturned earth, and snow. Sterling found the steer. It was bawling pitifully and flailing with three legs while the fourth was bent and twisted, obviously broken. To the right, amid rock and dirt-strewn ice, lay Ben's tractor, still churning with its motor running. Blood was smeared across the driveway in icy puddles and long red streaks. It was everywhere.

He searched frantically for Ben to no avail. Everywhere he searched he screamed his friend's name and listened for a response. As he turned toward the back door of the house, Sterling caught what he thought was a muffled cry from down the icy driveway. There he found his listless friend beneath the scraggly evergreen, his fingers clenched tightly around the ice-covered bough.

Sterling's panicked screams had been muffled by the wind, but the sound was audible enough that Natalie ran to an upstairs window to look out over the driveway. The sight nearly buckled her. She leaned heavily on the handrail as she descended the stairs and then ran for the door just as Sterling burst in with a bloodied Benjamin in his arms.

"Call 911!" he screamed.

"Oh no!" she groaned as her fingers wiped at the blood in order to see her husband's eyes.

"Not now, Natalie," Sterling ordered. "First make the call."

Half talking, half crying, she made the call and returned to where Sterling had laid Ben on the floor so he could apply pressure to his friend's torn thigh. "Get me some clean rags, Natalie . . . anything!"

Natalie ran to the laundry room and produced a white towel that quickly turned crimson as Sterling pressed it against the wound.

Ben was unable to keep his eyes open. He lay on the floor listening for Natalie's voice. He could tell from her horror-tinged inquiries that he was in dreadful shape, and one thought became foremost in his mind. He summoned all the strength he could muster and spoke her name. "Natalie . . ."

Natalie crouched beside him with her face so close he could feel her tears falling across his own cheek. "Oh, Ben!" Her voice broke. "The ambulance is on its way and you're going to be fine . . . just fine." She dug her hands into her mouth to prevent her cries from undermining the resolve of her words.

"Natalie," he repeated, this time forcing his eyes to make contact with hers. "My journals . . . read them . . . start with '60 . . ."

"Please, Ben, don't talk," she pled.

Again Ben's eyes fluttered. He forced them to focus on her face in case the darkness swept over him again. "1960, Natalie . . . read it. Promise me." Then his head slumped to the side.

The paramedics struggled to get up the increasingly icy driveway, and Sterling turned the job of applying pressure to Ben's leg over to Natalie as he went outside to help. Ben was completely unconscious now, his breathing more shallow, and a fear like none she had ever known gripped her. Never at any point in her life had she known she loved him more. Never before had she realized how inseparably inter-twined his life was with hers. She considered how ludicrous it was that they had practically made a pact to live as emotionally separate as possible, and now she realized that all they had truly done was thrown away nearly forty years of opportunities.

It was nearly ten o'clock when the ambulance was finally on the road to the hospital, with Sterling and Natalie following close behind. Natalie sat silently, her eyes glued to the back door of the ambulance as she clutched a book to her.

"What made you come tonight?" she asked.

"I can't explain it, Natalie. When Ben brushed my offer of help aside I went upstairs to turn in early, but I couldn't get him off my mind. I just . . . I knew I had to go . . ."

They drove on in silence but Natalie's mind replayed the horrific events of the evening. Then she began to wonder what events Ben had recorded in his 1960 journal, the year Martha was born.

The paramedics were unloading the gurney while the emergency room staff prepared to take over. A lady in a blue suit led Natalie to her office and began the registration process, but all Natalie wanted to do was sit by Benjamin's side. When the paperwork was completed the blue-suited lady then led her to the waiting room where Sterling sat, waiting for her. Natalie slumped into his supportive embrace, then sat up and opened the leather cover of the book labeled "1960."

Chapter Three

Aside from the physical differences between the striking nineteen-year-old young man and the fortyish-looking fellow with the smiling eyes and receding hairline, it would be hard to believe they were not already father and son. Their long conversations were alternately punctuated with laughter and periods of serious reflection, and then there were hours where they could sit quietly enjoying one or the other's favorite CD or movie.

It had been hard for Martha Johanson to share her son so completely with a new person. At times, the closeness between David and her fiancé Sam had almost made her jealous, but the past twenty-four hours helped her turn the corner on those feelings. She'd received the call the night before at eight. Her mother had called from the hospital to let her know about the accident, and from that moment on, everything was reprioritized. She took off work, David begged to skip his classes, and Sam arranged for another doctor to cover for him in case they needed to make an emergency flight to Maryland.

She had been inconsolable. She was found either glued to the phone with her mom or preparing to cancel her wedding and take the next flight east. David had taken the news hard as well since, aside from his mom, "Pap" and "Omma" were all the family he had. But Sam had been great. It was as if security and serenity walked in the door with him. In a manner that was as natural and unassuming as bandaging up a wound, he invited them to pray together, gave both David and Martha blessings of comfort, and then gave his support to whatever Martha wanted to do regarding the wedding. The calm he brought each time he entered a room was palpable.

Each call from the hospital brought good news about Ben's overall condition, but when Natalie called that evening with the latest report, the wedding plans had still been hanging in the balance. As soon as Martha entered the room, the look of relief was so apparent on her sun-freckled face that David and Sam instantly knew that not only would Ben be okay, but that the wedding would proceed as planned.

"Mom and Dad both want us to go ahead with the wedding," she said, smiling as she walked over to Sam and kissed him. "They feel that since they can't attend the ceremony anyway, we should get married here and then come east for the Thanksgiving holiday. Dad should be up and about by then, and he could use our help with the festivities—plus of course, they're anxious to meet you." She smiled teasingly, knowing how nervous he was about the first meeting with the new in-laws. "What do you think?"

"Oh, Sam, you will love the day after Thanksgiving on the farm!" assured David. "Next to Christmas Day, it's the best day of the year."

Sam looked curiously at David and then drew Martha into a loving embrace. "I think it's a great idea. Since we really haven't planned much of a honeymoon, maybe we can negotiate some things so we can stay awhile."

Martha beamed at David and whispered, "Thank you," in Sam's ear.

David noticed a curious look that hung on his mother's still-smiling face. "What are you thinking?" he asked.

"I don't know. There was something in Mom's voice. That's all."

"She's been through a lot the last twenty-four hours. She's probably exhausted," offered Sam.

Martha considered that possibility against the strange timbre of her mother's voice. "Yes . . . but it was more than that."

"What do you think she sounded like?" asked David, growing concerned.

"Don't worry, David. It wasn't a bad sound, in fact, just the opposite. When she spoke about Dad, aside from the expected mix of concern and relief, she sounded sort of . . . I don't know how to explain it . . . like a love-struck schoolgirl."

Sam looked questioningly at her. He was disarmed to think that such a sweet attitude from her mother would seem strangely unfamiliar to her. Admittedly, his wife was a shy woman, but she personally possessed a warm, affectionate manner. Still, he couldn't doubt the honesty of her bewilderment as she stared absently at the wall, tugged at a lock of her auburn hair, and finally answered his look, "You don't understand, Sam. My parents are not demonstrative people. They're very pragmatic with one another. It just seemed really odd."

* * *

Martha and David's favorite activity that evening, as it had been for the last twenty-four hours, was to rehash old Johanson memories, partly as a release from all the tension and fear, and partly to bring the newest Johanson adoptee up to speed on the family lore.

Sam seemed more worried the longer they talked. His future wife and stepson were whispering back and forth and snickering at his furrowed brow.

"Alright, alright, you two . . ." he protested. "No more family secrets."

Martha reached over and rubbed his earlobe. "Sorry, Sam, it's just that the more we talk about introducing you to my folks the deeper the lines grow on your forehead. What do you think, David? By the time we get to Maryland, Dad will be able to plant trees in those rows."

David laughed softly. He loved this banter and teasing. He finally knew what he had been missing out on. After spending the majority of his twenty years as the "man of the house," he was thrilled to see his mom in love with a man to whom he could so easily feel like a son. During the past few months he'd carefully observed the two of them. Although they had fallen in love quickly, and though marriage meant complete changes in all their lives, they were good changes that fit well. More than that, they had satisfied longings in both their hearts that, despite their best combined efforts, they had never managed to fill in one another, but which when offered to them, were immediately familiar and good. He had not fully realized how fragile his fatherless childhood had left him until genuine, solid, spiritual Sam entered the picture. It wasn't that he completely lacked a good male figure who was devoted to him. Pap had dedicated himself to trying to fill that role, but it wasn't the same as having that man there every day, on hand at a moment's notice, nor was Pap and Omma's love able to bring the sparkle into his mother's life that in turn blessed David as well. He finally understood the magic of having two happy parents.

Still, in spite of the lack of a loving father, he tried not to let the past bother him. He was the undisputed "golden child" of the Johanson family, and to him there was little difference in the depth of love he felt from grandparents or mother. They had all contributed to the man he had become, and now, with the addition of Sam, he couldn't believe that he could feel more loved or be more happy.

The first four years of his life had been spent on his grandparents' farm in Maryland. Living there allowed his mother the support she needed to finish high school and get her nursing degree, and it filled his early years with more joy than a child could wish for. His "Pap" had been more a father than a grandfather during those years, and "Omma" somehow managed to love him desperately without crowding the sacred niche reserved for his mother.

After graduation, ready to try her wings, mom and son left their idyllic farm life and headed south to Virginia, far enough away to feel independent, but close enough to make it home for long weekends and holidays. In Virginia, his pretty, petite mother had no shortage of male suitors and one, a Mr. Reed, eventually convinced her he was Mr. Right and they'd married. It was a brief union as Mr. Reed discovered, unfortunately, that he was not yet ready for a family, leaving Martha and David zero for two where husbands and fathers were concerned. David seemed to take it personally for a while. In fact, he was so despondent after his mother's marriage ended that Martha decided to hold him back from school that fall and let him heal a little. Luckily, there was still Pap and Omma.

David spent most summers on the farm, and every Thanksgiving and Christmas he and his mother were drawn back as well, so Pap had been a great influence on him, imparting invaluable gifts from his "old soul" that helped his grandson see and understand things beyond the wisdom of his young years.

It was a mixed blessing to both mother and son when, in 1993, a position opened in California for a nursing director's job at a small hospital. But Martha felt a change would be good and off they went.

With no family nearby and their small-town values seemingly challenged at every turn, the adjustment was difficult, but she was determined to make a go of it. Then Martha met Sam.

Doctor Samuel Pearce was a pediatrician at her hospital. She had seen him and noted the frustration of nurses whose passes went unrequited. One of the senior residents finally explained his shaken past. He had been in love only twice, first pledging himself to his high school sweetheart. But that relationship had ended abruptly while he was out of the country, serving his church as a missionary. Following his mission he'd tried to bypass romance, choosing instead to throw himself into his studies. Then he met another woman and had fallen deeply in love during his residency. The normally guarded doctor had thrown caution to the wind and become engaged in twelve weeks. Three days before their winter wedding day, his fiancée was driving through the snow-laden mountains of Utah when her car slid off the road and rolled, killing her maid of honor instantly while she lingered for four agonizing days, never regaining consciousness. After that tragedy, Dr. Pearce threw his love solely into the children he treated and dedicated all his energies to their care.

Martha had treated him with professionalism but found that she, like the others, was drawn to his gentle, caring manner and lifted by the great respect he showed everyone. She noticed he did not spend his discretionary time in the lounges relaxing with his colleagues, but instead chose to keep himself busy consulting with specialists, visiting the children in his charge, and comforting their families.

Then, two summers ago, while taking a hike along the Appalachian Trail with Pap, David had unknowingly been bitten by a deer tick and contracted Lyme disease. By the time he reached California he was showing flu-like symptoms that steadily became worse. Unsatisfied by the casual approach her physician was taking, Martha had asked Dr. Pearce for a second opinion. After a few calls to colleagues at Johns Hopkins, Sam began a medical protocol that had brought almost immediate results.

Martha had already arranged to stay the night at David's bedside, and the hourly visits Dr. Pearce made to check on David's progress afforded them opportunities to get more personally acquainted. On one of his visits Martha had offered him a cup of coffee. He awkwardly thanked her for the invitation but declined, sharing that he was a Latter-day Saint, a Mormon, and then explained that he lived by a health code that cautioned him to abstain from coffee and other harmful things. His awkwardness quickly passed as Martha and David asked him question after question. With his rounds officially over, he enjoyed his enthusiastic audience and spent hours discussing the doctrines of his church and stories of his pioneer ancestors who were driven from their homes because of their beliefs, then crossed the plains and settled in the Salt Lake Valley.

Martha and David were fascinated, as much by the earnestness and honesty with which Sam embraced these teachings as by the emotions they felt as he spoke. At first they felt a kinship with him over his love of family and heritage. They understood these principles. You could not be a Johanson and overlook the importance of heritage. But after he left David's room, Martha and David had spoken long into the night and discovered that each of them had experienced a feeling of rightness about the things he explained. There had always been a religious undertone in the Johanson home, where a prayer of gratitude for simple blessings of food and shelter was a staple of life, but Ben and Natalie Johanson had never affiliated with any one particular religion over another. They found good in every church, but there were always questions left unanswered and some points of doctrine that left them unwilling to commit to one theology over another.

But the feelings David and Martha felt that night while talking to Sam left them curious to know more, and the Saturday after David was released from the hospital they asked Sam for the address of his church. Although he seemed pleased by their inquisitiveness, Martha had felt a distance grow between them. For three weeks she and David read the copy of the Book of Mormon Sam had loaned them, attended church, and spent many evenings with missionaries who answered their questions and put all the pieces of information they were learning into an ordered, beautiful gospel plan. The missionaries had asked them to pray together to ask if what they were learning was true, and they each received a different but undeniable witness that it was, then agreed to be baptized. Pap and Omma received this news with some skepticism, but as time passed and they saw the happiness this choice brought Martha and David, they made peace with it.

On the day of their baptism, Sam reappeared. He apologized for having been somewhat aloof and sat quietly in the back of the room during the service. Although the chapel Martha and David would attend was a different one than the chapel Sam attended, he began showing up occasionally for their services. On those days Martha would invite him back for supper. After months of this "friendly" routine he finally asked Martha out on a real date. She knew immediately that she loved him, and David was convinced that it was just a matter of time before Sam would let go of his fears and admit that he too had fallen in love with this little family. It was almost one year to the day of David's hospitalization that Sam asked Martha to marry him, and now they would be wed in less than two weeks.

David was amused by how nervous Sam was over his impending first meeting with the in-laws—to face the couple whose twice-burned daughter and grandson he had stolen and changed with a new religion. *What? Him worry?* But David did share his new stepfather's nervousness about their possible reaction to the news of David's plans for the next two years, another result of Sam's influence. "Sure, they're going to just love meeting you!" David laughed jokingly.

"Sam, my parents *will* love you. Please don't worry," Martha said reassuringly.

"Sure, Sam," David chimed in, "Pap just loves new sons-in-law."

"David, stop," his mom laughingly scolded.

"Listen, college boy," Sam comically pled, "since you're the family golden child, cut your stepdad a break and build me up big time. Tell lots of stories about how I saved you from near death and kept a selfless vigil by your bedside when you were sick."

"Oh yeah," laughed David, "would that be before or after you started hitting on my mom?"

Sam's face blushed red as the laughter broke the tension in the room. After a few moments of silence Sam broke in more seriously. "Okay, so I am a little nervous here. I don't know much about your family, but holidays, at least in my family, tend to be all about old times and old history, so I am just warning you up front that I might feel a little awkward."

As Martha and David shared apologetic glances, Martha tried to put Sam's fears in perspective. "All you really need to know is not to mention anything about TJ unless someone else brings him up, and, well, you've already heard about all the important family stories. Other than that you'll just need to be your wonderful, charming self."

A worried look crossed Sam's face. "I remember you telling me some family folk tales or something, but I really didn't pay too much attention to them. Is it important that I know them?"

David jumped in protectively. "Sam, stories of David's Tree are not folk tales to Pap. To him these are sacred experiences and they're an important part of our family history, so make sure you don't make light of them."

"I wasn't trying to make light. I guess I just need a refresher course."

Martha looked at David. "You've probably heard the stories more than I have by now, so why don't you do the honors."

David leaned forward as if the telling of these stories required an emotional intimacy with the hearers. He bent his head down for a second. Sam wasn't sure if he was praying or getting his thoughts together, and then he began.

"To understand Pap's reverence for David's Tree you'd have to go back to the difficult time right after Mom was born . . ." David proceeded to tell of the miraculously good fortune his grandparents had in finding the farm just when their military housing was up, and how they found the struggling evergreen.

Sam considered the facts as well as the passion David obviously felt, but he was slow to ascribe the term "miracle" to just anything. He tried to see the event through David's eyes, to set logic aside and accept each remarkable piece on faith, but his voice betrayed his words.

"David, a miracle to me is so . . . so sacred that I don't like to throw the term around casually." He finished in a more quiet and apologetic tone. "That said, I do realize that this is sacred to you guys and I want to share in it . . . I really do."

Martha and David looked quietly at one another. Because Sam was so like Pap in his steadfastness and ability to cut through the muck of life, he had become a spiritual barometer to David and Martha. And David wanted, no . . . needed Sam to at least understand. Whether or not he accepted it as a miracle, they needed him to at least fully appreciate the impact this event had had in shaping their family.

David smiled a "last chance" smile at his mom and started in on the last leg of the tale. "Okay, Sam, for something to be a miracle, would you expect it to have some purpose?"

"Yes, David." Sam drew a deep, audible breath as the memories of his own past struggles over God's will and His ability to perform miracles settled over him. He had once wrestled with the when's and why's of the Lord's intervention, and was finally at peace.

David was encouraged. The next part of the story would powerfully make his point.

"Okay, normally an evergreen will grow about a foot a year, but this little sprig, because it was planted in the middle of a row, was constantly getting trampled on and roughed up. Pap struggled with the decision to move it in order to protect it, but somehow felt that its placement was part of its miracle. So he nursed it, but in spite of all his efforts, it was always a scraggly, little tree—but a scraggly little tree that saved my life."

Sam's face registered intrigue, and pleased that he again had Sam's interest, David began recounting the story of the Christmas when he was four, and how his Santa-requested sled had become so much of a temptation that the normally obedient son ignored his mother's and grandparents' warning and stole out of the house to take a first ride down the orchard hill.

Then Martha picked up the story. "Mom noticed that the sled was no longer under the tree, and so we began to panic and ran around the yard to find him. Dad followed his footsteps in the snow and visually traced the path up to square number five in the orchard where the steepest slope ran directly toward the pond at the bottom. He screamed and Mom and I immediately knew what was about to happen. All three of us began a stunned race for the orchard. Before we could reach David he was jumping on the sled and careening down the slope." Martha shuddered as she spoke, and David, noticing how his foolishness still haunted her, offered her an apologetic smile and continued.

"All I knew was that I was moving way too fast. I saw the little pine tree in front of me and the partially frozen pond at the bottom and I started screaming. It never occurred to me to just roll off the sled—no, I just screamed and held on for dear life," he laughed.

David's mood became more serious, though, as he focused on the last few seconds of the experience. "I closed my eyes and rode on screaming. I know it sounds silly, but I still expected that Pap or Omma or Mom would save me. Anyway, the little pine was right in front of me. The sled ran right over it, and even though I was really moving, somehow the blade of the sled got tangled up in its weak little boughs and I stopped completely. When everybody got to me, I was kneeling by the tree, sobbing, because I knew how much Pap loved that little tree, and how it was all bent over, its bark scraped off like a potato peeler had run over it."

Martha's eyes were moist as she smiled. "They really were the sorriest tears I've ever seen. He wasn't crying because he was afraid. He was trying to hold one of the broken boughs up in his hands and he kept telling Dad how sorry he was and begged him to fix it."

David smiled wistfully. "Pap got to me first. He just scooped me up in his arms and fell to his knees sobbing. Then Mom and Omma knelt down and cried with me. I had grown up with the miracle of this little tree, so I thought when I ran it over that I had committed a mortal sin or something, but back at the house, Pap snuggled with me under a quilt on his big chair and told me not to worry, that he thought the little tree had served its purpose that very day by saving me, and that maybe that's why it was placed there in the first place. That evening we dug it up and carried it back to the cattle barn. We wrapped the broken boughs as best we could and replanted it in an old barrel. Then, when Mom and I came back up for Easter, Pap and I planted it in a safe place near the barnyard where we could protect it.

"The doctor who checked me out the day of the accident called the *Herald,* and the story of my miraculous rescue was in the morning paper. 'David's Tree' is now a certifiable celebrity in Smithsburg, and every Christmas season it's one of the main attractions at the farm.

"But there's one more part to this story, Sam. You know this accident Pap just had? Well, the tree saved Pap's life too."

Sam's eyes grew wide and he looked at Martha for confirmation. She smiled an affirmative yes.

"Tell me more, David. You just might have a miracle on your hands after all."

Chapter Four

Jeff Johnson had eight minutes before his next appointment. He moved folders around until he located Meredith Davenport's file. He juggled his sandwich, another desktop lunch, wolfing down big bites while he perused her report. It was another story of a lonely but good kid who was uprooted by a move and who latched onto the first group that embraced her, but unfortunately it was the wrong group. Her circle of friends had suddenly changed, and before her parents realized it, there were other, more serious changes in grades, attitudes, and dress. Jeff flipped back to the front page of the file and looked again at the photos there. It was a dramatic transformation. If he hadn't known better he would have thought it was a joke. Photo one, taken in June, before her arrest, was her senior portrait. It reflected an attractive, seventeen-year-old woman with shoulder-length brown hair that casually framed a fresh, lightly blushed face. In photo two, taken the night of her arrest, she was almost unrecognizable. The changes in hair and makeup only enhanced the hardness of her overall appearance. Her dyed-black hair was cut in a short, jagged style with spikes and primary-colored highlights. Her makeup was as severe as her hair. Gone was the fresh face and youthful glow. In its place was an angry countenance.

Jeff took another huge bite and flipped back to the arrest record. A Washington County patrol car had pulled over a car matching the description of a vehicle reported stolen. When the officers approached the vehicle, two young men abruptly opened the door and confronted the officers. The scene was more insubordinate than dangerous, but things heated up quickly and the two young men, eighteen and nineteen respectively, were charged as adults while Meredith was held as a minor.

The car turned out to be the vehicle of one of the young men's uncles. The car-theft charges were dropped the next day at the request of the car's owner, but the insubordination and presence of alcohol, plus the DUI charge, became the primary concern for the guys.

Meredith's situation hit a panic button in the court system, however. The judge, who had seen too many minors come through his court, considered her arrest the "last straw" in a rash of recent juvenile offenses, and placed her into the county's "At-Risk Minors" program—ARM. Kids placed in this program were evaluated, assigned a caseworker, and placed in a program of supervised modification. Their caseworker met with the individual each week for the allotted amount of time and arranged for the offender to fulfill an assigned number of hours of community service, continue counseling, comply with the terms of a behavior modification contract, and basically keep his or her nose clean until age eighteen. If at that time they had fulfilled all the court's recommended requirements, any and all charges were expunged from their juvenile record and all court costs would be forgiven. If they failed to complete the agreement, the court costs, including fees for weekly assigned counseling, were billed directly to the youth's family, and the full weight of all the charges would return.

Meredith, or Merit as she reportedly preferred to be called, had been assigned to Jeff several weeks ago though they had not yet met. He felt optimistic about the possibility of salvaging what he believed was a basically good kid, but felt strongly that a positive first meeting and a good service assignment were going to be critical. *I've only got the rest of today and tomorrow to place her before Thanksgiving . . .* He flipped the chart back to see her address, and though he didn't recognize the street, the zip code and town still sent a shiver down his spine. "Smithsburg." He popped the last onion ring into his mouth just as his phone rang.

"Hey, Jeff, it's Dennis. You asked me for this stuff a while ago, didn't you?"

"Yeah, but I should have followed up on it. Too many cases I guess . . ."

"Or maybe this one's just not for you."

"I'm fine, Dennis," Jeff replied curtly. "Just tell me what you've got."

"Okay." Dennis backed off. "What part of Washington County does your minor live in?"

"Her address is listed as Smithsburg," Jeff replied with feigned ease.

"Oh." Dennis played along. "Okay, well, I have four service opportunities in Washington County, but only one in the Smithsburg area."

"Give me a quick rundown on that one," Jeff urged.

"Okay, it's service at the Brighton Children's Home. Brighton is a private foster care home situated on the edge of town. They began operating from grants and a large one-time endowment, but that money is dwindling fast so they've had to make some deep program cuts and could use some extra hands."

Dennis's voice continued, but Jeff's mind was stuck on the name. "Brighton Children's Home?" he interrupted Dennis. "What's the address of this place?"

"It's 4023 Brighton Lane, off Mountain Valley."

He didn't recognize the street address but he knew it was the same place. It had to be. Mr. Brighton once owned a moderately sized farm on the side of the mountain with a spacious, friendly home he had built to house his large family. *How many hours did I spend there?* Thousands, he guessed. The two families spent many evenings together playing games and sharing meals. Both sets of children had been more like one family, separated only by sleeping arrangements. He brought each of their faces to his remembrance, then paused longingly on one face. Then, as the thoughts became painful, he pushed the memory away.

After he left the area he had periodically subscribed to the local, weekly paper, and remembered reading an old article explaining that the county's need for a competitive truck route led to their decision to place it through the Brighton farm, leaving the old gentleman's home cut off from his barns and fields by the busy pike. After a few close calls on his tractor, he decided to sell off the bulk of his land, reducing his once-beautiful farm to a twelve-acre lot. Finally he sold the homestead and moved to Florida to be near two of their sons and their families. Jeff supposed that some investor bought the place and turned it into a children's home, and the unfamiliar address was most likely due to the new road. *Fitting,* he thought. It was a home that was always meant for children.

"It's an unfortunate situation," rambled Dennis. "They're really trying to run a family-style home for these kids with all the extras, but they've had to cut their music program back to almost nothing. The endowment is gone and the grant ended, so they can't afford to pay the teacher anymore."

Jeff's eyes kept scanning Meredith's bio throughout the conversation. When Dennis mentioned music, a bell went off in his head and he quickly searched for a particular paragraph. "Oh man, this is great," he exclaimed excitedly. "My client was an all-county violinist. She also plays the piano and guitar."

Debbie, the office secretary, knocked briskly and cracked the door open. "Jeff, your one o'clock is here."

"I heard that. I'll bring this over to you right now," Dennis replied and hung up.

Jeff cleared the lunch litter from his desk and stood up, brushing the crumbs from his shirt. After one quick survey of the office, he opened the door. Standing outside the doorway was Meredith and her parents. He invited them in with a warm "nice to meet you" and a welcoming smile.

Carol Davenport, Meredith's mother, entered first. She was a short, thin woman with sad eyes, about forty years of age. The slump in her posture made her look much smaller than she was, Jeff thought. He had seen that slump many times before. To him it was the ultimate symbol of the weight of the responsibility of raising children. He had seen countless numbers of loving parents caught up in the despair of their children's problems, a despair that seemed to physically buckle them. Still, Carol Davenport seemed somehow different. She moved numbly and offered a polite but forced smile, as if she hadn't used those muscles in quite some time.

Michael Davenport, Meredith's father, was a tall, evenly built man. He had a few extra pounds here and there that gave him a rounded, approachable look. His dark hair was thinning, and strain showed on his face as well, but he demonstrated a caring manner with his wife, and Jeff immediately liked him.

Unspoken 57

As Mr. Davenport led his wife to a chair and settled her in, Meredith passed through the doorway. It was apparent that every effort had been made to restore her appearance to resemble her earlier image. She wore just a hint of makeup and her clothes were again modest and classic. Jeff prided himself on having a natural ability to read people, and Meredith's overall countenance confirmed to him that she was indeed a basically good kid who'd temporarily run amok. He felt a sense of optimism that these were parents who could and would support their daughter through what lay ahead.

After the cursory introductions and review of the file with the family, Jeff spent a few minutes talking with the parents to get their spin on the situation and then suggested that they visit the snack shop to give him a chance to visit alone with Meredith for thirty minutes. As they left the room, Carol Davenport slid a gentle hand across her daughter's stiff shoulders and offered her an encouraging hint of a smile. Though not cheerful, Carol was obviously a caring mother.

As Jeff returned to his chair he noticed Meredith's eyes scanning the room and saw them shift from the tree to the aerial photo of the farm and back to him again. Each was assessing the other—she, through the things he surrounded himself with, and he through the way she responded to them.

"I understand you prefer to be called Merit," he began.

"Whatever," she replied disinterestedly.

Jeff smiled. *So we're going to be that way, are we?* he thought. "Well, Merit, I've heard what your parents have to say and now I'd like to hear what you think of all this."

"I think everyone is making a big deal out of nothing since I'm going to be eighteen in a few weeks," she replied. "But I'm here, so tell me what my penance is so I can pay it and get everyone off my back."

Her acrid voice took him by surprise. *Maybe I misjudged her. Maybe this kid really is further gone than I thought.* He looked at her for a moment—silently, intently. He could tell the silence unnerved her and he liked how easily her stubborn attitude shifted to discomfort under his gaze. He was reassured that his first assumption was right. She was successful at playing tough, but it was more performance than personality.

"I could be wrong, but I didn't see two parents who appeared to be on your back. My impression was that you're an incredibly lucky young lady who has two very scared parents in her corner."

Merit sat in silence. She fumbled with her hands and Jeff could tell that her eyes were moist. It was judgment-call time. He knew if he pushed her she would become emotional very easily, but he also knew from personal experience that that approach could backfire. He decided to change the subject and try to build her trust.

"Merit's an unusual name. How did you go from Meredith to Merit?"

Merit never met his eyes. Her only visible acknowledgement of the question was the skeptical arching of her eyebrows.

He smiled awkwardly. *Strike one,* he thought and tried again.

"The word implies worth and value. Do you think your parents were giving you a nickname to live up to?"

Merit's head popped up, and she rolled her eyes back in her head. Jeff felt the sting of her reproach. *Strike two,* he thought, but he decided not to move on and instead waited in confronting silence until she responded. Finally she replied.

"My parents had nothing to do with the name. I started it myself my freshman year."

Annoyed, but talking, he mused. "Really?" He sat back, tapped a pencil on his knee and offered her only mild interest. "Well, that tells me when, but I still don't understand why." *Keep her talking. It doesn't really matter about what, just keep the conversation focused on her.*

Merit tried to stare him down, to see if he would blink first, but again his silent stare won out. She leaned forward in her seat and looked at him as if he were dense.

"Do you know anyone named Meredith? Anyone under eighty? Well I don't. And I got tired of people too lazy to pronounce my name properly taking it upon themselves to rename me Mary, so I changed it to something I liked. End of story." She slumped back against the chair, moving her gaze from spot to spot, attempting to feign boredom but in actuality doing anything to avoid Jeff's eyes.

Her comments had been insightful, but Jeff decided to take the focus off of her and approach her from another angle. He leaned forward and reopened her file. He scanned the arrest report and began. "Merit, tell me about Brian Hartman and Zach Messerly."

Relieved to have the subject shift she responded with a flippant, "Tell you what?"

"What do want to tell me?"

"Nothing."

"Then why are you here, Merit?" Jeff sat back in his seat and paused. "This program is for kids who are *interested* in getting their life back on track. Now whether you succeed or not is going to have very little impact on my life, but it will make a very big difference to your future, and it means everything to your parents. So, should we just call it quits for today and I'll report to the judge that you're just not interested, or shall we begin again?"

Jeff's words were firm and again he backed up his tough position with silence. She studied his face, and Jeff knew he was being sized up personally, but as he bore her scrutiny, he watched acceptance soften her expression.

"Shall we try again?" he repeated, offering her a smile of hope, and she nodded. "So, tell me how you came to know Brian Hartman and Zach Messerly."

Merit closed her eyes, ordering the events in her mind. When she began she spoke in soft, sad tones, and Jeff knew there was obviously a lot of hidden information behind her words.

"Up until my sophomore year we had always lived in Frederick. I wasn't homecoming queen or anything, but at least I had friends at the church we attended and at school, and we hung out together. Then, after my little brother Markie died, Dad thought we all needed a fresh start, so we moved to Smithsburg."

This revelation was news to Jeff. He didn't know anything about another sibling. His mind raced, putting a thousand different pieces of the puzzle into place: Carol Davenport's deeply sad eyes, Michael Davenport's vigil over his wife, and Merit's sudden changes. He had so many questions, but instead let Merit continue on.

"I mean . . . no one ever asked me what I wanted . . . how I felt about moving . . ."

"Did you ever try to tell your parents how you felt?"

"How could I? Mom was crying all the time and Dad didn't know what to do. From the time Markie got sick it was like floating down a river toward a steep waterfall. You know you're going to fall, you know you're going to crash, but you float along trying to enjoy the ride as long as you can. Then one day, we crashed, and it was like no one had any idea how to be a family without him. Dad thought the answer was to move and start over.

"For a while I felt guilty because all I wanted was for things to be normal, to be the way they were, and then one day I realized they never would be. And then I just got really sad, like, it wasn't just about Markie's death. Somehow it seemed like it was about me . . . that I just wasn't enough, that I could never fill the emptiness Markie left behind, and I felt so . . . invisible. At home, at school, everywhere . . . I just felt . . . invisible." Her voice begged Jeff to understand.

"And then, one day, someone noticed me. Brian Hartman was a guy struggling in my art class. We worked on a couple of projects together. He would talk to me about his girlfriend and parties—the whole 'weekend connection,' not my style at all—but at least he talked to me. They broke up just before school ended and he got me a job at the gift shop where he worked. I guess I wanted to try to be what I thought he liked in girls, so I changed my hair a little and bought different clothes. Around July we started going out. I never did drugs with him, but I did drink a little and I started smoking. I knew it was stupid, but it just felt so good to have someone care about me. Can you understand that?"

Jeff's mind was haunted by an old memory of another fresh-faced, innocent girl who felt lonesome and unlovable until a young man spun her level head 180 degrees. He knew the story.

Merit's heart spilled on. "Brian lost his license on a DUI. I let him drive my dad's car and he was pulled over again. This time he was thrown into a treatment program. My dad took my license and forbade me from seeing him, but we found ways. We'd meet at friends' houses or catch rides with people. The night we got picked up there was a big party on High Rock."

High Rock was another uncomfortable flash from Jeff's distant past. High Rock was a cliff that jutted out about 600 feet above the ground where large crowds gathered to watch the hang gliders. But at night it became a dangerous party scene as kids filled with liquid invincibility came for the spectacular view of stars. He shuddered inwardly at the memories.

"Brian had called his friend Zach from Frederick and told him he could get him into this great party if he could give us a ride and some beer. When he showed up we knew he was already pretty wasted, but we didn't know he stole the car. Brian started in on the beer right away. They were so drunk they couldn't find their way to High Rock. They wandered around the mountain, driving in and out of private drives and smashing cans and honking the horn. When they heard the cops' siren they got really agitated and tried to lose them. Brian knew he would end up in treatment again, and Zach was squealing about breaking probation. When the police stopped them they were crazy and yelling, and the cops pulled their guns and cuffed us all." Quiet sobs interfered with her story. "The lady cop kept trying to scare me with threats of what happens to young girls who spend the night in jail. I was so scared. By the time my folks came to get me, I didn't care if I lived or died."

Her hands rubbed deeply into her eyes. Jeff laid his hand on her shoulder briefly, then pointed toward the bulletin board of photos. "See all these kids, Merit? They sat in that very chair and said the same thing to me at one time or another—and now almost every one of them has a new, wonderful life. You will too, and your parents and I will help you, okay?"

She sniffed and nodded slightly, taking the tissue Jeff offered her. "Now let's get your parents back in here and make a plan."

Chapter Five

It was a chilly day, perfect weather for the day before Thanksgiving. The dawn sky was a frothy, cloud-scattered canopy of orange, gray, and white. The breeze nipped at Natalie Johanson's wind-burned face and tousled her graying hair as she scurried from the hen house with fresh eggs in her pockets. There were so few eggs this time of the year, and she had been tempted to forego her usual check on her layers' progress, but there was a day full of baking and cooking ahead, and every little contribution would come in handy.

She laid her three little treasures near the sink and hurried over to the banister to listen for a sound from upstairs. Hearing none, she checked the clock for the time. "Hmm . . . 6:33," she read. "It's not like Benjamin to sleep in so late . . . especially not today." Her brow wrinkled as she wrestled with the question of whether or not to awaken her husband, and then, after great deliberation, she decided to risk annoying him and let his body enjoy the extra rest it so sorely needed. She turned from the stairwell and peeked into the living room to make a quick assessment, but the disheveled mess around Benjamin's favorite old recliner marred its tidiness. As Natalie picked up the dishes, remnants of Benjamin's evening snack of popcorn and cider, she noticed the paper was folded to reveal the classifieds. She knew Ben had been scanning the paper to make sure the ads were correct, so she took a second to look at them as well. The Boy Scouts' ad was nice.

CHRISTMAS TREE SALE
Cut and tied. $5.00 per foot.
Featuring beautiful Johanson trees.
12 South Main Street.
To benefit Boy Scout Troop 328.

This would be the seventeenth year they discounted two hundred cut trees and sold them to the Scouts for their annual fund-raiser. The fee they charged the Scouts barely covered the cost of cutting and moving them, but it was one of their favorite ways to give something back to the community that had been so good to them. Even though Ben cut his trees for the Scouts, he could never understand the "stop and shop" mentality of Christmas-tree shoppers who simply grabbed a pre-cut tree with no thought to the sacrifice being made in their behalf. Because of this, he only sold "cut-your-own" and "balled" trees at the farm, hoping to awaken people to appreciation for the trees and what they represented. Thus, Ben did have one condition attached to his deal with the Scouts—none of the trees was to ever be left without a home on Christmas Eve. Every year Ben made an agreement with the Scoutmaster of Troop 328 that he would refund the cost of any tree not sold, and so, at 6:00 P.M. on Christmas Eve, any pre-cut Johanson trees not sold would be given away for free to ensure that their precious lives, symbolic to many of the Savior's, had not been sacrificed for nothing. No, Ben regarded their lives as sacred, especially since David's Tree.

Natalie's eye now moved to their own advertisement. "Johansons' Annual Christmas Tree Sale and Fair" topped the ad in large, fancy print, while smaller captions invited families to come and enjoy the living Nativity and an evening reading of "The Night Before Christmas" on December twenty-third, featuring Santa as the guest reader.

> Gingerbread Men and Hot Cider Free for the Children.
> Fresh Pine Roping, Boughs and Swags.
> Handmade Crafts, and International Delicacies.

The last two items were fund-raising booths manned by local charities and clubs. The bottom of the ad featured a coupon for a five-dollar savings on any of the various types of trees. Natalie was excited, yet exhausted just from thinking about the upcoming month.

She could remember the pleasure she received from traipsing through the farm to select a tree with her own children, and then the supreme joy she and Ben experienced each year when they walked their precious grandson, David, through the same process. Tomorrow, on Thanksgiving, while the turkey finished roasting and the side dishes were placed on the bottom oven rack, Natalie, Benjamin, David, and Martha would all take their traditional hike around the farm to cut their perfect Christmas tree. But this year, a new family member would be initiated into this sacred family ritual.

She tucked the paper under her arm, then gathered up the heating pad Ben used for his back and the ice pack he'd used to soothe his injured leg. She moved to the fireplace and caught her image in the mirror above the mantel. She smoothed an errant strand of hair back into place and paused to be sure it remained. She smiled at the reflection staring back at her. It was both foreign and familiar. She looked much the same as she had twenty years ago, but the gray hairs were beginning to outnumber the auburn ones of her youth. She chastened herself for the melancholy that started to settle in and returned to her work.

Even though she had just dusted the day before, a white residue had already settled on the mantel, compliments of the fireplace below. Natalie folded up one of Ben's dirty socks and began pushing it along the shelf. As she shifted the photographs displayed on the mantel, her eyes settled on two family portraits, one taken right before Martha's birth, and one from the fall of 1975. The first photo was taken from the most supremely joyous period of her memories, when life held boundless possibilities. The faces of herself, Ben, and two-year-old TJ reflected that bliss. The second picture, the 1975 shot, was the last family photo Natalie had that included TJ, and that Christmas was the last one they had spent together. Every year after they moved to the farm, Natalie, Ben, and the children had stood before the same evergreen and posed for a picture to send in their Christmas cards. When it became evident that TJ was not returning home and Ben could no longer bear the hurt, he took all of the old photographs and placed them in a box in the attic, but Natalie had slid these particular photos in a kitchen drawer. When she finally replaced them on the mantel several months later, her unspoken demand was clearly understood by Ben. These pictures stayed.

The face of the handsome, dark-haired young man was burned into her memory. She did not want to forget that face. *What does he look like now that twenty-one additional years of living have etched their* *lines on it?* He would be nearly thirty-nine now. The holidays always made her long for TJ, and she became more melancholy as she recalled how Benjamin and she labored over a name for the wondrous little child—he wanting a name his son could live up to and she wanting a name her son would not want to run away from, and so they decided on the name Thomas Jefferson Johanson, TJ for short. She began to feel the burning in her eyes that always preceded her tears. It was a familiar though undesirable side effect of the holidays, and she brushed her forearm across her eyes and scolded herself.

Her reflection caught her attention again and she compared it to the face of the younger woman in the old photo. Her opinion of her appearance changed. Yes, she thought she was still rather attractive, her smooth face still close to the image in her late thirties, but at fifty-nine years of age, she could see changes that reflected more about the journey of her life than the duration of it. She wondered if anyone else could sense her return to the bliss of the portrait from the early days of her marriage. It was a very recent change and she caught herself looking in the mirror more and more frequently to see if the happiness burning in her heart had made its way onto her countenance yet. Or did people still see the old, steady Natalie, the woman who locked away her heart in 1960 after the difficult events of Martha's birth, the woman who slowly allowed her husband back into her world on a basis of courtesy and duty, the woman who had been a devoted mother and neighbor but who had never allowed her tender heart to be in a position where hurt or disappointment could wound her again? Sadly, she never allowed her heart to be in a position where love could warm it either, until recently.

She again considered her graying hairs. She had earned them. She had even deserved many of them. That unwanted change had begun about the same time as TJ's tortuous departure. Natalie thought the day he slammed the door on the devastation he left behind was going to be the darkest day in her already-clouded life, yet there were worse days to come. But after Martha's confession, Natalie had pulled herself together quickly, realizing that her daughter's needs superceded her own. But both Johanson women knew the hardest moment of their lives would be the moment they would have to tell Benjamin. Martha's

FIRE SAFETY
CERTIFICATE

Ashton C
Name

has demonstrated
Fire Safety!

Stop, Drop, and Roll
Safety Crawl

Miss Sean and Justin
Teacher

April 10, 2008
Date

FIRE SAFETY
CERTIFICATE

Ashton G
_____
(name)

has demonstrated

Fire Safety

Stay Crawl
Stop, Drop and Roll

August 2008
Date

Miss Castillo and Justin
Teacher

body had shuddered as she struggled to speak the words, and more painful still was the agony she had felt as she watched her father's steely shoulders slump. He never spoke. He simply offered her a shaky hand that drew her onto his lap where the pair sat and rocked for hours. Natalie had never been prouder of him and she longed to join the embrace and have him hold her as well, but she had foolishly allowed herself to be imprisoned within the boundaries she had drawn.

The winter and spring following Martha's news were painful, and it had become clear to the Johanson family who their true friends were. To casual observers, Natalie and Benjamin Johanson had appeared to be failures as parents. Their only son was a runaway with a questionable past and their only daughter was unwed and pregnant. There were other pregnant girls at the school, but the prominence of the Johanson family made Martha's situation the chatter around town. Though the principal never forced her to leave public school, enough suggestions were made about having her consider finishing at a local private school, that Martha agreed it would be best. The decision turned out to be a blessing in disguise. Martha signed up for nursing and science courses not offered at the public high school and, after graduation, she was able to become an RN in record time.

During her pregnancy, the rumors and snickers from the community had caused her proud Danish-American father to stiffen and blush. She had tried to reduce her public appearances with her father to spare him, but Benjamin instead strengthened his resolve and became more determined than ever to demonstrate where his heart lay. When Martha finally delivered her beautiful baby boy, no grandpa was ever more public in his pride.

It was ironic, Natalie thought, that although she had faced several bleak moments in the past twenty years, two of them had produced her greatest blessings. From the sorrow of Martha's pregnancy came their precious, adored David, and as she reflected on that great joy, she touched the frame on the mantel that displayed a montage of photos spanning his life from birth to twenty. But as wondrous as that blessing was to her, she knew the greatest blessing was the one that had recently come to her. She had won her marriage back.

This blessing in disguise presented itself on the night of Ben's late-October accident, when not only her faulty marriage hung in the balance, but the life of her husband precariously hung there too. Natalie's knees still went weak as she remembered her horror when Sterling carried Ben through the door. At first she thought he was dead, and she was astonished at the buried emotions that fear stirred within her. After his accident Ben had spent several days in the ICU and she had maintained a vigil by his bedside or in the waiting room down the hall, which she had only recently discovered, he had done when Martha was born. In the face of his own mortality, and fearful he might die, Ben had wanted to clear the air forever and leave no regrets behind. He urged Natalie to read from his private journals, recorded regularly for over forty years, so she would finally know the things he had never found the courage to say. She had pored over each volume night and day. Page by page she had come to know her husband again, and she was finally able to admit that her pride and insecurity were as much an accomplice in their years of trouble as were Ben's.

She wept over the entries of 1960, entries describing his hurt and confusion while she had hovered between life and death following Martha's birth. He tried to explain how his fear of losing Natalie had pushed his emotions to the brink, until he felt compelled to withdraw from her side so he could be strong and think clearly and wisely. In those pages she found sweet release from all her fears. She had discovered that Ben's love had never wavered. All he had felt was terror, and fearing his frightened spirit would falter, he girded himself with years of military discipline and became stoic, which she had mistaken for disappointment. His entries described how, while she lingered at the edge of death, his fears took him back to the war in Korea where the safety of others had been commended to his care and yet some died. Nearly every day since then he had grilled himself to see if there was anything he could have done differently to save more lives, and as a result of that personal recrimination, he knew he could never survive the agony of losing his wife, not when he should have had the power to save her. So, laying the consequences aside, he focused on the practical matter at hand, overrode her will, and gave consent for the surgery. *So many wasted years,* she mused sadly.

Hungrily she had opened the other critical volume, the one that contained Ben's entries following TJ's departure, the one that would describe how he felt after the second time she had slammed her heart shut to him. Again, amid his own loss and anguish, she found that his predominate desire had always been to win back the love of his wife. Instantly, Natalie vowed to erase the boundaries that had kept them apart. Finally, the casual courtesy they had labored to establish, and sadly substituted for love, was replaced by devotion once more.

Two of her bleakest periods were now awash with happiness and hope. Only one still remained. She had to find TJ.

Natalie headed toward the kitchen and paused at the stairs to listen for any sign that Ben was awake. Hearing none, she moved past Ben's desk and affectionately touched the worn pine wood. The drawer was slightly open and a corner of Ben's current, precious journal peeked out. Her hand was drawn to the black leather cover, and she reverently stroked it. She opened the drawer to the right of her knee and let her fingers caress the many volumes of past journals that stood chronologically. Instinctively her hand paused on the binding of the journal from 1960, the volume that had changed their marriage. It was like scripture to her, and just as Ben's beloved evergreen was his sign that God loved him and loved his family, so had these volumes become sacred signs of love to her.

She again listened at the foot of the stairs for some hint of Ben's rising. Hearing none she continued on until she passed the table where a note scribbled out in her husband's handwriting caught her attention. She read,

> *Natalie darling, please set a pan of hot cider on the stove in the morning. The weatherman is predicting a chilly day tomorrow.*
>
> *Ben*

His name was written within the confines of a lopsided heart. Natalie smiled. That recent endearment pleased her so.

That explains why he's sleeping in this morning, she thought. Benjamin was an early-to-bed, early-to-rise kind of a man. From his youth on his parents' farm to his days in the military, the workday began when the sun first broke and likewise, when the sun set, he believed a man should also settle in for the evening. His regimented sleep pattern had taken a beating lately as his internal clock responded erratically to the medicines and discomfort since the accident, so on those nights he would entertain himself with the late news. The price paid for last night's eleven o'clock weather report was sacrificed sleep—sleep that was badly needed. Still, Natalie knew he would be cross that he had been allowed to sleep in on the morning of the annual tree harvest.

Every Thanksgiving Eve since 1965, Sterling Davis honored his standing appointment to bring his crew of seasonal workers to the Johanson farm to cut trees and wire boughs for swags and garlands. Then, the Friday morning after Thanksgiving, the fun would begin as the excited, early-bird families rolled in to select their perfect tree. Ben would sweeten the experience with a free cup of hot cider and a homemade gingersnap for the children. It was like hosting a Christmas party every day, and Natalie and Benjamin loved the hubbub. Yes, he would be upset at her for not waking him today, but Sterling would handle things. After all, he more than anyone else understood how close they had come to losing Ben, and since that night she had watched as the bond between these two resilient men deepened until their decades' long friendship made them more brothers than friends.

She hummed as she whipped around the kitchen, contentedly attending to her tasks as she contemplated her recent blessings. Benjamin was home, improving daily, love was back in their home as well, and tonight her daughter Martha would arrive with her family. Ah, yes. She was thankful, so very thankful.

By 8:00 Natalie had already placed a pot of cider on the stove to warm, laid the bread out to dry for stuffing, made piecrust dough, and set the next day's turkey in the huge canning kettle to soak in salt water. A bowl of hot cereal with pears sat ready in the microwave, and she started up the stairs to awaken Benjamin, but she was too late.

"Natalie!" she heard him holler. She loved the way he pronounced her name. "Naa-ta-leee," a long first syllable divided by an almost indiscernible "ta" and a "lee" sound that seemed to resonate forever. That was one of the things about Benjamin that she had first fallen in love with. She had always hated being named after an unfriendly aunt and was considering changing it when she turned twenty-one. Then, on that fateful day while working in the canteen on the local army base, in strode the man of her dreams. He walked with a confident stride, holding his head at an angle while he looked at her in humble, caring glances. But it was his voice that melted her. It was an American voice with some lilting tone that ran through it that she could neither identify nor hear enough of. She discovered later that it was the result of his having learned English from his immigrant parents who spoke it as a second language. Whatever it was, it was enchanting, and when he spoke her name, "Nat-t'-lee," it truly was the most beautiful name she had ever heard.

His parents' old-world influence was as evident in his values as it was in his voice. From his mother he had learned the importance of family, of heritage, and of culture. From his father he learned the ethics of education and hard work, and the obligation of patriotism to the land that had made their dreams possible. Anna and Peter Johanson challenged their children to search for these things, and Benjamin answered the challenge. God, family, and country—these became the very beat of Benjamin Johanson's heart.

Peter Johanson thought no prouder day could have dawned for him than the day in 1952 when his eighteen-year-old son announced he was enlisting in the United States military. But when his only son was wounded and finally returned home, Peter Johanson cared little about the decorations or promotion. He was simply glad to welcome him back.

In 1956, after Ben's whirlwind marriage to Natalie, his sixty-two-year-old father received a request from his aged friends in the Danish government to return with Anna to again pursue a position in the Department of Agriculture. Knowing his son was well-loved and that his future was secure, Peter's sense of honor left him unable to decline the call to serve, and so he sold his farm, gave each of his children a ten-thousand-dollar inheritance, and left for Europe. This tidy nest egg became the deposit they'd used toward their beloved farm.

"Nat-t'-lee," Ben called out in a pitiful singsong voice that made Natalie chuckle.

"I'll be right up, Benjamin," she called up the stairs, scolding herself for musing so long.

"Nat-t'-lee, my darling. Am I your captive up here or are you planning to come and bring me my britches?" His voice had a teasing tone, but she knew he was concerned about the hour. The workmen would already be out in the fields cutting the previously marked trees, and although Benjamin's presence wasn't critical to the progress, it was critical to Benjamin.

"I'm sorry, Benjamin. I'm just in one of my moods this morning." She headed straight for her husband, placed a kiss on his lips, and handed him his pants.

"Natalie darling, the morning's half over. Why in the world did you not wake me? The boys have probably nearly finished the first three squares by now! What if Sterling isn't out there to direct the new men? They'll be chopping the balled trees and digging up the babes."

Natalie placed a quieting finger to his lips. "Don't get all flustered with me, Benjamin Johanson. If your head is too tired to tell your body to wake up, then far be it from me to drag you out of bed. You know what the doctor said."

"Oh, blast the doctor, woman! A man ought to know the limitations of his own body, shouldn't he?" He reached a playful arm out to draw her close. "In all our thirty-six years on this farm, I've never missed one harvest day and I'll be hung if I'm going to let an overprotective, though lovely, female keep me from it today!"

An ornery, devilish tone stole into his voice and complimented his wife as he raised a flirty eyebrow at her. She took his hands to help raise his stiff body from the bed. His medical recuperation was nearly complete, but weeks of confinement left him weaker and stiffer than normal, and as frustrating as it was for him, it was equally unnerving for Natalie. As she braced herself, using her weight to counterbalance his and bring him to his wobbly feet, he pulled back hard and drew her to his lap. In his enthusiastic play he miscalculated the angle and he drew her to his wounded leg. He tried to smile but the wince on his face and sudden shocked intake of air made Natalie jump up and bring her worried face to his. He squeezed her hands reassuringly and made a face that begged her not to scold him, so she just slid her hands to his face and smiled back.

Ben rose to his feet and slipped into the bathroom while Natalie busied herself laying out his clothes and selecting a warm work jacket for him. She buried her face into his favorite, old, green plaid jacket and drew her breath deeply. She loved the mixture of smells that permeated Ben's clothes. Aftershave, mingled with the lingering aromas of pine and other tree oils, made up the soothing, familiar essence. Even when few words were spoken between them, Natalie had found immeasurable comfort in that aroma. So did the children. "Daddy" became a scent of its own and it lingered even in his laundered clothes, which had always made his T-shirts the preferred nightshirts and cuddle cloths. She smiled fondly, remembering playful tug-of-wars between Ben and the children as he tried to wrest his shirts from their clutches. They would scream for Mommy to intervene, and Ben would argue that it was either victory or nudity! Yes, the more she thought about it, even back then, there were many wonderful moments.

Ben came out from the bathroom and sat on the edge of the bed. With his freshly shaven face and his thick, silvered hair combed neatly back, she could barely help stealing long glances at him. She longed to sit on his lap and ring soft kisses around his proud Danish neck, but she knew it would be a long while before his limbs could bear her weight. And so she satisfied her desire by tilting his head upward so she could place a warm kiss on his brow. She held his head, softly cradled in the crook between her own head and shoulder, and Ben sensed that the moment had moved from one of playful fun to one of silent understanding of how close they had come to losing one another. He pulled his head away from hers to look deeply into her moist eyes. He was still amazed at how little the years had diminished her loveliness. Her petite frame was only slightly thicker, and the beauty of youth was now somehow enhanced by a strength and experience that dazzled him.

Natalie was still adjusting to this new way Ben held her in his eyes. She regretted that her pride had kept her from welcoming his affection for so long.

Ben noticed the faraway look in her eyes that always appeared when her thoughts journeyed to the past, and he pulled her back to the present and to him. "It's as I told you, darling. All will be fine, and we'll have a most wonderful Thanksgiving, now won't we?"

She nodded silently, their eyes never breaking the moment. He reached his hands into her hair and let it glide between his fingers, stopping to gently hold her face in them. Their eyes still locked, he drew her face close to his and kissed her long and softly.

"So, Mrs. Johanson, is this another of your devilish ploys to keep me locked up here in your love chamber forever? You're a wicked one, you are. Now, off with you, woman." He gave her a comical scowl as he tapped her on her nose. Natalie welcomed his mischievousness. To her it was the best indication that his body was finally mending. With the steady return of his health and their renewed closeness, thirty-six years of suppressed playfulness now erupted daily and they felt like young lovers again.

Natalie smiled brightly, wiping her tears with a corner of her apron. Her hands had slid from his face to his shoulders, and she affectionately squeezed them. She felt the muscles that decades of hard work had built, and she knew without question that such a man could not be dissuaded from the tree harvest.

She handed him his crutches and watched as he struggled to get on his feet. The mornings were always the worst. She shuffled toward him to plant a final kiss on his cheek and remind him that his breakfast was in the microwave. The dreadful sounds of his hopping from step to step down the stairs made her struggle to keep from rushing to his aid, but again she remained still, allowing him his dignity.

Natalie remained upstairs to make the bed while Ben had breakfast. Before he sat down to eat he peeked out the kitchen window. He drew a deep, almost passionate breath at the scenery before him. "Dear God, I do love this place," he said thankfully. To Benjamin, the farm was so much more than soil and outbuildings; it was the womb of his family, their life's spring and the very symbol of their love. Before the farm they were young, impetuous individuals. After the farm, and through their trials, they were forged into a family. This passionate love he felt for the mountain land ran deeper than even Natalie could understand. It was his hope that his children should love their home in a manner equal to his own. He had dreamed they would bring their children here and that perhaps one of them would live there when he and Natalie were long gone, not necessarily to work the farm, but to love it and pass on what they had learned there. When TJ left home, Ben had regarded it as the betrayal of a sacred family trust, but years of understanding and forgiveness had softened his heart and now he believed that in the end, it would be on this farm that he would yet see his family reunited.

He pulled out his wallet and found the old business card from Riley's Aerial Photography. He had never told Natalie about the conversation with the man who came to their door asking if he would like a *copy* of the aerial photo he was commissioned to take of the property. When Ben pressed him for information on the person who had hired him to take the original, the photographer only remembered that it was a male who'd paid cash in advance. Ben could imagine only one other man who could possibly love the farm enough to request such a photo.

A lump formed in his throat. He looked over the fields of trees—squares and squares of them. Each and every one of them, in some measure, a product of his very own hands. And then he glanced at David's Tree.

He sat down to eat at his honorary place and his eye glanced at the empty chair to the right—TJ's seat. Even now, years later, his empty spot still burned a hole in Ben's heart. He pushed the grief aside and drew in the sweet aroma of the hot cider, triggering fonder memories of past holidays. He found great comfort in knowing that soon Martha and David would be here, and with them, a new family member. Their family tree was growing.

As he bowed his head to bless his food, he added the same plea he had uttered every day for twenty years. "Please God, bring our son home soon."

Chapter Six

Sterling Davis followed Ben through the kitchen door and kicked his boots off near the woodstove. The smell of Thanksgiving hung in the air like a warm, inviting comforter.

"Can I get you some cider, Sterling?" Natalie offered.

"You won't have to ask me twice," he replied with a hearty laugh.

"Ben?" she offered, and he also accepted. "So are you boys all finished?"

"Pretty much," Ben replied. "All the balled trees are dug and wrapped, and the men are just finishing wrapping up the Scouts' trees now. That reminds me—Sterling, what's the matter with that new fellow on your crew?"

Sterling took a minute to stare into his cup of cider before responding. "Did you have a problem with one of my men today, Ben?" he asked guardedly.

"Just that young, red-haired character. Every time I turned around he was scooting off on his own. I don't think he put in an hour's worth of work the entire day. I mean, it's no concern to me, but it's just not your style to carry dead wood on your crew. That's all I'm saying."

Sterling again paused before answering, "Bill." Sterling nearly spat the words out in disgust. "He's my sister Judy's son. Somehow she got it in her head that a season of manual labor on my farm would undo twenty years of neglect from a drunken, abusive father and instantly make him a new man. He's got some big problems, Ben. I can't say that I know what they all are, but even though I've warned him about drinking on the job I know he sips from some little flask from time to

time. The men are tired of carrying his load, and all I can say is that I
can't wait until spring when I can ship his lazy behind home for his
own folks to deal with."

Ben was quiet now. He had also tried to salvage a youngster he
loved through "sweat therapy," and to no avail. The silence hung
heavy in the room until Natalie broke the awkwardness of the
moment.

"Well, I'm just glad it's finished. I knew there was no way I
would be able to keep Ben out of the thick of it today, but I was
worried it might be too much too soon. So now that it's done," she
paused and stood behind him, wrapping her arms around his neck,
"I can have him back to myself until Friday morning when we start
the holiday sale."

Sterling smiled. "Well, Natalie, all I can say is Ben is twice the
man on crutches that most of these young boys are on two good
legs." With that Sterling placed a gentle, affectionate slap across the
knee of Ben's injured leg and they nodded thoughtfully, remembering
that frightening October evening a month ago.

Traditionally, fall and winter—the slower holiday-filled months—
were Natalie's heaven, but the almanac had been right so far this year.
From fall to spring, this was expected to be a very harsh winter and it
had been proven accurate. Generally, October weather in the area was
predictably autumnal. The fruit stands that dotted the roads in this
part of the eastern fruit belt were loaded with apples, squash, and
harvests of broccoli and cauliflower. The packinghouses still held a
few bushels of late peaches and pears. Pumpkins and mums flamed
roadside stands with fiery colors, while scarecrows and hay wagons
invited families to stop and look around. From late October into
November the vibrant fall colors would fade and darken as if in
response to the turning back of the clock and the early setting of the
sun. The children complained about the shortened time for play, but
it brought families back together for early suppers and evenings of
fun. Yes, Natalie loved fall and winter the best.

Spring was lovely, but spring meant long days of hard work
repairing winter's damage to land and limb, and summers were hot
and humid. Work began at first light, broke in the afternoon, and
then continued late into the cooler night. And although fall was a

busy time of picking and canning, it was joyful work. When they were little, the children and she had spent hours singing songs or telling stories while they raced to see who was the fastest apple peeler or pear slicer. Martha had been meticulous and therefore dreadfully slow, while TJ believed faster was always better. How clearly now she could recall the personality traits that had later defined her children's destinies.

* * *

Marty had been Sterling's contented crew chief for almost twenty years, but since Sterling's nephew arrived, he found his attention was either diverted to tracking down the boss's lazy kin or redoing his poor work. His biggest concern lately was the negative impact this lazy buck was having on the other men as they made sniping comments regarding the little prince.

While Ben and Sterling enjoyed a cup of cider in Natalie's kitchen, the last stack of cut-and-bound Boy Scout trees was being loaded by four of the five-man crew. Two were passing the trees through the baler and two were tossing the bound trees onto the back of the truck, but the fifth man, Sterling's nephew who was supposed to have already loaded the truck, was nowhere to be found. As the last of the trees was being loaded, Marty decided to make his obligatory attempt to find Bill. He wished he could just pack up the men who had done the job and drive home, leaving the slothful nephew to face his uncle alone. But loving Sterling as he did, and knowing the embarrassment this whole mess was causing him, he began to search the barnyard.

The barn was an ad for Christmas fun. Any space not filled with evergreen products was the residence of igloos, wooden cutouts of snowmen, Santa, and other holiday totems. Lights, bows, and candy-cane trellises rounded out the lavishly gaudy yet wonderful decorations. In spite of all the glitz and glitter, the highlight of the display was, without question, David's Tree.

David's Tree was an island of reverence in a sea of dazzle. Blue twinkle lights were woven through every bough while silver birds hung from transparent threads, appearing as though they were hovering around the little tree. An electric glass star sat upon the top, with fiber optic strands hanging down. When lit, the scraggly evergreen was a magnificent sight.

When Marty was content that Bill was not hiding in the barn, he made his way behind the truck and around the gauntlet of trees, carefully traversing past David's Tree. After making a futile sweep of the entire vicinity he headed for the Johansons' kitchen door to find Sterling and make his sad report. It caused Marty pain as he watched a cloud roll over Sterling's face at the news. The foreman was grateful for Mrs. Johanson's perfect timing. Just as she did every year, she rang the old dinner bell that hung over the porch calling the men in for fresh pie, bread, and hot apple cider. The clang was an annual invitation to several of these men and they responded swiftly.

It pealed loudly enough to also awaken the sleeping slacker hidden under a roll of burlap tossed into the cab of the truck. Bill was startled at first to find himself awakening in the truck. He had lost track of time but vaguely recalled Marty sending him to load the previously cut-and-bound Boy Scout trees. Unfortunately, he had decided to warm himself up first with a little swig of booze and he had fallen asleep without doing the work. He was the disappointment again. He knew how his uncle felt about him. Every day since he was a child he had seen that same look in his own drunken father's eyes, and now Marty and his coworkers reflected it also.

He wiped the liquored drool dribbling from his mouth, then raised his spinning head enough to see over the door's edge. Without realizing that the other men had already completed his assignment, Bill decided to back the truck up a few feet nearer to where he remembered the pile to be. He turned the key in the ignition and slid the transmission into reverse. He belched at the very same moment he pressed the accelerator, catching himself off guard. He slammed his foot to steady himself, hitting the accelerator, and the truck leaped into reverse. His reaction time was sluggish, and by the time he hit the brake, the damage was already done.

He jumped out of the truck and ran to see what he had hit. There, bent and splintered under the huge wheel of the truck, lay the crippled remains of David's Tree. Small branch ends wrapped in crushed blue twinkle lights reached from beneath the black rubber tires, and a few silver birds, knocked free by the impact, lay scattered on the ground.

At first Bill was grateful that he had only crushed one tree, but as he looked more carefully at the decorated remains, he realized that he had destroyed the one tree whose value exceeded that of any tree, and perhaps of all the trees on the entire farm. Suddenly he panicked.

His eyes darted around, searching for witnesses, as he jumped back into the truck and inched it forward. He ran back to the tree and gasped over the scene. It was completely splintered through at the base and all the branches on the tire-damaged side were crushed flat. With just a few firm twists, Bill broke it free of its ties to the earth and unceremoniously tossed it into the back of the truck with the load of wrapped trees. Within a few minutes, he'd buried the carcass of Ben's sacred charge beneath them. Content that his victim was sufficiently concealed, he jumped back down to gather up the evidence that lay upon the damp, muddy ground.

It was nearly dark now. Bill had a good plan, or so he thought. It would require some Academy-class acting, but it would get him away from here and provide him an opportunity to dispose of the evidence. He could see the silhouettes of the men through the Johansons' window, outlined by the glow of the kitchen lights. He wiped his mouth and straightened his jacket as he made his way to the door. Ben answered and Bill sensed his disdain for him. For a second he thought, *Good riddance to your stupid, ugly tree, old man*, but self-preservation kicked in. He smiled a sugary smile and inquired if he might speak to his uncle.

Sterling made no attempt to hide his anger over Bill's latest disappointing day of work. Bill did not argue. He worked with it. He feigned expressions of great sorrow and embarrassment and agreed with his uncle point by point. Then it was time to play his hand.

"I really feel lousy, Uncle Sterling. I know I've let you down and I've let the men down, and I want to make things right, or at least try to make up for me slacking off."

The words were right, but Sterling just stood there, sizing his nephew up. "Why the sudden remorse?" he asked skeptically. "I've been on you all season and so has Marty. What's different about today?"

Bill was sick of Sterling's condescending tone, but recalling that his neck was at risk, he held his temper in check and kept up the performance.

"I guess when I saw everybody laughing together through the kitchen window it hit me that I can choose to be a part of this crew or be an outsider the rest of the season, and I'd like to try to make the best of it and begin pulling my own weight," he crafted remorsefully.

Bill wasn't sure his uncle was buying it, but finally Sterling's face softened and he replied, "Okay. You say you want to make things right? What do you propose?"

Bill smiled inwardly. He couldn't have asked for a more perfect set up. "I haven't done much today. How about if I deliver these trees to the Scouts myself?"

There it was. An unexpected offer his uncle would be unable to refuse. It would give him the opportunity to get off the Johansons' place and dispose of the tree before anyone noticed, and by the time his accusers came he would have a new plan or maybe even be out of there.

Bill's uncharacteristic generosity caught Sterling off guard. Once he felt confident he'd heard Bill correctly, he shook his redeemed nephew's hand, and Bill was on his way.

Once at the tree lot, it took him several minutes just to unload enough trees to free up the scraggly, broken evergreen. He grabbed angrily at David's Tree and tossed it to the ground. He searched the lot for a spot to hide the evidence and soon found a ditch about thirty yards behind the crude office shed. He laid the wounded tree in the ditch, and, as an afterthought, tossed some straw over it for camouflage, then trotted back to the truck to finish unloading and consider his next plan. He would sleep tonight and head off first light for Myrtle Beach. The guys at the bar said there was always construction work there. He had just enough cash in his wallet from last week's check to buy a few nights' stay at a cheap motel if he traveled by thumb. Then he remembered the cookie tin on Sterling's desk that held the daily receipts from the greenhouse sales. Some days there were a few hundred dollars in it.

There was a momentary tug at his conscience, which he easily dismissed as he considered the possibilities a few hundred extra dollars would open. He would grab the cash tonight and hit the road before first light. Anyway, that would be tomorrow. He was safe until then. Nobody would notice the little tree until the morning and by then he would be long gone.

* * *

As Bill finished up at the Scout lot, his uncle was leading the crew out of Natalie and Ben's house to head for home themselves. As soon as they opened the door the motion detector switched on the lights that illuminated the entire driveway and barnyard. In perfect timing with the switching of the lights came Ben's gasp. David's Tree was gone!

* * *

Sterling was angrier than he could ever remember being in his entire life. He had intended to merely pull back the blanket covering Bill, but instead his hand landed more on his nephew's face than on the quilt. Amid the babbling confusion of expletives and thrashing limbs, Bill scrambled to keep pace with his infuriated and humiliated uncle who was propelling the younger man's body toward the cold, damp yard. He threw the sniveling young man to the ground and started firing questions at him. Bill, now awake and hot from humiliation, popped up from the ground and aimed his fist at his uncle's jaw. Sterling broke the incoming blow with his left arm while sideswiping his nephew with his right. Bill hit the ground hard this time, face first. He quickly flipped over and started to rise again, but Sterling anticipated a second threat and pinned him down with his mighty foot. Bill knew enough not to struggle further. He was no match for this man on a normal day, and now, the ferocity of his uncle's disgust truly terrorized him. He lay there silently and waited to hear whatever tirade was about to come.

Bill's body heaved in breathless fatigue. From an equally heaving chest Sterling's voice spat forth. It had a strange and eerie tone as if the voice were issuing from a dark and loveless place. Bill knew that timbre of voice and knew there would be no reprieve from this fury.

"I have just left the side of my dearest friend, who nearly collapsed in my arms when he saw what you had done. And I had to stand there and try to apologize for something that I can't even begin to understand or repay."

Bill miscalculated the timing and the message of his one and only response. "I thought it was just another stupid tree." The foot pressed deeper on his sternum and he wheezed.

"Liar!" Sterling spit back at him. "I warned you, the men warned you! Everyone knows that David's Tree is sacred to Ben. It doesn't matter whether or not you understand or care. What I can't tolerate is that you didn't have the decency to tell him. To be man enough to face your mistake and take responsibility for it. No, instead you compounded your crime by calculating a scheme to hide your guilt and then you just sneaked away like some slimy vermin."

Sterling's voice quieted and the rage gave way to hurt and disappointment.

"And you know what breaks my heart the most? That for a few hours I was proud of you, boy." He swallowed hard. "Even as I was climbing the porch tonight, after leaving the Johansons', I kept hoping I'd find out that it really was an accident and you didn't know what you had done. When I walked through the kitchen I noticed that the lid was off the money tin, but it didn't register until I opened your door and saw the wad of bills on your dresser."

Again his voice was thick with disappointment. "Well, I'm done coddling you. It's over. No more." His voice was cold and controlled once again. "First light, you are going to take me to that tree and you're going to face Ben Johanson like a man. Maybe he can get some cuttings from it, I don't know. We can't make it right, but you're going to try to do all that you can to restore what you've taken from him. Do you understand?"

Bill dared to do no more than nod his head. His uncle's foot lifted from his chest and he drew a full, hungry breath. Sterling said no more. He turned and walked back toward his house where his wife stood shaking from the scene she had just witnessed. With a final look back at Bill's panting body, she entered the house, closed the door, and then pushed the knob until it caught.

Bill sat there, shaking, until his anger exceeded his fear. It took him twenty minutes to pack up what few belongings he felt were worth carrying and he headed out the door and down the road. Within an hour he was on the state road with his thumb up. By first light he was on Route 95 headed south, about an hour from Myrtle Beach, South Carolina.

Chapter Seven

If Sam Pearce thought his new family had exaggerated the importance Ben placed on the little tree, his doubts were now laid to rest. When he first drove up the picturesque Johanson lane, he had an instant feeling of being caught up in a Currier and Ives holiday painting, except that the peace was broken by scurrying ATVs, headlights ablaze. Martha and David knew something was wrong as soon as they pulled into the yard, since the homestead would normally be settled on the night before Thanksgiving, the last quiet spell until Christmas Eve. After a few seconds of hugs and introductions, the reason for the activity was revealed. David's Tree was gone. Ben Johanson tried to quell his distress in the pleasure of having his family home, but his true inconsolability could not be hidden.

Sterling's crew and his men had been searching for the tree in every nook and cranny of the barnyard until Ben finally hailed his friend down to call off the search for the night. Sam was still completely befuddled over the extreme emotion the loss of this tree was causing for so many people. Natalie took him under her wing and tried to explain to him that, until tonight, even she had not fully comprehended how deeply Ben had been tied to the tree he had nurtured. Only now was she beginning to understand the very deep sense of reverence and duty he had attached to the care of this heaven-sent treasure, and that he saw its loss as a personal failure of some divine stewardship.

* * *

In spite of how strange Wednesday evening had been, Thanksgiving started out to be a fine day as far as Sam could tell. The breakfast was lovely and elegantly served; then the family had enjoyed the parades while being tempted by the sinful aromas that crept into the family room prefacing dinner. The conversation had been warm and comfortable, and he thought his new in-laws seemed genuinely interested in all the details of his, Martha's, and David's new life together. He noticed the small affectionate touches, looks, and kind-nesses that Ben and Natalie stole when they thought no one was looking, and it warmed his heart. After dinner, David and Ben had slipped off somewhere while he and the ladies looked through old family photos, further drawing him into their circle. It wasn't until the pie was eaten and Martha called him into the kitchen to help with the dishes that he had any inkling that the day didn't seem equally perfect to the rest of the family.

He complimented Natalie on one of the nicest Thanksgivings he had ever enjoyed, and she responded with a quick smile and then left the room tearfully. Martha looked at him as if he were daft. She tried to explain to him that although those things might all be parts of a lovely, traditional Thanksgiving, they were not the elements of a traditional "Johanson" Thanksgiving, and it was that lack of tradition that was making them all sad.

Martha explained the traditional Thanksgiving hike to select the perfect tree. They would have cut it and decorated it that very night and sung the first carols of the season to welcome in the Christmas holiday. Of course, today no one could bear to ask Ben to look at the trees. Martha then went on describing the other little tidbits of a true Johanson Thanksgiving, and in spite of having just expressed his appreciation for so lovely a day, Sam realized that he too would have enjoyed experiencing the holiday in their traditional way instead of all the alterations used to fill the silence of Ben's despair. Yes, it was a very nice Thanksgiving, but the Thanksgiving of Martha's expecta-tions would have been almost magical.

"Something else was different too," she mused distantly.

"What was different?" Sam asked.

"You mentioned it just now, how Mom and Dad could hardly pass by each other without touching or glancing at one another."

"Yeah. I thought it was lovely to see how affectionate they are," Sam replied. Noticing how quizzical her face appeared he countered, "But as you mentioned before, they haven't always been like that, have they?"

"No," she replied. "I mean they have always been courteous and respectful to each other, but I don't recall them ever being so . . . snuggly. You know, I don't think I've ever seen them kiss in front of me until this weekend. David was surprised by it too."

"Maybe nearly losing your dad made them appreciate what they have in each other."

"Maybe . . . I don't know, it was just . . . I guess it was weird."

"Weird? I thought it was wonderful. In fact, it made me comfortable. It's how my parents are with each other and how I hope our kids will see us."

Martha stiffened slightly. "It's just a little surprising, that's all," she replied, quickly changing the subject. "Everything just seems a little different this year, I guess. It's definitely not the traditional Johanson holiday."

Still, by 6:30 A.M. on Friday morning, the day after Thanksgiving, the magic seemed to be in the air after all. Vendors were already setting up in the barnyard, and Martha and Natalie were busy directing people and handling last-minute details. Sam noticed Ben engaged in what appeared to be an uncomfortable conversation with a man near the splintered spot where David's Tree should have stood. He was amazed by the disparity of the scene before him. A festival-like atmosphere filled the air of the barnyard, completely encircling yet unable to brighten the depressing scene where Benjamin and company stood in the center. Sam stared out the kitchen window, wide-eyed and childlike, at the organized business of the fun, and then shook his head in sorrow that the potential joy of the occasion was lost to Ben and diluted for the rest of the family. Still, knowing what this day meant traditionally to his bride, he remained focused on the happiness, so he drifted out of the kitchen and approached Martha.

"This is so neat," he swooned in childlike pleasure.

Martha smiled and hugged him. "I love Christmas Day, but to me, this day is the spirit of Christmas. People who come here on this first day of the Christmas celebration are usually in a magical mood. They're so full of holiday anticipation, their voices are soft and their faces are bright and smiling . . ."

It was clear to Sam that she was delighted to share her favorite day of the year with him, but as she spoke her voice become thoughtful and Sam wondered about the change. He gave her a quizzical look but she brushed it off with a smile and hurried to attend to another truck that had pulled in, loaded with holiday crafts. Martha directed them to their stall when Sam noticed the conspicuous absence of Christmas's number-one, self-proclaimed elf.

"Where's David?" he inquired over the festive din.

Martha shook her head. "He's still searching for the tree." Her eyes then shot a quick glance in Ben's direction where two reporters were questioning Ben and Sterling.

Sam slowly mouthed in her direction through his frown. "Why are they here?"

Her face clearly registered displeasure as she crossed to him. "One of Sterling's men stopped by a store last night and mentioned that David's Tree was gone. The store called the paper and now they're here to make it a 'human interest' story. It's upsetting Dad, but I don't know what to do."

With his uncomplicated logic, Sam inquired further, "Why doesn't someone just go and ask Sterling's nephew where he tossed it?"

Martha's frustration showed for a second at the lack of understanding Sam was affording this great family crisis. "He took off last night and no one knows where he headed. I feel bad for Sterling too. Looking at him reminds me of the look on Dad's face after TJ left home."

Sam understood and yet continued to marvel at the reach of this scraggly little tree.

* * *

Normally on the Friday after Thanksgiving, Jeff Johnson would be engaged in a sunrise, life-or-death battle of touch football on a Frederick County elementary school field with many of his "former kids," but now many of them had babies to tend, in-laws to visit, and work to do, so only a few showed up at all, and even fewer played ball. So, in spite of having already wolfed down a convenience-store muffin, he treated the gang to some pancakes at the local diner. Afterward, everyone shared their last pre-Christmas hugs and went their separate ways, leaving Jeff feeling a little glum.

His melancholy was personal. He marveled at how he was able to successfully get other people back on a normal, healthy track, but he couldn't quite get his own life together. He decided the best way to throw off the negative mood he was in was to busy himself with work. Surprisingly, and possibly to his own chagrin, his last-minute call to the Davenports' was fruitful, and he was able to move the meeting between Merit and the people at the Brighton Children's Home to this morning.

His hands alternately gripped and released the steering wheel in a nervous rhythm as he drove through the town that was both haunting and home. He had pressed himself to drive this route a few other times in the last few years, but this time was more disconcerting. Perhaps it was this morning's realization of his loneliness, or perhaps it was the holiday season coming on, but whatever the reason, he found himself both wanting to flee these familiar streets and to race up the lanes and cry for entrance at the doors of places where he'd known love and peace.

A new subdivision called Peachtree now filled the acreage where he and his best friend, Kevin Brighton, used to pick peaches. When very young and filled with the orneriness that consumed little boys during the last weeks of school, he, Kevin, and their little posse would load their pockets up with the small, solid, seed peaches on their way home from school. All the way down the road they would pelt each other with peach ammo. Once, a few extra rounds of ammo made it back to school and were hurled across the playground during lunch. He threw one with particular accuracy and caught Kevin's sister square in the forehead with it. At first he thought it was hilarious until he realized that his scrawny eleven-year-old frame, although over a year older, was about fifteen pounds shy and three inches shorter than hers and that he was no match for the pummeling fists of scrappy Cassidy Brighton. The screaming crowd that gathered to witness the fight drew the teachers' attention, and within half an hour both of their mothers were there to join them for a meeting in the principal's office. Their penance was one week of lunch detention, which they shared from a bench at the edge of the playground. At the end of the week, Jeff had a hard time deciding whose company he preferred, Kevin's or his little sister's, whose quick wit and take-no-prisoners mentality captivated his prepubescent heart and held it tight-fisted, although basically unrequited, for the next twenty-eight years.

His knees began to shake nervously as he passed the stone-gated lane that led to Sterling Davis's property. He could feel the warning knot forming in his stomach as he caught sight of the old, weather-beaten sign that directed customers through the wooded entrance to the greenhouses. He wanted to turn the Blazer and flee back over the mountain to the safety and anonymity of Frederick, but like a moth drawn to a flame, he continued on past the Kellinger property and the pond where he and some friends used to ice-skate in the winter. It was much shallower than the pond on his own family's farm and so it was the first and safest place to skate when winter bit the earth. A melancholy smile crossed his lips as he recalled the feelings of being twelve and carefree. How badly he wished he could go back to those days and start fresh.

His nervous eyes followed the Kellinger property line to the very corner where the Johanson and Kellinger properties met. Although the one pond served as the local skating rink, it was to the Johansons' deeper, colder pond with a dock and tree swing that the local kids gravitated for a summer afternoon dip. It was also to this magical place during the summer before his senior year, that his thoughts drifted so many times. That old swimming spot was the place where he had watched a girl become a woman, shared his dreams with her, and fallen in love.

A lump formed in Jeff's throat as his car slowly passed the Johansons' property. Through stinging eyes he counted every fruit tree in the first row. Twenty-six mature apple trees—once the babies of the orchard but now longtime fruit bearers—were lined up along the fencerow. At the end of the fencerow, by the twenty-sixth tree, he saw the big, white, friendly sign, which seemed to Jeff to stand as a sentry this day. Bedecked for the holidays, it extended a warm welcome to others who came to the Johansons' Christmas Tree Sale and Fair, while offering ominously contradictory messages to Jeff. He slowed to consider the madness of simply driving up the lane for a quick, surreptitious peek at what was his most wonderful single memory, but as he realized the impossibility of it, a wave of depression hit him, sending him reeling emotionally. He shook his head angrily for letting this happen when he had so carefully prepared against this exact emotional eventuality. He swallowed hard to clear the lump from his throat and then he sat there blinking away the sting in his eyes. *Is it time? No. Definitely not. Soon? Maybe. Not today, but maybe soon.*

His head slumped and his shoulders sagged as the weight of his losses bore down upon him. He wanted to return to the safety of the cocoon he had built around himself. He hated being here. He feared being recognized and equally feared the possibility of being unrecognizable. Through the years, a thousand dreams of reconciliation had awakened him from restless sleep. In some he was welcomed into loving arms, and in others he was rejected. But even more agonizing than the latter were the ones in which he was unknown, a blank face in a crowd of people who had moved beyond the spot in time where he once mattered—and those dreams, which hurt the most, were haunting him now. He coughed to clear his tight throat and sniffed hard.

He slapped his left blinker on and waited, panicked, as an ATV approached from behind. A handsome young man with dark hair, and eyes framed by thick, black brows, pulled up beside him. Jeff's heart stopped beating. The face that was now reflected in his side mirror was a specter from twenty years past. *Could it be?* He gasped. Sitting there at the edge of the Johansons' property during the holidays, he knew it was possible, but . . . Was this the boy? He stole another nervous look as the amiable young man got off the ATV, approached, and spoke.

"Lost?" The voice was cheerful and confident as he approached the car. Jeff sat mute, on emotional overload, eyes red and cheeks flushed as he wound the window down. The cheery young man noticed Jeff's pained countenance, took on a worried expression, and came again with a more concerned inquiry. "Are you okay, sir?"

"I'm sorry." Jeff held a napkin to his nose and blew in an attempt to explain his appearance. "Darned allergies," he replied with a wry smile. He struggled to slow his racing heart.

"Oh," replied the young man curiously. "Are you lost?"

"Actually," Jeff took the opportunity to change the direction of the conversation, "I'm . . . I'm trying to find the Brighton Children's Home." It was as if twenty years had suddenly evaporated and he was catapulted back with the other half of that ill-fated friendship, whose visage stood eerily before him. Equally unnerving was the reality that his own countenance, some twenty years younger, was reflected in the boy's face as well.

His handsome face immediately brightened and he smiled warmly. "You're practically there." His arm pointed down the road to a stand of Christmas trees flanked by a sign that read, "Boy Scout Troop 328 Christmas Tree Sale—$5.00 per foot."

"Just go about a hundred yards past that Boy Scout sign and you'll see Brighton Lane on your left. Turn in there and the home is just about a quarter mile down that lane. You'll see a big yellow barn and some crayon-colored sheds and outbuildings. It's a crazy-looking place . . . looks kinda like a kiddie park or something, but it's really cheery and the kids sure love it there. If you follow the lane around, it'll take you right up to the front door."

Jeff liked this guy. He had an easy way about him that immediately made you want to know him better—obviously bright, but no pretentiousness at all.

"Is the main house rainbow-colored too?" Jeff said with a smile, realizing it felt good to relax a bit.

The boy laughed in response. "Nah," he said as stooped beside the car door. "The house is pretty normal. Mrs. Sherman runs a pretty tight ship there, so Ms. Prescott has to have her fun on the outbuildings and such. Really, I've probably misrepresented the home. It's a wonderful place for kids, but those ladies keep a good balance between order and fun. My grandpa is like an adopted grandfather to those kids."

The last sentence was too much and too close for Jeff's already fragile emotions. He quickly slid the sleeve of his navy blue sweater up his arm to reveal his watch.

"Thanks for the directions. I've got a 9:30 A.M. appointment, so I'd better get moving." He took one last look at the young man and tried to hold his image clearly in his memory. The young man moved away from the vehicle after a warm good-bye was exchanged, and then Jeff saw him get back on the ATV and head up the lane. A part of his heart wished he were going too.

* * *

David had been up since dawn's first light searching for the tree. It wasn't that finding the tree was so critical to him. He would miss it and miss being a part of its legendary history, but he could accept that the little conifer was simply gone now. What he couldn't bear was the sad expression on Pap's face every time someone mentioned it. Pap did attribute reverent qualities to it, but the miracle was a very simple one—that a good man, living on a leap of faith, saw God's hand in something other men would perhaps have esteemed as nothing, and that in noticing God's handiwork, he had been blessed three times.

In the midst of all the conversations he and Pap had had about the tree, the most important lesson David had learned from them was the probability that miracles happen all the time to those who see God's hand in things. After planting the tree, Pap admitted to noticing God's handiwork in many places and events and he taught David to notice it as well. So like Pap, whether others would call certain occurrences coincidences or curiosities, to him they were little miracles, and it seemed that the more of these wonders they noticed, the more there were to notice, until life was more like a series of small wonderful miracles surrounded by daily life than mundane daily life sprinkled with an occasional miracle. No, Pap wasn't going to fall apart over this. That wasn't David's motivation in searching for the tree. He simply wanted to give his grandfather the opportunity to say good-bye to an old friend. But after hours of searching, David figured there were only three possibilities left—either the tree was left at the Boy Scout lot, or maybe tossed somewhere on Sterling's property, or it would never be found.

Chapter Eight

Jeff Johnson was mesmerized by the Brighton Children's Home. He could see Christmas lights woven in among the branches of the pear trees that lined the drive, and he imagined how beautiful the entrance must look at night. The big yellow barn was connected to a small barnyard and pasture where a few calves, goats, and ponies roamed. The crayon-colored sheds were neat and tidy and did indeed make the property look more like a children's park, except the grand old house was everything he remembered and more. It took Jeff's breath away.

The large, white house had been re-sided and now looked even better. Flower boxes filled with colored ornamental cabbages lined the sidewalk, and two potted evergreens swathed in lights stood at either side of the large double doors. The columns supporting the roof over the big front porch had rings of handprints with names and dates painted on them. He wondered if they were the names of the current residents or those who had been adopted.

He walked up to the front door and rang the bell. From the inside he could hear the sound of thumping little feet and then a small voice projected from the intercom hanging nearby.

"Huwo," the excited little voice offered.

"Hello to you," Jeff responded with a laugh.

Through the speaker he could hear the frustrated chatter of at least three little voices and he could only assume that a battle was under way for control of the intercom button.

"I have an appointment to speak with Ms. Sherman. Could you tell her Mr. Johnson is here?"

The request sent a scurrying set of feet bounding down the hallway. He could imagine them running down the long wooden hall that led to the kitchen where he and Kevin had spent hours rolling cars and balls. The first voice was yelling, "Miz Sherman, you gots a pointment."

"Simon is getting Mrs. Sherman, mister," another voice assured him. Jeff laughed until a tall, imposing, middle-aged woman of sturdy build finally opened the door and caught him up short. Mrs. Sherman was probably in her late fifties, Jeff guessed, by the graying hair and the laugh lines around her lips and her speckled eyes. As she was ushering the children away from the door, scolding them in a deep, stern voice, a trace of a smile tugged at her lips. The holiday sweatshirt she wore, covered by a gaudy, flour-coated, appliquéd Christmas apron, blew her cover, and Jeff sensed she was more bark than bite.

"Mr. Johnson?" she inquired. "You are welcome to join us for breakfast."

The children, sensing that this stranger was now a new friend, went wild anew in their unsuccessful attempts to get him to accept the invitation, prompting Mrs. Sherman to resume her more stern demeanor and order the rebels back into the kitchen to finish their chores.

As Jeff watched them turn and scoot back into the kitchen, he counted five little ones. He guessed that they all ranged from four to seven years old. One little boy, slight of build with huge, sad, brown eyes, turned around and called back a wispy good-bye, and Jeff immediately knew that his was the voice of the captivating waif named Simon.

"It's a lovely place. The children seem . . ." he paused, struggling to get the compliment right, "so . . ."

"Hyperactive?" she replied with a laugh.

"No, no . . ." Jeff laughed in return. "They seem comfortable . . . happy, I guess, for want of a better term."

"Well, most of them have been here as long as they can remember. When it opened, the goal of this home was to provide a long-term, stable, family atmosphere for children whose parents were struggling to get back on their feet, but as it turned out, most of the children placed here had parents with so many problems that their parental rights were never reinstated. We do get a few children who are placed temporarily and a few who are 'adoptable,' but most of these guys are lifers, as we say around here." She smiled affectionately. "They're our lives." Jeff just nodded and smiled.

"Well, Mr. Johnson, as much as I would have enjoyed another adult at the breakfast table, I'll just pass you off to Ms. Prescott and go it alone in the galley today until the cook arrives."

"Is Ms. Prescott your assistant here at Brighton?" he inquired.

"Actually, she is the owner of Brighton. I am her assistant, although sometimes I feel like everybody's mommy, but we get along famously and we both adore the children."

"I have no doubt," he replied. So the amenable woman he had been making all the arrangements with wasn't the person he would be dealing with today. He hoped this Ms. Prescott would be equally gracious. He had a feeling that this was the right placement for Merit.

Mrs. Sherman led him into the office that was once the Brighton's old sitting room. He was surprised to see it decorated with photos of the Brighton family. He stared hungrily at each one and was astonished to find himself in one group picture. It was Christmas, 1964, and Cassidy was in a cast after falling from the loft of the barn. He remembered the day clearly.

Ms. Prescott, an austere but attractive woman probably in her mid-thirties, rolled into the room in a wheelchair, obviously engrossed by the interest Jeff held in the photos. At some point he noticed her, and though she had startled him, it seemed he had startled her as well. Her attire was professional, though somewhat stuffy. *Undertaker gray,* Jeff thought. Her hair was brown, cut short, and impeccably coiffed. Jeff squirmed. He was suddenly concerned she might think his attire too casual for their first professional meeting. *A little stiff,* he assessed, though his attention was so diverted by the wheelchair that he never really looked carefully at her face.

"Oh . . . I'm sorry," he stammered. "Lovely photos."

"You looked as if you recognized them. Did you know the Brighton family?" she inquired with an expression that belied her disinterested voice. Jeff was disarmed by the contradiction.

"So, are they the original owners?" He sidestepped the question, trying unsuccessfully to appear disconnected from the people whose images he was studying a few seconds ago.

"Yes." With raised eyebrows she rolled her chair up close to his side, brushing his leg. Jeff shuffled his feet and moved sideways, his comfort zone clearly compromised. "This was once a working farm." She pointed to a photo of the Brightons. "They are both gone now."

The news upset Jeff, and as he struggled to regain his composure, he abruptly offered his hand to the lady. "I'm sorry. I haven't introduced myself. Jeff Johnson from the ARM program. Please, call me Jeff."

Ms. Prescott took his hand limply, and spoke with cool detachment. "Very nice to meet you . . . Jeff. Please, sit down." Then she added, "And you may call *me* Ms. Prescott."

The formality of her request startled him and he caught himself as he sat, shook his head in amazement, and, with a bemused grin on his face, thought, *If there's a Mr. Prescott, I pity the poor guy.*

* * *

When Carol and Merit Davenport arrived, Jeff quickly jumped up and answered the door. He looked as if he had spent hours being interrogated by the FBI, but before either Merit or Mrs. Davenport could question his demeanor, Ms. Prescott came rolling through the doorway welcoming them with a voice that dripped with honey.

Jeff's head jerked in her direction to see if her head was spinning *Exorcist*-style, or if some gentler, kinder entity had entered her evil body. This was not the same woman who had spent the last fifty minutes dissecting him in the most anxiety-riddled meeting of his career. He now thought she was a grade-A snob and he was no longer interested in placating her. Just when he was about to flash her one of his most arrogant looks she sweetly introduced herself to the ladies.

Ms. Prescott made gentle eye contact with the nervous Carol Davenport as she took her hand and gave it a reassuring squeeze. Then, in the most endearing voice imaginable, she said simply, "Welcome, Carol." Next, turning her complete attention to making Merit feel comfortable, she smiled and said, "And this beautiful young lady must be the talented Merit Davenport who is going to save our children from musical deprivation." The ladies blushed.

Jeff was totally perplexed at this complete reversal in attitude. He wondered why she had seemingly singled him out for abuse. *Does she just hate men generally or is this some sort of power game?* he wondered. But then, as Ms. Prescott introduced herself to the women, it all became irreversibly clear. This was solely about him. She'd turned to face the women while still in complete view of Jeff and said, "Come into my office so we can finalize our plans, and please, call me *Cassidy.*"

Then she looked directly at Jeff, flashing him the same ornery smile he remembered from his youth. His heart stopped and he froze, unable to breathe or move. Cassidy Brighton Prescott directed the women to go on ahead into her office while she and Mr. Johnson tied up a few loose ends.

She had her back to Jeff as she closed the door to her office, giving them some privacy. As she spun her chair back around to face him, a soft laugh escaped her and she said, "You have to admit, you deserved that one, TJ." But no humor showed on Jeff's face. His eyes were pools of confusion that broke her heart, and she knew she had carelessly overplayed her hand. She should have known whatever pain had been poignant enough to persuade TJ to stay dead to his loved ones for so long could never have been bridged by a moment of fun, and now, no words could soften the cruel shock.

In that five-second introduction his world had been completely compromised. He had left his apartment a lone man living in a shallow world of his own design. Suddenly his walls of carefully built defenses were crumbling and he didn't know how to rebuild them, or if he even wanted to. He was totally unprepared for this. Twenty years of sidetracked possibilities began to pass through his thoughts. Every lonely day and night, every hopeless holiday, and his equally hopeless-looking future was laid open in that moment; he felt emotionally naked.

Cassidy's expression changed from concern to empathy. She rolled her chair toward him but he recoiled from her and headed for the door. His hand was on the knob when she reached up to put hers on top of it. "Please don't run again, TJ," she pled.

He closed his eyes and let his head fall forward to rest upon the door. He focused on the feel of her small soft hand over his, and he remained.

"It'll be all right," she promised soothingly, and for the first time in over twenty years, he believed it could be so.

Chapter Nine

Carol Davenport had understood the nervous pause on her husband's end of the phone when she told him Jeff Johnson had called and arranged to move the Brighton meeting to today. Mike had been right to be concerned. The change in the meeting now meant that Carol would have to face Brighton, and all its mother-deprived children, without him, and at a time when she was just beginning to cope with Markie's death. The sounds of children's voices and the clumping of little feet in the room above had unnerved her at first, but as she sat there with Merit during the long wait for Jeff and Ms. Prescott, something inside her suddenly clicked on and she managed to turn her attention from her own worries to those besetting her daughter. She chatted randomly with Merit about the charm of the house and the kind disposition of Ms. Prescott, attempting to reassure her daughter that Brighton would be a comfortable place to work. Merit soaked up her attention. In fact, Merit responded so eagerly to her mother's conversation that it shamed Carol to consider the toll her own self-pity had taken on her surviving child.

It had been a painful about-face for her to sit and listen to Jeff Johnson's recounting of Merit's story, but every word spoken had been true. So much of Merit's rebellion was tied to Carol's handling of Markie's illness and death. Then one day they looked up and the daughter they had raised was as lost to them as was their son. But Carol and Mike had sensed a spark of cooperation in Merit since that first meeting with Jeff. They were cautious not to make too much of it or to press their daughter, but Carol sensed that Merit had long felt backed against the wall and now Jeff Johnson was offering her a way out.

After Jeff and Cassidy returned to the room the meeting went wonderfully. A rigorous schedule was worked out for Merit and she enthusiastically agreed. Not only would she work with the children and provide a daily music hour, but she was also offered the opportunity to plan and produce Brighton's Christmas program. Carol was at first worried that all this might be hard to juggle alongside Merit's academic load, but seeing her daughter's eyes sparkle with enthusiasm made it clear it was worth the challenge to Merit.

When the details of Merit's schedule were arranged, Mrs. Sherman took Merit and Carol out on a grand tour of Brighton so Merit could meet each of the fourteen child residents and the other staff members. The rest of the day was to be spent observing the staff as they worked with the children, helping in the kitchen, and then getting her special assignment revealed.

As soon as the Davenports left the room and the door was closed again, Cassidy turned to Jeff and spoke. "Would you give me a hand?"

He walked over to her tentatively. They could both feel the tension in the air. He was scarcely able to believe that he was sitting in a room with the woman whose adolescent face and voice he had summoned to memory time and time again to help him through his darkest moments. So strong were those memories that despite their twenty-one years apart, no other woman had filled her place in his memory. Still, two obvious issues bothered him. The first was his inability to recognize her. *She's changed so much . . . Have I changed equally?* he'd wondered several times that day. And the second was that now he'd finally found her, she was apparently married to some guy named Prescott.

She raised her arms as he lifted her and placed her on the sofa. He sat down tentatively beside her, taking several seconds to meet her gaze. "TJ, I am so sorry about the way I set you up this afternoon. I had no . . . I didn't expect . . ." Her voice trailed off.

TJ. The name that for so long had epitomized his shame and regret sounded sweet to his ears. "How did you know who I was? How long have you known I was Jeff Johnson?"

"At first it was just a suspicion," Cassidy confessed, "but the name intrigued me. I mean, it's not a quantum leap from Thomas Jefferson

Johanson to Jeffery Johnson. I made a few inquiries and heard glowing reports about your work, but no one knew anything about your past. Then I went to the Frederick County website and found your picture. I still didn't recognize you at first. I mean, the last time I saw you, you were eighteen and had more hair than I have now. But as I studied that face I recognized those eyes and your father's strong chin—in spite of this." She'd reached a hand out to brush along his beard and he shivered. "And then I was pretty sure that hidden somewhere beyond that distinguished, graying hair and the tie was that wild young man that once made me swoon." Her nervous laughter trailed off when he didn't join her.

Now her voice came in soft tones. "It really wasn't until I saw your reaction to the photos that I was sure it was you. You were so captivated by them, and I knew it wasn't because of the beauty of the subjects." Again, her attempts at humor fell flat.

"They're beautiful to me." His voice trailed off softly.

There were so many places she would have liked to take that comment, but she knew that now was not the time. *Small steps, Cassidy,* she thought.

Jeff took the lead and she gratefully followed. His eyes scanned her frame from head to toe and a concern and sadness showed in his glistening eyes. "Your hair . . ."

Her hand instinctively touched the darker, shorter strands. "I guess I've changed a bit too. Rather than let nature turn me into a dishwater blond, I decided to call the shots and go for something more sophisticated, so I chopped off my hair and started coloring it." Her voice became wistful. "Wow, that was almost sixteen years ago . . ." Jeff cringed at the time lapse.

"What . . . happened to your legs, Cassidy?" he asked gingerly.

"I had a car accident in the fall," she replied guardedly.

He probed gently. "What are the doctors saying? Will you walk again?"

Cassidy paused and Jeff could tell she was carefully measuring her words. "They tell me I will get out of this chair . . ." She broke their gaze. Her eyes would not meet his. It was clear this was a conversation she didn't want to pursue. He reached across the sofa and took her left hand and squeezed it gently. For the first time he realized she wasn't wearing a wedding ring. He rubbed his fingers over the spot where her band should have been.

"How is Mr. Prescott handling your accident?"

Cassidy again paused before answering. It was a long pause. This question obviously hit a spot that drew more hurt than the previous one, and he regretted his intrusion.

"I'm sorry . . . I just was wondering since you're not wearing a wedding ring."

"It's okay, TJ. William bailed out of our marriage about ten years ago. He couldn't take the routine of marriage—you know, coming home to the same woman every night. By then everyone knew me as Cassidy Prescott, so I didn't want the hassle of changing my name back." Again her humor bridged the awkwardness. "Don't worry. At least you won't have to run out and beat him up because he ran out on a poor little crippled girl."

"You give me far too much credit," he answered shyly.

"I don't think so," she assured him as she lifted his chin, forcing his eyes to meet hers. "In the back of my mind you've always been my knight in shining armor."

They sat in silence for a few moments. It was both awkward and innocently familiar. In Cassidy's mind the twenty-year abyss could be easily crossed. It seemed natural that he should take her into his arms and kiss her, and although Jeff had imagined such a kiss a thousand times, in truth, that level of intimacy was now well beyond his self-imposed barrier.

The long pause became awkward until Cassidy dropped her hand from his chin, and asked, "TJ, where have you been? Have your parents seen you?"

His response was immediate and urgent as he took her by the shoulders. "Cassidy, you've got to promise me that you won't tell them you've seen me. Not yet." He could see immediately that he was placing her in the middle and he hated it, but he needed time to regroup before he could even consider a homecoming.

"Believe me, whatever happened in the past, is past. You can't begin to imagine what seeing you would mean to them. They live every day just wondering if you're alive."

He knew she was right. He had always known his parents would welcome him home. The problem wasn't them. It was him. The pain of facing the simple questions, "Where have you been?" and "What have you been doing?" terrified him until having no contact became more comfortable than the truth. How could he explain this to her though? He suddenly felt like the kids he counseled, trapped in a corner thinking there was no positive way out and fighting the urge to bolt. He closed his eyes to think. How could he avoid the confessions that had haunted him for more than twenty years, but still leave the room with Cassidy's respect because he'd answered her? And then he had an idea. "Cassidy, do you remember the summer our parents rented those cabins on the steep side of Peacock Mountain in West Virginia?"

Confused by the change in mood and direction of the conversation she answered hesitantly, "Yes."

"Kevin and I tried to play soccer on one of the decks even though our dads told us not to, warning us that the ball could go over the rail and roll down the mountain. Five minutes later we were sneaking down the mountain so our dads wouldn't know they had been right, but it was too steep and we fell about a hundred times until we were all skinned up and bloody." He smiled a sad little smile and continued. "Getting back was worse. We would drag ourselves a few yards up the steep rise and then we'd slide right back down again, scraping our bodies against every limb and briar growing along the way. After an exhaustive hour, having made very little progress, our dads' voices rang down from the ATV path about fifty yards above us. Too proud, we declined their offer of help, so instead they suggested that if we crisscrossed we could cut the angle out of our ascent.

"As much as we hated to admit it, they were right again, and although we had to walk about three times farther that way, the course matched our strength and we made it."

He turned now and faced her. His voice was strong and resolute. "That lesson turned out to be the allegory of my life. I fell, Cassidy, down a long steep slope that left me bloodied and bruised. But the worst part was that I took others along with me. I sat in a kind of hell I had built, too stupid to admit I was wrong, and too proud to ask for forgiveness and help. My day of reckoning came when one friend just gave up and killed himself." Jeff visibly shuddered. "He died in my arms. That day and a thousand days after I wanted to call my father and say, 'Please come and carry me, Dad,' but I realized that what he taught me was true. He could carry me back up, but what if I had learned nothing and would maybe even repeat my mistakes and fall again? I'd have rather died than face those demons again.

"So I tried to learn from Dad's lesson, that I could master the way if I matched the ascent to my strength and skills. I made a conscious decision to fight my way back, slowly and steadily, until I could face him with a life I could be proud of, tell him how much I love him, and ask everyone for their forgiveness. I have been slowly coming back but it's taken me fourteen years to get to this point, and I'm just not quite ready to face him yet." His head dropped into his hands.

After several minutes, he lifted his haggard face, looked into her eyes and pled. "Finding you today almost knocked me back down. I wasn't ready for all this. I . . . need a little more time. I feel like I'm almost ready, but I just need a little more time," he repeated. "Can you understand that?"

Compassion flooded Cassidy. She could see what this confession had cost him. She clutched his tense shoulders and pulled hard to slide herself across the sofa. His body remained rigid and unsure, but she threw her arms around him and drew him close to her in a tight embrace. This time Jeff did not pull back. He buried his face in the softness of her hair as she held him in her arms, then his arms responded as well.

Cassidy slowly relaxed her embrace and pulled away. Jeff's confusion was evident. Her arms slid down his shoulders and took his hands in hers as a look of embarrassment registered on her face.

"What is it, Cassidy?"

She could barely meet his gaze. "Jeff, I've done a terrible thing here today. I hope you'll be able to forgive me."

Jeff visibly tensed and Cassidy tightened her hold on his hands to reassure him.

"You've poured your heart out to me, shared things that clearly cause you pain, and I've been awful." Jeff's brow wrinkled, begging her for clarification. "This whole thing has been a test, Jeff, a charade. Yes, I was in a car accident, and yes, I was stuck in this wheelchair, but only for a few weeks. Actually the medical supply people pick it up tomorrow. I just thought, if Jeff Johnson did turn out to be TJ

Johanson, it would give me a disguise, an opportunity to distance myself enough to see what kind of man you've become—if you've become the man I knew you could be. And you've shown me today that you're a finer person than I."

She lowered her eyes in shame, and this time it was Jeff who reached out with comfort.

After a few moments of holding each other in mutual understanding, he whispered in her ear, "Please, keep my secret a little while longer, and I promise, Cassidy, I'll tell you everything."

* * *

Carol was invited to stay as long as she wanted, but she knew she would soon have to leave so Merit could bond with the Brighton family. She lingered behind her daughter and Mrs. Sherman on the tour, content to enjoy the beauty of the house and watch the children at play.

Brighton was a home teeming with happy, loved children, everything she and Mike had longed for. Two children had made their family happy and complete, but Markie's death was like the death of their entire family as she knew it, and try as she did to rally, she couldn't get past her grief to keep her home alive for Merit. The good members of their Protestant congregation had reached out to her family, but as Markie became sicker she had stopped attending church, and though she never really stopped believing in God, she was angry that He chose to heal other people's children but had not answered any of her prayers. Mike tried to take Meredith from time to time, but the half-filled pew was a reminder that they were losing Markie, so father and daughter eventually stopped going as well.

After Markie's death, Carol pulled back even further. The retired violinist from the Baltimore Symphony Orchestra, who served as the church organist, had been Meredith's musical mentor since she was five, but Carol suddenly found her sympathy and questions too intrusive. Despite Merit's pleas, she decided that lessons were no longer needed. In response, Meredith doubled her practice times, until one day Carol just stood in the doorway of the room with her hand to her head as if in agony. Meredith stopped playing that day and she hadn't played a note since.

The move had helped Carol temporarily, giving her plenty to keep busy, but eventually as the routine of life settled in, the hole that could not be filled, and the ache that couldn't be soothed reappeared and again she fell into a walking sleep. However, when she saw the effect her malaise was having on Meredith, she tried to compensate by denying her rebellious girl nothing. She placed Mike in the uncomfortable position of either playing accomplice to his daughter's ruin or of playing "bad cop" against Carol's "good fairy" role, which was tearing what was left of their family apart.

Then Merit had her midnight adventure. In many ways, Carol believed it to be the salvation of their family. She came to a renewed awareness that she had to come back from the dead herself to help her husband save their daughter. Small steps like talking and rebuilding a routine helped, and even though they were investing all that they emotionally could in Merit, they finally knew enough to reserve some of themselves for each other. She was still struggling, but she was at least fighting back now.

This twenty-eighth day of November was warm and pleasant, and Carol felt doubly blessed to be outside in the sunshine watching the children at play. These energetic, happy children drew her attention so fully that she wandered over to a bench and sat down. She counted fourteen children playing or doing chores in the yard. The four oldest children were busy feeding the calves and pets, while another group of six children of varying ages were playing in the playhouse. Two of the youngest children were in the care of two little girls who appeared to be tiring of their assigned duties. One girl held the hand of a wide-eyed little boy who kept staring at Carol. She smiled at him and he immediately dragged his companion along to Carol's side.

"How are you?" Carol asked in a child-friendly tone she hadn't used in years.

"He doesn't want to play today," said the girl.

"Oh, a tired one," teased Carol. "What's your name?" she asked.

Again, it was the girl who responded. "He's Simon. He's three."

Amused by the maternal tendency of this little girl, Carol inquired, "Are you his sister?"

"Not really," she replied. "Mrs. Sherman and Ms. Cassidy tell us we are all brothers and sisters in the Brighton family, but we don't have the same mommies and daddies."

"Oh." Carol was stunned by the child's candor. "What's your name?"

"Meghan."

"How old are you, Meghan?"

"Seven," the blond imp replied.

"Seven? You are very grown up for seven. Have you always lived here?"

"Since I was three. I used to live with my mommy, but she's too sick to take care of me, so I live here till she can take me back."

"I see," Carol replied, uncomfortable that she may have opened a painful topic. "It's nice that you have such a big and happy family here at Brighton," she offered.

The little girl simply nodded. Simon, who had been staring at Carol ever since the conversation began, looked up to her with soulful eyes and asked, "Are you my mommy?"

Carol was unnerved by such an inquiry, but Meghan, who had obviously been through this conversation on previous occasions, tried to straighten out the details.

"He asks every lady that." Then to Simon she added, "Simon, you know your mommy is in heaven and your daddy lives in Chicago."

Carol was astonished that these children lived in a limbo world of nonparenting parents. "He has a daddy in Chicago?"

"Yes," replied Meghan simply. Then, again attempting to clear the details with Simon, she explained, "Remember how he sends you presents at Christmas and your birthday?"

His sad eyes never left Carol's. A slight nod was his only response.

What a twist of fate, thought Carol. *Here sits a woman who lost a son, talking to a little boy who lost his mother.* An idea struck her and she posed the question to the girl.

"How would you like it if I watched Simon so you can play with the other children?"

The girl paused to consider the arrangement and then in her most responsible voice she asked, "Is it eleven o'clock yet? 'Cause Simon is my responsibility until eleven."

"Well, it's a little earlier than eleven, but I would be happy to sit with Simon, that is if you think that would be all right."

Again the little girl considered that option, and finally, after careful thought, she agreed. Simon sat down beside Carol and placed his little hand in hers. The woman and the little wide-eyed boy sat there on the bench saying very little, but communicating love in the best of ways.

* * *

It was nearly three o'clock when the crowds of shoppers started thinning out. The first day of the Christmas-tree season had been brisk at the Johanson farm. David made some vague reference to errands he needed to run and out the door he slipped. His plan was to search the two last places where he thought he had a prayer of finding the tree—the Boy Scout lot and Sterling's place. He drove his ATV to the Scout stand and noticed a wooded area a few hundred yards behind the shack, bordered by a long ridge with a sizeable drop-off that ran parallel to the road. He started walking the length of the ridge, kicking at the dirt, when he stumbled upon a trench filled with debris and straw. He kicked at the debris absently and began to walk past it when his eye caught sight of something beanbag shining amongst green foliage and straw. David reached his hand into the trench and pulled out the object. It was broken and dirty, but it was unmistakably one of the silver birds from David's Tree. David cheered and whooped as if he had found the Holy Grail, and he called the Scoutmaster over to help him pull the tattered, treasured evergreen from the trench.

It was *the* tree. He had no doubt. Completely assured that this was the answer to his prayers, David now set about to determine the damage done to the evergreen. He slowly turned the tree around, trying to lift the smashed limbs, and he found to his surprise that none of the major limbs were broken, merely flattened. And so, although David's Tree could never be replanted or saved, it could enjoy one last glorious Christmas.

David's first reaction was to ride home, get the truck, and haul the tree back to its old spot. He could have it decorated and ready for Pap by morning, but then he wondered what Pap would feel at the end of the holiday as he watched his sacred tree go brown and brittle and die. He shared all these concerns with Sid, the Scoutmaster, who added his own wisdom. "It'd be like cutting a dog's tail off an inch at a time, David. Right now Ben's facing the loss, and he's dealing with it and getting through it—one clean chop. But if you take this sad little tree home, he'll hurt every day— chop, chop, chop."

David agreed and decided against taking the tree home. The analogy was a little graphic but it was the truth, and David's elation departed as suddenly as it had come. Now he was filled with confusion. He couldn't let the legend of the tree end with the coda, "and it was tossed into a ditch." He carried the tree near the road and leaned it against the shack while he worked to straighten and lift the flattened limbs. Sid brought over a saw to clean up the splintered trunk, and then he and David lowered the tree into a bucket of water. A few of the limbs went cooperatively back into their normal fall, but seven of the most badly damaged ones would not rebound. David borrowed some baling twine from Sid and started tying up the limp limbs. After about an hour of loving artistry, it was hard to tell that the evergreen had suffered such an ignominious assault. Now David knew for sure that the twelve-foot, miracle evergreen was fit for a special final Christmas home, but where?

* * *

Carol Davenport literally forced herself to leave Brighton before Merit's tour ended. She wanted to stay and play with Simon and hear his precious voice pose incredible, unanswerable questions all afternoon, but she knew this was Merit's day and she needed to respect that. As her car pulled out of the lane, an idea formulated in her mind. She would call Mrs. Sherman on Monday and volunteer to work some day shifts. The plan made her giddy with excitement. Mike would be happy. He had practically begged her to find something to fill her time, and she and Merit would have something in common to share. *Or should I tell Merit?*

She considered what to do and decided that she would hold off telling anyone about her plan and would instead just see how things unfolded. Her first concern was to support her daughter in her own new adventure. Time would tell her how to proceed. For now it was just her wonderful, thrilling secret. She glanced in the rearview mirror and saw Merit, Mrs. Sherman, and a gaggle of children walking out from around the big yellow barn. *Got out in the nick of time,* she giggled inside.

Chapter Ten

Merit was in love with the Brighton Children's Home and its residents. When Mrs. Sherman gathered the children for lunch it hardly seemed like three hours could have passed so quickly. After lunch it was suggested that Merit lead the children into the great room for music time. The great room was a spacious, modern addition to the original home. Its two outer walls were made up almost entirely of shade-topped windows that overlooked a patio and garden area. It also had a huge stone fireplace. The wall opposite the fireplace was an entertainment paradise made entirely of built-in cabinets whose shelves boasted a TV, VCR, DVD player, and stereo equipment, all bearing nameplates of the donors and the dates of their bequests. Most of the equipment had been there for years. Shelves filled with toys, board games, and movies filled every other inch of space.

The center of the room was crammed with sofas, beanbag chairs and quilts, all of them seemingly suggesting, "snuggling encouraged." An old, but handsome, black baby-grand piano beckoned to Merit from the other half. Except for a door that led to the kitchen, the wall attached to the main house featured floor-to-ceiling shelves. Half were stuffed full of children's books and classic literature recycled from the local library, whose name was stamped on the spines, while the other half stored various used musical instruments. After months of neglecting her music, Merit was suddenly thrilled by the thought of being surrounded by so much opportunity.

The children surrounded the cluttered piano bench and waited for her to begin to play. She smiled nervously, laid the songbooks aside, and began to play a favorite classical piece from memory. Her

confidence quickly returning to her, she then played a few contempo-
rary pieces the children recognized. It felt wonderful, but when she
began to play Christmas carols and the children joined in with their
angelic voices, it was heavenly. She switched from piano to guitar and
then to the little, slightly battered violin. The children were captivated and she was reborn. By the time three o'clock rolled around and
Mrs. Sherman returned, Merit was teeming with ideas for the children's Christmas program.

Mrs. Sherman led Merit back to the garden where a tired but
glowing Jeff Johnson and Cassidy Prescott were sitting. He rose as she
entered and his smile told her that she had passed her orientation with
flying colors. "Thank you, Mr. Johnson," she whispered softly to him.

"It was all you, Merit. You earned this chance," he replied with a
wink.

"Well, since you two get along so well together, I'm going to let
you help Merit with her last assignment today, Mr. Johnson," Cassidy
said in mock authority.

"Uh-oh," Jeff groaned comically. "See, you do a good job and—
bang—homework!"

"Ahhh, this is a fun assignment. I need you two to go to the Boy
Scout stand and select a Christmas tree that we can decorate by
Monday. How's that sound?"

He realized that Cassidy was sending him to the stand that sold
Johanson trees and he questioned her motivation. *Is this another one of
her tests?* But he knew Merit couldn't do it alone, so he agreed.

Merit had never selected a Christmas tree. To her dismay, when
she asked Jeff how many Christmas trees he had ever purchased, he
shrugged his shoulders and replied, "Just one, the little Norfolk pine
in my office." Merit felt certain they were perhaps the two *least* quali-
fied people in the town to fulfill this mission, but her fears were
surprisingly laid to rest at the lot as Jeff Johnson went row by row
through the trees naming each variety and listing the pros and cons of
each one. Merit was flabbergasted, but he dismissed her awe of his
knowledge by quickly attributing it to being a "botany nerd" in high
school. He rattled off the information with the acuity of her former
biology teacher, who, unfortunately, had spent many mind-numbing
hours regurgitating botanical information that sent him into scientific

nirvana while boring the students to death; but somehow, listening to Mr. Johnson was a pleasure. He touched limb after limb of each tree as if greeting old friends. A contented, faraway look shone on his face, and Merit allowed a few feet to separate them as they continued on through the rows of trees so she could study him. He became a different person—his normally controlled, proper gait replaced by an easygoing stroll that better suited him.

After an hour, the two shoppers found themselves debating over their two "tree finalists" when a young man jogged up behind them breaking the silence.

"Ummm . . ." a voice whispered near Merit's ear. "I couldn't help noticing that you two were about to make a grave mistake." It was David Johanson.

Merit and Jeff turned to see who was trying to throw a monkey wrench into the culmination of an hour's worth of earnest and painstaking labor. Although annoyed, she softened slightly at the sight of the intruder's dazzling, dark eyes, but Jeff stiffened and resumed his formal stance. David sensed the awkwardness his inter-ruption caused, and then suddenly, recognition flashed across his face and his attention focused on Jeff Johnson.

"Hey, you're the guy from this morning, aren't you?"

Jeff nodded guardedly.

"Then I guess you found your way okay," he added, confident he was about to find a fitting final home for the miraculous little tree. "What I was trying to say was that I noticed you were searching for a perfect tree and I happen to know that neither of these is *the* perfect tree."

"Oh, really?" challenged Merit. "And what would make your choice the 'perfect tree'?"

David threw his whole body into an excited rundown of his product. "The perfect tree has to have more than a nice shape. It should have a great story. I have a tree with a great story, and it deserves a great home."

"And what makes you think we'd give it a great home?" Merit inquired.

"Well, you're from Brighton, right?" he asked the curious pair

Merit cautiously questioned his assumption while Jeff stood

silently, mesmerized by the familiarity of David's features and voice, with traces of memorable intonations from his father's Danish lilt.

David summoned all his charismatic charm to soothe the awkwardness. He took a comical step backwards, spread his arms wide, and with an all-knowing shrug of his broad shoulders and tilt of his head, he replied, Mafia-style, "I told ya. I know things." Merit broke into a smile at the inconsistency of appearance and language, and Jeff could no longer resist his humor either. Pleased that he had succeeded, David extended his hand and formally introduced himself.

Jeff was nervous as to how to safely return the introduction, but before he had time to decide, Merit was already halfway through the response. "Hi. Merit Davenport. Nice to meet you. This is Jeff Johnson." Jeff liked the firmness of David's handshake and the confident eye contact—traits not inherited from his father. "How did you know we were . . . ?" Merit began.

Jeff jumped in. "David and I met this morning, Merit. He was nice enough to give an out-of-towner directions to Brighton." Merit noticed that the stiffness was back in his voice.

"Oh," she replied with sarcasm, "and I thought I was having my first experience with a real psychic."

"Psychic or not, I do have the perfect tree," David replied with a wink in Merit's direction. "And it does have a great story, and Brighton would be a great home for it." He walked backward as he spoke, beckoning them with his curled index finger. They followed him in pied-piper fashion to the wounded tree soaking in a bucket of water. It was not a particularly attractive tree, being neither as tall nor as full as either of their other choices, and their disappointment showed.

David made a sweeping gesture with his right hand, showcasing the less-than-obvious advantages of this tree while giving his best sales pitch. "Have you ever heard of 'David's Tree'?" he asked, receiving no response. He walked over to the sales shack and came back with a copy of a newspaper. He held it up and pointed to the lead article, "Town Faces Its First Christmas in Thirty-Seven Years Without Miracle Tree."

"You're looking at the star of that article." He spoke more softly, pointing again to the damaged tree. "This tree has special significance to this town and to my family. Its trunk was broken in an accident and I'm just trying to find a deserving place for it to spend its last Christmas. I think Brighton is the perfect place."

David spent time recounting the miraculous stories of the precious evergreen while a small group of shoppers and Scout helpers circled about them, adding to the story or at least nodding their agreement. Merit gave him her full attention. Jeff listened carefully for a few minutes until forgotten childhood memories flooded him. He walked over to the tree and ran his hands along the trunk, still crooked from being battered by hurried tree shoppers. The knots were also there, due to the ties he'd attached to the tree in the past to secure it; ties which had bitten into the flesh of the then-scrawny sapling. Yes, though he didn't know it as "David's Tree," this tree was also his old friend.

Suddenly Jeff was utterly surrounded by memories of his father. Sorrow swept over him as he considered how the loss of the crippled old tree must be affecting him, and he waited for a break in the conversation to make the delicate inquiry.

"So, uh, this tree really has significance for your grandfather?" Jeff asked guardedly.

"Yeah," David replied sadly, "it was a family treasure, but it was a miracle to him."

"Then this must be really upsetting for him . . . ?"

David paused, most likely considering how to best answer the question while honoring his grandpa. "The whole thing has been very hard for him. The circumstances . . . well, it's a long story, but let me just say that Pap doesn't know I've found the tree yet, so I don't actually have permission to give it away, but I think he'll agree after I explain my plan to him." And then to Merit he added, "So do you think Brighton could find a spot for my old friend here?"

It was clear that she was enchanted by the thought of providing a last Christmas for the miracle tree, but she was nervous about how Ms. Prescott would feel about a damaged tree with a crooked trunk. Jeff could read the dilemma in her expression and offered her his reassurance.

"I bet Brighton would get a lot of publicity as the final resting place of David's Tree." He said it so nonchalantly that it came out almost like an uttered thought. "You know, Merit," he continued, planting his little seeds of encouragement with greater enthusiasm, "if you were to advertise that Brighton had the famous tree, why, I'd bet people would stop by to see it, and who knows, maybe some of them might even make contributions to Brighton as well . . ."

Merit pondered what he was saying. It made sense. She had just learned how financially strapped Brighton was at the moment, and even if no one made donations, it couldn't hurt to have the community be more aware of the home. "How much will this tree cost us?" she bartered.

David leaned his six-foot, two-inch frame close to the face of the captivating girl. "That's the beauty of a miracle, Merit. You can't put a price tag on it. So I guess it's yours for free."

That clinched it. David still had to present the plan to his grandfather before it could truly be theirs, but he felt confident Pap would agree that this was a fitting farewell to David's Tree.

Chapter Eleven

When David arrived at the farm Friday evening it was dusk, and the Johansons had settled in for a quiet evening. Ben and Sam were engaged in a spirited debate over a football game while Martha and Natalie were preparing dinner. When David walked in, Ben noticed how he seemed to have frozen in the doorway as he scanned the scene. A warm feeling flooded Ben as he recognized the expression of pleasure wash over his grandson. Normalcy had settled back into the family.

Supper became a long, pleasant affair. Ben finally stood up, shaking the fatigue and stress out of his bones, almost missing the support of his recently abandoned crutches. Natalie rose to his side, planted a kiss on his cheek, and hugged him close. Martha, still awestruck by these displays of affection, caught her mother's delighted attention and soon an arm was extended which drew her in as well.

"We're ready to call it a night," explained Benjamin. "Are you three ready to turn in?"

Martha smiled at David and Jeff, and in a soft voice replied, "In a few minutes, Dad."

Ben and Natalie exchanged quizzical glances over their daughter's mysterious response, then turned to begin the labored climb upstairs. At the top of the stairs Ben stood quietly for a moment with his ears finely tuned to the voices below. Natalie shot him a scolding look, but he raised a finger to his lips to shush her. He strained to listen, and then a contented smile spread across his face. *Praying. That's what they're doing down there—having a family prayer. How many times did Natalie and I kneel at our children's bedsides teaching them to pray? It* had once been so easy, so right. But somewhere between puberty's angst and the frenzied pace of the teenage years they had simply let the moments slip away. *When did we lose that?* he wondered. And when it came to Martha's own family, not since David was small could he recall her praying by David's side, but here was her little family, praying together again. He assumed that this was, at least in part, Sam's influence, and he added one more item to the ever-increasing list of qualities he admired in his new son-in-law. *I like Sam. He's a keeper.* Contentedly, he and Natalie entered their room and closed the door.

As soon as Sam closed the prayer, Martha leaned across the table and kissed his cheek. Then she placed a loud smacker on David's cheek, eliciting loud protests and laughter. How she loved her little family. David looked into his mother's face and could see that she was again moving into that sad-proud place she went whenever her thoughts raced ahead to January and to the time of his departure. "Mom," he said in a mock scold.

"I know . . . I know," she surrendered. "It's just hard . . ."

Sam was dealing with his own case of separation anxiety, but secretly, he was humbled and pleased to think his example and the stories of his own mission had stirred these desires in David. It hadn't required any encouragement on his part. David had already been filled with a spiritual hunger, he simply hadn't known how to satisfy it until he and Sam had spoken. Soon thereafter, he announced his desire to serve a mission. He and Martha wrestled with the conflicting emotions of sad and proud, but their greatest concern had been the reaction this news would bring from Natalie and Ben.

"You need to tell Omma and Pap, David. They need to hear it from you," Sam advised.

"I know. I've been thinking about it a lot today. I'll tell them at breakfast tomorrow. Plus, I have something else to tell them first and I think it will make the news a little easier to take."

Sam and Martha both looked at David, expecting him to be a little more forthcoming, but he gave them a wry smile and stood up. "I guess you'll just have to wait until tomorrow like Omma and Pap," he said with a wink as he bounded up the stairs for bed, leaving his parents to wonder.

"I hope I can hold it together tomorrow when he tells my folks. If I fall apart, Dad will be sure to protest," Martha said worriedly.

"It might be easier to let David go if . . ."

Martha stood up abruptly. "Don't press me, Sam," she begged. "You told me you would give me time and let it be my decision."

"I was just suggesting that—"

"I know what you're suggesting and I've told you up front how I feel about this."

"I just thought that since the visit is going so great . . . I mean you've seemed so happy. Well, I hoped that maybe it's given you some time to think about it."

"You mean to think *differently* about it. I don't want to talk about this right now, please."

Sam reached for her hand, but her arm was stiff by her side and she did not respond. Once he held her hand in his she softened, but she averted her eyes, making it clear that she was upset.

"I'm sorry, honey. I shouldn't have brought it up," he said softly.

Martha melted into her chair, bringing her forehead to rest in her hand. "No, Sam. I don't want you to hide your feelings from me either. I just thought we were in agreement on this. I grilled you on this a hundred times and you told me . . ." Her voice dropped off in despair.

Sam ran his fingers through her hair and conceded, "I know, I know. And you're right. I love you, Martha. You've made me happier in a few weeks than I've been my whole life. If nothing ever changed I'd count myself the luckiest man in the world."

Martha met his gaze. He looked at her with love radiating through his smile. She didn't question his love for her. If anything, his feelings had only deepened since the wedding, but she knew something else, something critical had changed in him as well.

* * *

Breakfast was early and simple since another busy day lay ahead. A sunny day wrapped in a cold snap would make everyone feel Christmasy, so customers would come in droves today. Ben sensed a little tension in the air and watched curiously as Martha and Sam continuously pushed the last remnants of food around on their plates. Unbeknownst to Ben, they both knew what was coming, and if it got as unpleasant as they assumed it could, they wanted a strategic reason to divert their attention—and those last bits of eggs and hash browns were their diversions.

Ben figured whatever was going on had to do with the newlyweds since David seemed calm and unflustered. Then David rose from his chair, tapping his fork against the side of his juice glass.

"First, I would like to thank Omma for another masterful breakfast. An egg is truly a work of art in her nimble hands." He again tapped his glass with his fork, and Sam, getting a handle on the routine, joined in with a tap-tap of his own, followed by a hearty, "Here, here!"

"Thank you, my good man," David encouraged. Benjamin was beginning to laugh, and Natalie bowed deeply, basking in the humorously indulgent praise.

He began again, but this time a touch of seriousness ran through his voice. "Now then," he drew a deep breath, "knowing that we have a busy and wonderful day ahead of us, I don't want to belabor things. However, I do have a few important pieces of news to share with you all."

He looked around the table but his eyes rested on those of his grandfather.

"Well, out with it, lad. Time's a wastin'," Ben said comically.

"Well, which news would you like first? The great news or the fabulous news?"

Ben cast a sideways glance. He knew his grandson too well to miss that these tremendous sales pitches were almost always intended to sweeten a bitter pill. He responded with an answer that was couched in skepticism equal to David's optimism.

"Let's just start out with the 'great news,'" he replied.

"A fine choice, Pap," David cheered. Martha held her breath. " . . . I found the tree."

There was a collective silence and then an equally collective gasp of shock. Martha clasped her hands to her mouth. Natalie turned to Ben and clenched his forearm in support. Ben just stared at David, trying to decide if this was a loving grandson's fabricated ruse to protect a man he loved, or the truth.

Finally, Ben spoke. It was a simple question filled with anticipation and hope, and upon which hung his peace of mind. "Really, son?"

David's face became as soft and tender as the timbre of his voice. "Really, Pap."

Another silence fell over them as Ben absorbed the impact of that knowledge. "Where?"

David answered this question carefully, with enough information to satisfy the question but not enough detail to restore any of the distress that had just been lifted.

"It was left at the Scout lot, Pap. I left it there because I wanted to run something past you. I fluffed it up and trimmed the trunk so it could soak. A girl and a man from Brighton came by the lot to pick out a tree for the children while I was there, and I got this great idea." He leaned in toward his grandfather to emphasize his desire for the plan's approval. "If this is to be our tree's last Christmas, what better place for it to be than at Brighton? You know it will get tons of attention there and that could be a big blessing to the home. Imagine how the kids will feel to have a miracle tree to decorate for Christmas."

Everyone sat silently, waiting to see Ben's reaction to the suggestion. Several seconds passed as he considered the proposal, and then he became aware of the awkward silence as his spellbound family members' next breath hung on his response. *What have I done?* he wondered. *How have I convoluted something lovely and divine into something so distressing and heavy?* He was ashamed. His grandson had a better perspective on the loss of the tree than he. *Sad? Yes. But devastating? No. It was tree, after all. A special tree, yes, but a tree nonetheless. Not a child, not a wife—a tree.* And it was time to count his blessings and move on.

He turned his eyes to David's and spoke in a strong voice. "I think that is a wonderful idea, David. I'm glad you thought of it. Will you make the arrangements?"

The mood changed instantly from tension to relief, and David simply replied, "Sure, Pap."

Everyone sat quietly for a moment, absorbing the relief of Ben's response, then Ben stood to leave the table when David's salesman voice again returned.

"Hold on a minute. That was just the great news. We still have the fabulous news left."

Martha sucked in air almost imperceptibly, and Sam grabbed her hand under the table and squeezed gently.

"I thought the Brighton plan was the 'fabulous' part," Ben said, confused.

"Nope. I have something else even more fabulous than that," he teased. Again his voice softened, and as he leaned closer to his grandparents they could feel a shift in his mood. "Pap, have you ever wondered where we came from and whether there's a purpose to our lives?"

Because it was more of a rhetorical question, Ben did not respond, though his eyes registered keen interest in where this conversation was headed.

"I've met a lot of people and it seems like everyone is searching for answers to these same questions. They started nagging at me when I was so sick. Some nights I'd lie in bed in the hospital and I'd wonder, 'If I do die, where will I go, and will my life have had a purpose?' And more importantly, 'If it does, would I have fulfilled it, or will I ever get the chance?'"

Ben's eyes become thoughtful as his mind converged on two points in time. First he recalled how he and Natalie were ready to fly to California to be with their grandson and his mother during that dark and scary time, and then he recalled similar questions that tugged at his own heart the night he lay on the frozen ground, preparing himself for what was to come. Natalie's face also registered recollection of similar thoughts.

"I feel I have those answers now, and after talking to Sam about his experiences, well, I've decided that I'd like to share those answers with others . . . as a missionary."

Ben's eyes immediately darted in Sam's direction. Sam held his breath, but surprisingly, Ben was receiving the news with little immediate reaction. Natalie appeared to be revisiting a thought that was not foreign to her. Her eyes seemed curiously focused on a point miles and years beyond the kitchen walls, and then some sort of recognition sparked in her memory and she turned to face Benjamin. His eyes were cast downward toward the table. Natalie squeezed his hand and he raised his gaze to meet hers. A silent conversation passed between their eyes and Ben began to nod, a subtle, almost imperceptible nod. A solemn acceptance crossed his face and he turned and spoke in a graveled voice.

"A missionary, you say? What does that mean, David?"

David, Sam, and Martha finally breathed. Ben particularly noticed the worry in David's face and was flattered that his and Natalie's feelings were so critical a concern to their grandson. He was not completely caught off guard by the announcement. He remembered the spiritual hunger David demonstrated even as a young boy and the long talks that hunger fostered. He knew this boy loved, honored, and respected him, and that he regarded his grandmother, his precious Omma, as a second mother to him. And because of those deep attachments, Ben knew he needed the assurance that they understood and would support his decision.

"I've made a two-year commitment, Pap. I'll leave after New Year's to enter the Missionary Training Center in Provo, Utah. I'll be there for about two months while I brush up my Spanish and improve my teaching skills, and then I'll fly to Central America."

Martha dug her nails deep into Sam's knee while he fought to remain quiet, and then Ben reacted. His voice did rise in volume and pitch, but it was controlled. "Two years? In Central America? David, there are people right here who you can help. Why do you need to go so far?"

Natalie touched Ben's arm and whispered his name softly. His voice immediately became contrite. "Can you at least fly home for a visit?" Ben asked more encouragingly.

"I can't, Pap," David replied with sympathy. "It's like you've always taught me, 'focus on one thing at a time.'" He smiled as he referred to their "how to become a man" talks. His voice wavered as he faced the confusion in his grandfather's face.

"It will be as tough for me to leave as it will for you to let me go, but I know that for me to give my best effort, I'll need to love the people I'm serving with all my heart, and to do that I'll need to lose myself in the work and let go of my old life for a while. So I'll only call you a few times, like on Christmas, but I'll write every week and you guys can send me lots of packages." He laughed and his eyes were now shining, but his voice was controlled. He walked over to the empty chair near his grandfather, pulled it around to face him, and sat down.

"Pap . . . Omma . . . I love you guys with all my heart and I owe you so much for the great part you've both played in making me who I am today." Ben's lower lip was tightly pursed and Natalie's eyes glistened as she listened to her grandson. "When I look at my life I can see that I've been blessed with so much, and I feel like I have a huge debt to repay to the Savior. This is how I want to do that. Can you understand?"

Silence settled around the table while everyone considered how David's decision would affect them. Ben fidgeted in his chair for several seconds, then stood without a word. The other three family members mistakenly assumed he was dismissing the entire discussion in a cursory fashion, but Natalie knew what he was about to do. Her eyes were set upon his destination, the old desk where he kept his journals. When he reached the desk he touched the spines of several books until his hand settled on the back of a particular volume. He pulled it out, thumbing through the pages as he walked back to the table and sat in his chair. He laid the book reverently on the table, continuing to search for a particular page. Everyone waited for him to speak. Finally, he found the page he wanted. His eyes met Natalie's and she smiled encouragingly, then he allowed his gaze to sweep around the table, settling on David. Old eyes and young eyes met, and Ben began.

"Many years ago I was facing the struggle of my life. The details aren't important now, but I was . . . lost. I had prayed but received no answers and finally, in desperation, I knelt in the corner of our old yard and I poured my heart out to God. I begged Him for help, for an answer, and I made Him a promise. Now, I'm wondering if He's calling you to fulfill that promise."

Ben's voice quivered and he cast his eyes downward to read the journal entry, written almost as a prayer.

> *Father, I have two weeks to find a place for my family to live. I know that sounds like a small task, but you know my struggles. I feel the very survival of our*

family hinges on finding a healing place to rebuild. I have prayed and prayed for an answer. Tonight I begged you for a sign. I know how faithless that sounds, but I need to know. Are we here for a purpose or is life just a random set of chances and sorrows? I need to believe that you hear my cries and know how much I love my family. I would give my life for them, and if I, only a man, can love so much, then I believe you who are greater than man must love greater than a man.

Of course you do . . . you gave your Son. And so, tonight I cried to you again, from the darkness of my yard, and I begged you for help, and I promised to dedicate my life to repaying the debt. Please help me, Father, and show me what I should do.

Ben closed the book. He coughed to clear the emotion from his throat. He continued, "One week later we signed the contract for this farm and about a week after that we moved in and found the little seedling growing in the orchard. Perhaps now you can understand why I attached so much reverence to it—it was my sign from God. But now, I'm thinking that maybe the tree was planted to save you, David, because . . . perhaps you are the answer to my prayers. You and your mission will help me fulfill my promise."

Martha and David looked at one another. So many little fragmented pieces of their family history suddenly fell into place and they understood more poignantly the depth of Ben's love. It was going to be all right. They knew it now, and Sam now understood the importance of the tree.

Natalie buried her face in Ben's cheek, and he took her chin and kissed her softly. "I love you, Ben," she whispered in his ear.

"Then I have everything, darling," he returned.

David looked around the table at the four teary-eyed people he loved most in the world, and now with the burden lifted from his anxious heart, he was elated. But there was still one more wondrous surprise to reveal, so he jumped up, cleared his own eyes, and began to wheel and deal in his best game-show-announcer voice.

"Sam, don't we have one last surprise waiting for our lucky couple?"

Sam knew where he was heading, and he joined in. "You're right, David!"

"Well, then, Sam, tell them what they've won," David encouraged.

Sam looked over at Martha's encouraging face and continued. "Mr. and Mrs. Johanson, you came to breakfast this morning believing that your beautiful daughter and grandson, and your new, incredibly handsome son-in-law were leaving Sunday—but guess what?"

Natalie and Ben's eyes were filled with hopeful anticipation as Sam rattled on. "If you can name a number between one and three you will win today's surprise itinerary!"

Natalie paused while she processed and then she jumped up in her seat, laughing and yelling, "Two, two!"

"That is correct!" David congratulated her. "Now, Sam, read that itinerary."

"Well, David, today's prize is one that is sure to please Omma *and* Pap. It's a three-week, all-expense-paid, business/belated honeymoon trip to Europe for Martha and Sam, who will be leaving the very precious and completely toilet-trained David through New Year's Day!"

"Very good, Sam," David bellowed, then turning his face into an exasperated scowl he added for Sam's benefit, "except for the whole 'toilet-trained' part." He then turned his attention to Pap and Omma. "Well, folks, what do you think about that prize?"

Pap smacked his strong hands on the table with pleasure. "We'll take it!"

Natalie clapped her hands together and looked at Martha for confirmation of the wonderful news she thought she had heard. Martha smiled back at her and took Sam's hand. "It's true, Mom, if it's okay with you and Dad."

Ben's big voice boomed out his reply with complete incredulity. "Okay? Okay? Are you kidding? Of course it's okay with us. It will be just like old times, eh, David?"

David nodded, his face completely glowing at the way this was all working out. "Just like old times, Pap," he replied.

"How is this possible?" Natalie asked. "What about David's college?"

Martha jumped in. "It's all arranged, Mom. David worked it out with his professors to complete his courses online."

Sam was delighted to see how much joy their last surprise was bringing Ben and Natalie. He added the final details. "We leave on Tuesday and we should return December twenty-third, just in time for a Johanson family Christmas, and then we leave New Year's Day for California. We'll have a few days to help David pack, and then he leaves on the seventh for the Missionary Training Center."

Martha didn't want the happiness of the last few minutes to be marred by reminders of David's impending departure, so she quickly interjected, "And until then, he is all yours."

Chapter Twelve

On Monday morning, Carol Davenport couldn't wait for Merit to leave for school. Her impatience sprang from several desires. First, the long weekend had afforded Merit far too many excuses to spend time with her new male friend, David Johanson, and although he seemed like a wonderful boy, Carol would prefer that things move more slowly, particularly in light of her daughter's previously flawed relationship. Merit had met him Friday at the Christmas-tree lot near Brighton. He offered to deliver her prized tree the next day, which ended up taking the entire morning since David decided to stay awhile and "help" with the children.

Saturday evening there was the invitation to see a movie with him, and then Sunday there was a holiday concert. He was always polite, and Merit mentioned he was going to be a missionary, but Carol was not yet ready to trust Merit's judgment where boys were concerned.

The other reason she was anxious to get Merit on her way to school was her excitement over starting her first day as a volunteer at Brighton. She had enjoyed Friday's visit with the children so much that she had called Ms. Prescott later that evening and inquired about a volunteer position. Today was day one of her new adventure.

Her husband Mike must have noticed something different in her attitude or mood because he made numerous comments, teasing her about "having a new boyfriend" or "winning the lottery." Finally, before he left for work that morning, he just looked lovingly into her eyes in a way neither of them had lately and kissed her on the cheek.

It pleased her that she felt a spark in their numbed marriage. She wanted to tell Mike about her new activity, but she decided to wait, wanting to see if she would be able to sustain this new happiness and energy, before she gave her husband a false sense of optimism.

Her reluctance to tell Merit was different. Carol could see Brighton's potential as an anchor in Merit's life, a place where she was trusted and needed. Perhaps someday there would be "room enough" for both of them to work together, but for now she didn't want to do or say anything that might derail the progress Merit was making. Cassidy and Mrs. Sherman agreed that for now, Carol's involvement would be their little secret.

When Carol arrived at Brighton's front door, her knock was greeted by Meghan's cheery voice over the intercom. Once inside the airy foyer, she was deluged with the children's greetings. She peered through the bellowing group looking for her special pal, Simon, but he was not among the clamoring assembly. After Mrs. Sherman gave her the rundown on the day's itinerary, complete with her assignments, Carol inquired about Simon.

"He's got a touch of the bug," Mrs. Sherman replied with a face full of compassion and concern. "Poor little tyke. He was up most of the night with a dreadful hacking cough. He coughed so long and so hard he made himself sick, so we ended up changing his linen and giving him a bath at three in the morning." The look of concern that washed over Carol's face must have stirred Mrs. Sherman. With her next breath she decided to change the hourly schedule of Carol's assignments and retrieved the old one from her hands.

"Why don't you head up the stairs and visit with Simon for a few hours. Cassidy's been up there with him for a while and she could probably use some relief."

Carol was elated. She found Simon curled up in Ms. Prescott's lap as the two sat in a beanbag chair. His eyes were tired and glassy, and although he had a cup with a built-in straw pressed to his lips, he wasn't drinking. Cartoons were playing on the TV, but Simon was barely paying any attention to them. Cassidy's fingers ruffled softly through his hair as his eyelids fluttered with the rhythm of her motion.

Carol was amazed at the strong emotions their closeness aroused in her. *What are these feelings? Jealousy?* She tried to push that notion aside, but even as she was attempting to dismiss the thought she evaluated her heart and knew it was true. She was jealous of Cassidy's relationship with Simon.

Carol had turned to leave when Cassidy noticed her standing in the doorway. Simon reacted to the change in her rhythm and stirred, catching sight of Carol. It took a moment for any recognition to register, but a smile spread across his face and Carol knew he remembered her.

"Well, Simon," Cassidy said, "I was afraid Miss Cassidy's arm was going to get too tired and I would have to take a break from rubbing your head, but now Miss Carol is here so you are a very lucky fellow." She gave his hair one last ruffle and stood to greet Carol, who was startled to see Cassidy out of her wheelchair and walking unassisted. Her amazement was apparent.

"Yep," Cassidy admitted, slightly embarrassed, "I'm fully mobile again."

"Oh . . ." stuttered Carol.

"Well, I'll leave my little pal to your careful attention. Bye, Simon. Maybe I'll see you at lunch later, okay?"

Simon's head nodded, but only slightly. Carol grabbed Cassidy Prescott firmly by the arm and led her to the doorway. It was an uncharacteristically bold move for the generally shy Carol, but Cassidy noted the concern in her face over Simon's situation, and spoke to her in calm, reassuring tones. "He's really just fine. He has a little cold, that's all. Our regular doctor stopped by on his way back from the hospital and he checked him over. Simon just needs a little rest and some snuggles and he'll be as good as new in two or three days. Don't worry."

Carol's face relaxed, and with her relief came the return of her shy countenance, now very contrite as she let go of Cassidy's arm. Cassidy then rubbed Carol's arm and smiled at her. "I know you two have become special pals. Sit with him awhile and if he falls asleep, come join me in my office. I have a ton of filing I could use some help with."

Carol agreed, then quickly headed over to visit with Simon. She had barely drawn near enough to sit in the vacated beanbag chair when Simon shifted his position to place his head in her lap. She sat there momentarily stunned by this gesture of trust and friendship, then she too began ruffling the small boy's hair.

An hour passed as Carol sang him songs, with the two just enjoying the pleasure of each other's company. Then the sound of twenty or so feet began to signal the approach of many of the remaining children. Despite their attempts to draw Simon into their play, he continued to lay his head in Carol's lap until his heavy eyelids closed soundly and small snores fluttered from him. Carol then picked up the little bundle and carried him to his bed as directed by the older children. She tucked him in close, kissed him on the head, and headed down to Cassidy Prescott's office.

A manila folder lay on the desk and several boxes full of thick file folders lay on the window seat. Cassidy was sorting the folders into piles and looked completely overwhelmed. "I don't even know where to begin," she said aloud to no one in particular, only now becoming aware that Carol had entered. "I got so behind while I was laid up. So did Simon nod off?"

"Yes, just a minute ago," Carol replied wistfully. "How could anyone give such a beautiful child up . . . and why has no one ever adopted him?" She tried to keep the comment casual, but she was fishing for information about the adorable little thief who had stolen her heart.

"It's a complicated situation, Carol. His mother died soon after she delivered him, and the man listed as the father on the birth certificate has never arrived, though a law firm representing him assures us that he's working to be able to provide a home for Simon someday. Gifts and cards arrive like clockwork on holidays, birthdays, and the like, and the father requests photos, but he has never seen Simon in person and won't sign his rights away to allow Simon to be adopted by anyone else."

Carol was angry. *So that's that? This beautiful little child is stuck in limbo. His own father won't love him and so no one else is allowed to?* A stabbing pain went through her heart, similar to the one she felt when Markie died. Another child lost to her.

"Carol?" Cassidy tried to jar her from her clouded thoughts.

"I'm . . . I'm sorry. I was just thinking. It's so unjust. A little child being denied a home because of the parental rights of a parent that doesn't care anyway? Aren't there laws?"

"Several of these children are in similar situations, Carol. They come from homes where one parent or another is trying to get on their feet and get them back, so in the meantime we try to love them and give them the best home and family situation we can. But," Cassidy cautioned, "we also learn that we have to be able to love them with the knowledge that we may have to give them up. We have to remind ourselves every day that most of these kids do have a parent out there, and part of our job is to help them transition back into that home if possible, and into another home if that option becomes available. I forgot that a few times in the early days of Brighton, and I nearly lost my mind when children—children I felt were my children—were taken away. Every day now I make myself remember that I am loving and nurturing someone else's child and that I have to be prepared to let go."

Carol wondered if she could continue to come to Brighton under those terms. *Can I love and invest in children that could suddenly be ripped away from me?*

"How do you do that?" Carol asked with incredulity.

Cassidy set the folders down on the table and walked over to her window, looking out over the children's play area. "It's a two-step process," she replied. "First, I remember that loving them is an honor. Their parents can't or won't for whatever reason, so we are all they have."

"But that leaves you wide open to agony. How do you insulate yourself from that?"

Cassidy turned to face her with eyes full of understanding. "That is where step two comes in. I'll explain. I got into this business because I longed for a houseful of children, and when it didn't seem like I would ever have a family of my own, the answer seemed to be to share the love I'd longed to give to my children with other children who needed to be loved. Of course, when I watched the first few children drive away with other families, I thought I would die inside.

"I had my degree in counseling and took several additional courses before I earned my license, so I understood intellectually that I would have to let go, but when it was time to actually do it, I fell apart, completely apart. My county supervisor suggested I see a counselor. I resisted at first, but she taught me something that has stayed with me ever since."

Carol was listening to Cassidy's story but her thoughts had turned to her own loss. No explanation was needed. Carol knew how deeply pain bit into the heart of a mother who loses a child. No explanation would ever be necessary to make her understand that. She looked up, letting her eyes inquire about step number two because her throat was too tight to speak.

Cassidy continued on. "This counselor asked me a lot of questions about the children who went home or were placed . . . and asked me to answer them all. As I spoke she taped the interview and played it back. Before she played it, though, she asked me to listen carefully to all my objections to their departure and make an *X* for every objection that was about the children's loss and an *O* for every objection about my loss. When the exercise was over, the number of *O*'s on my sheet was far greater than the number of *X*'s. And then she said this, 'Real love requires us to lose ourselves in the loving. No matter how noble our intentions, if we can't love *without* measuring *our return* then we're setting ourselves up for hurt.' She then suggested that if that was the case, then I should relinquish Brighton. But, if I could forget my own needs and just love the children, she promised me that what I would receive would be beyond my expectations. It has been absolutely true."

Carol thought about Markie again. His short life had been filled with needles and surgeries and medically required separations from home. She thought about Merit's childhood, being shuffled off to relatives so Mom could be with Markie. And she thought about Mike and the agony he suffered being powerless to do anything to comfort his little son those last weeks. She could see the wisdom in Cassidy's words. Her depression had been completely about her loss. There had been little consideration of anyone else's or about the relief Markie must have felt to be free from his sickly body and the fear that accompanied its care.

But she still missed him. Perhaps someday she would achieve Cassidy's level of selflessness, but not today. Not yet with Markie, and not yet for Simon. Markie was gone, and though she thought of him every moment, she had battled through that pain and said her goodbyes. But Simon was still here and he needed a parent, and she resolved to either be that person or find that person.

Carol nodded understanding nonetheless. "So tell me about these folders," she inquired, quickly changing the subject. "What do you want done with them?"

Cassidy was caught off guard by the rapid change in the conversation, but she followed Carol's lead. "Well, this stack is medical forms that need to be filed into the children's individual folders." She pointed to a small pile of typed forms. "And these boxes are full of press releases and fund-raising information that need to be assembled into packets before Saturday."

"What's happening on Saturday?" asked Carol.

Cassidy looked at her in amazement. "Didn't Merit tell you? Every year we host a 'Santa Breakfast,' but this year, since the word got out that we're giving David's Tree its final Christmas, the paper called and they want to take pictures of the tree and the children. A few of the children can be photographed but some can't by law, so we're sorting all this craziness out. Didn't you see the photo in this morning's paper?"

Again Carol responded with a blank stare as Cassidy plowed on.

"Merit offered to help the children make ornaments for the tree and to prepare a few songs for next Saturday. A photographer came by Sunday afternoon and took photos of Merit, David, and the children working on the ornaments. The photo and the story were printed in today's paper. It's pandemonium, but, as David says, it will give us a great opportunity to get sponsors and do some fund-raising for the home, so we need to get these fund-raising materials into packets before the breakfast."

Cassidy concentrated on the press packets as she scurried around the room to Carol's curious amazement. Other than a slight limp, she showed no residual signs of injury and she could outwork a three-man team. Cassidy put Carol's various jobs in priority order with the medical filing being the most critical. Carol picked up the medical folder and read the name on the first form, then halted. She turned to the file cabinet and opened the top drawer, thumbing nervously through the folders, searching for the name whose tab matched the name on the paper in her hands. At the same moment she heard an excited gasp escape from Cassidy. Cassidy stood frozen in her tracks for several seconds, then bolted for the door. In passing, she rattled off a few last-minute instructions to Carol, then closed the door firmly.

Carol glanced cautiously over her shoulder to see what had caused the nervous reaction, and knew in an instant it was the unexpected approach of Jeff Johnson coming up the walk. His arrival barely registered with her. Her entire attention was riveted on the folder hanging before her entitled, "Confidential: Simon Allen."

Chapter Thirteen

Cassidy's heart was pounding at the thought that he was standing just outside her door. She had given him her phone number, and they had spoken three times since their chance encounter Friday. Jeff had asked a thousand questions about his family. As she tried to bridge the twenty-year gap for him, she had become acutely aware of the pain each revelation caused. He was particularly interested in knowing how Martha was, and obviously found comfort in hearing good things about her son David and of her marriage to Sam Pearce; however, the toughest questions had been about his parents. It was apparent that he still agonized over the impact his leaving had on them, and regardless of her assurances that they would joyously welcome him home, she could not convince him.

Saturday night she pressed him harder to contact them, but he had become distant, and when he hung up, Cassidy feared she had pushed so hard he might run again. She held her breath and then, miraculously, he called again Sunday night. She had turned the tables on him, this time posing questions to him. She needed to know if the spark from their youth that haunted her for twenty years had left him thinking of her occasionally as well, hoping that he might find strength in knowing that her desire to identify him was not just launched out of curiosity but from caring. It had been a presumptuous thing to do, totally out of character for the shy girl she once was, but losing him, and realizing she could survive a failed marriage and the social dearth that followed it, had since convinced her that if her heart ever felt inclined to someone again, she would stick her neck out and take a chance for happiness. Past experience had taught her that all pride got you was a table for one. Her heart definitely still felt inclined toward him, and now he was at her door!

Her first view of him was unsettling. It was immediately apparent that he was more nervous today than he had been on Friday. She smiled apprehensively at him and began to apologize for being so pushy, but Jeff gestured for her to stop, smiled weakly, and gave her arms a gentle squeeze. Cassidy mistook the gesture and tilted her face to kiss him, but he only offered his cheek, withdrew quickly, and fumbled to move on.

"Where are all the children?" he asked.

"They are . . . uh . . ." She was so distracted. *What is going on in his head? Is this where he'll make his farewell and sail into the sunset again?* She was becoming angry. "They're having their regular 'quiet time,' which they do every day after lunch."

"Oh," he replied blankly. Silence. Cassidy wanted to kick him, but softened a bit when he suddenly spoke in a sad voice. "How would you feel about a walk?"

Something in his voice told her he wasn't a man on the run but a man looking for a hand to pull him in, and she relaxed. "I'd like a walk. My jacket's over there, on the coatrack."

Jeff helped her into the brown suede jacket and led her out the door and onto the sidewalk. It was a brisk fall day, slightly cloudy, but when the sun broke through it was in bright, searing shafts. They went on in silence for several minutes, watching the leaves skid across the path, as they headed off toward the large lawn swing in the corner of the yard. Then they stopped. Jeff stood there surveying the property, noting all the similarities and the changes, and he sighed. Cassidy knew he was measuring the passage of time and she didn't intrude. Eventually, he motioned for her to sit and he took his place beside her. He cupped his face in his hands, rubbing his fingers into his eyes. Then he raised his face to meet her eyes, noting her confusion and concern. "Hi," he said, smiling apologetically.

"Hi," she answered nervously, her expression speaking volumes.

"I've done a lot of thinking since Friday," he began. "Every time we've talked on the phone since then, part of me has been constantly amazed at how utterly comfortable and right it felt to be talking to you, and then there's a part of me that just wanted to jump out of my skin or run away because it was so uncomfortable . . ."

Cassidy listened silently while her mind and mood seesawed up and down.

"I struggled with all those feelings, trying to decide whether or not it would be a good idea to pursue this thing that's still between us. I know I can't handle another hit in my life, Cassidy, and I don't want to do anything that would risk hurting you either, but I really didn't want to walk away from this without a fight."

She held her breath.

"And then I realized what's tearing me up. It's the secrets. I'm afraid the feelings you think you have for me might be destroyed when you come to know the man I've been. So that's why I'm here, to begin to clear out the secrets. I want you to know the truth about me, Cassidy. And then you can decide if there's still any reason for us to pursue this."

His head dropped in relief. As he began to raise it up, her hand was on his, gently touching him, comforting him. He moved it to his mouth and kissed her palm. His eyes closed, savoring the scent of her skin. He moved his cheek against her skin, loving the feel of her touch, then opened his eyes, fearing his expression revealed too much.

"I'm afraid if you were willing to castigate yourself for something as minor as your 'wheelchair test,' you'll have a hard time understanding what I came here to tell you." Jeff stood and cast his eyes across the property again. Cassidy stood quickly also, fearful of the apprehension creeping into his eyes.

"How about that walk you promised?" she asked, taking his hand and leading him.

"Are you allowed?" he replied, looking concerned.

"If my leg gets tired, I'll just lean on you a while. How would that be?"

He laughed shyly and wrapped his hand over hers as she clutched his arm. They walked for several minutes or so while Cassidy, applying every skill she'd learned in her counseling courses, rambled on about anything that would keep him walking and adjusting to having her by his side. Jeff looked at her, having figured out her plan, and smiled from time to time. When she questioned the reason for his humor, he chuckled. "Psychology 231?"

She wrinkled her brow, and then as she got his point she laughed. "Can't pull anything over on you anymore, eh?" Then she exaggerated her grip on his arm and rolled her hand in a circle in front of her, gesturing while she told him in a mock Freudian imitation, to keep talking.

Jeff laughed. "Oooh . . . patterning, reflexive listening, and conversation stimulation. You're good. Maybe I should tell my boss to hire you."

"Nah," she countered with a comical nasal snort. "See, I'm really only going through these exercises so I can hold your arm longer and feel your muscles."

Jeff now laughed so hard he nearly cried. It was the first truly hearty laugh he could remember in years, and for the first time, being with her actually felt like being home.

"So what did you think when you first suspected that Jeff Johnson was TJ?"

Cassidy wanted to come back with a flip answer to keep the mood light, because something told her Jeff, or TJ, or whoever he was, was pressing on with his agenda, but she didn't want to relive the past. There was hurt waiting there and she'd had enough of that. She was ready for a dream or two to actually come true, and as reckless as it might have been, she was ready to put her money on the man whom she'd been praying would return home.

"What did I think?" She leaned back and paused, carefully selecting her words. "I thought it was kismet."

The pair resumed their stride but silence hung in the air until Cassidy had to explain. "You know how people say you never forget your first love? Well, I believe that . . . and that was you. After you left I blamed you for every miserable thing that happened or didn't happen in my life. I just kept thinking that I was supposed to be with you, and that every other man that came along was, at best, just a substitute, and that meant that I would never be as happy as I would have been if you hadn't messed everything up. So I guess I was angry with you for a long time, but I always believed you would eventually come home. I suppose if I were really honest with myself, that's the reason I opened the home here and didn't follow the majority of my family to Florida."

Jeff was disarmed by her candor. He lived so guardedly, and she leapt out with unabashed courage. *I was once like that,* he marveled. *Will I ever be that secure again?* They walked on.

"Tell me what you remember about that last summer, Cassidy," he prompted. His eyes probed hers to measure the damage his selfishness and departure had caused her. She realized they couldn't move forward unless she could help him face it and then get past it. She drew a deep, long breath. She had replayed that summer so many times in her mind, slightly altering the facts each time to accommodate her ability to handle the pain. What had begun at age seventeen as the anticipated "spring of her dreams" became the summer that nearly broke the spirit of Cassidy Brighton. For months she had been filled with an anger and pain so excruciating, she locked herself in her room for days at a time, barely eating, barely speaking. As Martha's crisis unfolded, Cassidy managed to let go of some of her self-pity as she invested her energy in helping her friend.

In one moment Martha had lost both of the loves of her life—her baby's father and her beloved brother and confidant—whom she needed more than ever. In time, Martha's forgiving nature softened Cassidy's pain until she was able to consider how terrible TJ's situation had to have been to leave everything and everyone he loved behind. Eventually, there was no anger left, only compassion. And now he was asking her to recall the agony of those painful days. They walked back to the swing. She took his hands in hers and focused her memory-filled eyes on his, allowing him to enter the dark places where her scars, once buried, were revealed a final time.

"I . . . I guess we'd have to go back to the summer before your senior year and my junior year." She paused, finding it all so surreal to be so affected by something long past and long put away. "I always loved our lazy summers, but that summer felt different to me, magical, because you . . . noticed me. I wasn't just as a pal anymore, but . . . a woman."

She stammered, realizing the disparity between those adolescent feelings and the words. She wondered if they still seemed as true to TJ. He didn't speak but the look in his eyes assured her he had revisited those feelings himself, validating her words, and eventually she continued. "When we swam that summer, we seemed to always break away from the group. Remember how we laughed and talked about our plans and dreams?" She again paused. "I felt as though I knew you better than anyone else in the world, and that I had shared more of myself with you than anyone else. That's why I felt so . . . so betrayed when you left."

Cassidy looked at Jeff to see how that disclosure affected him. He still didn't speak, but his hands gave hers a gentle, encouraging squeeze and he nodded somberly for her to go on.

"I told you things I had never told anyone else . . . and I felt with you like I'd never felt with anyone else. I'd had had a crush on you since grade school, but that summer I knew that I was falling in love with you."

She cast her brown eyes downward. Still silent, he cast his own head down and pressed his forehead against hers. "I'm so sorry, Cassidy. I can't begin to tell you how truly sorry I am. If I could change it all, you've got to know I would, but first I need to understand." He raised her face to meet his gaze and asked, "Tell me everything, Cassidy. I need to know."

"Why do you need to dredge this all back up, Jeff? Why can't you accept that we've moved past this and start fresh? What good can come from rehashing decades-old wounds?"

"I threw away twenty-one years, Cassidy." The regret was heavy in his voice. He looked into her face, trying to help her understand. "Don't you see? Until I know where I left things, I can't know what and where we are now, and I can't move forward. You may be able to say you forgive me and really mean that, but I need to know what damage I caused, or I will just keep churning the scenarios I've imagined over and over in my mind the rest of my life, and believe me, I've imagined that I left behind dreadful harm, so the truth can't be worse than my nightmares."

She winced, imagining what his last twenty-one years had been like. "Alright, what do you want to know?"

"Everything you want to tell me," he replied.

Cassidy shifted her position and closed her eyes to order her thoughts. "Okay. Well, I guess I set myself up for disaster when I dared to dream that what we'd shared in the summer would continue, but as soon as school started I could feel you pulling away from me and then, I heard . . . things."

Jeff could imagine the "things" she had heard, the things he had tried to keep from her. *No matter now,* he mused. What she didn't know he was going to have to tell her anyway.

She used humor to ease the message. "I can't believe the levels of degradation I allowed myself to sink to," she smiled, her humiliation still apparent, "because in spite of everything you did to push me aside, I was willing to accept any scrap of your attention. I bailed you out when your homecoming date got sick, and then I begged Martha to tell you she was sick so I could be the one to take you shopping to buy a gift for your girlfriend." She punched him in the arm.

Jeff smiled back at her apologetically and rolled his eyes. "I was such a jerk. How could you have even liked someone like that?"

"Potential. I saw potential," she insisted, laughing. "But I agree, you were a real jerk," she scolded with mock seriousness. "Kevin started telling me to stay away from you because even he could see that I was about to get steamrolled." She considered her brother's warning. "Now that I think about it, he really never said a kind word about you after that winter. I don't know what happened between you two, but it must have been terrible for two great friends like you to split."

Cassidy detected something in Jeff's expression that told her she had hit a nerve. At first she considered passing it by, and then small fragments of memories came together, illuminating a terrible recognition. "It was Kevin, wasn't it? Kevin did this! He told you to stay away from me, didn't he?"

Jeff was stoically silent. He tried to maintain a blank expression, but it was apparent that she was right. He simply responded, "Where is Kevin now?"

That was a confirmation to Cassidy, who at this moment wanted to hop a plane and grab hold of her brother's neck and wring it until he confessed. Instead she replied through gritted teeth, "Florida, he lives in Florida with his perfect wife and their three perfect children."

Jeff smiled, pleased that his former friend had obtained a happy life. His pleasure just infuriated Cassidy, who was now as driven to know the truth as Jeff had been previously.

"Don't blame Kevin, Cassidy. I'm the one to blame for this."

Jeff stood up and walked over to the fence that surrounded the pasture, separating it from the play yard. He leaned against the freshly painted white post with his back toward her and sighed, loudly this time. Cassidy followed him. She followed her instincts and allowed her tall, slim frame to rest against his back. She enjoyed the nearness of him yet, and she leaned there quietly for a few moments, feeling the rise and fall of his breathing, and then softly encouraged him. "Please help me to understand all this, TJ."

He kept his back to her. It was easier this way he guessed. "Cassidy, all Kevin did was try to protect you from being hurt and to prevent me from complicating your life. Don't be angry with him. He was just being a good brother. I wish I had done the same for Martha."

"No. No way, TJ," she said firmly. "You aren't going to leave it like that." She pulled away from him and grabbed his shoulder, forcing him to face her. Her eyes were filled with conviction now, and Jeff knew she not only deserved more information, but would settle for nothing less. His earlier commitment to total disclosure wavered when he realized how fresh some of the pain still was. But buoyed by the depth of her need to understand, he faced her, traced his fingers along her cheek, and made a joke about how he always loved tough women. Then he turned back around to lean against the post, pulling her in beside him.

"I carved your name into the old tree at Veterans' Park that summer. I fell for you too, but I didn't know how to handle it. I can't explain it simply, except to say that I loved you as a sister before I ever thought to love you as a girlfriend, so imagine how weird that will make a seventeen-year-old guy feel." He laughed nervously, but was surprised to realize that her attention was still fixed on his first confession.

"You carved my name into the old tree at Veterans' Park? I've read all those carvings hundreds of times—praying to find my name so I could imagine it was from you. I've never found anything."

"You'd have to know where to look," he replied mysteriously. "Remember how I missed the first football game my senior year because of that sprained elbow? Well, I sprained it falling out of the upper boughs of that tree, after I finished carving our names up there."

Cassidy stared at him, trying to figure out if he was telling the truth or teasing her. "Why did you hide it way up there? Were you ashamed to have anyone think you liked me?"

"I was still trying to reconcile my feelings for you. I guess I figured that if it didn't work out, no one would ever need to know, and if it did work out," he teased, "you were scrappy enough to climb up there and see it for yourself."

Cassidy scowled over yet another reference to her as "scrappy," but Jeff took hold of her hands and pulled her so close to him that she could feel his eyelashes brush her forehead. In a whisper he added to his confession, "Do you want to know the truth? I had it all planned out that if you and I ever did get together, I would bring you way up into the top of tree and show you the carving, and we would sit there in the moonlight and I would kiss you for the first time right there, close to the stars."

He held her close to him and wrapped his arms lightly around her. He wanted to hold her closer, to never let her beyond his grasp again, but there was so much more he needed to tell her. When he was finished he would see if she would still allow him that privilege.

"So, you see," he whispered, "you weren't imagining anything." He slowly released her, but her arms remained firmly around him. Cassidy could not imagine that anything he could say could ever make her want to leave his side.

"What changed things?" Cassidy asked in a small, quiet voice. "How did you go from loving me like that to treating me like you did that night at the prom?"

Jeff wondered where he should begin. Each false turn and erred choice seemed linked to some prior event. It always seemed like the beginning of his troubles was tied to the end of that precious last summer, so that's where he began.

"It was so easy during the summer. There were no pressures. We could just let our friendship slowly ripen into something deeper, but the trouble was, we ran out of summer. As soon as school started we had no time together. I just got . . . distracted."

Cassidy knew who the "distractions" were. With her he had been a gentleman, almost shy, filled with dreams and plans, the sharing of which made him almost nervous and boyish. Around the "distractions" he was loud and flirtatious, and Cassidy could neither imagine him sharing the tender things of his heart, nor could she imagine those girls caring about them either. So she had sworn her heart free of TJ Johanson and thrown herself into her studies until he yanked her back into his world.

"It wasn't a good crowd for me, but after I started hanging out with them, I didn't feel comfortable around you or Kevin anymore either. I was so . . . lost, but I didn't even realize it."

Jeff's eyes were fixed on some spot way ahead of him, as he wallowed in the regret of his squandered youth and innocence, hoping against hope that she really could handle the truth. "You know the stupidest thing? None of that ever made me as happy as the simple moments we shared together just talking, but I discovered that too late. Innocently enough though, I made the mistake of finding some measure of comfort in a friendship with the very girl Kevin had secretly fallen for. He hated me after that. We never *did* anything," he said carefully, trying to make her understand, "we were just friends, but because of my reputation, Kevin just assumed things. He thought I had purposely derailed him, that I had completely betrayed him. He told me to stay away from you, and that if I didn't he would tell you all the details of my . . . experiences."

Jeff winced as he considered the incongruity of living such an unbridled life—hating his behavior so much that he spent hours in strategy to keep the stories from his parents and from Cassidy. Despite his efforts, Cassidy had nevertheless been hurt by it, and his parents were sufficiently suspicious to begin the constant barrage of questions that was catalyst to his final door-slamming exit.

"The thought of you knowing . . . everything . . . made me sick, so I promised him that I wouldn't pursue seeing you."

Cassidy's stomach tightened. Her brother had destroyed her chance to be with TJ. He hadn't even given her the chance to decide whether or not to forgive him. She was so absorbed in her thoughts she barely heard Jeff continue.

"I promised him I wouldn't *pursue* seeing you, so instead, I found ways to bring you to me." He finally turned to face her and his eyes were sparkling with pleasure at his caginess. "Remember homecoming? My date didn't get sick," he confessed. "I broke our date and then I had Martha call you to tell you that. I was praying you would offer to help me out, and as it turned out, I ended up with the girl of my dreams on my arm that night. And that Christmas shopping trip? Martha didn't get sick and cancel. I asked her to tell you that in the hopes you would again offer. There was no girlfriend to shop for. I hadn't even gone out since homecoming. I used that trip as an opportunity to be with you and to have you help me pick out a gift for you."

Cassidy stared at him in disbelief as he went on. "I remember we lingered at the jewelry counter for a long time, and while I looked at rings for my supposed 'girlfriend' you turned and turned the carousel filled with silver charms. I went back the next day after our shopping trip and bought you a silver charm bracelet with three charms—a sunburst to remind you of that wonderful summer, a silver tree to symbolize the tree in Veterans' Park where I carved our names, and—"

"A silver heart," finished Cassidy numbly. "That was from you?"

"Didn't you read the card? Martha secretly placed the box under your tree with a note tucked inside from me, because I knew if Kevin found out he would never let you have it."

Melancholy swept over her. "Oh, he let me have it all right," she said wistfully. "He must have figured it out and changed the card. He said it was from him."

"That little rat," Jeff said, half chuckling in wonder. "Pretty gutsy thing to do though . . ." He laughed again and then got very quiet. "Well, that explains why you never responded. I just assumed . . ."

Opposing thoughts crossed her mind. She had a gift from Jeff. She had always had it and didn't even realize it. Then she considered how hurt he must have been, believing she had rejected him and his gift. Some things were becoming clearer, but some still didn't add up.

"I still don't understand, TJ," she probed. "If you loved me as you say, how could you have done what you did to me?"

He knew exactly what she was referring to. When he had received no response to the note he tucked into the charm bracelet, he assumed she didn't want any contact with him, so he honored his promise and stayed away. It was the beginning of the end of life as he had known it. Even when their families would get together, he would concoct excuses to be unavailable which fueled the brewing stress between him and his father.

"A month before the prom, Kevin let me know that you had a date and it totally threw me. I could handle not seeing you as long as

I assumed you were locked up in your bedroom like Rapunzel, studying and not seeing anybody, but the thought of you being with someone else bothered me more than I ever imagined. I was so upset. All I could think about was that more than anything in the world I wanted to be worthy to walk up to your doorbell and ring it, talk to your parents like old times, and then wait for you at the bottom of the staircase and be the one who would hold you in my arms." Jeff's voice broke and he quickly caught himself and continued. "But I wasn't worthy. So don't be angry with Kevin, Cassidy, because he loved you, and he knew I was really messed up right then and worried where I might lead you. And looking back on it now, I know that if I had just swallowed my pride and asked for his forgiveness, and told him the truth about how I felt about you, we could have worked it out. But I was too proud."

Cassidy stood silently, considering it all. She didn't speak. She didn't move. She just wept silently and wished things had been different.

Jeff took her by the shoulders and turned her to face him. His sad eyes peered into hers. "That night, I was so rude to my date. About thirty minutes into the prom she dumped me. I didn't care, because she wasn't the one I wanted to be with anyway. I waited around the doorway so I could see you when you arrived. It was raining, do you remember? Your date let you out near the door and then drove away to park. You headed toward the coatroom and I couldn't take my eyes off you. I don't know if I was nuts or if I didn't care about the consequences. I just remember thinking that if I let that moment go by without telling you or showing how I felt, that I might never get another chance. So I acted on impulse. I walked over to you and . . ." His voice fell.

Cassidy had replayed that moment over and over in her mind a thousand times, the cut of his tux, the tousled look of his hair. She closed her eyes and could clearly recall the musky smell of his cologne that seemed to match the haunted look in his eyes. She remembered how those eyes had frozen her to the spot and how she felt like she might die if he approached her and passed by. But he didn't. He stopped in front of her without saying a word and took her shoulders tightly, walking her backwards into the rows of coats. He looked down at her and the only thing he said was, "Cassidy . . ." And then he kissed her with a long, hard kiss that left her breathless and shaken. She remembered looking up at him and watching the look in his eyes shift from total adoration, to shock, and then to shame. He pulled her body against his and cried, "I'm sorry, Cassidy . . . I'm so sorry . . ." and then he turned and ran out of the room leaving her alone to try to understand what had happened and what it all meant. It was the only kiss they ever shared, and the last words he had spoken to her for over twenty years, until last Friday.

Jeff and Cassidy leaned back against the fence, no longer touching—each instinctively needing to be alone. After a few silent minutes Jeff spoke up.

"I don't know if hearing all that has made things better or worse, but it's the truth. Regardless of whatever else you feel when you hear the rest of the story, I want to be sure that you know that you weren't mistaken about how I felt back then. Always remember that I loved you too."

"What's the rest of the story? Did loving me drive you away from here, from your family?"

"No," he replied emphatically. "Never think that. It was loving you that gave me the courage to survive."

"Survive what, TJ?"

He silently took her hand and led her away from the fence. "Wanna walk back to the house?" he offered with a smile that signaled that the soul searching was over for the day. She walked beside him with her arm draped softly across his back. He gave her a hug and left her standing by the doorway.

"Will you call me later?" she called after him.

He stopped and looked back over his shoulder. "Let's sleep on what we've talked about today. We've both got a lot to think about. I'll call you tomorrow."

"Promise?" she whispered to herself, unsure if she would ever see him again.

Chapter Fourteen

It was Friday evening, December fifth. Natalie stood ironing Kris Kringle's red fleece britches while Benjamin fluffed his beard in preparation for his annual appearance at Saturday's Santa Breakfast. He marveled that he and Natalie would have three weeks to enjoy David before the newlyweds returned for Christmas, and though only TJ's absence prevented the upcoming holiday from being perfect, Benjamin was still somber. Not even the news that Sterling was stopping by could cheer him. In fact, the news had actually deepened his moodiness.

David was so wrapped up in Merit Davenport, he was completely oblivious to his grandfather's malaise. He had found an excuse to see her every day since they met, most recently under the ruse of helping the Brighton children make new ornaments for David's Tree, which would have its grand unveiling tomorrow morning at the annual Santa Breakfast. The Johansons had portrayed the Clauses for years, with David and Martha filling in as elves when needed, but this year David's assistance with the ornaments was a little more "hands on" as his hot-glue burns attested. The ornaments were three-inch mirrors edged in ruffled lace. A two-inch photo of one of the children occupied the center of each mirror. Each ornament was backed in Christmas-colored satin with a ribbon loop for hanging. When David's Tree was illuminated, the ornaments reflected and magnified the light, showcasing the images of the Brighton children. All that remained tonight was to help the children hang the last of the ornaments on the tree and lay their gifts out for Santa to share with other children in the community, and then David would sweep Merit away for a special evening.

As pleased as Natalie was to see David so happy, she could see trouble on the horizon. Each of his new passions, this young girl and his impending missionary work, were in direct opposition to one another. The attainment of one spelled the doom of the other. So she held her breath as he sauntered into the room, hoping her usually wise grandson would proceed with caution. As soon as she saw her dashing David, her hopes for caution were lost. He was dressed to impress, wearing a black, knit turtleneck with a pair of tan khakis. He had a brown leather jacket slung over his shoulder and he was purposely swaggering. In spite of his silliness, the effect was sophisticated and stunning, and Natalie knew it was the very effect he had sought. "Ben, get a look at David. I'd say he's the spitting image of his grandmother," she teased.

Ben just looked up with raised eyebrows. "Pretty fancy tree-decorating outfit, I'd say."

David caught the sarcasm in his grandfather's voice and responded defensively. "We'll have the tree finished by the kids' bedtime and then I'm taking Merit out. She needs a little break since she's been spending every free minute at Brighton."

"Oh sure, sure," Ben scoffed. "Just doing your civic duty."

David turned and smiled an exasperated smile, a little irritated to be the object of his grandparents' humor this evening. That feeling was amplified by Ben's final comment as David turned the knob on the door to leave. "I hope you have another civic-minded replacement lined up to keep her feeling welcome after January."

David rolled his eyes and closed the door behind him. He sat in the car for a few seconds scolding himself for not taking the opportunity to clarify things with his grandparents. *Why do they have to make such a big deal about Merit, anyway? I can enjoy her company now and still do the things I need to do to prepare for my mission, right?* Ben's comments reminded David of the last conversation he and Sam had shared before his parents left on their honeymoon. Sam had tried to keep the mood light but his warning was not lost on David.

"You know what the hardest choices are?" he had asked. "Not between good and evil. Most of us are pretty clear on those. They are between good and good, or good and better. A relationship with a nice girl is a good and wonderful thing, at the right time and under the right circumstances, and a mission is a wonderful and noble thing. It's possible to have both, just not at the same time. Don't fool yourself, David, and think that you're the *one guy* who can do both and not get distracted. I'm not saying don't be her friend. I'm not even saying don't care for her. But what I am saying to you is that the closer you get to her, the harder it will be to leave, and the adversary will use that against you. He will plant doubts in your mind and make you question what you already know to be right, so be careful."

Sam had shared his own heart-wrenching story about a girl he'd loved so much that he'd tried to justify how it might be just as noble to stay home and marry her as to serve his mission, and how he had made a list of all the good things he would do to serve God in place of two years in the mission field. He described the agonizing days he spent in fasting and prayer to get peace with his plan and how, finally, in spite of all his efforts to convince himself and the Lord that he had a better idea, he received his confirmation that he was mission bound. He told David that he and the girl had spent a harrowing, tear-filled final evening, thinking they both would just die, pledging their unfailing, eternal love, and then three months later, he'd received a wedding announcement informing him that she would now be pledging her unfailing, eternal love to yet another. David had laughed at the story, but he got the message. If strong, vigilant Sam could get so distracted, then he would have to be very careful. *I'm being careful, aren't I?* He was keeping his eyes wide open and being perfectly honest with himself about Merit.

He had dated in the past; no one steadily, but a few girls frequently. They were each very different in appearance and interests, with the one common trait being the ease he found in talking to them. It was probably the result of growing up with a single mom, but David loved talking things over with women. He enjoyed shooting the breeze with his guy friends, but when something mattered to him, he just seemed drawn to get a "second opinion" from one of his girlfriends. He had known a few flaky girls, but they didn't hold his attention. That was what he found most intriguing about Merit. There was a sadness buried deep inside her, the source of which was still a mystery, but she radiated so much happiness. That desire to seek joy beyond hurt had given her compassion he valued.

She was easy to speak with and although she was not forthcoming about herself, she had strong, passionate views on everything else, and she was always open, always willing to listen.

The one thing he had not been able to share with her was his testimony of the Savior. They had discussed religion, and he was very open about his mission, but his comments had been general and dispassionate, mere intellectual ideas on the topics of faith and God. He had not shared with her the gospel fire that lit his heart and which suddenly made life miraculous and invaluable. It was becoming easy to share this part of himself with his grandparents and he wanted to share it with her too. *Why haven't I?* He thought long on that question. He knew, but he didn't want to face it. He was afraid of what he'd do if she rejected the tender things of his heart. *Would it rattle my testimony? No, that's not it. What if it scared her off? What if I lost her?*

That was his fear, and he knew he had to face it. In truth, he no longer had a "missionary" feeling about Merit Davenport. What began for him as a chance to enjoy a satisfying friendship, and a chance to share the gospel with someone before he entered the MTC, had become much more personal to him, and strangely, fear of Merit's rejection of those things had kept him from being bold. He had tried to convince himself he was building trust first, but he knew he was justifying his fears. He had compromised her chance to hear the gospel because he feared she might reject it, and he didn't want to face the choices that position would leave him. Not yet . . .

David considered at what moment he had realized that. It had been Sunday evening, two days after he met Merit. Merit had invited him to her house after the choral concert they'd attended, and he had asked her to play some music for him. After much cajoling on his part, her humble protests stopped and she agreed to play. She picked up the violin and he watched with fascination as she and the violin became one. It was her hands, those beautiful, nimble, yet commanding hands that held his attention. Her body swayed with the music, and her head and shoulders swept and stalled with the music, emphasizing each measure. He played a game, closing his eyes to see if he could imagine her movements by the sounds of the instruments, then he would open his eyes to see if he was right, and soon he had become as susceptible to the power of her playing as she was.

When she finished, she placed the violin in its case, signaling the end of her performance, but David, who was visibly touched by her music, smiled approvingly and nodded for her to continue. She sat down next at the piano and warmed up on a small, classical piece. David was mesmerized, watching her delicate hands masterfully dance across the keys. She moved on to a moody, slow piece, not normally to his liking, but which she dressed in rhythmic nuances that were subtle, yet captivating. Her body moved as she played, as if in a dance. As the piece swelled and became powerful, she too became powerful. The music was beautiful but she became the music, and he had found himself unable to separate them. He was unsure if it was because her technical ability was so superior or if it was that watching her play was like peering through a window to her soul, but when she finished the piece and met his gaze, their connection was electric.

She invited him to join her on the bench and took his hands, placing them on the keys to teach him a simple melody. He quickly surrendered his awkwardness, enjoying her touch and the intimacy of sharing her music. He learned quickly and the pleasure his interest gave her was evident. She offered to give him lessons and he immediately agreed, although he wondered if she knew his motivation. He felt it. She felt it. It was unspoken but apparent, and they each performed brilliantly, denying the attraction the evening uncovered, and returning to their portrayal of two casual friends when it was time to say good night.

Monday and Tuesday were comfortable but strained as they made polite conversation, shared silly jokes with the children, and worked on the ornaments. Merit had even given him another piano lesson, and even though giggling children surrounded them, he again felt the spark that warmed him as they sat closely, her hands guiding his across the keyboard.

But something changed Wednesday when they worked on the ornaments at the Johansons' farm. The fire was crackling behind the glass doors of the fireplace, and Merit took her cup of hot cider and sat on the rug by the hearth while David loaded the car. He came inside breathing on his hands, trying to warm them up. Then he took his cup of cider and moved to the rug. He drank his cider quickly, set the cup aside, then leaned back to enjoy the beauty and warmth of the fire. His hand had barely brushed hers, but he felt instantly warm, as if electricity had passed between them. Curious about the electricity of their touch, he readjusted his position to allow his hand an excuse to brush hers again, with the same results. He smiled at this childish game, wondering about the effect this girl was having on him.

The intent of his move was not lost on Merit. She responded by rubbing his hands between hers, seemingly to warm them, while smiling innocently at him and acknowledging the shyness of his gesture. David remembered the hundreds of times he had seen some modestly loving gesture extended between Sam and his mom, and the new spark that seemed to pass between Omma and Pap when their hands touched briefly, and he resolved at that moment that he'd look for a woman that appreciated the seemingly small allure of the touch of a hand.

That was all that had transpired between them by the end of the evening—looks, music, the touching of hands—but those things had been enough to convince David that Merit was someone he could love, and that made him nervous. He had always been cautious with his emotions. A few girls had stirred him and he'd quickly ended those relationships. One thing David clearly understood was the sorrow and anguish the irresponsible exercise of those passions could cause. He had seen it in his mother's life and he saw it in his peers; and he vowed he would never let his heart rule his head until he was in a position to properly fulfill the promises that were tied to those passions. And now there was Merit.

The timing couldn't have been worse. He had no fears about crossing his moral boundaries, but his focus was blurred. He knew he was exactly on the very precipice about which Sam had warned him, and he could see all too clearly the potential for pain and tears and heartbreak. Still, he was unwilling to admit he was on a course he couldn't handle, so he planned to proceed cautiously, to nurture the relationship but make no promises. *Piece of cake,* he resolved.

* * *

Natalie and Ben worried at the delay in David's departure. They saw him sitting in the car, thinking, a worried look on his face.

Natalie regretted their teasing him. Ben left the table and sat in his easychair. He had worries of his own, nagging worries that had been disrupting his sleep and which left him feeling heavyhearted. Natalie had noticed the restlessness in him. At first she thought he was agonizing over David's mission, but she heard the pride in Ben's voice every time he spoke of his grandson's future plans and she knew it had to be something else.

Ben was staring at a Christmas card that had arrived in the mail that day. Curious about the level of interest this one card was getting from her husband, Natalie quietly walked over to his chair and placed her hands on his shoulders to catch a peek. The envelope was embossed from "Davises' Tree Services and Nursery." The card's cover was a photo of Sterling and his men standing in front of a beautifully decorated Christmas tree, and Natalie instantly knew that one face staring off the card was haunting Benjamin. Sterling's nephew, Bill.

She questioned whether or not to say anything. She wanted to comfort him, but she knew this hurt was not just about Ben's part in Bill's departure. She knew the roots of this anguish ran deep, back to TJ, and she didn't want to harrow up that hurt, not tonight. Instead, she was spared the need to fill the silence when Sterling rapped on the door. She opened it, shared a friendly but brief exchange, and excused herself to go upstairs.

"I can't stay, Ben. I just wanted you to know that I dropped off another three hundred feet of roping and thirty more wreaths. I'll send your invoice in the mail." It was awkward now. Everything was awkward between them now. "Well, just wanted to let you know."

He fumbled with his hat brim and turned toward the door when Ben held up the card with the photo front and said, "Sterling, I owe you an apology."

Sterling could barely meet his gaze. "You don't owe me anything, Ben. I just wish things were different, like before. I feel terrible every time I drive up here and that spot is empty," he said. "So I know it must hurt you even more. I'm just so sorry . . ." His voice trailed off.

Ben stood and walked over to his friend. He put his strong hand on Sterling's shoulder and squeezed. "See, I've got us all thinking crazy. It was a tree, Sterling, a tree. A special tree, yes, but nonetheless, a tree. Never was and never will be as important as a person, but I had everyone so worried about how I would miss it that we completely overlooked that we drove away your nephew, and for that I'm begging for your forgiveness."

Sterling took the card from Ben's hand and spoke with a husky voice. "I almost retook the photo after that night, but it was too late. It haunted me with the signing of every card." He ran his hand over his tired eyes and shook his head to clear his thoughts. "I was rough on him, Ben. Too rough, I know. But he made the decision to lie and he's the one who chose to run instead of handling his troubles like a man. He made choices too."

Ben laid his hand on his old friend's shoulder. "Being right is often shallow comfort. All I can say, is if the chance comes to make things right . . . well, my advice is to take it, my friend."

Chapter Fifteen

Cassidy Prescott was nearly sick Friday, wondering if Jeff would call. Several times she picked up the phone to call the Frederick ARM office to see if he had shown up for work, but he had recently mentioned that they were so short staffed that he and the other caseworkers often had to answer the phones if the secretary was ill or called away from her desk. Cassidy didn't want to take the chance of dialing right into his office, so she had resisted the temptation.

She was grateful the Santa Breakfast was tomorrow morning. With hoards of human-interest-loving media people and local dignitaries expected, she had her hands more than full, and the diversion had kept her busy until well after supper. After the children were tucked in for the night, and once she and Mrs. Sherman felt confident that everything was in perfect readiness for the morning's festivities, she began to climb the stairs for an early night's sleep. But her thoughts came back to Jeff and the knot in her stomach formed once more.

Just as she crested the top step, a soft tap was heard on the front door. She hurried down, a little alarmed since no one was expected. "Who is it?"

The nervousness in her voice must have been apparent because Jeff immediately picked up on it. "I'm sorry, Cassidy. It's J . . . TJ. I'm so sorry. I should have called first."

Cassidy's fingers flew over the locks and the door was open in record time. "No, no. It's fine," she assured him as she took his extended hand and drew him inside. "I'm just so glad to hear from you."

Jeff sidestepped the inclination to make excuses for not having called sooner. He scanned the beautiful decorations visible at every view and commented, "The place looks wonderful!"

"Thanks," she replied, distracted. "Tomorrow's the Santa Breakfast."

"Oh, that's right." He chastised himself for not remembering. "I bet you have a thousand things to do tonight. Maybe I should—"

"No, actually we just finished up about five minutes ago. Mrs. Sherman's head hasn't even had time to hit the pillow yet."

"Do you want to get to bed? I mean, I can come another time," he stammered.

Cassidy was becoming exasperated. If every meeting was going to require her pulling him in, then she might want to consider asking Santa for a winch. "Jeff," she blurted out, "the work is finished, my time is my own, and there's nothing I want more than for you to sit down . . . breathe . . . and talk to me."

Jeff Johnson visibly relaxed and sheepishly followed Cassidy back down the darkened hallway to the large family kitchen. She flicked on the lights, and he stood there smiling, noticing the changes in appliances and paint, but otherwise he commented on how pleased he was that the important things, the tall glass-paned cabinets and warmth of the old room, were still present.

He wandered over to the door of the old pantry and opened it, revealing a fresh, clean piece of molding on the other side of the doorjamb. His face fell but Cassidy encouraged him to look further. He stooped down and saw that dozens of tiny hash marks were scored across the paint. Most of the names were unfamiliar to him, and the dates were too recent to be those for which he was searching, but eventually his fingers crossed lines with fond, familiar dates and his face lit up.

"When we applied for our license we had to replace all the old wood because of lead paint. When the carpenter pulled the old piece off that jam I kept it, and when the new jam was built and painted, I retraced all the height marks Dad scratched on there for every one of our birthdays. Now these kids line up there on their birthday mornings. It's an important rite of passage even today."

Jeff beamed and leaned against the counter while Cassidy fixed two cups of steaming cocoa. As she was squirting whipped cream on top, Jeff leaned in close to her and teased. "You slipped up back there."

"I what?" she asked.

"You slipped up back there. You called me Jeff." He waited for her response.

Cassidy wanted to enjoy his attempt at playfulness, but this was a sensitive area for her and she didn't think it was entertaining. "Well, what do you expect? Who the heck are you anyway? One minute you're TJ and the next you're Jeff, then for few brief seconds you act like some swashbuckling flirt, and then you close up and seem ready to bolt and run. You know, I'm trying to be patient here, but I have some trust issues too. I'm willing to stick my neck out but you can't keep cutting it off and expect me not to get a little cranky." She drew a deep breath and wondered if she had undone the fragile trust they had rebuilt, but he was still standing there and she felt her indignation was justified.

Calmer now, and struggling to get back to the launch point of her tirade, she countered, "So what do you want me to call you?"

"What would you like to call me?" Jeff asked, more contritely.

She clenched her jaw, wondering if he was purposely baiting her now. "Could you please not answer my question with a question? Could you just give me a straight answer on this?" Her nerves were raw now. The Santa Breakfast was stress enough, but she suddenly realized how much of her energy had been subconsciously focused on him all day, and now she was walking on eggshells, trying not to unnerve him, trying to maintain his trust. Well, she had fears too, and her reserves were gone. Her lips trembled as she carried the two cups to the table. As she passed, Jeff took her arm and squeezed it affectionately.

"I'm sorry, Cassidy. My comic timing was a little off back there." Then, in a voice tinged with regretful realization, he added, "It's not going to be as easy as we would have liked, is it?"

She rested her head against his chest and shook it slightly. He kissed her hair and lingered there. "I've been Jeff Johnson legally now for ten years, Cassidy. I haven't heard the name TJ for even longer, and wasn't sure I ever would again. It feels good to me, it's just that . . . we've all been in time warps where I'm concerned. I'm TJ Johanson in yours, and Jeff Johnson in mine. Neither fellow is too steady on his feet, but for now, at least until I square things with my family, I think it would be best if you called me Jeff."

She paused as she considered the implication of his request, and finally conceded sadly, "You're probably right." She pulled away from Jeff as she became even more pensive. She felt as if a door to their past had been slammed shut. Her connection to this man was *TJ*. She had little experience with "Jeff," and though, logically, she knew he was one and the same, the request to lay aside the persona that was familiar to her rattled her security. A self-defense trigger went off in Cassidy as she considered the potential for happiness TJ's reappearance offered, balanced against the potential for further hurt if Jeff decided not to stay. "You told me you couldn't take another hit in your life. I thought I . . . could and would do anything to make this work, but I'm beginning to realize that I can't take another hit either. So if you're willing to try and make this work, then I am too, but if you believe there's a chance you're going to bail out on me again, then I think I'd rather you just go tonight." She carefully measured her next words. "I know I love you. I can feel that the things I loved about you are still inside you, but the longer I let myself become attached to you, the bloodier this is going to be for both of us."

A hunger to protect her filled him and he stepped up. He placed his hands firmly on her shoulders and pulled her close. "I don't want to go anywhere, Cassidy. I just want to be here with you." He closed his eyes, wishing she could know how true those words were. "I want to tell you the rest of my story tonight, and after you hear it, if you still think I'm a man you could love, then I'm here to stay."

She nodded and they began gathering mugs and jackets. The night was chilly and clear as they carried an old green quilt and their cocoa out to the old swing. Wrapped in the warmth of the quilt and comforted by Cassidy's willingness to strive with him a little longer, Jeff began the telling of the worst days of his life.

"After I kissed you on prom night, I was so ashamed that I ran to my car and sped away. I was afraid that when Kevin found out about the kiss he would tell you everything and all I wanted was to be far away when that happened. So I drove up to High Rock because I had heard that a lot of kids that were boycotting the prom were having a big party there. On the way up the hill some guys who were leaving handed me a half-finished pack of beer. At the summit, I found a spot where I could be alone and I sat on the edge of the cliffs looking over the city. There was a kid nearby that was totally wasted. He could hardly even walk. He staggered over to me, saw the cans sitting beside me, and asked me if he could have one. I knew he was senseless, but I wasn't thinking. I just said, 'Sure, take them all.' He picked them up, popped one open, and started chugging it down while he staggered away along the edge of the cliff. A few seconds later, I heard a scuffling sound and I saw that he had lost his footing. He was screaming and clutching for something to grab. A bunch of guys tried to get to him, to grab his hand, but none of us got there fast enough. His terrified eyes looked straight into mine right before he slipped over the edge and into the darkness." Jeff paused and shuddered, the memory still horrifying.

"Maybe he was already too drunk to make it down the edge, maybe he would have fallen anyway, even if I hadn't handed him that last drink, but all I knew was that he fell holding the can I had given him, and I had done nothing to stop him, or to warn him, or anything." He blew out a deep breath as if to cleanse the image from his mind. "Luckily, no one I knew was up there, but I lost it. I completely lost it and ran as fast as I could through the trees down the backside of the mountain to my car. I could hear the sirens screaming behind me and I saw people running up the trail. I drove around for hours, so when I went home my folks would think I had stayed until the end of the dance, but my clothes were muddy and my car looked like I had been off-road.

"The next day when the paper arrived, the headlines were all about the tragic accident up at High Rock. I could tell my father was suspicious. Aside from asking me how the dance was, he grilled me on details that I knew were related to his suspicions of my presence at High Rock. He threw question after question at me, probing about the dance and my date, and then he began interrogating me about the mud on the car and my clothes.

"I lied. Lie after lie, I crafted a rational enough story to satisfy the point of the questions, but I never satisfied his suspicions. He never came right out and accused me, but I knew he didn't believe I was telling him the truth. When his interrogation began to upset my mother he finally stopped." Jeff sighed and stared into his steaming cup. "The sad thing is that a couple of times he really had me on the ropes, and I think if he had pursued a little harder I might not have been able to withhold the truth, and who knows, maybe I would've moved out of the path of the train I was in front of."

He took a long sip and muttered, "Who knows . . ."

He continued, "Anyway, what needed to be said never was, and instead the situation just festered between me and Dad. I hardly went to school after that. I couldn't bear the tearful girls or the grief counselors and press hanging around. I came late, left early, and barely passed my finals. I told the school I was needed at the orchard and told my folks I was helping out at school. After graduation I went to Ocean City for senior week as planned, only I didn't come home in a week. I told my parents I'd found a job on a crabbing boat making great money and that I would be staying the summer. They were furious but they didn't know how to reach me, so what could they do?

"During the summer, finding a place to crash was easy. Lots of kids had an open-door policy where people freely came and went from one apartment to another, and as long as you tossed a few bills on the table to help cover expenses, they were happy. It sounds ridiculously dangerous to me now, and it should have even then, but to a sheltered, small-town kid, I felt as if I had arrived.

"One guy I met down there was a potter and an artist who lived in his van and sold his work on the boardwalk. He was everything my conservative parents detested, but he was a poor, gentle soul who had barely ever known a home or a family all his life. He had taken me in for a while when things were tight, so when summer ended and I got laid off and his business slowed down, I took him home with me."

"Was that David's father?" Cassidy finally spoke, but Jeff had been so lost in his thoughts he had almost forgotten anyone else was with him and he turned abruptly to face her. The connection between the memory and the name "David" seemed incongruent to him and he pushed it far away, passing over the question.

"You probably know more about what happened next than I do, Cassidy," he said as he shifted in the swing and repositioned the quilt around her. She didn't pursue her question. "All I remember is that

Dad suddenly felt that the cancer that was destroying one of his children now threatened both, and he was ready to cut his losses and let me go if it meant he could save Martha. That's how it felt to me at the time anyway, and that's how I responded. Looking back, I can understand his fears, but I was angry, and still hurt and reeling from all the memories at High Rock. I hurled unspeakable, vile things at my dad; slammed the door, and never went back. Years went by before I found out that Martha had a son." His voice trailed off sadly.

"Where did you go after you left home the second time?" Cassidy asked softly.

"Back to the ocean. I got hired as a cook in a bayside seafood restaurant, a local dive, not a tourist spot. They ran numbers out of the back room and lots of cash flowed through there every night. They treated me like I was their best friend." His voice dripped with sarcasm. "I got tickets for concerts at the arena, clothes, anything and everything I wanted. The owner offered me a chance to make some big money serving as a courier, ferrying money back and forth from one place to another. He said he preferred his couriers to travel in pairs for security so I made arrangements with my friend, and offered him some fast cash for a few hours of what I called 'security work.' On our first night out we were asked to drop off a package at a hotel room and we got busted in a sting operation."

Cassidy lowered her eyes and moaned while she took Jeff's arm.

"As it turned out we were carrying a lot more than cash. The owner knew his operation was being watched so he decided to have some stupid expendable kids take the heat, only I compounded the tragedy by involving an innocent guy who thought he was going to be some big-shot security man for a few hours and score some big pay."

Jeff leaned forward, placing his head in his hands as he worked to clear the images from his mind. "We ended up in jail, screaming our innocence, and three hours later our bosses bailed us out. They made it *really clear* to us that we would be better off taking a little heat and toughing out a little jail time than talking too much." Jeff rubbed his hand across his bearded chin that bore the deep, jagged scar from the blows that were delivered along with his bosses' message to keep silent.

"The DA knew we were nobodies, but when we refused to talk they made it clear they would prosecute us to the fullest, and my friend cracked. Caught between the threats from our former employer and the promise of extended jail time, my friend lost it. I stopped by the parking lot where he was living in his van and found him semi-conscious in the back." Jeff's voice became thin. "I ran to call for help, but by the time I got back to the apartment he wasn't breathing. He died in my arms of an overdose."

Jeff paused and Cassidy placed a comforting hand on his back. His body shuddered as if he were freezing, and she tucked the quilt around him as he tried to compose himself. He turned to face her but she said nothing. She simply sat there and put her arms around him.

He continued to shiver and she tightened her embrace. He barely responded but he didn't push her away. He no longer wanted to meet her gaze, but allowed his head to rest against hers and eventually his body stilled. He finally pulled away from her and looked deeply into her eyes to determine what they would tell him. He found unlimited compassion there that gave him the strength to finish.

"He died in my arms, Cassidy. I killed him. It was as much my fault as if I had shot him. I killed him. I spent seven years in prison, at Jessup, for carrying what I thought was a bag of cash three blocks." He laughed sarcastically and then quickly sobered. "No, that would be minimizing all my mistakes. I brought this on. The timing and the reason of my reckoning might not seem fair, but the totality of my choices earned me what I received. I had broken every standard by which I had been raised. I let pride separate me time and time again from the people I loved, and I drew others into my shame—twice they paid the highest price. I let my family pick up the trash I left behind and then, perhaps the cruelest thing of all, I allowed them . . ." he paused, looking sadly into her eyes again, " . . . all of you, to wonder if I were even alive or dead.

"So many times, as I laid there, crying myself to sleep in Jessup, I wanted to call up my folks and beg their forgiveness. I wanted to tell them how sorry I was and ask them to come and visit me. I wanted to tell Martha I was sorry that her big brother messed up her life and then just abandoned her. And I wanted to tell you how sorry I was for not loving you as you deserved and for confusing you again when you were finally getting your feet under you. I really did want to say all of those things, Cassidy, but I was too proud and too afraid to make the calls. So I made my decision to help other kids avoid the mess I had made of my life. When I got out of prison I earned my degree in social work and counseling, but I still couldn't make those calls.

"When I graduated from college my only guest was my parole officer, Dennis Martin. When he left that department and moved into the ARM program he recommended that I join him. I want you to meet him, Cassidy. As I've tried to build an honorable life from the shambles of my past, Dennis has been the only person I've ever let in, until now. That is if you still want me."

Cassidy looked up at Jeff. Her face was resolute but loving. She took his face in her hands and brought his eyes to meet hers. "I love you, Jeff. I don't care what you've done. I know what kind of person you are inside, and the kind of man you're working to be. And I want to be with that man if he'll let me."

She pulled his head down and placed a kiss filled with promise and hope on his lips, then paused as her eyes held him in a long visual embrace filled with the same assurances. They walked back toward the house yoked in one another's arms. Some bridges could be crossed, Jeff realized, even burned ones.

Chapter Sixteen

The next morning, Saturday, December fourth, Cassidy bolted upright from her bed in a cold sweat. Two intense thoughts gripped her. The first was that at nine o'clock, in just over two hours from that moment, more than a hundred guests and members of the press would converge on Brighton for this very special Christmas-tree lighting and Santa Breakfast. The thought of all that confusion worried her, but the second thought terrified her. She realized that she might have forgotten to remind Jeff that his parents, in fact most of his family, would be there as well.

Panic flooded her mind with every possible, terrifying scenario. After their soul-bearing talk last night, Jeff had begged her for more time to prepare to reconcile with his parents. Would he think she had purposely withheld warning him to force an unexpected, seemingly random meeting. And if so, despite his assurances to the contrary, would he feel betrayed and bury himself for another twenty years? Could he believe that in the bustle of the last twenty-four hours she had simply forgotten to tell him? The worry made her sick.

She picked up the phone and tried to call him but there was no answer. *Where could he be?* She knew he ran almost every morning before he showered. She had to catch him before he left the house. *Answer the phone!* she silently begged.

The minutes sped by with all the preparations that needed tending. The children were all hurrying to dress in the beautiful, new, and highly anticipated Christmas outfits given to them by the local department store. Cassidy gave each of them an admiring compliment and smile, but her thoughts were distracted by her worries of Jeff. She tried to call him four more times, but there was still no answer. She said a silent prayer that whatever happened would turn out for the best, and she dove into readying the children.

Merit met David and his grandparents in the driveway at eight. Natalie and Ben hurried off to dress in their costumes while the younger pair took the children into the music room to rehearse their songs. That freed Cassidy to welcome the press and pass out the fundraising packets to the invited guests while Mrs. Sherman reported to the kitchen to fuss over the staff and check the breakfast menu. By a quarter to nine all the preparations were ready, and Cassidy tried to force her mind to stop fretting over Jeff's arrival and instead enjoy this beloved tradition.

The Brighton ladies laughingly joked that benevolence must somehow be tied to the aroma of turkey, since every year, right after Thanksgiving, packages would begin showing up on the Brighton doorstep. The women feared that the overindulgence would create more havoc than happiness, so they devised a plan to bless the children and teach them at the same time, and the traditions had stuck ever since. First, they began requesting that all donations arrive, unwrapped, by the first of December. All the items were then set out in a spare room, which became "The Brighton Christmas Shop." For one week the children could peruse the shop and select the items they wanted on their Santa list as well as "buy" gifts for one another at five to ten cents on the dollar, using money they earned throughout the year. Additionally, they each were encouraged to select one gift for an anonymous child in need in the county. So much good had come from this plan. The children learned generosity and gratitude and they no longer saw themselves as disadvantaged or needy, but instead considered the needs and concerns of others. It was the most beautiful part of Mrs. Sherman and Cassidy's Christmas.

Getting all the material expectations of Christmas out of the way early allowed the Brighton family to focus on the other wonderful aspects of the holiday. They would be secret-service buddies, doing acts of kindness for one another. They would read wonderful stories each night and sing every day. They would carol in town and give their annual Christmas concert on December twenty-third. And then, on Christmas Eve, they would gather at the Johanson farm and act out the Nativity for the town.

But today's festivities were about to begin. Cassidy continually scanned the area for signs of Jeff, but there were none. It was time to get things moving, so she told Merit to bring the children in. They lined up in front of the magical tree and introduced the very special guests of the morning, the Johansons, dressed as Santa and Mrs. Claus, who then made their entrance. It was time for the program to begin.

When all the guests were seated in their places, Cassidy welcomed them, then she introduced Merit and the children who quickly began their introductory number. The adults sat in silent awe at the perfection of the children's voices. Every entrance and cutoff was performed together and the tone was sweet and angelic. When the piece was finished they beamed proudly at their conductor. The Davenports, bursting with pride, led the others in appreciative applause, which would have lasted longer except for the gasp of wonder that erupted from everyone when Santa Johanson turned the switch and lit David's Tree. Even in the morning rays, the mirrors caught the reflection of the twinkling lights making the tree glow with majesty. Each of the photos of the children appeared radiant, almost ethereal, and the effect was so captivating that the journalists hurriedly scribbled to capture the moment while camera bulbs flashed.

David watched closely for his grandfather's reaction as the tree came alive with light. He saw Omma take his hand, beaming a bright smile in her husband's direction as if to will her happiness into him, but it was unnecessary. The stalwart patriarch's face also glowed. Whatever trace of loss he felt seeing his old friend in a pot instead of in its honored spot at the farm had been dealt with, tucked away, and seemed now to be inconsequential in the totality of all that had transpired since. David's worries dispelled, and sensing that the timing was right, he took his place at the podium and prepared to offer the blessing on the food.

He was handsomely dressed in a black, well-tailored suit. Just visible under the jacket was a red vest set off by a red, green, and black Christmas tie. He caught Merit's smile of support for the outfit. He had told her that his grandmother bought these items as a conciliatory gesture after he declined the very "tempting" offer to, once again, be Santa's Elf, but he also recognized something more complimentary in Merit's smile. He knew that just as she was brightening his life, he was making a positive impact on hers, and knowing that gave him indescribable pleasure.

When the room was quiet, he folded his arms, bowed his head, paused to let the impressions come to him, and then offered a heart-felt prayer. Such a responsibility would have been difficult a few years earlier, but David recognized it as another manifestation of how the gospel was molding him, raising him up and preparing him for his mission. Additionally, he seemed to find frequent opportunities to share some sliver of his testimony or a favorite scripture with his grandparents, which often led into sharing long, spiritual discourses with them, and it felt delicious. He was often amazed at the spiritual sensitivity they possessed, which he had never fully understood or appreciated. Even now, as he concluded the prayer, he noticed how they fought to restrain their tears. He smiled, knowing how upsetting it would be for the children to see the Clauses cry, so after the reverent amens were whispered around the room, David turned the podium back to Cassidy, drawing the guests' attention away from the Clauses.

The breakfast was wonderful and full of lively conversation, and Cassidy was finally relaxing, realizing that the day was a dazzling success. The children began to take their turns visiting Santa and handing their precious gift offerings to Mrs. Claus while the guests examined the tree and the press people conducted interviews. As Cassidy surveyed the scene, a lump formed in her throat; there, in the doorway leading to the kitchen, stood Jeff!

Her eyes tried to signal to him, to warn him not to enter, but it was apparently unnecessary. He seemed glued to the doorway, either unable or unwilling to move from the spot. Cassidy waited for an opportunity to slip away from her guests, then headed toward him. As soon as she was within his grasp, he reached for her and pulled her tightly against his chest, swinging her around beyond the view of the crowd. She pulled away to look into his face, but instead of seeing ardor she saw panic, and immediately she knew he had seen his parents.

"I'm sorry, Jeff," she began quickly. "I've been worried sick trying get a hold of you to tell you your parents are Santa and Mrs. Claus. I tried to call you but you didn't pick up." He didn't answer. Cassidy tried to read whether he was ready to bolt and run, but oddly, what she perceived was that he was as equally drawn to peer around the doorway at his family as he was compelled to hide from them behind it. His breathing was rapid, his body tense, and he continued to hold her tightly though he still didn't speak. She was dismayed by the severity of his response, dashing her hopes that after their long, candid talk Jeff might let his guard down somewhat and be more open about seeing his folks. She could see that that day was still far off. Yet, he was so compelled to see them . . .

"I saw their truck outside with 'Johansons' Orchard and Tree Farm' lettered on the side. As soon as I saw it I knew they were here. I wanted to get back in the car and drive away but I just had to catch a glimpse of them. Then I couldn't leave. I couldn't take my eyes off them."

He shivered and Cassidy wondered how long he had stood peering around the corner of the doorway, stealing glimpses like a little child, and then a smile stole across his face.

"Man, Cassidy, they look so good. It's almost like no time has passed at all. My . . . dad . . . has a few more wrinkles." He'd struggled with the word *dad*. "And Mom is a little more round and gray, but they look great. Don't you think they look great?"

Cassidy smiled at the affection in his voice. "Yes, Jeff, I think they look wonderful." They stood quietly again. She knew he had so much to say, but it would come in his own time.

"Did you see how proud he seems of David?" Jeff asked. The regret in his voice betrayed his pleasure. "Dad makes a great Santa. He's so patient with the children. And Mom . . ." His shining eyes sparkled, celebrating a step toward the fulfillment of an improbable dream.

"Cassidy, I can't stay, but I want to get one more peek at them. Then I've got to go, but I'll call you later. It appears your event has been a great success. I'm so proud of you." He squeezed her tightly and looked happily, lovingly into her eyes. "Thank you," he whispered huskily as he pressed his lips against hers. In a second he released her and took a step into the doorway with Cassidy right behind him, but suddenly he stopped. She tried to accommodate his halted motion but was nearly trampled as he jerked backwards in retreat. Jeff scrambled to press himself against the wall again, trying to be invisible, but why? Instantly, Cassidy knew. His worst fear was being realized. There in the doorway was Natalie Johanson!

Cassidy's mind raced at lightening speed. Had Jeff's mother seen him? Of course she had. Did she recognize him? It was too soon to tell, but it was apparent by the quizzical look on her face that she was struggling to satisfy the questions forming in her mind. Cassidy knew she had to act quickly and calmly or either Jeff, or Natalie, or both of them would have a breakdown right there in the doorway. She decided that the best response was a matter-of-fact one. She smiled at Natalie and turned her attention back to Jeff. Her determined eyes bore into his panic-stricken ones trying to make him understand. She would have to hope for the best, so she began the ruse.

"See you later, honey." She laughed, taking his arm and turning him so that his back was to his mother. Then she kissed him and as she pulled away she whispered quietly, "Just go, Jeff, and I'll cover for you." Jeff didn't move at first, as if his body were suffering from his brain being thrown into overdrive. Cassidy tried again. "I know I'm irresistible, sweetheart, but you have to go now." She moved behind him playfully, and as she began to push him, Jeff moved slowly toward the exit. Finally, he understood and rushed through the door without looking back. Cassidy took a deep breath to steel herself against whatever response Natalie would have.

As she turned and faced her mother's dearest friend, it was evident that Natalie had suspicions. There were hopeful questions in her eyes. Cassidy's heart was ripped in two. She wanted to grab Natalie's shoulders and scream, "Yes, yes, it's TJ! Isn't it wonderful? He's come home!" but she knew it was not her place, so instead, she decided to simply walk up to Natalie and begin a casual conversation.

"The whole day has just been better than I dared hope. You and Ben are the best."

Her casual chatter wasn't allaying the woman's suspicions. She just looked at Cassidy with questioning doe eyes, silently begging for the truth. Cassidy knew her pretense was slipping and she also knew that if Natalie kept eyeing her she would cave, which would be disastrous.

"Well, I'd better go and say good-bye to my guests," she tossed out lightly as she tried to slide past, but Natalie caught her arm with gentle firmness.

"Who was that man, Cassidy?"

"That's my new beau. Isn't he handsome?" She was amazed at how easily she was throwing the story together.

Natalie nodded, her eyes fixed on Cassidy's. "Who is he? He looks . . ."

"He's a local boy," Cassidy cut in. "Made his fortune in the big city," she laughed nervously. *Where am I getting this stuff?* "Maybe you knew him when he was younger."

Natalie wasn't satisfied one bit. "What is his name?" she asked suspiciously.

"He's a Johnson boy. They had a little farm . . . then he moved to Frederick."

"Cassidy . . ." Her eyes were pleading now and Cassidy was crumbling. What could she say that would give Natalie hope and still keep her promise to Jeff?

She put her hands on Natalie's shoulders and looked straight into her eyes as she spoke slowly and deliberately. "Natalie, we've only recently become reacquainted, but he's a wonderful man, very sweet, and I'm in love with him. He's a little . . . shy . . . about introductions, so we're taking it slow . . . but I promise, as soon as he's ready to visit, I'll bring him over, okay?"

Natalie pulled back slightly. There were volumes of answers hidden behind Cassidy's eyes, but Natalie didn't press her. No definite confirmation was given, but the women were each satisfied that the other understood. Natalie's eyes glistened and her voice was shaky as she replied, "We'll look forward to it." She squeezed the younger woman's hands, smiled gratefully, then turned her numb body around and made her way back to her seat.

Chapter Seventeen

The Brighton Santa Breakfast, with the unveiling of its miraculous tree, was *the* news item. Local families and out-of-towners were stopping to see the beautiful tree adorned with the faces of the Brighton cherubs. David's tree had been a great blessing. Thousands of dollars were pouring in from individuals and organizations, staving off the financial crisis and providing a sizeable nest egg from which the women could draw to offer trips and classes for the children that otherwise would have been impossible. And even new interest had been expressed over the few children who were eligible for adoption. In any case, she knew much unanticipated good had come from the breakfast, and the townspeople had rediscovered the Brighton Children's Home, seeing it in a whole new light.

The ripples of that day had spread wide. Jeff had been panic-stricken but giddy while viewing his parents that morning, but when his mother had walked into the doorway and faced him, it had thrown him into a tailspin. He had called Cassidy later that afternoon, so concerned about his anonymity that he grilled her for information about the conversation that had taken place after he fled the room. She told him over and over that she had explained to his mother that the handsome man was her new beau, which she seemed willing to accept. Ironically, as relieved as he was that his secret was still safe, Cassidy could tell there was a trace of disappointment in his voice that his mother hadn't known who he was, when he'd recognized her immediately. She didn't tell him that Natalie had suspicions.

On Sunday, the morning after the breakfast, Cassidy cleared her calendar to spend the entire day with Jeff. She had pulled out photo albums and reels of old home movies, anticipating a chance to get reacquainted and fill in the gaps of time they'd lost. They spent the greater part of the day upstairs in her private apartment, rolling with laughter one minute and quietly reflective the next as they each dealt with the lost years.

When the last album was closed and the projector was put away, Jeff still held one photo in his hands. It was a photo of his mother taken at the previous year's Santa Breakfast.

"What are you looking at?" Cassidy asked as Jeff turned the photo in her direction.

"Yesterday during the breakfast, her eyes seemed so happy. And then when she came back to the kitchen, I saw something else hidden there."

"What did you see?"

"I don't know. Confusion? Sorrow? Pain? I couldn't help but think that I etched those lines on her face." He touched her eyes in the photo gingerly, then laid it aside and looked at Cassidy. "Don't worry, Cass. I'm still not ready to go up there, but I'm more determined than ever to get ready. First I think I want to get to know David better."

* * *

Cassidy and Jeff spent some fraction of each day together since the breakfast, though some of those days were spent in sleep-deprived comas of sorts. They had each been burning the midnight oil and the cruse was getting low. Cassidy also found herself increasingly drawn into the relationship that was growing between David and Merit. They had continued to find daily excuses to run into each other and to meet at Brighton or at one another's homes. There was always an errand to run or a piano lesson. Cassidy laughed at how they concocted a thousand and one stories, all in order to disguise what everyone saw blooming between them. She could hardly imagine the pressures they were under. She had loved someone desperately at that age and he had been ripped from her, but she couldn't imagine how difficult it would be to love someone knowing each day was a countdown to separation.

She wondered if Carol was as aware of the depth of the attachment developing between the couple. Like Merit, Carol also seemed to have found an almost daily excuse for stopping by Brighton. Cassidy still wasn't sure whether she had told Merit she was a regular volunteer at the home, or if Merit just thought her mother stopped by frequently, but all the children enjoyed her, and she was warm and kind to each of them. Still, it was clearly evident that Simon was the focus of her attention and that worried Cassidy. She analyzed her concerns a hundred times and had even sought Jeff's advice on the matter to be sure she wasn't simply jealous of the woman's special friendship with Simon, but Jeff had seen it also. Carol had a professional, nurturing relationship with the other children, but with Simon it was different. She hovered over him, and her concern and praise for him far exceeded that which she offered the others. In short, she was filling the role of mother, and Cassidy feared that one or both of the pair was becoming vulnerable and would get hurt.

On Saturday, December thirteenth, Carol came to Brighton to drop Merit off for work, but she couldn't resist stopping by the great room to see the children first. She and Cassidy exchanged a casual greeting and soon cheery hellos reverberated in the house as the children greeted her as well. A few minutes later, however, Cassidy poked her head around the corner and the other children were off playing together while Carol and Simon sat off to themselves, curled up in a beanbag chair and sharing a picture book.

Cassidy called her to her office and closed the door to keep the conversation private. Carol's face was immediately apprehensive.

"I only planned to pop in and say hello," she tossed out defensively.

"I'm worried about you two," Cassidy warned.

"You don't need to be."

"Carol, you're becoming far too attached to Simon, and what worries me even more is that he's becoming dependent on you. There's no future in this for you, but the potential for hurt is great."

Carol's hands went up to stop the conversation. She looked at the floor and wrung her hands nervously. "Perhaps you're right. If you feel I need to spend less time with Simon, then I will. I'll do more paperwork and confine my contact with Simon to times when I'm with all the children. Would that be acceptable?"

Cassidy became even more concerned as she watched Carol, seemingly unraveling before her eyes. "Carol—"

"Please, Cassidy," she begged. "Please don't tell me I can't come anymore. I love the children—all the children. I haven't been this happy . . . for a long time. Please."

"Alright, Carol, alright then," Cassidy agreed reluctantly.

After Carol left, it took Cassidy a while to shake the feeling of foreboding that hung over her as a result of their conversation. She slunk down into her desk chair and rested her head in her hands. Her life was suddenly filled with complicated people, and at times the weight of their concerns overwhelmed her. Her thoughts ran back to Jeff. She saw great progress in him and it made her smile. Running into his mother had rattled him, but pulling out the old photo albums and home movies had somehow centered him, and each day throughout the following week he'd been thoughtful, even pensive at times, but consistently positive and comfortable.

Cassidy used her daily contact with Merit and David to assess the residual effects Natalie's brush with Jeff was having on her, and the only insight it yielded was David's comment about how Natalie had pulled boxes of old photos down from the attic with no argument from Benjamin. Cassidy had primed the waters intentionally when David was visiting on the pretense of "checking the lights on the tree." She casually mentioned that Natalie had "met" Jeff at the breakfast and wondered if she had said anything about him. David winked at Merit and began to tease Cassidy. "Oh yes, there was *that* little piece of information. And I thought the thing between you two was purely professional."

Merit's face flushed at the word "professional" and she cast a wondering glance at Cassidy who now speculated that Merit had never told David the truth about her own "professional" relationship with Jeff, or how she came to work at Brighton. Cassidy shot Merit a reassuring glance and teased, "Oh, David, you thought he came here just because of the children?" But it was clear that Merit was holding her breath until David responded.

"Well, I knew he was social worker here, but what had Omma called him? Hmm . . . Let me think . . . Oh yes," he joked, dragging it out sarcastically. "Your 'beau'? Hmm . . ."

Everyone in the room laughed and Merit finally drew a normal breath.

"You two work pretty fast, I'd say," David continued on teasingly.

"What do you mean?" Cassidy questioned humorously, but her guard was coming up.

"Well, the first time I met him was on the morning of the day I first met the lovely Merit." He pumped his eyebrows and rolled the corners of his invisible handlebar mustache. "It was the day after Thanksgiving. He was just sitting in his car at the corner of our farm. He didn't know who you were or where Brighton was. I thought he might need some directions, so I went up to his window to check. He was a wreck. I think I must have scared him to death because at first he looked at me as if he'd seen a ghost, and then I noticed that his eyes were red. He tried to tell me it was his allergies. Maybe, I guess, but I don't think so. Something was bothering him."

Cassidy could easily imagine what that morning's drive must have done to him. And then all her games and antics. She felt ashamed again.

"Anyway, a few hours later, when he and Merit came to buy a tree, he seemed so different." David's voice became soft and thoughtful as he considered the change, and then he returned to his silly antics and responded, "And the rest, ladies, is history." He paused and then his voice again returned to the soft, serious tone Merit loved and through which Cassidy felt the maturity of his spirit. "All I can say is that whatever you have, Ms. Prescott, you should bottle it, because a few hours with you made him a new man." Laughing again, he added, "And in two weeks he's your 'beau'? Merit, these two had better never say another word about us."

Merit blushed. He had referred to them as "us." Did he see them as a couple? Did he even realize what he'd said? Again, Cassidy picked up on Merit's mood. She understood. She had been hurt once herself. After that she had carefully weighed every little gesture, every innuendo.

David left the room to get a few spare bulbs, and Cassidy took advantage of the opportunity to whisper quietly to Merit. "Merit, haven't you told David about . . . everything?"

Merit cast her eyes downward. "No, since he's leaving in a few weeks I didn't see the point. I guess I should tell him." It was more a question than a comment. "I'm just afraid . . ."

"You really like him, don't you?"

"More than I've ever cared about anyone. It's really hard though, knowing he's leaving. He's so good and he understands what I feel without me having to explain every detail. I don't know what I'll do when he leaves. I just thought, well, I'm a different person now than I was when . . . all that stuff happened, so maybe, since he's leaving soon and we might never see each other again, maybe I could just not tell him."

Cassidy stood there, remembering how it felt to be seventeen and in love. "Merit, only you know the answer to that. I don't want to give you the 'I know what you're feeling' speech, but someday, very soon, I'll tell you my story and lots of little pieces will fall into place. You'll see how small secrets, that would have been okay if they were just shared, ended up tearing two people apart who loved each other very much." Merit cast her eyes down as she listened. "So let me give you two pieces of advice," Cassidy continued. "First, my experience is that secrets have a way of getting out, and if there's a chance that might happen, who would you want him to hear it from? And second, if you believe David really is all those things you said, good and kind, don't you think he'd understand?"

Merit didn't say anything. There were tears in her eyes. When David walked into the room he could sense the change in the mood. He looked tenderly at each of the women, paused without changing any bulbs, and then exited again. Cassidy put her arms around Merit. "You *are* a different person, Merit. No . . . I take that back, I think you *were* a different person back then for a little while because of difficult circumstances, but I think inside you have always been a wonderful, talented, wise young woman, and that's who David knows and cares about. But more importantly, that's who you need to know and care about. Okay?"

Merit clung to her and whispered thank you in her ear. David saw them from the corner but retreated again until he heard the cheery chitchat return. When Cassidy left the room he looked at Merit with concern etched into his handsome face and said, "Everything all right?" Merit only nodded with a grateful smile.

"Wanna get something to eat?" he asked, and again her response was a smile and a nod. He placed his hand on her shoulder and gave it a gentle squeeze. Cassidy caught the loving gesture and thought how much David and TJ were alike—TJ who twenty years ago had shared his dreams with Cassidy while swimming in the pond and who had carved their names high up in the tree at Veterans' Park so they could sit there and share a first kiss near the stars. David was, at that moment, what Jeff was just rediscovering about himself. And Ben. This was how Ben was. He was the root of the gentleness in both of these men. *Good fruit from a good tree.*

Cassidy suddenly wanted to call Jeff more than anything else in the world. The Saturday volunteers would soon be bringing the children in from play and then Mrs. Sherman would oversee dinner. Cassidy had an hour or so to herself before she took over the evening activities and supervised getting everyone ready for bed. "Well, you two. I hate to throw out good help, but, as David so eloquently put it, I have a beau to call . . . and heaven forbid that the word should get out that Cassidy Prescott enslaves men *and* her volunteers!" Merit and David laughed. "So you guys can just finish up what you're doing and then get out of here and have some fun."

Within ten minutes they were in David's Jeep, and Merit called her parents from his cell phone. It was already dark and there was a frosty bite in the air. Merit shivered in the cold, rubbing her hands together to warm them. David cranked up the heat and took her hands in his and blew on them. His lips brushed them and Merit wondered if that was his intention or if she was reading into things again. He did what he always did whenever the mood began to shift, he made a joke, "That's the one advantage of going out with a guy that's full of hot air."

Going out? It made her shiver. Everything was making her shiver tonight. She couldn't keep her knees still. They shook uncontrollably, making her appear colder than she was. It was her nerves, she knew it. She needed to talk to him and she was nervous. They went through the drive-through of a little dive outside of town, picking up some fried chicken and french fries.

"How about a picnic?" David asked.

"We'll freeze to death, or at least the chicken will," Merit quipped.

"We'll have a car picnic. Presumably the chichen will already be dead," he countered humorously.

Merit knew what he was doing. He knew she needed to talk and he was trying to give her the opportunity. She shivered again. They drove up into the mountains and David took the Jeep off the road onto a well-worn path. There were other cars there as well and Merit knew this was the local "parking spot." David threw her an apologetic smile, and parked away from the others.

"I had hoped we'd be the only ones up here since it's so early and so cold tonight, but it appears they're making their own heat." He laughed nervously but Merit could see he regretted his choice of location. "Maybe we should go somewhere else," he said as he began to restart the engine. This place, spotted with a few steamy-windowed cars, implied everything he did not want to imply, but Merit put her hand over his and shook her head.

"It's okay, David. I know that's not why you brought me here. I've never been here before but I've heard about it. The view is amazing though. It's okay." David relaxed. Merit reminded herself that everything she said was true. She knew where she was. This had to be High Rock, the location of the party she and the boys were trying to find the night they were all arrested. But they'd never *arrived*. And the view was amazing. It was the highest vehicle-accessible point in the area and it overlooked hundreds of square miles of the Piedmont Valley. The stars were magnificent, unhampered by city smog or lights. The few lights nearest to them were from the farms and small housing developments in the fringe communities, like Smithsburg, that formed a ring around the sprawling city of Hagerstown. Even though it was a large city by Smithsburg standards, there were no skyscrapers or buildings with double-digit floors, but there were enough lights to form a bright cluster in the distance that looked almost like the center of an iridescent flower.

David opened the bag of food, which had miraculously remained warm sitting near the heat vent of the car. They ate in relative silence, still feeling a little awkward about the location. One by one the cars began pulling out, and David noticed that the passengers were dressed up in semiformal attire. He realized that these were probably kids going to their high school Christmas dance that was about to begin. Most of them appeared to be about sixteen or seventeen and they probably had early curfews, forcing them to get their "parking" done early. He shook his head and smiled with sadness that these girls, who had probably spent hours on hair, nails, and makeup, were allowing themselves to be crumpled and contorted in cars with puberty-driven boys, and then they would make their grand entrance into the dance looking like they had been run through a trash compacter. It was so ridiculous. A loud horn honk broke the silence as the last of the cars pulled out, leaving Merit and David alone on the hill.

"Some guy must have hit the horn during one of his smooth moves," David said with a nervous laugh. "Lucky for you, you're safely in the care of a future missionary." He said it as much to remind himself as to reassure Merit. He was twisting the steering wheel nervously, then a thought occurred to him. "Merit, this is your school district. Is your Christmas dance tonight?"

Merit squirmed as she decided how to answer that question. "Uh, yeah, I think it is."

"Didn't you want to go? I would have been happy to take you." She didn't answer, but merely smiled. Another thought crossed his mind. "Oh . . . I've been completely monopolizing your time, haven't I?" David was instantly apologetic.

"Oh, no. No, David. If I had wanted to go, it would have been with you." Her voice was soft, embarrassed by the confession. David comically rushed in to support her.

"I knew it. It's the vest. You were afraid I'd wear the 'dazzling' Christmas vest Omma bought for the breakfast. Although I adore it, as a favor to you, I would have agreed to leave it at home. Now I *could* go home and slide into a powder-blue polyester leisure suit. Very classy."

Merit laughed. He never pressed her. He simply accepted her position and made her feel wise for taking it. She wanted to tell him how desperately she wanted to show up at the dance with him on her arm, but she was too afraid someone would make a comment or a gesture, and he would find out everything. Now she understood what Cassidy was trying to tell her this afternoon.

"David, I know a lot about you. You've told me some things, and Cassidy has told me a lot of stuff about your family, but you really don't know very much about me."

"I know what you let me know about you, and that's enough for now."

"Is it?" she countered seriously. "I thought so too until today. Cassidy and I were talking and I realized that maybe it's not enough."

David squirmed inside. He knew Merit needed a safe place to talk, but now that the conversation was beginning, he was torn. He could tell that this was going to come from someplace tender within her, and that his inclination would be to console and comfort her; this was the wrong setting—too secluded, too vulnerable. This is what Sam had warned him about. He needed to think. *Move the car, David.* But how could he interrupt her when he could see what it was costing her just to broach the topic? His eyes were on her but his mind was engaged in a silent prayer that he would not misstep. It was obvious to him that Merit was struggling, not only with what to say but also with her emotions. He wanted to touch her, to hold her, but he didn't dare. He took one finger, lifted her chin, and smiled at her. It was enough.

"I don't know what we are to each other, David, friends, or a couple or . . ." Her voice trailed off. "But I feel like whatever we are, I need to know 'we' are honest and that there aren't any secrets between us."

David relaxed a little. *That's it,* he thought. *It's the mission . . . She has questions. She wants to know more about it. I can handle this.* And then something Merit said caught his attention.

"Jeff is not the Brighton children's social worker, David. He's mine." There, it was out. She paused to detect his response. It was slight. His eyebrows were arched, questioning what she meant by that and his head cocked toward her as if to hear more clearly.

"I made some mistakes, David, some pretty big ones a few months ago. I'm not just a volunteer at Brighton. Working there is part of my probation."

David sat silently, absorbing what she had said. He had so many questions. So many things he wanted to ask her, but he wasn't sure whether he should or whether he even wanted to hear the answers. He knew the answer to her first question, about what they were to each other. He was invested in this girl and he felt suddenly threatened that whatever she was about to tell him would change things. It was crazy. In a few weeks his mission would split them anyway. *Yeah, but that will be different. We'll still be on good terms, we'll still care, and we can write. What if what she's about to tell me ends that?*

David's silence unnerved Merit. She wanted to crumple up in a ball, but instead she was committed to plowing through the can of worms she had opened.

She told him everything, from Markie's illness and death to the painful revelation about the unraveling of her family. She tried to help him understand her loneliness and her feelings of worthlessness, and then she told him that she gave up her music, her "beautiful, magical music," as David referred to it.

David listened intently and his fears began to allay. He felt safe enough to take her hand. His thumb began to rub circles in her palm, and she calmed somewhat as she spoke of her fears and sorrows. She seemed to draw strength from his support, but then her story took a turn as she mentioned the name Brian Hartman, and David no longer drew the little circles in her palm. Merit noticed it immediately.

Brian Hartman, although a year younger than David, was a former friend of his. His father managed a dairy farm in the valley but had moonlighted for Sterling Davis for years. Every Thanksgiving Eve, when Sterling would come with the crew to work, he would bring his son Brian along to play with David. Even though they had only spent a few days together some years, Brian had been a favored childhood friend. After David and his mother moved to California, they either lost or forgot to make contact for several years, until two years ago when he came back to the farm for a visit and inquired about his old friend. His grandparents didn't say much, but what they did say broke his heart. Brian had been in and out of trouble that year and his parents had sought counseling for his drug and alcohol use. David went to see him one day, but it had turned into a disastrous mistake. Brian asked David to take him out for a ride and then wanted to stop by the local convenience store. He came back to the car with a six-pack of beer as if he were a conquering hero. David told him to dump the stuff and the boys fought. Since Brian wouldn't get in the car without the beer and David wouldn't drive with it, he left Brian standing by the road and went home to call the boy's parents so they could pick him up. Later that evening David got a call from Brian, apologizing and trying to explain about his "problem." David had felt bad for his friend that day, but now, after hearing his name linked with Merit's, he just seethed.

Merit began to explain her relationship with Brian. The more she told him, the sicker David felt. Brian had changed her, changed her lifestyle. She pulled out an old photo of her and Brian from behind several others in her wallet and showed it to David. It was taken at a party she attended with him. Her hair and makeup made her mean looking, and her clothes made her look easy and cheap. David fought the vile images of the pair that flashed through his mind. *This is not my Merit.* He didn't even want to see her looking like this.

Merit plowed on. She told him about the party at High Rock and about Zach. She went through the tale of the drinking and the arrest. She told him everything. And then she ended and sat quivering, with her body turned toward David, waiting for him to respond.

David hated how he felt. He was sick. He was caught up in his own hurt. If she had been some casual friend or acquaintance he would have reached out to comfort her, to tell her it was okay and that her decisions were not who she was. He would have told her that he understood the pain and confusion she was experiencing with her family and could see how a person would reach out for someone, anyone, for acceptance and love. He would have said all those things because he had been touched by the Savior and was supposed to be filled with Christlike, unconditional love. He was supposed to know that it wasn't his place to judge, that it was his place to love and forgive. He was going to be a missionary in four weeks! But he couldn't say those things because it was all too personal to him. He could understand her hurt and he could separate the actions from the person, but not right at that second. He was being ripped apart by the recognition of his own inadequacies. He was too caught up in himself, in what *he* was feeling, and what *he* might lose, to put her needs first. Suddenly, he doubted himself, doubted his commitment, and his worthiness. He was choking in a sea of doubts. He needed air.

Then he remembered Sam's warning. *I'm not saying don't be her friend. I'm not even saying don't care for her. But what I am saying to you is that the closer you get to her the harder it will be to leave, and the adversary will use that against you. He will plant doubts in your mind and make you question what you already know to be right, so be careful.*

Father, help me, David prayed silently, then he looked over at Merit and finally realized what his silence was costing her. "How about if we walk awhile," he said.

He didn't even wait for her response. He went around to her door and took her hand to help her out. They walked one of the trails that meandered near the cliff. He breathed deeply and thought, stealing glimpses of her sweet, familiar face. He watched the nimble way she maneuvered along the rocky trail, and the stark images of the photo were replaced by the memory of her moving lithely as she played the violin. Peace began to wash over him. He liked the way her smaller hand felt in his and he knew this wasn't a charade. *This* person was who Meredith Davenport was. The other person was the charade, the illusion, and he felt better having wrestled that fear out of his mind. His thumb again began drawing small circles on her palm and he could feel the tension begin to dissipate.

He led her over to a rock that sat atop the cliff. They sat there quietly as he gathered his thoughts. In spite of the angst he felt over her disclosures, he admitted that he had been as unwilling to share the corners of his heart as she had been. He tried to sort all his tender feelings into some order so they could finally know what they were dealing with and where they were headed.

"I understand all those feelings you talked about . . . feeling lonely, abandoned, frightened. My mother is wonderful, and Omma and Pap have filled in almost all the gaps, but there is an emptiness that comes when you lose family, whether it's a brother that dies, or parents that withdraw from you, or . . ."

" . . . or parents you've never known?" Merit asked.

David smiled. They were back again where they began earlier. They were in sync, close, and there was understanding between them once more. "Yes, or stepfathers that make your mom cry and then leave. For the most part, I've never felt that anything was missing, but then, sometimes I feel an empty spot, like an unanswered question that hangs around nagging at me. It's like the way Omma must feel every time she dusts off TJ's photo. I know my grandparents would have loved me even if TJ had stayed around, but I know they loved me fiercely because he didn't. It doesn't change anything about *how much* we love each other, but about *how* we love each other. I'm always aware that their greatest fear is that I'll leave or be taken from them. That's why I thought they would flip out when they heard about my mission. And it's why I have always lived my life so carefully, especially since that sledding accident. I've always known what something like that would do to them. So I've been the good boy—the quiet, thoughtful child, the responsible son and grandson—because the thought of hurting them is unbearable to me. I love them all that much. But I've had days when I thought I would explode with anger. Why did my father never want to see me? Why did he abandon my mother and me? Was I just an accident, born because of an impulsive moment, or was I supposed to be born, born to be David Johanson or somebody else? I was a perfectly loved, perfectly loving, totally messed-up person, until Sam introduced us to the gospel."

Merit was listening intently. The only difference between her and David could be that he had found answers and purpose through his newly found faith, where she had tried to find it in other people. The thought intrigued her.

"Sam taught me that we lived before we came to earth and that this life is a time to gain a body, grow in faith, and be tested, like one long, amazing day of school. He told me that each of us has a mission to fulfill in this life—people whose lives we may touch, work that we may do, but the thing we must realize is that we have *choices*. That made sense to me. My father and mother made choices, but those were *their* choices. They don't affect my worth, only I can do that, and even if I totally blow it and do everything wrong, it can all be made right. That's what the Savior made possible with the Atonement. Have you ever heard of the Atonement, Merit?"

The realization that he now had the chance to share the tender things of his heart with her excited him, but he could see by her expression that he was overwhelming her, so he slowed down, considered how to approach it, and then an idea caught him. He picked up several large stones near him.

"None of us will leave this life without having done something wrong." He picked up a stone and placed it in the front pockets of her sweatshirt. "Like lying or hurting someone or . . ."

" . . . getting drunk and arrested?" Merit offered contritely.

David smiled, rolling his eyes affectionately. "Yes," he replied. "That was very wrong." He tossed four large stones into her pockets with exaggerated effort and continued more soberly, "Or having failed to do something we should have done, like helping a neighbor in need. These errors are called sins." She seemed interested so far and it delighted him.

"Now, imagine tossing in a stone for every single sin you've ever committed," he challenged. Merit thought carefully and tossed in a few and then sat back thoughtfully.

"What are you thinking?" David asked.

"How I might need bigger pockets," she laughed nervously. "There's more than—"

David held up his hand to stop her. "You know what? I don't need to know. In fact, I don't even want to know, and soon you'll see why. Now stand up."

Merit awkwardly complied, but she had to use her hands to support the weight of the bulging front pockets.

"This is what most of us do all our lives, Merit. We walk around yoked by our sins, carrying them alone, adding to them every day, until many of us break under the load—physically, emotionally, or spiritually. Imagine also adding to your emotional load all the stones for every sin against you, then heaping on top of that all the hurts, sorrows, and anguish that others bring to us accidentally, or that life throws at us." He opened his hands, filled with more stones, and he added softly, "Then consider how little joy life holds as we are left to carry that all alone, forever. Sadly, this is what most people do. For our own sins, the load is called 'justice.' We reap what we sow."

"David, I don't want to carry these anymore," said Merit. David rose to help her.

"And that's the point of the Atonement, Merit. You don't have to," he added as he began removing the stones.

The lesson was powerful and Merit could see the importance it held for David.

"The Savior offers us another way, a better way. Rather than carry our own burden forever, He offers us mercy and freedom from pain and sorrow. He's willing to take all our burdens upon Himself if we'll have the faith to take His name upon us through baptism—to be made clean. He was perfect, Merit. Consider that His single, perfect, sinless life was sufficient to pay the debts of every other child of God. It's His gift to us, and because He loves His Father, and because He loves us, He wants to give each of us the chance to repent and be forgiven of all our mistakes. We can be free of our burdens and be made clean and worthy to someday go home to heaven and be with Him and with Heavenly Father when our day at school is over."

Merit sat silently, tucking herself into a ball, considering all that David had said. He was expecting the joy he felt to fill her too. But when she finally spoke, her tone wasn't joyful. It was disheartened. "But I mess up every day, David. And even though you talk about understanding my mistakes, you're practically perfect. No wonder you can feel free of all of your sins. You hardly have any. But I'm still digging out. I don't know if I'll ever feel good about myself again. Not the way you do." Her eyes welled up and David could feel despair settling back in. He countered quickly.

"It's a day-to-day process, Merit, for each of us. But you're right. It does get easier as we understand the plan and learn to listen to the Spirit."

She looked confused again. "The Spirit?"

"Before the Savior died on the cross and was resurrected, He knew we would need help to get through this life successfully, so He promised the disciples He would not leave them alone. Since He couldn't stay with them all the time, He left behind the Holy Ghost to be a comforter and to guide them, and that same gift is promised to us."

David noticed a beam of moonlight and got another idea. More than anything else, he wanted the power of the gospel to touch her heart. *Please feel it, Merit.* "Merit, think of this beam of light as something called the Light of Christ," he said, indicating the shaft of moonlight. "Some people call it a conscience. It represents truth and those things that bring us closer to God. This light is constant. Just like truth, it never changes. We can count on it, and the scriptures tell us that 'the light of Christ is given to every man who cometh into the world.' Everyone who is born has the Light of Christ to help them judge right from wrong. But the Holy Ghost is an even greater gift to those who exercise the faith to take Christ's name upon them and be baptized, and it works like this."

David's voice was soft and intense. "Now imagine that my hand represents you after baptism." He moved his hand into the beam of light. "Look where the light hits the rock wall. What do you see?" he asked, yearning for her to see and understand.

Merit saw the shadow of his fingers on the rock wall.

"That shadow represents the Holy Ghost or Holy Spirit. The Holy Ghost can teach us, guide us, comfort us, bring us peace . . . It's the greatest gift that we can enjoy on the earth, Merit, and those who repent of their sins and get baptized can have Him as their constant companion. Then as long as we stay in the light and follow what we know is right, the Holy Ghost is with us. Now the light never leaves *us*, Merit . . ." David now moved his hand back and forth across the shaft of light. " . . . but we can move out of the light by making bad choices or by turning away from what we know is right. That's the secret. The Holy Ghost will let us know when what we are doing or thinking is right or wrong, and then, if we listen to the promptings and move back into the light of Christ, He will continue to stay near us and guide us. Do you understand?"

Merit sat very still for several moments. It all sounded so good. She wanted to believe it, to believe that she could feel clean and innocent. She would give anything if she could get rid of the weight of guilt she carried when she met people who knew her past or when she had to talk about her mistakes. And David . . . the way his eyes shone with the fire of what he was saying. She wanted to feel that too. But even more than that, she wanted his eyes to shine that way when he looked at her. After what she had told him, could he really ever see her that way, clean and good again?

"What are you thinking, Merit?" David asked cautiously.

"That I now see how passionately you feel about this," she said almost sadly.

"That's why I want to serve a mission. To help other people discover that the Savior can lift the yoke from all of us, and to baptize them into the kingdom of God so they can go back to Him someday." He smiled at her but he didn't see the joy he felt shining in her eyes. His heart sank. *What have I done wrong? Where did I fail?*

"Talk to me, Merit." He was afraid. *What if she never feels the way I do about the gospel? What would I do? Where would that leave us?* Her head hung down. He put his hand on her back and stroked it gently. "Please talk to me, Merit."

His hand gently touched her chin, pulling her face around to meet his eyes. She was crying. Silent, tiny tears were falling from her dark lashes, streaking her face. The thought that something he'd said had caused her hurt pained him. She shivered. He had been so caught up in talking that he didn't realize how very cold she was and how blue her lips were becoming. "Let's go back to the car."

He pulled to help her up but he pulled too hard and she fell against him. He caught her and softly pushed her slightly away, although it took all his effort not to cling to her. Instead, he compromised and tucked her shorter frame beside his and walked her to the car. He opened her door and paused as he went around back. He was grateful for a moment apart from her. He needed a chance to clear his mind of her sweet face and to clear her scent from his head. He looked at her through the back window and saw her reflection in the mirror. She was leaning against the seat. She was no longer crying but her face was wet and the streaks were still apparent on her cheeks. *She's so beautiful. What have I started?*

David got into the car and paused as he placed the key in the ignition. He couldn't leave things like this. He turned to face her. "I'm sorry, Merit. I wanted to share the things of my heart with you, so you can understand what I believe and why I believe that you can change too. I didn't mean to upset you."

She sat there and the tears began again. "Please, Merit. Please tell me why you're crying. What did I do? What did I say?"

How could she tell him that she loved what he said and at the same time was afraid of it, because the conviction that made him so wonderful, so easy to love, was the same thing that would take him away from her, dashing her hope that maybe he would choose to stay here with her. She saw that tonight. She had confessed all her flaws and he hadn't judged her, but she still didn't have that peace, that serenity that he had. He offered her his best gift, but she still couldn't feel what he felt. It was the great divide, the line in the sand that would separate them.

"I saw this light in your eyes tonight, as if you were so far beyond me, so far beyond ever doing anything wrong, and I felt like I could never be . . . good enough. But I understand why your mission is so important to you. You'll be a great missionary, David. You need to go. They need you to go and give them this hope, but I feel like I . . ." Her voice trailed off and she sobbed.

David was crushed. "Merit, don't be so hard on yourself. I think you're wonderful. I think you're the kindest person I've ever met. You make me excited to share these things I feel. I've never expressed them out loud to anyone but my mom and Sam, and I've just barely begun sharing them with my grandparents. Do you understand what I am saying?"

She looked up at him. "I'll hold you back, David. To be a good missionary you have to let go of me, tonight, because . . ."

David panicked. " . . . because of what?" he said in desperation.

" . . . because I'm falling in love with you and I don't want you to leave me."

He saw it in his mind like a movie scene where the plane nose-dives directly into the ground. He could see where he was headed, but he chose not to stop it. And though he could hear Sam's words in his head, he dismissed them as well. Instead, he scooped Merit into his arms and held her tightly. And then he kissed her. It was the kiss he had told himself would never happen, the kiss into which he poured all the feelings he had vowed to avoid. Sam had jokingly told David that if he ever got into a position where he "had" to kiss a girl, that he should never kiss longer than the time it took to say "Mississippi." Well, tonight he was well past Mississippi. He could have rattled off the entire map and half the capitals before he regained his senses. When he finally did, he pulled away from Merit, and she saw confusion wash over him. He scooped her back into his arms to avoid her eyes, but she could feel the difference. He was stiff and rigid, and though his arms were around her, he wasn't embracing her as much as clinging, and not to her as much as to his mission decision, which his feelings for Merit now placed in peril. After a few minutes he released her, lowered his eyes, and simply said, "I need to get you home." They drove in relative silence, each of them confused by what had happened but even more confused about what lay ahead.

Chapter Eighteen

Tuesday, December thirteenth, was a happy, hectic day. Carol Davenport had been at Brighton for the first time since their tense conversation on Saturday, and to Cassidy's delight the day went splendidly. She greeted all the children, paying personal attention to each one, and when Simon tried to pull her away individually she had encouraged him to join the others, to which he finally agreed. She had been a pleasant assistant in the office also, accomplishing more filing in a few hours than Cassidy would have asked her to do in a week. And when Merit arrived to conduct the practice for the Christmas concert, Carol scurried off to help Mrs. Sherman in the kitchen with the assembly of a gingerbread house for the children to decorate that evening in preparation for their upcoming gingerbread-inspired field trip. She waited around for Merit to finish, and since David was conspicuously absent, she busied herself back in the office with more filing. By the time the Davenports left, Cassidy scarcely recognized her tidy office.

Jeff arrived in time for supper and found *his* spot at the table, as he was now a regular fixture at the Brighton supper table. He convinced several of the boys to don aprons and clear the table while he filled the sink, proclaiming dishwashing to be "manly work." Cassidy marveled at the effect a man around the house was having on the boys. Content that the galley was under control, she strode down the hall to admire her beautifully organized office. She smiled and sighed at the wonder of order, then reluctantly admitted that it would be a fleeting thing. Determined to enjoy it while it lasted, she sat in her chair and spun around a time or two, giggling with pleasure at the thought of actually being ahead in her paperwork for the first year's end in Brighton history. Carol's organizational efforts had given her a blessed gift. She would be able to relax and enjoy the holidays, and what made it more wonderful was that this year she had someone to enjoy them with.

She sorted through the day's mail and went to the file cabinet to put a few newly arrived documents away. One document concerned Simon Allen, and she pulled his folder from the drawer and laid it on her desk. When she opened it she immediately noticed that the documents were out of order. *No matter,* she thought. If Carol had moved things around a little, well, it was a small price to pay for all the work she had accomplished, but after Cassidy had searched the file for the third time she became alarmed. The document containing Simon's birth father's information was gone.

* * *

For the first time since Merit began working at Brighton, she wasn't following her cheery routine of hugs and kisses, then homework and calls from David. Instead she had been quiet and subdued. She had arrived home from her Saturday night date with him an hour before curfew, and then she went immediately to her room. Though she had told her mother earlier in the week that she planned to go to church with David, he never called. And despite the countless, brief calls Carol caught her daughter making to him, David did not come by.

It was apparent that he was also avoiding Brighton, and so each day Carol arranged to bring Merit home. She had tried numerous times to talk with Merit about the situation, but it was clear that the hurt was too raw and, unsure about what to do, she simply honored her daughter's privacy, waited for Merit to come to her, and held her breath, hoping that Merit could handle the apparent breakup.

Tuesday, on the way home from Brighton, the floodgates opened. Merit didn't reveal any of the details of their split, but her hurt was immense and all Carol could do was offer her daughter a listening ear and tissues. The two women sat in the driveway for thirty minutes while Merit expressed in a dozen ways how much she missed David's company, and it was only when her father came home and peered anxiously into the car window that Merit was able to gather up her things and go inside.

"How's she doing?" Mike Davenport asked hopefully, but his wife's worried expression answered his question without need for further explanation. "Darn shame," he said with a frustrated sigh. "He's been such a blessing to Meredith. I hadn't seen her that happy in a long while. It was like we got our little girl back. Darn shame."

He began to open the car door, but Carol waved her husband on into the house, giving herself time to ponder what she had just come to realize—that even this hurt, the hurt her daughter was now experiencing with David, was related to that period of time when Meredith had felt alone, motherless, abandoned, and unloved.

Carol struggled all night over her new dilemma. She had made a plan. It was a plan borne of desperation and hunger, and she had felt morally compelled to follow it through. She had stolen Simon's family-data sheet and was planning on taking the morning shuttle from Baltimore to Chicago to confront the man whose name was linked with the child. *Simon needs and deserves a family,* she had told herself. *Every child deserves a family . . . a loving home and family . . .* And yet now she doubted herself. As right as her *desires* were for Simon, she knew her *reserves* were limited. Her conversation with Merit proved what damage her limited reserves had previously inflicted on her daughter. Could she, in her current state, be sure that she could now give her daughter all she deserved—and meet Simon's needs as well? Maybe someday . . . but now?

Carol opened her purse and found the wad of tissues, makeup-smeared and still damp with Merit's tears, and her priorities became clear. She jumped in her car and headed back to Brighton. It was after ten when she knocked at the door. Jeff answered and the disappointed look on Cassidy's face made it apparent that Carol's deceit had been discovered. She reached into her purse and withdrew the document.

"This belongs to you," she said as she handed the form to Cassidy.

Chapter Nineteen

On the fourth day without word from David, Merit stopped dragging her pitiful broken heart around and instead she just got mad. She tried to push "What's-His-Name" out of her mind and threw herself into school and her work at Brighton. Her parents were pleased to notice some of her spark return, and equal to the changes they noticed in her were the changes she finally noticed in them and in their home. It seemed to Merit that her mom had been getting prettier every day since Thanksgiving. She was again making the effort to fix her hair and add a little makeup to brighten her face, but she was also smiling and humming again. That night, Wednesday evening, when she got home, she smelled the aroma of cookies coming from the oven, a wondrous scent that had not filled the air since Markie died. And to her amazement, a beautiful Christmas tree stood in the stand with boxes of ornaments scattered on the floor ready for a family night of decorating. In spite of Merit's less-than-perfect mood, she couldn't help but relish the thought of witnessing the rebirth of her family.

The most amazing development though, was the change in her parents' relationship. She nearly fainted when she saw her father pick up the plant mister and spray her mother, who didn't brush him off or ignore his approach. Instead, she crumpled up on the sofa, shielding her head with her hands amid laughing protests until her father relented from his attack and took her hands to help her up. When they noticed Merit's stunned pleasure, her father stretched out his hand to draw her in and the three of them fell back down on the sofa and admired their undecorated tree.

* * *

Natalie and Ben had fully enjoyed the last four days. They'd had
David completely to themselves, with time out only for his studies. It
had been like old times, with David working by his grandfather's side
until supper, then he would haul out the old board games and they
would play until Ben began to yawn. Yes, it had been heavenly, except
for the phone calls from Merit, which David had either refused or
quickly dismissed since Sunday. It was easy for Ben and Natalie to
convince themselves that the first few days were David's effort to set
aside a little time for his family, but it was obvious he was troubled
about Merit. Natalie had overheard David say something about
"catching up on his studies," which she had accepted as truth. And
although he sat at the table with his laptop turned on and plenty of
books sprawled across the table, his attention was everywhere but on
the work before him. By Tuesday, even Ben began to worry. He treasured any time with his grandson, but even he preferred a few hours
with the bubbly, effervescent David to an entire day watching David
lament.

On Wednesday evening Merit called again and Natalie took the
call. She could tell that Merit was no longer willing to accept the "he
says he has homework" excuse David had been hiding behind. Natalie
was beginning to feel like an accomplice in David's deception, so
when Merit asked for him and David tried to wave the call off,
Natalie instead told her how much they had missed seeing her and
handed the phone directly to David. He winced as if in pain and then
gave her a look of such panic that she almost regretted having
betrayed his wishes, then she firmly took her ground again. She
figured that whatever the problem was, it was better to lay it out in
the open. She was, after all, an expert on the damage of nondisclosure
and stubbornness.

David pressed the phone to his forehead while he considered what
to say, but it was obvious this call was very direct and to the point.
Very little conversation was required on his part.

"Hello, Merit. Sorry . . . I . . . what? Oh . . . that's right. I guess I
forgot. Well . . . umm . . . I don't know . . . let me think a minute. I'd
like to but . . . sure. I understand. In that case . . . I guess so, I mean,

yes. I'll be there. Yes, yes, I promise. I'll be there at three. Okay. Merit? . . . Merit?"

Natalie feigned disinterest with the entire conversation, but Ben stepped in with his normal delicacy and provided the conversation starter. "Sounds like you got cut off at the knees, son."

"Did I even get a chance to speak?"

"Did you need one?"

David looked hurt by Ben's obvious reproof. "What do you mean?"

Ben picked up the bowl of nuts and sat at the table opposite David and began to crack and eat them. Some men smoked when confronted with a problem, some paced, but Ben Johanson cracked and ate nuts, and David knew his grandfather was taking this issue very seriously.

"Well, David, that girl has called here several times a day for four days and you never seemed very interested then."

"I've been busy."

"Well, that kind of busy worries me, son. When a boy is obviously as smitten with a girl as you've been, and then he suddenly tries to avoid her, well, that usually means there's a problem. And some of these problems are more than just troubling, David, they're dangerous."

David knew what worries were filling his grandfather's mind. "No, Pap," he assured. "It's not like that. It's my mission. The more time I spend with Merit, the more confused I get about going. I just needed some time to sort things out, that's all."

An immediate brightness returned to Ben's face. He sighed deeply, smiled at his grandson, and said, "Then you need these more than I do." He pushed the bowl and cracker toward David and they laughed, flushing the tension from the room.

David cracked a few nuts with Ben, and Natalie smiled at the two of them. She wished that Ben and TJ could have settled the questions between them so simply, but that was then and now was now. And her son was coming home! It was TJ she had seen at Brighton, wasn't it? Cassidy hadn't actually admitted to her that the handsome man at the breakfast was TJ . . . but she knew it was what Natalie suspected and she hadn't discouraged her from believing it, so it had to be true! The thought made her so giddy that Ben looked on curiously, trying to decide if she was daft or hiding some secret. He decided it was some secret, but being that this was the secret-hiding time of the year, he gave her a smile and a wink and didn't pursue it any further. Natalie winked back, increasing his curiosity even further, and he raised an ornery eyebrow at her. David saw this moment of playfulness in his grandparents as his opportunity to sneak away. He walked Omma over to Pap and sat her down on his lap, scolding her for being ornery and thus being in need of a stern talking to, and turned to make his exit to sounds of the lovingly happy laughter of two of his most beloved people.

The night air was crisp and his breath made clouds every time he exhaled. He beat his hands against his legs while he walked to the barn and found a bale of hay to sit on. He had a lot of thinking to do tonight, as if he hadn't been thinking nonstop since that kiss Saturday night. He hadn't broken any moral laws, although he definitely compromised his judgment. The kiss? He hadn't gone up to High Rock with a plan to kiss her, but he surely didn't make a plan "not" to. Like a calculator, his mind tabulated all his errors in judgment. *Let's see,* he thought. *I took a girl I am crazy about to a notorious make-out place, alone, at dark. Then, after she told me lots of very personal things about herself, I upset her and she started crying, so I tried to console her by . . . kissing her . . .*

He hit himself in the head. After she had poured her heart out to him about things she had been afraid to tell him for fear he would reject her, he responded by teaching her about repentance, then he kissed her, *and then* he rejected her. *Great plan, Davie boy!* The most unsettling thought was that the decision to kiss Merit hadn't been beyond his control. He *chose* to kiss her and he knew it. He had heard Sam's warning ringing in his ears, but he'd pushed it away. He knew he had made a conscious decision not to let his growing feelings for Merit distract him from his more immediate goal of preparing himself to leave in January, but there he had been, ignoring Sam's counsel, turning down the volume on the promptings of the Spirit, and in short, completely threatening every goal he had set for himself. So what did that say about his qualifications to be a missionary? *Well,* he thought, *it's hard to be a missionary and a boyfriend at the same time.* He hit himself in the head again as if mock brilliance had just struck him. He leaned back against the barn wall and started pulling wisps of straw out from the bale.

He wasn't so much angry as he was afraid of his feelings for Merit, and doubt was melting his resolve. He wanted to talk to Sam. He needed to talk to Sam, but Sam and his mom were on a train trip and couldn't be reached for two days, and now he had a new complication. Merit had called to remind him that tomorrow was the children's walking field trip to the library for "story time with the Little Gingerbread Boy" and then a visit next door to the bakery. Weeks ago Mrs. Sherman, the professional worrier, had asked David and Merit to go along to provide extra pairs of eyes and hands. She asked Merit to call and confirm that he was still going, and because it was easier to go than to make an excuse, he agreed. *Why doesn't Merit's mom just go?*

Now the clock was ticking. He had until three tomorrow to sort things out and explain to Merit what he could barely understand himself. He again thought of Sam and how much he needed a father to talk to who understood his situation and could give him some advice, and then a light went on in his mind. He slipped to his knees and began to pray. Heavenly Father already knew all his concerns, but still he poured out his heart, point by point. It was comfortable and easy, and though he didn't know how long he prayed there, when he walked back into the house he was a happier young man.

Natalie and Ben immediately noticed the complete change in both David's countenance and attitude and they smiled in wonder.

"What do you think caused that?" Natalie asked Ben.

"I don't know, but I'd like to bottle whatever it is as a miracle cure," he said laughing.

"Maybe we're due for some miracles. We've had a few before," she said wistfully, as she brought TJ's image to her mind.

"That we've had, darling, that we've had."

* * *

"How about letting me take you to lunch tomorrow?" Jeff coaxed over the phone.

"Oh, I can't tomorrow, we have a packed day. How about Friday?" Cassidy countered.

"I can't, I have a day full of meetings. In fact, I'm supposed to have my weekly meeting with Merit but her folks can't get her here. Hey, I bet if you called and offered to drive Merit, Carol would be relieved, and then I could take two of my favorite ladies for a late lunch."

"Well, it's not as exciting an offer as I'd hoped for, but . . ."

"Cassidy Brighton! You're making me blush."

"Oh, brother . . ." she groaned. "In that case . . ."

"Around 3:30 P.M. then, unless I hear from you."

Chapter Twenty

David arrived ten minutes before three, just as Merit was turning the corner down Brighton's Lane on her walk from school. David ran to meet her, prepared for any scenario from tears to incoming blows. What actually happened scared him more than the threat of physical injury. She was courteous but cool, as if he were no more to her than a mere acquaintance. At first he thought she was stringing him out until he had sufficiently groveled, but he realized that it was no act; something had gone cold in her heart where he was concerned, and it was the one scenario for which he had no plan. David made small talk, but every time he tried to express his apology or talk about last Saturday night she would put up her hand or close her eyes shutting him out. In the worst case, she looked at him with cold, disinterested eyes until his rambling words froze in the chill of her gaze. He gave up. He knew the timing was wrong. He would simply fulfill his obligation and hope that as the afternoon went along she would soften.

The children went crazy when he appeared in the doorway. For a few moments he forgot about his troubles with Merit and basked in the capacity of little children to make him feel adored. As things quieted down he stole a quick glance in Merit's direction but soon realized she had gone directly to the kitchen to check with Mrs. Sherman on last-minute details. *She doesn't even want to be in the same room with me,* David thought to himself.

Merit handed David a packet with the names of the three children for whom he was directly responsible, the name tags for him and those children to help identify them to the people they were visiting, and a red piece of rope he and his children would use to hold onto while they walked. Her eyes met his in a distant, business-only contact. As he took his packet he tried to touch her hand, to see if there was any spark left there. She didn't recoil, nor did she respond. She simply looked at him until he felt her rebuke and let go.

The walk to the library was uneventful. The librarian met them at the door dressed as the Little Gingerbread Boy, and the children squealed with delight. She led the children to the story room, all decorated for Christmas, and she began with a song. The children loved to sing anyway, but this song had hand motions and dance steps that prevented the librarian from playing the piano. Merit volunteered to play. She looked over at David, expecting him to make some goo-goo gesture at her, and sure enough he did, which she refused to acknowledge, so David decided to simply focus on the children and follow the librarian. He mastered all the hand motions and the steps and, adding a few extra "cool" moves of his own, he turned a simple, adorable children's song into a funky piece of choreography. The children squealed with pleasure and Merit had to fight not to enjoy the moment.

After the song, there was an interactive story about the Gingerbread Boy and then a craft. Soon it was time for the adults to bundle the children up and gather their groups for the short trek next door to bake cookies. David exited the library first with his little group, and as he stepped outside he caught sight of a familiar face leaving the liquor store across the street. It was Brian Hartman. According to Merit he had been remanded to a treatment center, but here he was, coming out of a liquor store with a bag in his hand. David couldn't take his eyes off his old friend and the intensity of his stare caught Brian's attention. Brian strained to recognize the person focusing on him from across the street, and then recognition must have set in, because he suddenly lowered his head and became cowed. Cassidy and her group came through at that moment, and as the little crowd began to exceed the capacity of the sidewalk, Cassidy urged David along into the bakery. He moved his children inside and greeted the baker, an old family friend, but as soon as Cassidy walked in and took over the introductions he moved back to the window to watch Brian.

Mrs. Sherman's group came through the bakery door and David knew Merit would be on the sidewalk now. *Did she see him? Did he recognize her?* David was surprised at how intense his feelings were concerning these two. *Try to be charitable, David. You're supposed to love everyone.* He wondered why her little group had still not entered. When he looked out the door Brian was no longer standing across the street. He now stood on the sidewalk, talking to Merit. She was obviously uncomfortable, torn between courtesy and duty. David suddenly stepped up beside her and she jumped at the sight of him. He struggled to compose himself and offered to take her kids into the bakery. Once inside he peered out the door again and Merit smiled and mouthed, "thank you," which he interpreted as a request for rescue and came to stand beside her.

"Man, Merit, I hardly recognized you. So you've gone back to the light," Brian teased.

"That's one way to put it . . . yes I have, and I'm happy again, Brian," she said assuredly.

"So what did they do to you? Rehab?"

"No, community service. But Brian, I thought *you* were in rehab," Merit said worriedly.

A look of sad resignation crossed his face. "I was, baby. Three weeks of residential therapy and now I follow up with AA. I just don't think I'm going to be an honor student," he said holding up the brown paper bag. He laughed, but there was no humor in it. His tone matched the sad look in his eyes. He stepped back to admire her. "But you look good, Merit. I'm really happy for you, really." His sincerity was genuine. He took her hands and smiled proudly at her. "You're going to make it, girl. At least one of us is going to make it."

No thanks to you, David thought to himself. Brian was again staring at him.

"So you're hanging out with Mr. Perfect here?" Brian continued. It wasn't intended to mock David. It actually carried a tone of admiration in it, but David barely smiled.

Merit looked at the sidewalk and tried to extricate herself from this threesome.

Brian spoke again. "Yeah, my dad told me you were going to be a missionary or something. I think he heard it from Mr. Davis."

David mumbled to himself but outwardly he politely smiled in response.

"Brian," Merit said, focusing on the bag, "please throw that away, whatever it is. Please."

"Don't worry about me, Merit," he said genuinely. "I'm really sorry about all the trouble I got you into. You always were a nice girl. You sure do look great." Then to David he spoke more arrogantly, obviously annoyed at David's coldness. "Doesn't she, or aren't you able to look at girls anymore, old friend?" Again, David just laughed softly.

"I've got to go, Brian. This field trip is part of my probation. Please promise me you'll throw that away," Merit implored with eyes filled with compassion and caring.

Brian felt her sincerity, shook his head and then, pausing momentarily, smiled sadly and said, "I'd like to, Merit, just for you, I really would. I owe you that. But you know that even if I did throw it away I'd probably just go to the next liquor store down the block and buy another one."

The look that filled Merit's face was not disappointment. It was complete sorrow. Both boys saw it and both were affected by it.

Brian cleared his throat and spoke. "I'll tell you what. I won't promise that I'll throw it away, but I'll promise you that I'll think about it . . . I'll really try. How's that sound?"

Merit smiled, placed her hand on his shoulder, and thanked him for the difficult gesture.

"Can I see you sometime?" Brian asked solemnly. "I, I mean, well I know we're not supposed to be together, but like if I were to see you in town, could we talk?"

Merit looked at him for several seconds and touched his arm. "Of course."

He stood there awkwardly, trying to determine what to do, and then he embraced her and kissed her on the cheek, whispering, "Bye, baby," in her ear as he turned and walked away. David stood there awkwardly, confused by Merit's reaction. He thought he saw a tear in her eye, and as she wiped it away she turned and headed into the bakery. David reached for her arm and turned her to face him, but her look was defensive, and he just stared painfully at her.

"You can forgive him but you can't forgive me?" he asked.

She looked at him and shook her head. "Is everything always about you?"

"What? I'm just asking you to forgive me."

"Why?"

"Why?" he asked confusedly.

"Yes. Why? Because you're lonesome, or because you hurt me? Because you left me feeling smaller and more worthless than Brian ever made me feel? Yes, he has problems, and yes, he introduced me to things I probably never would have gotten involved with otherwise, but you know what else he did? He befriended me when no one else noticed I was alive. He let me cry on his shoulder when my family was falling apart. He made me feel like I mattered in his life. So yes, he wasn't good for me in some ways, but he cared for me despite all his problems. Can you say that, David? Can you say that you want me to forgive you because you care about *me* or because you need holiday entertainment, because I am not willing to be your yo-yo! You can't keep pulling me in close, and then when it gets uncomfortable just toss me aside and then expect me to be willing to come back because you feel lonesome or guilty. Got it?" Merit then hurried into the bakery leaving David alone on the sidewalk.

He sat there on the antique park bench staring up at South Mountain until everyone exited the bakery with their gingerbread treasures in tow. He had done a lot of thinking about what Merit had said. He knew most of what she had said was right, but he also knew she didn't understand the extenuating circumstances his looming mission created. Part of him considered that the best decision may have been simply letting her go, but he knew he would regret not having attempted to set things right. The voice of reason cried loudest in his head and told him to leave her alone and cause no more harm until he had his own thinking cleared. So he had sat there and thought, long and hard.

They needed a fresh start and a little time under the right conditions. No more long talks in the dark at High Rock. When they had returned the children safely to Brighton, he asked Merit if he could give her a ride home. She hesitated, mumbled something about having not called her folks yet, and then agreed. It was only a three-minute car ride. There had been no time to talk, and David sat as plastered to his side of the seat as Merit was to hers.

"You were right back there," he said as she reached for her door handle.

"I know I was," she replied stoically.

"It's not that I didn't want to call you, I was just confused, maybe a little afraid of everything I was feeling. I just needed some time."

"What did you think I was feeling? Maybe a little confusion and fear too? Or did you think you were the only one entitled to that privilege?" Her words were harsh but her voice was soft and achingly gentle.

"I don't want to fight anymore," he pled.

Merit sat silently and then replied, "What *do* you want?"

"Things I have no right to ask for," he said. "I guess I want a fresh start and for you to care enough to give me one. I saw today that you still have feelings for Brian, and I need to deal with that. I'm not in much of a position to ask you for anything, but if you'd be willing, I'd like to see you tomorrow."

Merit turned her head away from him to look out her window. She tried not to let him see the tears, but he caught her reflection in the window and his heart broke. He was the cause of this hurt as well. Perhaps he really was no better than Brian Hartman. Brian had caused her harm but was this hurt any less damaging? He could barely bring himself to consider it.

"Alright," she said softly without turning her head. "But it will have to be late in the afternoon. Cassidy is taking me to meet with Jeff at three. I'll call you when I get home."

David's heart leapt at this modest sign of hope. "How about if I drive you both over?"

He realized how intrusive his offer might have sounded and he began to backpedal when Merit responded. "Alright. Meet me here at 2:45, then we'll pick up Cassidy."

It was a terse conversation, but it was more than he had hoped for. He jumped out of the Jeep to open her door but she was already out and closing it. She did not wait for a good-bye, but headed directly up the walk to her front door. David stood there watching her until she was safely inside. Only then did he jump back into his Jeep and head home. It was a small thing, but it was a start.

* * *

Carol Davenport was surprised when her daughter walked through the front door. "I was waiting for your call. I told you I'd come to pick you up."

"It's alright. David offered," she said matter-of-factly. "Don't read anything into this, Mother," she cautioned as she headed to her room, then turned to apologize. "I'm sorry, Mom."

"Merit, can't you sit and chat with me for a while?" Carol asked.

"I've got a ton of homework and a term paper to write. I'm running out of time with all the rehearsals for the Christmas concert on the twenty-third. I've got to dig into it tonight."

"Alright, sweetheart," Carol Davenport replied. "You do understand that Cassidy will be taking you to Frederick tomorrow instead of me since I have an appointment of my own?"

"Yes," Merit answered. "Actually, David is coming along also. It's all covered," she added with feigned indifference as she slipped quickly behind her bedroom door to conceal her surfacing tears.

Chapter Twenty-One

David waited nervously in Merit's driveway. Yesterday she'd been in an unpredictable mood, so he was unsure what to expect. Her bus dropped her off promptly at 2:45 and he stepped out of the Jeep to greet her.

"So, how was your day?" he asked, beginning with what he thought was a pretty safe opener.

"Fine," she replied and then fell silent. She was more uncomfortable with the awkwardness than with the attempt to make casual conversation so she added, "I'm getting a little swamped between studying for finals and all my work at Brighton, but I'm managing." Then she threw in a little zinger to remind David why making casual conversation was so difficult at the moment. "How's *your* paper coming along?"

David tried not to flinch at Merit's reference to the term paper he'd used as an excuse for not calling. "Good . . . really good . . . yep . . . done, in fact."

"I bet," she answered as she headed for the house to drop off her books.

What's that supposed to mean? he thought to himself, wondering if he had just been rebuked, but he quickly chastened himself before he took a simple comment and created another quarrelsome topic. They drove the short hop to Brighton in relative silence. David was beginning to wonder why he had ever offered to come. He parked the car a short distance away from the entrance to give them a few minutes to talk.

"Merit, are you ever going to speak to me again?"

"I've been speaking to you," she said defensively.

"You know what I mean," he replied. "Is it ever going to be . . . comfortable between us? I'm really sorry I hurt you, and I've tried to apologize and explain myself, but if I have caused you unforgivable hurt, and you really don't think we can ever be close again, then what's the point of any of this? You don't need to humor me or entertain me. I mean, I've only got a few weeks left. I'd rather end it now and save us each any more pain than to prolong the inevitable."

Merit looked at him, utterly shocked that he could even suggest such a thing.

"Could you just walk away from this . . . from us, so easily, without trying to set things right?" she asked, her lip quivering.

"I don't want to. Ever since the morning I met you at the tree lot, I wake up excited to see you and just be with you. It's wonderful. I've never known how much fun it could be just to be with someone, not doing anything in particular, just . . . you know, talking and hanging out. But lately, I wake up miserable. I go to bed miserable. I can't study and I have to pretend to be happy for my grandparents' sake. I just can't go on like this anymore."

He gripped the steering wheel firmly and looked straight ahead through the windshield. Feeling the silence beside him, he finally looked over at Merit. She too was staring blankly out through the windshield and her expression was again filled with surprise. "I thought only I was feeling that way, kind of melancholy," she said sadly. "Nothing is as wonderful as it was, not even Brighton. I don't even want to play my music anymore."

Hearing those words pierced David's heart. He considered how the breakdown of this relationship was like a scalpel, cutting away the joy and leaving scars behind. He laid his arms across the top of the steering wheel and rested his heavy, confused head on them, moving the wheel from side to side. Merit could hear him murmuring something softly under his breath.

"What?" she asked.

"It's just so stupid," he replied.

"What is so stupid?" she inquired again.

He lifted his head to look at her. "I am miserable without you and you're miserable without me, and yet we can't find a way to get back to where we were. It's just so stupid." A few seconds went by with both of them looking crushed and then he asked her, "Do you even want to get back to where we were?"

"See, you think it's stupid. I'd call it sad." Her expression matched her words. She had a faraway look on her sad face as if saying good-bye to something irretrievable. "It was so wonderful when our relationship was growing and we were just discovering things about each other, but now it's like it's dying. Being apart makes me sad but so does being with you. The clock is winding down, David. All this time I had hopes that we could write to each other while you're away and I could ask you questions and you could teach me about your faith. Then I could grow along with you and see if what we were building could continue, but now I just feel like you're about to enter a world that I'll never understand, and even worse, where I'll be unwelcome. So in answer to your question, yes, I wish every minute that we could get back to where we were, but I really don't think that's possible."

She didn't cry. She didn't turn away. Instead, David felt sure she had just defined all her fears and offered him a door. Now it was up to him to walk through it and push those fears away.

"Merit, there's nothing more important to me right now than to have your support on my mission." He paused and she held her breath. "That's not true. I don't just want it. I need it. And do you know why? Because while I talk about love and try to understand love and forgiveness, I've discovered that you already know more about it than I do."

He broke his gaze with her and turned his head away, embarrassed by his honesty. "I've always appreciated your sweetness and kindness, but yesterday, watching you with Brian made me do some serious thinking." He returned his gaze to her again and it intensified when he saw how her hope was hanging on his words.

"At first I was just flat out jealous when he called you 'baby' and flirted with you, and . . . I have to admit, I was getting a little nutty when you were so kind to him after all the trouble he's caused you. But when I got home, I thought and thought about everything that had been said and about how you treated him, and two thoughts occurred to me. First, when I thought about the concern you showed for him, it was one of the most generous things I have ever seen. You could have simply brushed him off or coldly told him to get out of your sight. Most people would have thought you were justified, but you didn't. Your reaction was completely selfless. You harbored no animosity. You just showed concern for him. I'm not sure I could have been so generous. Actually, I'm pretty sure I wouldn't have since I've been writing him off as a waste of my time for the last couple of years already.

"The other thing that amazed me, Merit, was the way he responded to your kindness. You gave him hope. All it took was a little of your time and genuine caring, and he was willing to try to change, to see his possibilities. I would feel it a privilege, and I would count my mission a complete success, if I could look into one person's face and know I had made that kind of difference in one life." He reached for her hands, cautiously at first, unsure if she would pull away, but she didn't. "So you see, Merit, you're welcome to share my mission with me. In fact, I need you. I've spent so many hours praying for the Lord to bless me with the gifts you already possess. You say you want me to teach you? Well, there are so many things I would love to teach you, about where we came from and why we're here and where we're going. I know these things, Merit. I have a testimony of these things. But I need you to teach me too, about love and mercy and forgiveness. You can teach me these things by your example. Please forgive me for hurting you and teach me to love that way. Will you?"

Merit closed her eyes against the moistness welling there and smiled. She didn't say a word but her head nodded slightly, and although it was almost imperceptible, David squeezed her hands in acknowledgement and drew her close to him. As he released her he blushed and knew they would soon have to get Cassidy or Merit would be late for her appointment with Jeff. Still, he didn't want to lose the opportunity to build on this moment. "Merit, no matter what happens or doesn't happen with us there are a few things I want you to know, okay?"

She tensed, but the gentleness of his eyes erased her concerns and she faced him, confident that he wouldn't hurt her again.

"Our kiss . . . It was the most wonderful and the most terrible moment of my life. I wanted to kiss you. I have for a long time. I've never cared about anyone so deeply or fallen so fast, but that's why it was also so terrible. For the first time in my life, my head and my heart wanted two different things and it really scared me. I don't want my last few weeks here to be a choice between you and my mission." He looked at her to try to read her response. "Do you understand what I'm saying?" he added softly.

She didn't answer immediately, but when she did her voice was soft but strong, and tinged with regret. "I do, David," she replied. "I wish you had told me these things last week instead of avoiding me. I spent every day replaying that night to understand what I had done, or what I had said that made you look at me so haunted and scared."

"It wasn't you," he assured. "Do you understand that now?"

She considered it carefully and then answered, "Yes."

He let out a big sigh of relief and she relaxed. It was better now. The comfort of before was still not completely restored, but it was better, much better.

The clock on the dashboard read 3:03 and David knew they had to leave very quickly or Merit would be late. Merit asked for a few moments to touch up her puffy eyes, so David offered to get Cassidy while she reapplied her makeup. He ran a finger adoringly from her forehead to the tip of her nose and told her he was sorry for making her eyes puffy. She met his gaze and smiled shyly, then playfully pushed him out of the car. As he headed toward the house he paused and looked back over his shoulder. His lips mouthed the question, "Really better?" Merit smiled genuinely and nodded yes. David smiled his pleasure back at her and his step was lighter yet as he headed into the house.

He had become such a regular fixture at Brighton that he now felt comfortable just walking in, unannounced. The house was quiet and he wondered where the children were, but then he remembered that Fridays at three was their art class and the children would be upstairs with the art teacher from the local elementary school.

David assumed Cassidy was in her office. As he approached the door he noticed that it was ajar and heard voices coming from the room long before he was there. He recognized them as Cassidy's and Jeff's and soon discovered that Jeff was speaking over Cassidy's speakerphone while she, too, was busy touching up her makeup.

"Soon, Cassidy, soon. I promise." Jeff said through the speaker.

"I'm not kidding, Jeff. I can't be caught in the middle of this. We're past the point of keeping this a secret . . ." David smiled thinking he had walked in on a discussion of their no-longer-secret romance. He was about to knock on the door when a change in Cassidy's tone of voice made him halt and listen.

"I didn't want to tell you this before, but that morning at the breakfast . . . she recognized you."

"What?" came the surprised reply.

"I'm pretty sure she recognized you."

"She" recognized you? She? Who was "she"? David wondered.

Jeff's voice sounded alarmed. "You told me you handled it . . . that everything was okay."

"I was afraid of what you'd do," she replied. "I didn't want you to leave again."

"How, how did she respond? What did she say?" Jeff asked nervously.

"She said you looked familiar and tried to accept my explanation. But even if she didn't, it's only a matter of time before David puts the pieces together. We're running out of time, Jeff."

David? Me, David? he wondered curiously. *What are they talking about?*

"My 3:00 P.M. is here," Jeff responded nervously. "We'll talk about this later."

His voice sounded final and Cassidy took the hint and ended the conversation. David's head was reeling with questions. *Who had recognized Jeff unexpectedly and what "pieces" was Cassidy sure this David would put together? Am I the David they were discussing?*

Rapid footsteps hurried to the doorway and David stepped back nervously. The door opened abruptly and Cassidy nearly ran him down. "David!" she said sucking in a startled breath. "You nearly scared me to death. What are you doing here?"

She seemed flabbergasted to see him, and he tried to direct her attention away from the fact that he had been standing outside her doorway. "Uh, didn't Merit tell you? I'm your designated driver today."

"No," she countered, seemingly confused and distracted.

It wasn't until they were all three in the lobby of Jeff's building that Cassidy was hit by a sudden concern that she should warn Jeff that David was with them.

"David, this is going to just be a short, routine meeting. Why don't you just wait here and we'll call you when the business part is over." Cassidy hoped he would buy it.

"No problem," he responded, not completely sure how proper it would be for him to sit in on the meeting in the first place.

Cassidy excused herself under the pretense of buying a pack of gum. As she fumbled in her purse for her cell phone, Merit took matters into her own hands. "Jeff won't mind, David. Come on up with me." She grabbed his hand and headed for the open elevator, pushing the button for Jeff's floor. "I want you to see Jeff's office. He keeps a decorated Christmas tree in there all year long."

Cassidy blurted out a terse warning to Jeff as she saw the elevator door close. Before Jeff could do anything about it, his door opened and his secretary let Merit and David in.

"Hi, Jeff," Merit said with delight, then pointing to David said, "I brought you a surprise."

Jeff stood frozen in his spot waiting to see if the few personal articles he had allowed himself would betray his secret. David extended his hand but immediately sensed the tension in the room and allowed it to drop back down by his side. He met Jeff's gaze with confusion and then his eyes were drawn past Jeff's face to the photograph on the wall behind him—a vaguely familiar aerial photo of a farm. A haunted look came over Jeff but David kept staring until the photograph captivated him. His eyes shifted back between the photo and Jeff's face, which was as riveted on David as David was captivated by the picture. Merit became quiet and confused by the strange moment occurring between the two men.

"Do you mind if I look more closely at it?" David asked Jeff as he took liberties and approached the photograph.

"It's just an old farm," Jeff responded nervously.

"Pap has a few of these," David muttered as his finger searched the corner of the photo for the name of the photographer. It was the same name that was embossed on his grandfather's photos. The date was 1990, the date on the first in Pap's collection. "He's had one taken every year since the photographer first approached him in 1990." He stared carefully at the photo and then added, "He uses them to chronicle the changes he makes on the place."

He knew this property. The farm's external appearance looked a little different now, owing to additions and renovations, but there was no doubt. This was his grandparents' place. But why did Jeff have this photo?

Cassidy came bursting through the door. When she saw where David's attention was riveted she gasped, confirming David's suspicion. He came back around to look at Jeff. The look of fear on Jeff's face was now replaced by resignation.

David began to scan the room for other surprises that might catch his attention. His eyes fell on the fully decorated Christmas tree, stopping momentarily at each beautiful ornament until he noticed the pot. The bright, happy, blue-and-gold pot was almost an exact duplicate of his whatnot pot back in California. He walked over to it and knelt down. He ran his fingers over the artist's initials, the letters "PW." *Peter Wallace? But how could that be?*

He knelt there for what seemed like minutes putting the pieces together. Then he remembered Cassidy's odd phone call. *Are these the pieces?* David wondered.

Merit's eyes went from Jeff's face, to Cassidy's, to David's. She was lost in this obviously private scene and felt uncomfortable. David stood up and walked right past her as if she were invisible. He stood directly in front of Jeff, cocked his head askew, and wrinkled his brow as he racked his mind to examine Jeff's face and his expression. There was something in this man's countenance that he had never seen before. He looked down at the nameplate that sat unceremoniously on the desk as he tried to order his thoughts. *Pap's farm, the pot . . . What's going on here?*

He looked at Jeff's face again and back at the nameplate. The similarity between Jeff's name and his own family name struck him. Similar name, same photo, same potter. His mind inserted an "a" into Jeff's name and the pieces finally came together! The light of recognition illuminated his face and his mouth went agape. Jeff seemed alarmed by his initial reaction, but as the seconds passed and acceptance smoothed David's furrowed brow, Jeff's expression radiated confirmation. *This is not Jeffery Johnson,* David thought, *this is Thomas Jefferson Johanson!*

In spite of the overwhelming shock he felt, a knowing smile crept across his face and suddenly, this kind man who had played so tenderly with the children, who had helped Merit reclaim her life, and who had captured Cassidy Prescott's heart was now very personal to him. The uncle extended his hand timidly to David, who returned the offer, then shook his head as if to knock the pieces of the puzzle into final perfect order. He tightened his grip on Jeff's hand and drew him close. His arms went around the broad shoulders of his uncle in a joyous embrace. Jeff reacted cautiously at first, still unsure how to respond, but soon the pleasure of having family so close filled the emptiness of two lonely decades, and his own embrace tightened.

Merit stood smiling in confusion at the pure joy she saw exhibited, but was still unclear as to exactly what was transpiring. Cassidy put her arm around her and led her from the room. She wondered how she would satisfy the questions Merit would hunger to have answered without violating the new pact these two men were entering. She simply trusted in the relationship she had built with the sensitive young girl and said, "I think it's David's place to explain it to you, okay?" Merit nodded and the two women sat in the outer office, giving the men time and privacy to sort out their feelings and decide where to go from there.

It took several minutes for Jeff to stop shaking enough to utter more than repeated comments about how many times he had envisioned the moment they would actually meet as uncle and nephew. He expressed his fears about "coming home," and David enthusiastically tried to put his concerns to rest. And then the questions began.

Jeff explained how the series of seemingly random events had brought him back to Smithsburg, leading him to Merit, to Cassidy, and to David. David shook his head in wonder, preferring to see it as Pap would see it—that God had had a hand in it—and then he nearly whooped with joy as he considered how Pap and Omma would respond when they heard the news.

That comment brought a complete change of expression to Jeff's face, and David seemed to understand that if Jeff had spent countless hours with him and had not yet revealed his secret to him, then he would need the privilege of revealing it to Pap and Omma in his own time. He promised not to say a word, bringing Jeff visible relief. Then David envisioned another wondrous reunion, the one between TJ and Martha.

"I wish I could tell Mom," David groaned. "She's always talked about you as if you were on vacation or something. She never gave up hope. Neither did Pap and Omma. I can tell by the way they say your name." Then David worried Jeff would misinterpret his remark. "Your name was . . . well, it's practically sacred to them. When I grew up I had this obsession about wanting to look like a traditional Johanson, so when I was about fourteen I told Omma that I really thought I was beginning to look like you, and she spent the next couple of hours poring over your picture to see if I made the grade. You'll see. You'll probably bump me right off my pedestal," he laughed, helping Jeff to finally relax. It was a brief moment of peace.

"Jeff, can you tell me anything about my father? Do you still keep in touch?"

Jeff knew it was going to come up—how could it not? But he had hoped he'd have more time for David to get to know him, to like him, and to trust him before he had to tell him the horrifying truth about what happened to his father. He considered sidestepping the question somehow, but he was trying to rid himself of secrets, not create new ones with new people, so he sat back on the edge of his desk and began to tell David about the summer of 1976.

"How much do you already know, David?"

"Mom told me that she fell in love with Peter Wallace that fall, and that he was some sort of an artist. Anyway, eventually Pap found out about some letter she wrote to him and there was a big fight, and that day was the last time the family ever saw either of you."

"That's the long and the short of it, David." Jeff took a long, labored breath. "Your father and I headed straight back to the ocean. We argued the whole way down the road about your mom. I wanted to kill him for the first hour of the ride because I knew for sure what had happened between them, but by the time we arrived at Ocean City we just felt it best to part company. We saw each other from time to time, and to be honest with you, David, your dad was just such a lost soul that I couldn't hate him. I mean I was still furious that at eighteen he hadn't had better judgment than to sleep with an innocent sixteen-year-old farm kid, but he had never known a real home and I think he saw something . . . I don't know . . . comforting and safe in the farm and in your mom's sweetness, and I do believe he loved her in some way. I also think your mom saw a wounded person and her compassion overruled her judgment."

David's eyes were glossy. "She said he sang to her."

"He did, David. Your father was a fine musician. If someone had taken the tiniest bit of interest in him he could have been a wonderful man."

"So what happened to him? You keep speaking of him in the past tense."

Jeff swallowed hard. He could barely look into David's shining eyes. He saw so much of Peter there that speaking of him was unbearable.

"I got a job at a dive restaurant as a food preparer and the owner offered me a 'promotion.'" He spat out the words. "He ran a gambling racket in the back room and he offered to pay me a week's salary as a bonus for carrying the night's take from the restaurant to a hotel room on the other side of town. The only hitch was I had to take another guy along. They told me that two guys were less likely to get robbed than one. I knew Peter was broke so I took him."

David's brow furrowed and Jeff knew he was running scenarios around in his head. "Did something bad happen? Did you guys get held up?"

"Worse, David. Much worse . . ."

Jeff explained about the set-up, the bust, and the beatings he and Peter took at the hands of their employers. He rubbed his hand across his beard.

"I was terrified, but my fears were nowhere near Peter's. I don't know what had happened to him in his childhood, but the thought of being locked away broke him. He completely fell apart. I didn't know what to do. I knew it was my fault, but I didn't see any way out. I considered calling your grandfather, but I was so proud I stalled on making that call."

Jeff paused, letting the implication of the ending sink in, hoping to soften the blow. "I stopped by the lot where Peter was living in his van and I found him passed out. He had overdosed on heroin. I called for help, but by the time the paramedics arrived, he was gone. Your father died in my arms, David. In truth, I'm responsible for his death."

The words hit David harder than he would have suspected. *So that's it . . . My father's dead and now I'll never know him.* His head dropped as he let that final truth sink in. After a few quiet moments he raised his head and asked, "Did he ever know about . . . about Mom and me?"

Jeff coughed to clear his own voice. "No, David, he never did. I never even knew about you until a few years ago myself. But Peter passed away three months before you were even born." Jeff looked up and saw that the news had not been the answer David had hoped for, so he added, "I think he would have been so excited if he could have known about you. I really do."

The room was silent and a difficult pall settled over the previously happy reunion. Jeff wondered if his return to his family was now sealed against him. No one knew what to say or do to break the moment, but David felt that it was his place to extend the olive branch.

"So why do you keep the pot? It must be painful to see it every day."

"It is," Jeff replied, rubbing his fingers over his stinging eyes. "I guess I keep it for two reasons. I try to remember how Peter might have turned out if someone would have loved him enough to have given him a chance, and, well, the pot reminds me of the tragedies that can happen when even good kids from good families get too far out on a limb."

* * *

Thirty minutes later the two emerged from Jeff's office, a little worn out but smiling. Jeff noticed that Merit was on the outside of the story and he walked over to her and put his hands on her shoulders, explaining, "Well, I guess this was a pretty confusing meeting for you today, Merit, but it was a very positive one for me. I'll let David bring you up to speed on all of this." He next walked over to Cassidy and clutched her to him, pressing his face against hers.

David walked back to Jeff and the men stood facing one another. David again reached out and took his uncle's hand. "Christmas Eve. That's it, and then I'm coming for you myself."

"That soon? Are you sure?" Jeff asked cautiously.

David nodded and gripped his hand more firmly.

"Alright then." Jeff smiled gratefully. "Cassidy and I will get in touch."

There was a last, gentle handshake, a quick embrace, and then David released Jeff and walked over to Merit. She touched the glisten of moisture that hung on his long, black lashes and spoke. "From the looks of your eyes, it must've been pretty intense in there."

"Do I look scary?" he asked sweetly.

"No. Nice, actually. You're vulnerable like the rest of us," she teased.

"You have no idea," he said thoughtfully.

"I'm trying to," she replied. He looked at his uncle and held the gaze for a long time. With one arm firmly around Merit he took the other and raised it over his shoulder to point in Jeff's direction. "I have your promise," he reminded more seriously.

"I won't forget," Jeff replied. Then he motioned Merit in for her appointment.

A few minutes later David and Merit headed toward home, leaving Cassidy to help Jeff sort things out. Merit looked at the completely mesmerized expression on David's face and punched him playfully in the stomach. "Okay," she teased. "Time to spill your guts. What went on in there?"

Contentment tinged with sadness colored David's face. "Merit, Jeff knew my dad. He told me that my father passed away before I was even born. He was one of his best friends and was with him when he died. Actually, he knows my whole family."

Merit's hand went to her mouth. "Oh, David. That must've been so hard to hear. How are you doing?"

"Hmmm," he replied thoughtfully. "I'm not sure yet."

"Well, at least you have some answers now. That's wonderful! But why didn't Jeff say something before?" she questioned.

"I guess he was just waiting for the right moment."

"But . . ." Merit tried to pursue the inquiries, but David put his finger to her lips and shushed her.

"I need to sort it out myself first, okay?" he asked softly.

She laid her head on his shoulder. "I'm just sad and yet very happy for you, David, all at once."

"Me too, Merit. More than you could possibly know."

Chapter Twenty-Two

Natalie climbed out of bed early on Saturday, just about a second behind Benjamin. He seemed to be his old self again, energetic and strong, and she was delighted to see his old spark had returned. This week had been exceptionally busy for their business, and now they had holiday preparations for their own family to attend to. On Monday they would make a late-night run to the airport to pick up Sam and Martha so the family could all attend the children's Christmas program at Brighton the following evening. The next day would be Christmas Eve and the Nativity pageant.

She pulled a piece of paper out of the cubby and began to plan her own holiday menus. Christmas Eve was always easy—deli trays and a few family favorite side dishes. For dessert she would bake pies and cakes and maybe a baklava, rounding out the dozens of cookies that already filled every tin she owned. But Christmas Day was another story completely. All her best china and silver would be set and the meal would be an intimate family supper. But for how many this year? She smiled in secret anticipation of what her Christmas dream and intuition promised to make come true, and planned her menu based on the traditional dishes TJ would remember.

David came bounding down the stairs whistling again as he had done when he came home the night before. It was the first morning he had awakened happy in many days, and she smiled lovingly at him and commented, "So, I take it things are better between you and Merit?"

David placed a loud, exaggerated kiss on her cheek and raised his eyebrows mischievously. "Yes, Omma, once again your dashing grandson is 'The Man.'"

"I never doubted it." She smiled again, placing an approving hand on his handsome chin.

"Where's Pap?" he asked mysteriously.

"He's moving the herd down to the lower pasture to get this one rolled and ready for parking for the Nativity," she answered with interest. "Why?"

David responded with odd pleasure. "I had a very wonderful day yesterday, Omma."

"I can tell. You're only *that* happy when you and Merit are getting along."

"Yeah," he replied. "We had a great afternoon. I took her to an appointment in Frederick to meet with her counselor." He slowed down and tread gingerly, weighing her response to determine how to proceed. "His name is Jeff Johnson, and he's dating Cassidy Prescott."

Natalie slowly turned around and met David's eyes. His vocal inflections were sending her the same double message Cassidy had sent her back at Brighton that morning.

"He is wonderful, Omma. His life has been difficult but he's in a good place now. He's well respected, and I think he and Cassidy are really in love. I'd like to bring him here Christmas Eve, but he's pretty nervous about meeting . . . everyone, especially Pap," he finished cautiously.

Natalie's eyes sparkled brightly and then closed as if in prayer. Her hands smacked together lightly in a joyful clasp that quickly released and then went to David's face like a frame.

"You tell this Jeff Johnson that he is, has always been, and will forever be welcome at this table. You tell him nothing in this world could bring Benjamin or me more happiness than to open that door and see him standing there. Tell him I know that for a fact, will you, David?" She drew him into her arms and held him close. David knew she understood and he would make Jeff understand it too, this very afternoon when he saw him again.

Ben stomped in through the door, blowing steam from the cold and shivering in the way that Natalie loved. He complained about the cold and yet thrived in it as well. She helped him off with his coat, rubbed his arms with her warm hands to get the circulation going, and then wrapped her arms around him and gave him a kiss. This kiss was more than the run-of-the-mill "hello" kiss, and it drew Ben's attention and a quizzical look.

"I'm just in a very good mood, Ben," she offered by way of explanation.

"David," teased Ben, "check the jug. I think the cider's gone hard!" Natalie protested, and as she handed him a cup of the comically suspicious cider, he gave her a wink and a teasing smile.

David slipped out of the house, anxious to get his daily responsibilities out of the way early so he could get to Brighton. He shivered with happiness. This was going to be a great day! He could now tell Jeff with confidence that he would be warmly received on Christmas Eve, plus, this afternoon Merit was going to give him another piano lesson. Although things were better, he still knew that the pressure they were living under was creating a strange dimension to their time together. It was as if every minute of the present was separate from the next, like a set of photographs in a scrapbook, instantly set aside like memories. He decided if that was how their time was going to be, he wanted one last, great, amazing evening he could share with Merit, a memory she could cherish during their separation and one that would be unforgettable.

He knew time was drawing short to plan and execute such an event. Tomorrow was the eighteenth, exactly one week before Christmas, and what a crazy time it would be. Once his parents returned and TJ was reintroduced to the family, he and Merit would have a hard time finding time alone together. After Christmas he was doubtful things would be any less scheduled since his departure date would be drawing close and family time would be at a premium . . . and as for finances . . . He had committed his savings to his mission and had only the small earnings from working with Pap to buy Christmas presents, as well as to fund this amazing evening. But what would he do?

He stumbled through his work, his mind only half on his tasks, and then showered, changed, and headed for Brighton. As he drove up he was surprised to see that Jeff's and Carol Davenport's cars were there. He could see Merit through the large glass windows of the great room. She had the children lined up in performing stance, but as soon as David opened the door, twelve screaming fans immediately broke ranks and attacked him, delighted that his arrival had secured their temporary freedom.

"Fifteen minutes, guys, okay?" Merit yelled as they then made a hasty retreat to the kitchen for cookies. "Hi you," she said to David, whose arms opened to receive her welcoming hug. "You're late," she teased.

"I'm still sort of in a fog. I see that your mom and Jeff are here. Where is everybody?"

"In Cassidy's office. Mom stopped by to apply to be a volunteer, but listen to this . . ."

Merit caught David looking at her, measuring her response to the news about her mom. "I'm fine with it . . . really," she assured him as the door opened and Carol Davenport's happy face emerged. "Hi, David," she said. "We thought you heard about the rehearsal and you chickened out," she teased.

"Why would I chicken out?" he replied. "I'm the audience. I have my part down cold."

Carol looked at Merit who shot her mother a rapid "hush" look that David caught and investigated. "What's going on here, ladies? I am just an audience member, remember?"

"David, I woke up this morning with a great idea to put the songs in order, like a cantata, and add some narration. It will be great! I just need a narrator," Merit hinted. David began a weak protest but Merit raised an eyebrow at him and said, "And you owe me . . ."

"In that case," he surrendered, "I'd be honored."

Carol laughed, enjoying the pleasure this match seemed to bring them both.

"Miss Carol," Simon called as he ran to Carol with hands filled with treats. "I made you sumfin." He handed her a slightly deformed sugar-cookie star blanketed in blue sugar. Carol had been watching her diet, but she couldn't refuse this love offering.

"Simon, did you decorate this cookie just for me?" she asked as she scooped him up.

"Uh-huh," he replied, nodding solemnly. "Eat it," he begged. "I put extra stuff on it."

"I can see that," she replied, squelching a giggle. Merit and David turned to walk away so they wouldn't betray Simon's vision of the perfect cookie. As they exited they heard Carol negotiate a compromise. He agreed to let her save the perfect cookie to eat later if she would agree to help decorate more of the masterpieces, and off the pair went, hand in hand.

"They really have become attached, haven't they?" David observed.

"Yeah. It's amazing, but I worry about her getting hurt. Cassidy told me he's not adoptable because he still has a father somewhere in Chicago. If he ever comes to take Simon away I'm afraid it will be like losing Markie all over again, and that will be another terrible separation for our family to get through."

Her reference to separation reminded David of their own upcoming separation and it stung his heart. He didn't want this wonderful afternoon touched by anything but happiness, so he quickly changed the subject. "What're Jeff and Cassidy up to?" he asked.

"That's what I was trying to tell you," she whispered. "Jeff came here early this morning and drove Cassidy up to High Rock to watch the sunrise. They've been laughing and giggling ever since. They must still be in Cassidy's office."

David knocked on the door and Jeff opened it and greeted him with a warm hug.

"David! Merit! Come in. We have wonderful news."

Cassidy stood in front of her desk, beaming as they walked in. Jeff stood behind and wrapped his arms around her. She leaned into him and raised her hand to caress his cheek. There, on her left hand was a sparkling diamond ring.

"You're engaged!" Merit squealed. "When? Where? At High Rock?"

The two stole a long, intimate look as their smile confirmed Merit's guess. "Yes," cooed Cassidy. "Jeff planned the most romantic proposal. He called me late last night and told me to be ready at 4:00 A.M. because he had a surprise for me. He picked me up and we drove to the end of the paved road and then we hiked up to the top. There, at the edge of the cliff he had a blanket laid out with a vase and flowers and a basket filled with croissants and fruit and a thermos of hot chocolate. He was up all night preparing everything. Well, we sat there and ate and talked and watched the sun come up over the valley, and then he asked me to marry him."

Merit's face was almost as radiant over hearing the tale as Cassidy's was from retelling it, and her enthusiasm was not lost on David. She walked over to examine the beautiful ring and gushed and squealed. "Oh, it sounds like a scene from a movie. I'm so happy for you."

Cassidy closed her eyes and snuggled against Jeff. Merit and David envied their happiness. After a few seconds of Merit smiling and David fidgeting, he cleared his throat and broke the silence. "Well," said David awkwardly, "I guess we'll leave you two alone."

Jeff and Cassidy laughed. "We're sorry. Did you two need something?" Jeff asked.

"Don't worry about it," David said laughing. "I was going to invite you out for a little guy time, but it would appear you have a better offer. I'll give you a rain check though."

Jeff smiled appreciatively, then David and Merit backed out of the room and closed the door. As soon as they were down the hall they erupted into giggles and whispers that drew Mrs. Sherman out from the kitchen.

"Merit, we're going to need a little more time in here on these cookies, so you may want to postpone the second practice with the children."

"It's okay, Mrs. Sherman. I'll just give David his piano lesson now and I'll work with the children when you're finished."

"Well, it'll be at least an hour then. The children aren't content with just decorating the cookies. Each one must be a masterpiece equal to the treasure Simon created for your mom." She feigned frustration, but there was a smile lurking there too. Mrs. Sherman, sometimes gruff and rigid, loved anything the children loved, so their added enthusiasm was like heaven for her.

"By the way," she added ominously, "have you heard the weather report? The radio just put out their forecast and they're saying the light snowfall they were predicting may turn out to be a big ice storm instead. It's predicted to hit our area by Sunday. You might want to have a backup plan for the concert." She turned and headed back to referee the bakers laboring in the kitchen.

"It wouldn't dare storm and ruin this concert," Merit moaned.

"The weather is so unpredictable in this valley, Merit, don't worry yet," David soothed.

"You don't understand, David. I have completely rearranged my entire life for this concert. I've been here every day after school and some nights until late. My schoolwork has suffered, I've had to sacrifice sleep to get my assignments done. Not to mention that all the time I've spent getting ready for this event will be wasted and would have been time we could have spent together. We have to have this concert."

Realizing that there was no point in arguing about something that might or might not happen, and over which they had absolutely no control, David surrendered his position and took his seat on the piano bench, ready for his lesson. Merit sat somberly beside him, but as always, as soon as their hands touched the keys, something magical happened between them that blotted out any prior disappointment. David stumbled happily through one of the hymns she had taught him from the old hymnal her piano teacher had used in her early lessons. It had been less than a week ago that David thumbed through the old book sitting on Merit's piano and began singing a few of the hymns. Merit had been astonished that he knew any of the old songs that had been the foundation of her own religious upbringing. They counted seventeen hymns that were common to both, and this common ground had been a blessing. First, it had proven to them that they agreed on more doctrinal points than they differed. More importantly, David used the themes of the music to bear his testimony of the Savior and to answer many of Merit's questions. It had been a treasured opportunity and a simple answer to his many prayers regarding the girl who had stolen his heart.

Next they played a simple little duet where their hands crossed back and forth over one another's, brushing softly. His heart melted. It was thanks to Merit, who had brought out the gift of music that David never before knew lay hidden within him, that they could share religion. He was now committed to do everything in his power to give her a special gift in return, but it was already the twentieth, which meant their time was running out, and the rest of the coming week would be filled with rehearsals.

He remembered the look on Merit's face when she heard about Cassidy and Jeff's sunrise at High Rock. He wanted more than anything to give her a moment, one wonderful, unforgettable moment that she could treasure while he was away. She would appreciate his help with the concert, his desire to share this experience with her, but he wanted to make her face illuminate the way it did just hearing about Cassidy's proposal. He would think of something, and he'd give her an incredible moment and a memory to last her for the next two years . . . or more.

Chapter Twenty-Three

Saturday was chaotic. Word of the approaching storm sent the usual Christmas Eve shoppers out earlier than normal. In addition to the last-minute rush of bakers and cooks at the local grocers, worried parents, fearing that "Santa" would be unable to make it out to find the wrapping paper and toys, also cleared the toy shelves. The mood was happy if not a little crazed, and Natalie joined right in with the rest of the merry mob, dropping her bags on the kitchen table to display her loot.

She cranked up the radio station dedicated to playing only Christmas carols during the holidays and set about to transform her purchased treasures into treats. Ben noticed Natalie's exceptional giddiness, and what he thought was nervousness, and wondered what was getting her all fired up. He guessed there were many reasons. It was going to be their last Christmas with David for two long years, and their first Christmas with their new son-in-law, Sam, and then there was an approaching storm. Natalie had always loved them and the way they made everyone hunker down with family and feel like baking cookies and playing board games, but she had a new respect for them since Ben's accident, and he assumed that perhaps all these events together had her wound tightly.

Ben was once fearless about the weather, but since his brush with death during the last ice storm, he also had a new respect for the danger of such weather. He prepared for the Nativity program but he worried that it would have to be canceled this year. By Sunday the sky was already strangely colored. The temperature was dropping and the wind began to barrel down from the mountains. Valley weather generally followed one of two scenarios. Either the storms vented their fury on the west side of the mountains leaving just traces of precipitation for the low-lying towns, or they crossed the mountains with their moisture-laden clouds intact and then hovered over the Piedmont, for hours or even days, burying the low areas. Ben prepared for the worst.

David was torn between trying to help Ben and Merit both. Merit had copied scriptural passages from Luke and interwoven them with familiar carols, creating a smooth, cohesive story, but even she could see that it lacked passion and intimacy. When David made some suggestions, she was so thrilled by his interest in the project that she handed the narration over to him with her blessing. He wasn't worried about the assignment. He had plenty of new thoughts and feelings about the birth of the Savior that he was honored to share. When he was finished, the script reflected the carefully documented events Merit had written, personalized by his own understanding of their meaning. His problem was time—time to help Merit, time to help Pap and Omma . . . and time was running out.

Knowing that only he knew the real reason for Omma's jittery joy, he tried to spend moments with her, never really saying much, but sharing her excitement in knowing glances and smiles. Ben thought they were both going daft, but took comfort that her hectic activity kept her from worrying about him.

Sunday evening the dreaded phone call came in. The airports were preparing to cancel all flights and close down the runways if the latest weather predictions came true. Martha and Sam's flight was currently delayed, but the family was told to keep checking the airline's website for arrival and departure information. Amazingly, Natalie's mood was not dampened by the news. *As long as they're here by Christmas Eve,* she mused.

David called Merit to see how she was handling the weather reports. Her voice sounded defeated. She had given so much. They had sacrificed so much, and now all their precious, irretrievable time could end up having been spent preparing for a canceled event.

Now more than ever he needed an idea. He couldn't let their remaining time together fizzle into a string of disappointments. He racked his brain trying to think of something grand that would brighten her voice and give her a memory that would always cause her to smile while they were apart. He had two ideas that offered possibilities but still lacked the pizzazz factor he sought. One idea was to take Merit to Veterans' Park and carve their names into the boughs of the famous old evergreen. It was a good start, but it still needed something more original. The other idea borrowed too heavily from Jeff's romantic proposal plan but was worth considering. The old barn loft had one door that faced the point in the sky where the winter moon shone. David considered setting up a romantic little moonlit dinner perched up there. It could be nice, but he wasn't sure that romantic was exactly the mood he was trying to achieve. Magical was more like it. A magical moment of their own that could never be duplicated. In frustration he pushed both ideas aside for a while and flipped the news on to catch the weather updates.

He looked out the door from time to time to see if the anticipated snowfall had begun, but although the air smelled like the coming of snow, and the stars were masked behind the heavy cloud-filled night sky, the ground was still dry. Ben turned in about nine and Natalie turned in soon after her last batch of pumpkin bread was cooled and wrapped. David couldn't sleep. His mind was like a highway with dozens of thoughts running around, cutting each other off and generally getting jammed up in one another's way. And then it began. The sleet began as a light scratching on the glass. The sound of the sleet and ice against the windows was a familiar one he had heard many times before, but this was quickly changing, becoming a pounding, powerful battery of ice and rain. He opened the kitchen door and within minutes the walkway was coated and treacherous, and the yews were becoming green, crystalline balls.

Pap did a good job of preparing for this, David thought. The animals were all snugly secured in the barn and the doors were locked tightly. Plenty of fresh hay and straw had been hauled up from the lower barn, and the watering troughs were filled to the brim. All was ready. There would be no more repeats of the dreaded night when Pap tried to rescue the stranded steer.

Omma had also been busy. All the bathtubs were filled with water for washing and flushing in anticipation of the electricity failing, leaving the well pump powerless. She had filled jugs with water for drinking and topped off the kerosene lamps and heaters. In the event the power should be out for an extended period of time, there was the old generator, which could power the family's needs but which was loud and smelly and required frequent refilling. Fresh batteries had been placed in the flashlights, and then there was the food!

Realizing that no power meant that cooking would become limited, Omma had a roast cooked and sliced, and loaves of fresh homemade bread were bagged for sandwiches. A large pot of chicken noodle soup was in the fridge at the ready, and the old Coleman camping stove was hauled up from the basement to warm it up. David smiled affectionately at his grandparents. They could face the same difficulties that would cause others to panic, and in their well-orchestrated and loving hands, an adventure was created. David loved life here on the farm because it was life with Omma and Pap.

He flipped on the TV to catch the latest update on the local forecast. The weather was the big news story on every station. The temperature in the upper atmosphere was the critical factor. If it warmed a few degrees the area would be pelted by ice and sleet, and if it became colder the precipitation would turn to snow. They drew a line across the map indicating how they felt the temperatures and snow lines would fall and there in the Piedmont Valley, it was up for grabs. He pulled the old down comforter from the quilt stand and made a bed for himself in Pap's old easychair. The smell of Pap's aftershave and the warmth of the comforter, so aptly named, calmed his thoughts and soon he was asleep.

* * *

Jeff was glad Cassidy threw him out early that evening. She had told him she hadn't waited for him all of her life just to have him end up as roadkill on the icy highway. It turned out to be a prudent call since the latest report indicated that the state police had decided to close the pass over South Mountain, the natural break between the Frederick and Hagerstown areas. That mountain range divided so many things. It broke the county boundaries, caused the weather to fall differently on either side, and had kept him a self-imposed prisoner for years.

His mind was calmer now, and he was sleeping better than he could ever remember, even though everything in his life was about to completely change. In a few days he would walk through the doors of his family home and try to reclaim a spot there. That thought once terrified him, but now he anticipated it with nervous longing. He was getting married in the spring, and soon even this old apartment would be a thing of his past. A new bride, a new home, an old home, and his own family. No one could have told him even a month ago that this would be the future of . . . Jeff Johnson? Of Thomas Jefferson Johanson?

He walked over to his window overlooking the frozen pond at Baker Park. It had just recently frozen and snow was landing on the surface, blending it in with the frosty grass. *A white Christmas perhaps,* he mused. He had loved them, prayed for them as a child when every kid's greatest joy was to actually get to use the new sled or skates left by Santa. But white Christmases had become painful, agonizing reminders of his aloneness and separation, and now, when he was about to bridge that gaping solitary abyss, God was blessing him with a white Christmas.

He realized how easily and how frequently he now attributed the good things in his life to God. *David's influence,* he mused. He cast a quick glance to the end table where the video *Together Forever* sat, another of David's subtle attempts to share his new faith with Jeff. "Together forever," he whispered as he considered the enormous implication of the words.

He watched the snow fall a little longer, all the while feeling that this was the most beautiful snow that had ever fallen, and the most joyous Christmas season in the history of Christmases. He wished Cassidy were there, right then. He wanted to hold her in his arms and watch the snow fall with her. He wanted to do everything, see everything, together from now on, *together . . . forever . . .* The title captivated him. Finally, his curiosity overtook him and he pushed the video into the VCR and became spellbound by the wondrous promises it displayed. *Can anyone really know for sure that we can be together forever?* He questioned the joy that possibility brought to him. A few months ago he would never have dared to believe such a thing, but tonight, deep inside, it felt right and true. More than just whimsy or wanting, the logic of it made sense to him. *Weak, mortal parents love their children . . . wouldn't a perfect God be capable of loving better than we? What does David call Him? Heavenly Father . . .*

Heavenly Father! Of course He would. Would a true father strip us from the people we love most? Deny us the chance to be with them after death? There was no sense in that. Suddenly Jeff knew that couldn't be right. Even he could see how that would be inconsistent of a just and loving *father.* He turned off the TV and put a classical station on the stereo, then sat down to consider the possibilities that he had never previously even dared to dream, and somewhere, comforted by these new revelations, he fell into a happy sleep.

* * *

Jeff awoke about 1:30 A.M. and was suddenly aware that the music had been interrupted by the news. He recognized the voice of the reporter as that of the morning DJ.

"Many thanks to the officers here in the Frederick Barracks for four-wheeling me in here tonight. I guess the station manager figured the only way I'd make it in here for the morning show was to have me spend the night, so anyone out there who sees my wife, tell her I love her and that I hope to make it home in time to see our four-year-old son graduate from high school."

Jeff wondered how much things had worsened in the short time he had slept.

"Okay, well folks, here is the latest weather update. It seems like the snow line is running pretty much along South Mountain. Folks to the east will have sleet and freezing rain. People living on the west side of the mountain should see the whole smorgasbord—sleet, freezing rain, some snow, and maybe a little hail. The fellows at the main weather station are going out on a limb and are saying that if this storm decides to hang around as long as predicted, this could turn out to be the worst ice storm since 1961."

Jeff remembered the family significance of the ice storm of early 1961. It had been the famous winter storm that transformed the old tree at Veterans' Park into a giant crystalline cone. It was on a trip to see the spectacle that they had seen the "For Sale" sign on the farm.

He finished a sandwich, clicked the radio off, and headed for bed. He considered the factors which led to his decision to go home on Christmas Eve. Of all the days that had passed and would yet pass, why had he felt so strongly that it needed to be that particular day? He supposed that part of the reason had to do with his fondness for that special night. Christmas was always wonderful, filled with family chaos and friends and neighbors popping in, but Christmas Eve was the perfect blend of both chaos and serenity. The Nativity usually brought crowds of people to the farm, most of whom left soon after the program and then headed home or off to a church for a midnight service. A few close friends would come inside afterward for pie and cider, but nearly everyone would be gone by nine, and then the family would sit near the fire and laugh or play games and eat and talk. Sometimes they too would attend the midnight service at the church down the road; however, sometimes they felt the most reverent way to celebrate was simply to be together in their home. It had left an indelible impression on Jeff, that he had missed and for which he had hungered since his last Christmas at the farm, and he was counting on the fondness of those memories to pave the way for his reunion with his parents. *Three more days till Christmas Eve. Three more days, and then I'll be completely home.*

* * *

Monday morning, Ben and Natalie slept in later than usual. The power had gone off and the alarm failed to sound. The darkness in the room warned them that the weather had not cleared, and as they opened the curtains to peer outside, they were both awed and alarmed by what they saw. Every tree, shrub, and blade of grass was encrusted with white snow and then covered in a thick layer of ice. Frozen rain was still falling, and icicles hung in thick, long spears from gutters and eaves. It was beautiful, but to those who had experienced the havoc this type of weather created, it was treacherous beauty.

Ben and Natalie dressed quickly and then headed downstairs. David was awake, sitting in the same chair, wrapped in the same comforter, with his attention riveted to the battery radio.

"What's the weatherman saying?" asked Ben.

"We'd better call the airlines, Pap. All the airports are closed and no flights are taking off or landing. The troopers closed Route 70 also, and most of the valley is without power."

Ben checked Martha and Sam's itinerary and then searched for the cell phone to call the airline. Natalie pumped up the old Coleman stove and set about making breakfast. David thought about Merit. She would be devastated about the weather. Merit's home sat on a steep ridge, which afforded a beautiful view of the surrounding area, but getting in and out was treacherous. David doubted if most of them could even get to their cars today. He took some comfort that he could at least call her after Pap got off the phone, but he sighed at the loss of one of their last chances to be together. Friday had been her final day of classes before holiday break. With the stress of studying and exams out of the way, they had hoped for a few days to enjoy each other's company, but this day would be lost to them.

Ben hung up and ran a hand through his hair. "It's pretty dicey. They might open one or two of the runways by nightfall, but they'll be so backed up they think they'll end up rerouting many of the flights south to Dulles or maybe as far south as Richmond, and then shuttle people north by bus. In either case I doubt we'll be seeing Martha and Sam anytime today."

"Maybe they'll call us, Ben," Natalie encouraged, "and then we'll decide what to do."

Ben looked at her in amazement. Was this his wife? Under normal circumstances, the loss of a day or delay of any kind in seeing her daughter would have sent her into a tailspin. He would have expected her to have him round up a sled-dog team to haul them in, but he never would have guessed she would so matter-of-factly accept this news and then turn around and make French toast. *What is going on?* he wondered. Then he considered the accident from which he had just recently recovered, and he assumed that she was more worried about taking chances than she was about the loss of a few hours with family. *Yes, that's probably it,* he decided.

David thought it was probably too early to call Merit, and he actually found some pleasure in being "trapped" at home. It was a comforting, relaxing feeling, and familiar . . . but what was it exactly? And then he realized what it felt like. It was the feeling of being a child! Freedom for a day from all responsibilities, schedules, and worries. He snuggled deeper into the comforter and suddenly wanted to watch cartoons or play outside. He thought back to the old days when he would spend holidays here at the farm, and he reminisced over the myriad ways he and Brian would entertain themselves. Suddenly he had a thought. "Pap, do you think the snowmobiles can get around in this mess?"

"Well, they aren't too good on ice, David, but if the ice isn't too thick they might be able to grab enough of the snow beneath to pull them along. I wouldn't trust them on a slope or anywhere you'd need to make a sudden stop though," Ben answered.

Natalie looked cautiously at her grandson. "David," she warned, "you're not going to try to get up the hill at Birch Knolls to see Merit are you? That hill is terrible."

"No, Omma," he answered reassuringly. "Actually, I had another idea. I thought I might swing over to Brian Hartman's and say hi."

Ben looked at Natalie and then responded, "Brian's had some trouble lately, son."

"It's okay, Pap. I know about the drinking and the rehab stuff. I bumped into him in town a while back and I just want to see him before I go."

David dressed in warm clothes and his down-filled ski set and headed toward the barn. Natalie met him at the door with a basket of breads and cookies for him to deliver to the Hartmans. He made his way to the barn, slipping and skidding all the way, and finally had the snowmobile packed and ready. He checked the animals as his grandfather had asked, and seeing that all was well, he headed slowly down the lane.

Brian's house was a small rental home on one of the large dairy farms in the valley. Neat and tidy, the home was provided by the farmer as part of Mr. Hartman's compensation for working on the farm. In addition, Mr. Hartman moonlighted for Sterling at the Johansons' and other orchards from time to time to supplement his income. His solid reputation for industry and honesty was well known in the community and had added to the community's shock when his son, who had also been held in high regard, was arrested in the fall. It had been made clear to everyone that Brian was not interested in pursuing farming as a career, especially on someone else's land where he was the "son of a hired hand," as he'd once called his father. He tried a variety of jobs but never found a niche. David guessed the job at the gift shop where he and Merit became close friends was probably another attempt to investigate a future vocation.

When David reached the house he untied the basket and slowly made his way to the door. He reconsidered the wisdom of his visit and then, looking at the basket he was now committed to deliver, stepped onto the front porch and knocked. Mrs. Hartman greeted him and immediately the aroma of wood smoke and soup filled his nostrils. Mrs. Hartman was a great cook and no blackout would deter her any more than it could deter his grandmother. The house was warm, cheery, and filled with Christmas spirit, and Mrs. Hartman received the basket with a smile and hugged him affectionately. They exchanged brief conversation and then she told David he would find Brian in his bedroom in the back.

David knocked softly on the door but there was no answer. He knocked again, and when there was no response he opened the door and peered in, expecting to find Brian asleep. Instead he found him lying on his back, staring at the ceiling, listening to music through headphones that were blaring so loudly David could identify the song. After a few moments, Brian noticed the movement by the door and lifted his head to see who had entered. His expression registered complete surprise, and David even suspected that there was at least some initial pleasure at seeing his old friend. But then a fog set in, probably brought on by memories of their last unpleasant conversation, and he flopped his head back down and scoffed at his guest.

"So, to what do I owe the pleasure of this illustrious visit, old friend?" he asked. "Are you here on a sobriety check, or are you on an evidence-gathering mission to prove to Merit that she ended up with the right man? Well, let me put your mind at ease. I plead no contest. You are the better man, David, so you can just go home victorious."

David wanted to turn and leave. He didn't need this. He came to be a friend not to be abused, and he was in no mood to put up with Brian Hartman's self-pity. He reached for the doorknob and said over his shoulder, "Good to see you too, man. Have a good one."

"Yeah, whatever," Brian replied, but there was something in his voice that sounded disappointed. David paused and thought again about the things Merit had said in Brian's defense outside the bakery, and he tried to see him as she did.

"You know," he offered, "I was sitting at home this morning thinking about old times, and all our grand adventures, and I wondered if you might want to take a final run on the snowmobile with me . . . for old times' sake."

"For old times' sake?" Brian countered. "I don't recall you wanting to get together for 'old times' sake' before."

David's natural instinct told him to blow the guy off and leave, but he thought about Merit again, and how she had seen good in Brian, and he wondered why he couldn't see him with the same Christlike eyes. The answer was simple. He didn't want to. A small part of him saw this troubled boy as a rival, a threat who would have the privilege to see and visit Merit long after David was gone. And though he tried to convince himself that he felt these feelings because Brian was no good for her, in that moment he knew it had little to do with Brian and everything to do with his mission. He faced the ugly thought that while he was excited about the course he had chosen, a part of him resented or feared his mission for causing him to leave Merit behind while Brian would be there, possibly hoping for a chance to fill the gap, and he realized that instead of facing his own fears, it had been easier to simply blame his old friend.

David knew he was at a critical fork in the road. He would go on his mission, of that there was no doubt, but he suddenly realized that *who he was* when he went on his mission would make all the difference. He could remain David Johanson, and *try* to love and teach the people the gospel of Christ, while fretting over everything he had left behind, or he could lose himself in the work and be an *example* of the love and teachings of Christ because, for a while, he had let go of the people and things he had left behind. This was the moment to choose.

"You want to know what changed, Brian," he asked with kindness. "I did, and I hope you'll forgive me for being judgmental or rude or whatever else I've been, whether you want to ride with me or not."

Brian looked at him, stunned and speechless for a long while until he broke the tension with a laugh. "Me forgive you?" He laughed again. "I like that . . ." He shook his head and sat up. "So, after all the garbage that's been between us, you want to forget it all and go for a ride, eh?"

"Yep," David replied simply, offering a hand to lift Brian up.

Brian looked at David's hand for a long time, leaving it dangling awkwardly in the air, but David did not withdraw it. Instead, he presented it firmly, intent on not being the one to surrender the offer of friendship again. Finally, Brian took it and pulled equally on David's strength until he rose to face his friend. They stood there, looking into each other's faces until their resolute countenances melted into smiles, and along with them, the years of separation melted as well. David was learning to lose himself.

The Hartmans, who had held little hope that Brian would accept the offer, grinned brightly to see the two friends together again. Within minutes Brian was dressed and the two were shooting over the hills, skidding and sliding out of control. They would tumble off the vehicle, rub the afflicted bump or scrape, and head off again. David recalled his grandfather's warning and heeded his advice, but only in the slightest. They crossed the road which was nearly vacant, and headed for downtown to survey the storm's damage.

It was as magnificent as any ice storm they had ever seen, both the beauty and the damage. The entire town had a gothic, almost eerie look. The glassy, ice-coated trees, posts, signs, and rooftops would have shimmered iridescently in the sunshine, but with the sky still obscured by thick gray clouds, everything appeared antiqued and surreal. Long, frosty icicles hung everywhere and the windows of the shops and houses were frosted and opaque. The streets and sidewalks were empty, and since the run on the stores had left the shelves nearly barren anyway, most of the shopkeepers felt obliged to stay home and enjoy the solitude of what would surely have been a low-profit business day. Only the pharmacy showed signs of any activity, and though David knew the mall on the outskirts of town would be bustling with the last-minute shoppers who could and needed to get out, here in downtown Smithsburg, it was another world.

The damage was equally impressive. Large heavy limbs wrapped in power lines were down with emergency crews cordoning off the area, already making repairs. Smaller twigs and branches were scattered all around, cluttering yards and rooftops and marring the pristine surface of the crystalline yards. Farther down the main street a large tree with shallow roots had become overburdened by the weight of both the heavy blanket of snow and the thick ice, and toppled completely over onto the roof of a van. A mobile news crew was shooting scenes of the damage and aimed their cameras at the boys, waving them over for an interview. They obliged, commenting more about the beauty of the ice than the danger it presented. The camera crew asked them for directions to Veterans' Park, the location of their next shoot, and the boys' curiosity was piqued. After giving the crew the directions, the two adventurers sped off to the park, where despite the relative quiet of the business district, many families had come to enjoy the majesty the storm had created.

The park was a small parcel cut from a local farm. A rambling creek that ran for miles through two counties took a sharp bend right at that point and bordered the property on three sides. Whenever a hard spring rain fell, the creek would flood its banks for weeks making that area undesirable for crops, so in 1949, the farmer leased it to the town for a dollar a year for one hundred years and dedicated it to be developed as a park. Most of the land had eventually been sculpted into ball diamonds, playgrounds, and soccer fields—but these few acres, which had long been dedicated to the heroes of the town, and which had served during three wars as the town's gathering point for celebration and memorial, remained a quiet place. Well-maintained gardens and a few carefully planned monuments were interspersed with benches and an old tree swing. Generations of children had splashed in the cool waters of the creek while parents sat under shade trees reading and sharing local gossip. Here could be found the pulse of the town, and that being the case, the undisputed heart was the old evergreen.

Every person who entered the park was magnetically drawn to it that day. Moms and dads towing mittened children on sleds, people clad in down and walking their dogs, and every other brave outdoorsman who ventured into the park came and encircled the ancient tree. It was a sickly old tree most days, beautiful only to those who understood its history and to those who had cut the emblems of their romances into its flesh, but no one who saw it on that day, robed in crystal majesty, could dispute the magnificence of its appearance. Burdened by the weight of the snow, it looked as if someone had taken an eighty-foot green cone, dipped it into a pot of liquid glass, and set it aside to dry. Its thick, flocked arms, encrusted with inches of ice, now hung down, pointing to the earth. Mysteriously, appearing through the translucent layers were the large, brightly colored balls hung weeks ago. It was captivating, and a spirit of community and reverence hung in the air. Very few words were shared. Most people merely smiled understandingly at one another or stood silently taking in the beauty of it, and even the boys, who had been raucous and rowdy minutes before, felt it and fell silent. The spell was only slightly broken by the sound of the TV news truck and the print reporters and photographers as they scurried about setting up lights and equipment. But even they, pressed by deadlines, couldn't help but pause and enjoy their magnificent subject.

The boys picked up bits and pieces of the interview questions and derived from what was being said that the press was drawing comparisons between this transformation of the tree and the legendary events that occurred in 1961, and because of that, the old evergreen would be the feature story in the news and the front page image in tomorrow's paper. The cameraman was walking around the tree to select camera angles, and as he navigated the perimeter he saw an overlap of two wide branches on the backside. From most angles this overlap seamed into the otherwise complete cone of ice, but from one precise angle it was apparent that the overlap created a gap in the tree's circumference. He pressed in closer and realized that this gap was an opening to a "room" created under the lowest boughs of the tree. David secretly watched him enter the cavern, ostensibly to film it, but for some reason he rejected the thought and backed out as mysteriously as he had entered. Instantly a perfect idea began to form in David's mind. He knew what he would give to Merit!

David never told Brian about the magical cavern under the tree, but with his spirits buoyed up by the innumerable plans formulating in his joyful mind, he became playful and animated, and the time passed quickly between the old friends. When another battery of freezing rain began to fall, David, feeling safe that the secret of the room would not be discovered, and content with the friendship he and Brian had renewed, suggested that they head home.

When they arrived, Mrs. Hartman stared at the countenance of her son. It was as if in those few short hours, years of tarnish had been removed, lifted by forgiveness and caring, and she again hugged David and returned Natalie's basket, refilled with culinary treasures of her own making. Brian walked David out to the snowmobile, placed a fond hand on his shoulder and said, "Thanks for coming by, I had a good time. I just want you to know that . . . well, I'm glad you're with Merit now." His voice became soft and he tipped his head down to hide his eyes. "I never meant to hurt her or get her into trouble. I really did care about her, David."

David didn't know what to say so he simply offered his hand in friendship.

"She's a great friend who loved me even though I didn't even love myself. And as much as I hate to admit it, she's more at peace and looks better now that she's with you than she ever did with me, so take good care of her, okay?"

The boys shook hands and David offered Brian a quick invitation to come to the children's program the next evening, then jumped on the snowmobile and drove away.

David left the Hartmans' wondering if he would ever see Brian again, and knew he had parted with the bigger burden lifted. He had Merit to thank for that.

Chapter Twenty-Four

The remainder of Monday was gloriously uneventful for David. He spoke with Merit on the phone for several hours, or so Pap said, and then he and Pap and Omma played board games by lantern light and ate popcorn until the lights miraculously turned back on around bedtime. After chuckling about the "perfect timing," they had family prayer, a renewed Johanson tradition requested by David, and headed off to bed. David picked up his scriptures and read until he too nodded off to sleep.

Around 5:00 A.M. a call came through. Natalie picked up the phone and told Ben it was Martha. They were still in England because no flights scheduled to land in the Atlantic Coastal area or New England were taking off. Fearing they would be stranded overseas for Christmas, they agreed to take stand-by status, flying into the Raleigh-Durham airport, and would then work out transportation north to Maryland. They promised to call as soon as they knew their arrival time in North Carolina, and Ben and Natalie assured them that once they got to the States they would find a way to get them home for Christmas Eve. Ben jumped up out of bed and set about to make plans to shuttle them home or pick them up himself.

A few of the major routes were partially open and moving slowly again, but the police were still advising people to stay home if possible until the back roads and side streets were cleared. With the temperatures still fluctuating hour by hour, surfaces that were wet one moment would refreeze and become treacherous again, and so it was with a little trepidation that David watched his grandparents struggle with what to do to rescue his parents.

Eventually, Ben decided not to leave the fate of his family to anyone else. He and Natalie began packing the old Suburban with food and blankets, then threw in some tools in case of an emergency, and planned to head down to Raleigh to greet the planes until Martha and Sam's came in. David laughed affectionately at the extent of their preparations and the quantity of their provisions. He asked them in jest if they were going to bring home his parents or if they were on a covert mission for the Red Cross. They laughed, but then all joking was set aside as Ben offered to pray for their trip. It was a simple prayer that echoed the faith of an uncomplicated man who had spent his life exercising what knowledge he had of God to its fullest. A year ago, such an intimate offering would have surprised David, but knowing what he now knew about the prayer Ben had recorded in his journal, he accepted that this was a bigger part of his grandfather's nature than he had previously understood.

It was nine o'clock when the fully stocked "rescue-mobile" pulled out of the driveway, and David ran inside to call Cassidy with his grandparents' regrets. She expressed her worries about the road conditions but confided to David that Jeff had decided not to attend the concert to avoid the possibility of having his first meeting with his parents be so public. Now he would come for sure, and since the weather had kept Cassidy and Jeff apart since the night they announced their engagement, Cassidy was anxious to call and tell him he could attend.

David was equally anxious to call Merit with his own surprise. When Merit answered the phone her tone belied her words. She said she was fine and that the concert was going to be fine, but her somber intonation made him all the more pleased that he had his plan for the perfect evening all figured out and was ready to give her the invitation. He had called earlier and solicited her mother's help in laying out a scavenger hunt in the house to lead Merit to a poetic invitation inviting her to be his date for a magical evening following the children's concert. Upon finally finding the invitation, she called him back in a completely changed mood and David's enthusiasm soared. He had so many preparations to make, and the timing was critical.

The concert was set to begin promptly at seven with David narrating. Since most of the preparations for his surprise had to be made near or after dark, everything would have to be popped into place in an hour's time. The overall plan was simple—a special dinner in a magnificent location. The dinner plan was flawless; it was to be chicken cordon bleu, which he had already ordered from the White Horse Restaurant and would pick up exactly at 8:30 P.M. But the location was the spectacular part. David was setting their dinner up in the ice cavern inside the old evergreen at Veterans' Park. He had a clear vision of how he wanted everything to be.

Omma's folding card table and chairs would be set with her good china and lace tablecloth. He had even ordered a bud vase with a single red rose for the centerpiece. To keep everything organized and easy to move, he lined Omma's laundry basket with a thick blanket and placed all the essentials inside. A box of matches and the three-armed candelabra that traditionally sat in the center of the dining room table was packed into the basket on top of the china, along with silver services for two and the crystal stemware that had already been wrapped and placed inside. He had his portable stereo filled with new batteries and armed with three carefully selected CDs, and to make sure the evening's memories could be enjoyed again and again, he purchased and packed a twenty-seven-exposure disposable camera with flash.

He ran through a quick mental checklist to make sure he had everything. He loaded it all into the back of the Jeep and ran the schedule through his mind again and again. At 5:45 he would gas up the Jeep and hurry over to the park. By then it would be dark and the park's Christmas lights, set on a timer, wouldn't come on until 6:00 P.M. And even so, at that hour, the dinner hour, there shouldn't be anyone milling about who would see him setting up. He would set the table and have everything ready to go by 6:30 so he could be back at Brighton and ready to narrate by 6:45. He knew if he were late Merit would panic and that stress would ruin the rest of their evening. The concert would end by 7:45 with a short reception following, at which he would make a brief appearance. Then he would excuse himself at 8:15 to pick up the food and be at the park by 8:45. There was one last detail to arrange. He still needed to get a chauffeur to pick Merit up at 8:45 and drop her off at the park by precisely 9:00 P.M. He was going to ask her parents to drive her to the park and walk her to the tree blindfolded. That was still a viable option, but now he could also solicit Jeff's help as a backup plan.

In either case, while she was blindfolded and brought to the park, he would have time to light the candles, place the food on the plates, serve the sparkling cider, and start the music. He got chills just thinking about how smooth this evening was going to be. He would ask Merit to write to him while he was away, no promises or commitments, just a beginning, and then he would tell her the exciting news about Jeff really being TJ. It would be an item of trust, a bond he would share with her that would draw her into the most intimate of circles—his family. He shivered with excitement again, and then, suddenly, another idea came to him. He had seen a trinket at the pharmacy that would add one final, perfect touch to the evening. A display had been set up on a counter featuring spun glass ornaments, one of them a tree. What a great lasting memento to give her!

By 3:00 P.M. the basket was packed and all the arrangements had been finalized. He figured he had plenty of time to pick up the glass tree, wrap it, then shower and dress. Suddenly the phone rang. It was Cassidy.

"David, sorry to bother you, but I may need a favor."

"What's up?" he asked as calmly as he could in spite of his fear that the "favor" would totally destroy his perfect timing.

"The man who's contracted to plow our driveway is sick and everyone else is so backed up they can't promise to clear our drive until tonight or maybe even tomorrow. If we can't get it cleared we'll have to cancel the concert tonight. I can't get out, and other cars and people can't get in."

David looked at his watch and began calculating. He knew he had to do it. If the concert got canceled Merit's inconsolable disappointment would spoil the plans for his magical evening. *Okay, plowing that drive will take up to two hours plus time to get there and get back, and I still need to pick up the glass tree . . . that'll make it 5:30 or 6:00 P.M. before I get home.* "I'll come right over, Cassidy, but I had some other obligations this afternoon, so if I'm a minute or two late getting back to the program, you'll have to explain it all to Merit, okay?"

Cassidy happily agreed to cover for David and asked if she could in turn help him. David thought for a minute and then two troubling details came to mind.

"Cassidy, I'm trying to trump Jeff Johnson, numero uno ladies' man, and pull off a very special evening for Merit tonight. I could use some help with two things. First, is Jeff definitely coming tonight?" David asked.

Cassidy chuckled at his description of Jeff. "Yep, he promised he'd be here early as a matter of fact."

"Great, then I actually can use both your help. And second, can I get you to run to the pharmacy for me after I clear the driveway?"

* * *

Merit tried to call David three times Tuesday afternoon and finally, worried that something may have come up and that he wouldn't show, she called Cassidy. Cassidy laughed and described the guy plowing her driveway, and Merit added another sweet kindness to her list of things to thank him for.

At 5:30 P.M., David hit a patch of stubborn ice that slowed down his already tedious progress. It was 6:15 before he pulled the tractor back into his driveway. His mind was racing as he tried to figure out how he could get showered, dressed, gas up Pap's Jeep, get over to the park to set up, and still make the concert. He mentally adjusted his schedule and called Cassidy.

"Cassidy, I am *really* running late. I can't possibly get to Brighton before 7:30 P.M. Can you stall for me?"

Cassidy paused as she considered her options. "Alright, how about if I ask Merit to lead into the program with a few piano numbers? I'll stall as long as I can without making her suspicious, but you're going to have to hurry, David, because you know she's going to give me the third degree, and I'll crack and spill my guts about your date."

"Alright, I'll hurry but try not to be too conspicuous, Cassidy, okay?"

"This is not my forte, David, but I'll do my best for my future nephew."

Now David laughed. "Thanks, Auntie," he said affectionately. "Oh, and one other thing, timing is everything tonight so I need to back all the plans up a half hour. Will you tell Jeff? See you soon." He hung up and raced to the bathroom to get showered and dressed. By 6:45, the time he was supposed to be pulling into Brighton, he was barely pulling into Veterans' Park.

* * *

The number, diversity, and dress of the guests amazed even Merit. There were many people attending that had strong, almost familial ties to Brighton and to Cassidy, but there were also many people present who were complete strangers to her.

Sterling Davis and his wife were there dressed in their Sunday best, and although Jeff immediately recognized Mr. Davis, Mr. Davis paused for a long time trying to place Jeff. Merit wondered why there seemed to be so many people who looked at Jeff, mentioning that he reminded them of someone.

The cameras were flashing and Merit was awed by the social spectacle her simple little children's concert had become. Nearly every chair was full and there was a line extending out the main door. Jeff had solicited the help of a few guests to hurriedly bring in all the dining chairs to accommodate the anticipated overflow. Merit saw her mother and father arrive nearly half an hour early and sit in the seats she had reserved for them in the front. She marveled at how wonderful they both looked. This evening was an emotional milestone for them. Her dad had brushed off his best suit for the occasion and her mom had shopped for a new outfit especially for this night, the first personal purchase she had made since Markie died. They waved to her and she smiled nervously at them as she caught a glance at the clock over the fireplace mantel—*6:45! Where is David?* She ran back down the hall to check on the children. Mrs. Sherman was warming them up with a few simple tunes. They were filled with anticipation, dressed in their very finest outfits, and beaming with excitement. Everyone was ready except for David.

Merit was vacillating between fury and worry. *David promised . . . he promised he would be here by 6:45 at the latest. Where is he?* And then another shock registered in her mind. There, coming through the doorway, was Brian Hartman! Merit's heart sank. *Is this why David isn't here? Did he see Brian pull up? Does he think I invited him?*

Cassidy had held off stalling the program until she was sure there was no hope David would show on time. When it became clear to her that Merit's mood was deteriorating she and Jeff decided to move to plan "B," with Jeff now assigned to the job of making the explanation to Merit.

"Have I told you yet how wonderful you look?" he asked as charmingly as possible.

"Yes, Jeff," she replied, annoyed by his third reference to her appearance in ten minutes. "You're stalling. Where's David? I know you two are covering for him. He isn't going to show, is he?"

"David's just running a little late, Merit. It took longer than expected to plow. He told us he would be here as soon as possible, so Cassidy was wondering if you could help us stall for time by playing a few piano pieces to lead off."

"He's not coming, is he?" she cried.

"Of course he's coming, Merit," Jeff tried to reassure her. "You know, it's a tough job being Sir Galahad and the star of the show all in one day."

Merit wasn't amused or calmed by Jeff's humor. She continued to fret and her eyes were welling up with tears. Jeff put his hands on her shoulders and fought the urge to tell her the truth.

"Merit, I happen to know without question, that wherever you are is where David most wants to be this night, and he will be here. I promise, okay?"

"Okay," she replied.

He turned her toward the piano. "So, will you go out there and play a few pieces before these well-dressed people turn into a raging mob and storm the stage?"

Merit smiled and nodded. "I will if you promise to signal me the minute he arrives."

"I promise," he said.

Merit turned and went immediately to the piano with Cassidy close behind. Cassidy made her apologies for the delay and transitioned nicely into an introduction for Merit that turned their dilemma into an audience bonus as the crowd responded with enthusiasm. As soon as Merit's gentle touch brought the still, black instrument alive, the room became almost reverent in mood. She had five suitable pieces she could play from memory, enough music to fill about thirty minutes, but beyond that, if David still hadn't appeared, she knew they would have to go on without him. The thought made her sick, partly for the blow it would mean to the program, and partly because she knew if he weren't there by then, he wasn't coming. Knowing how clearly he understood the importance of this evening, that would be a signal that something was terribly wrong. But she pushed those concerns away fearing they would betray her hands, and she put her faith in Jeff's reassuring words.

* * *

At 6:47 P.M. David quickly unloaded the table and chairs and ran with them near the tree. Despite the half moon and the twinkle lights on the tree, the darkness made setting up too difficult. When he ran back to get the basket of essentials he started the Jeep and turned the headlights on. They fell slightly left of the tree, but the added illumination was helpful. Just in case though, David grabbed his flashlight too. Once all the items were near the tree he turned on the flashlight and got to work. He carefully entered the "room" and inspected it. It was even more amazing in the night than it had appeared during the day. The moonlight filtered through the ice, creating an eerie glow accented by brighter beams of light that passed through gaps in the tree and ice. The shifting temperatures had altered the consistency of the ice, and David could see fractures and cracks running deeply through it.

The "room" was only about five feet tall, far too short for standing, but suitable for sitting and dining. Several shimmering icicles hung from below the branches, another evidence of the partial melting that had occurred during the day. The long, lower boughs of the tree that protruded from points slightly less than five feet up the trunk, and which once hung above the ground, now scraped the icy earth. David noticed this change and felt momentary concern for the damage the heavy ice was causing the old tree, however he brushed these worries aside and set about performing his tasks. He removed his gloves and worked from a bent position as he laid the lace tablecloth over the table and nimbly set Omma's good crystal and china in their places. He set the candelabra in the center and placed the bud vase and rose to the right of Merit's plate. He then laid the bottle of sparkling apple cider in the snow and stood back to evaluate the effect. Within fifteen minutes he had everything ready to go, but he couldn't resist pausing momentarily to admire his handiwork. A thrill shivered over him at the excitement of pulling off such a perfect gift. It was a silent, magical fairyland, and he was giving it to Merit.

Just then a nearly inaudible creaking sound caught his attention, but he identified it as the sound of the boughs straining under their icy burden and dismissed it. He checked his watch—7:02. *I'll be at Brighton in eight minutes and then, after our 'only slightly delayed concert,' I'll give Merit the most memorable dinner of her life . . . Dinner? Oh no, the dinner!*

David had backed up the schedule to accommodate everything but the delayed pick-up of the gourmet dinner he had insisted must be ready precisely at 8:30 P.M. They wouldn't be ready to eat till later now. And not only would he look like a fool, but the expensive meal would either be overcooked and ruined or cold and ruined. In either case, the most important component of the evening was botched and his frustration hit him like a kick in the stomach. In his haste he had walked out of the house and left the cell phone lying on the table. Now there was no way to call the restaurant and no time to get there and change the order. He put his hands to his head and stomped the ground as he calculated his options. The pressure to get to the concert weighed on him heavily, overshadowing any alternative plan he could imagine, and he realized angrily that his choices were to attend the concert and scratch the dinner, or run to the restaurant and plead with the maître d' to resubmit the order for pick-up at 9:00 P.M. Neither option was good. Missing the concert would disappoint Merit so completely that nothing he could do would make things right, but what was the point of all these carefully crafted plans if they had no supper to share? He had never been so frustrated.

He stood up angrily, in disgust at his failure. As he did, his tall frame crashed into the low ice ceiling. His head snapped up hard, directly into a jagged point of ice formed by the day's melting and refreezing, and it cut a deep gash into the back of his head.

Reacting to the shock of the blow, David stumbled backward and tripped over the chilling bottle of sparkling cider. Disoriented and foggy, he thrashed about, instinctively searching for a handhold to steady himself. As his fingers scraped and clutched for something upon which to rest his staggering body, he became aware of the sounds of crashing. It was bits of ice, breaking loose along the fractured lines on the limbs, mingled with the crashing of the crystal and china. The assault of the ice pelting him added further to his disorientation. Blood ran down his head and face from the gash to his skull, and as the ice hit him it dyed red and melted on his clothes in patches of muted crimson.

As he recognized that the warm ooze in his eyes and on his hands was his own blood, fear took over. He raised his arms to protect his head and for a second remembered where he was. He could hear the creaking of the heavily overburdened limbs and knew that every touch, every panic-driven ounce of his weight that bore upon the branches made the groaning worse.

He saw the headlights of the Jeep and thought it was the way out. He made one final, lucid decision. He would throw his weight in the direction of the exit before the groaning limbs broke away from the tree and crashed down upon him. His vision was blurred both from the blow and the blood, making his only navigation point the bright beam of the headlights. Like a two-hundred-pound sledgehammer he threw his weight into one powerful forward thrust toward what he perceived to be the way to safety, but the recognition of his error in judgment was instantaneous. The brief afternoon warming had offered the upper branches an hour of melting. A large, heavy inner limb on the west side of the tree had caught and held the moisture and then refroze. It had become as clear as glass. It caught the bright beam of the headlights and further magnified the light. What David perceived as the ice-free exit was instead a broad, thick sheet of treacherous, glistening ice.

The weight of David's body crashed through the razorlike sheet, cutting and scraping his face and hands. The force of the impact was his last fully conscious recognition. Everything after that was blurred. He landed facedown with a heavy thud. A searing pain bit into his left cheek and radiated into his brow. Somewhere in an unidentifiable place he heard a loud splitting sound followed by what seemed to be the sound of hail, as his rapidly numbing body felt the increasing weight of unknown pressure and then a coldness that began to burn, but he was unable to fully register or care about the peril. Buried under a blood-tinged mound of ice and snow, he laid still and listened to the groaning. He knew it was coming from somewhere above him and that it was getting louder, but he could not decipher its source or the reason for it. His eyes fluttered in a vain, instinctive attempt to clear his mind one last time, but the required effort was beyond his capabilities, and he could feel himself moving further and further away from caring about his situation.

The burning cold, the red ooze, the grinding weight upon his back, they were all inconsequential to him, but one last sound demanded his clouded attention. The limb, whose creaking sigh had become a warning cry, now screamed as it separated itself from the blow of David's impact. The woody tendons, twenty feet above the ground, strained to hold it in its place, but gravity won the fight. Ripping and tearing at its joint on the tree, the icy, snow-laden branch surrendered its grip and fell with full force. The ice-covered greenery pitched upward and down again, crashing against David's head like a plank. His unconscious body lurched involuntarily and he was blessed not to know what was coming next as his back took the blow from the heavy twelve-inch-wide branch that crushed down upon him. Freed from the sagging limb, the tree jerked back and forth a few times sending ice and snow falling all around, and then it slowly came to rest. All was silent except for the sound of the Jeep's engine running in the parking lot.

Chapter Twenty-Five

Merit had already played three beautiful pieces to rousing audience approval by the time the clock read 7:15 P.M. At the end of each piece she would look over at Jeff and Cassidy for a sign that David had arrived. Jeff's heart broke each time they signaled no. He was worried sick that only something dire could be keeping David from being there that evening, but Cassidy had other concerns. She knew from the bakery trip that there was residual animosity between Brian Hartman and David, and with Brian in attendance, she wondered if David's absence was a simple case of jealousy, so her first concern shifted to the program and to Merit.

"Jeff, what are we going to do if David doesn't show? He's the narrator! I could just throttle him for doing this to that poor girl."

"Cassidy," Jeff replied sharply, "do you really think he would just arbitrarily miss this?"

"You're really worried about him?" she asked more contritely.

"Think about it. What would keep him from being here after all the fuss he made about covering for him?"

"Brian," she replied through her tightened jaw.

"No," Jeff said, waving her comment aside. "David told me they made peace yesterday."

Cassidy's expression changed from suspicion to concern. "I didn't know. What should we do?"

"I don't know where to begin looking for him. I'm going to call his cell phone and see if I can track him down, although I'm sure he would have called if he could. In the meantime, do you have a written copy of the narration?" he asked.

"There's one in my office." Her face showed relief. "Will you read it?"

Jeff knew he'd rather do anything than stand in front of a room full of people—*this* room full of people—and perform, but he didn't want to make this any harder on Merit than it already was. "Yes, I'll be the narrator."

Cassidy gave him a grateful look and hurried to her office to find the script while Jeff called David's cell phone in vain. She returned as Merit finished her final piece and watched as she made another appeal to Jeff for word of David. When Merit rose from the bench, the entire room immediately stood to offer the talented pianist a standing ovation. She smiled through glossy eyes as she numbly accepted the recognition and then panic crossed her face as she wondered how to proceed.

Cassidy came to her rescue by announcing another slight change in the program with the narration now to be read by Mr. Jeff Johnson. Merit smiled sadly as Jeff stepped up to his place. Mrs. Sherman, on perfect cue, led the children into the room and onto the risers David had built three days earlier. The audience gushed over the beautiful faces of the wiggly children, their expressions bright with excitement and anticipation. Merit swept her hands in front of the group to acknowledge them, and the audience responded with a round of gracious applause.

As soon as the applause died down, the room lights were softened and the program began in the glow of David's Tree. Jeff read the first paragraph of dialogue while Merit played soft background music between the carols and nodded entrances and cutoffs to the children. Back and forth the program continued as Jeff told the story of the birth of the Christ child in word, and the children testified of it through their songs and expressions. Merit listened carefully to the script and felt a chill run through her. Something tender and new about the Christmas story touched her heart in a way she had never felt before. She noticed Jeff's voice breaking, and looked at the audience and saw them wiping at their eyes, and she knew it was David's words that touched them all. Somehow he had captured the same tenderness in prose that the children were able to convey in song, and she knew that it was his personal understanding of Christmas that was elevating the program. These were the beliefs he had tried to help her understand that night at High Rock when she had felt so threatened, but tonight, they seemed to be more of an invitation, to her and to everyone, to feel what he felt and share in the joy this understanding of the Savior brought him.

She recalled how she had responded that evening, and the recollection of her response now seemed so selfish. David had merely tried to share the gift he was ready to take to strangers with her, and she had only been able to see what it would cost her. And when, in his confusion, he had withdrawn, she had focused only on her hurt, and again made him the villain. A lump caught in her throat, making it difficult to focus on the concert, but as another of David's beautiful passages caught her attention she knew she was now ready to accept the invitation his words offered—and suddenly, she missed him more than ever.

As soon as the program concluded, Jeff headed straight for Cassidy, who pulled herself free from the guests to speak with him. Merit also forged past the well-wishers as quickly as courtesy would allow and headed straight over.

"He never made it?" she asked, already knowing the answer.

Jeff looked at Cassidy, afraid to meet Merit's gaze. Cassidy's expression was filled with concern, and Merit looked at Jeff and found the same.

"What is it?" she pressed.

"Maybe nothing, Merit," Jeff tried to say reassuringly. "I know David planned to be here, that's all." And to Cassidy he turned and said, "I'm going to go look for him."

"Where will you even start?" she asked.

"I'll start at the farm and then head over to the park where he was supposed to end up."

Just then Brian Hartman approached the group to congratulate Merit. "I just wanted to shake the hand of the star," he said with a smile. Merit offered him a cursory smile and then cast her eyes downward to hide her tear-filled eyes. "What's the matter, Merit? You look upset."

Merit said nothing, but the looks on Cassidy's and Jeff's faces told him something was terribly wrong. "Is something wrong with David? I was surprised not to see him after he made a point to invite me. What was he doing over at the park tonight?"

"The park? When?" all three repeated loudly.

Jeff turned to face him and grabbed his shoulders firmly. "What time did you see David?"

Brian was startled by the depth of emotion his simple question raised, but he answered calmly, "Around seven. He and I went snowmobiling there yesterday and saw the old evergreen. I drove past there on the way to the concert tonight to see it lit up. I thought I saw Mr. Johanson's Jeep sitting in the parking lot with its headlights on and the engine still running. It was weird. I figured it was David."

Jeff looked at his watch and calculated in his head. "It's 8:40," he breathed, his brow creased in worry. "That was almost two hours ago. I'm going to head over there."

"I'm going too, then," Merit said firmly.

"I don't think that's a good idea, Merit," Jeff said cautiously.

"Merit, why don't you wait here with me, and Jeff will call us if there's any news," Cassidy offered, but Merit wasn't interested in any other options.

"I'm going," she said determinedly. "You know he'd come looking for me." Jeff and Cassidy protested no further. They knew she was right. "Cassidy," Merit added, "will you explain to my parents where I went? They're talking to some people in the corner." Before she had an answer or could be further dissuaded, Merit had her coat and was on her way to Jeff's car.

"Call me as soon as you know something, Jeff. Okay?" Cassidy called after him.

He came back, hugged her tightly, and pulled away to look in her eyes, whispering, "Stay near the phone." His eyes could not hide the worry and fear written there, and Cassidy was suddenly frightened too.

Jeff and Merit rode in silence on the short yet interminable ride to the park. A few hours ago his world was filled with anticipation of family joy and reunion, and now he was praying that his newly found nephew, the joy of the family, was simply all right. He knew it was selfish of him, but he couldn't help but consider the bitter irony that if anything was indeed wrong, his return would be remembered as the day something happened to David. Nausea swept over him. He offered what he thought was an inaudible plea to God to keep David safe, and then he felt Merit's hand on his shoulder, her own eyes as worried as his, and he knew she had heard his prayer.

Jeff's headlights swept the parking area, illuminating the Jeep as his car pulled into the lot. He drove straight toward it and jumped out of the car. He approached from the passenger side, and from first observations, everything seemed normal. The engine was quiet, the hood was cold and the lights were off, but when he crossed to the driver's side he noticed that the door was ajar. Jeff began to yell David's name, but there was no answer.

"Maybe he left a note," Merit suggested. Jeff looked inside and found no note, but what he did find was disturbing. The key was in the ignition and was turned to the "On" position. He tried the key anyway, and after the engine sputtered momentarily it fell silent. *It must have run out of gas . . .* Jeff speculated. He also noticed that the headlight switch was in the "On" position and set for high beams. *How long would the lights have had to be on after the gas ran out to run the battery down?* The last piece of evidence was even more compelling. There on the seat was a menu from the "White Horse Restaurant." Jeff recognized two sets of notes in David's handwriting, scribbled along the borders. The first set was a schedule of tonight's itinerary that had been scratched out. The second set of notes was the same itinerary with different times penciled in. The clues began to fit together, and Jeff was beginning to understand that this was David's plan for his special date with Merit.

He paused to put it all together. *David came here about 6:45 P.M. The headlights were on at 7:00 when Brian drove by, but it's stone-cold now . . . and the door was ajar. Why would David walk away and leave the Jeep door open? He wouldn't,* was Jeff's analysis.

That left two disconcerting possibilities. The only reason David would have left the Jeep that way was if he had stepped away for just a minute, but he was clearly nowhere to be found. *Where is he?* Jeff wondered in panic.

Jeff ran through the possibilities. The only way David would have left the park with the Jeep in this condition would have been by force or accident. He doubted that David was the victim of force. If he had been mugged, would the perpetrators have left an open, at that time, supposedly running Jeep behind? And if he had been whisked away from an accident, his rescuers would have turned his engine and headlights off and closed his car door. No, that left only one possibility. David was here, somewhere, and he was in trouble.

Merit stood silently by, watching as Jeff weighed the evidence and drew his conclusions. He checked his watch again. It was nine o'clock and, true to the schedule, the timer for the lights switched and the old evergreen went dark.

In his hurry Jeff had parked the car perpendicular to David's Jeep. But now he needed the headlights' illumination and he needed to keep Merit occupied. "Merit," he said taking her gently by one arm, "turn my car around beside the Jeep and put the high beams on, then call Cassidy and ask her to see if she can round up Sterling Davis and a few other people to come down here, okay?"

He could feel Merit tremble. She looked at him with wet eyes full of fear, but he had no words of consolation to offer her.

"What should I tell her? What do you think is going on?" she asked fearfully.

"I don't know," he said, trying to get her headed toward his car.

"But what do you *think* is going on?" she pursued. He stood silently looking at the Jeep and rethinking his theory. She waited for his response, and realizing he was trying to avoid her, she grabbed his arm, but he still wouldn't face her.

"Jeff!" she screamed tearfully in his face. "What are you thinking!?"

He spun around. Confusion filled his eyes and anguish filled his voice. His words came out in a rush. "I don't know for sure. I only have a feeling, but I don't think David would just walk away and leave his Jeep running and unlocked for two hours, Merit." He handed her the menu. "He had special plans for this evening. He expected to be at the concert and then back here with you tonight for supper."

Merit looked numbly at the menu. Her heart was twice broken, once at the thought that he had planned something so special and so personal for her, and once again from the fear that was gripping her.

"What could have happened?" she asked through her tears.

"Just call Cassidy, Merit, and get some help here, now!"

Merit ran to the car and started putting it into position. Jeff scanned the moonlit park again and saw something near the darkened tree. It was a glowing object in the snow. As he struggled to get a bearing on it, the bright lights of his car flooded the tree and it was lost again. He hurried over to Merit and waved forcefully for her to kill the lights. Again he found the glow, and once he had the spot marked in his mind, he again signaled for Merit to turn the lights on.

He began to walk in the direction of the glow when he became aware of several sets of footprints pressed into the white earth that headed to and from the back of the tree. Straight ahead, poking out from under the tree, he noticed a large limb, downed and lying on a snow mound and surrounded by littered debris in the otherwise flat, smooth snow. As he drew closer he kept his eyes focused there and then was able to see a dark, shadowy patch in the snow. His pace increased and he heard the sound of his car door opening far behind him. His mind tried to identify the form—and a reason for a single dark shadow to fall on the snow on a dim, moonlit night.

Soon he was upon the glowing object. It was a flashlight, lying in a low area, encrusted with snow, as if it had rolled and scraped along the surface. Jeff picked it up and aimed it at the mound. In one second he heard his mind scream and Merit's footsteps closing the gap.

"Stop, Merit!" he screamed with authority. "Call 911!"

"Jeff?" Her voice was small and timid and frail. "Jeff?" she spoke again, and her feet took a step in his direction.

He spun and pointed fiercely back toward the car. "Go, Merit! Now!"

She ran back, her wailing, broken voice echoing in the still air. He wondered if she would be able to control her voice enough to even make the call. He wondered if it would even matter.

Jeff's knees were like jelly, and nausea cramped him. He wanted to run away as well but he was compelled to go forward. He aimed the light, not wanting it to find anything, but its beam illuminated the dark patch in the snow that extended five feet in front of the mound. Red and frozen, Jeff knew it was blood. He aimed the light at the mound and saw a hand peeking out from scattered icy debris, lying still and blue against the red-tinged background. He stumbled and caught himself. Half running, half tripping, his breaths coming in terrified gasps, he made his way. He saw the fabric at the wrist of the cold, blue hand. He knew it was David's leather jacket.

He fell down to his knees and began clawing at the snow and ice, pressing with all his might against the heavy limb, but his strength was swallowed by his frenzy and he worked in vain. The first of four sets of headlights pierced the night, and Jeff thanked God that help was coming. He sobbed and tore at the mound and screamed David's name but there was no answer. He tried to find a pulse at the wrist but his own fingers were now numb and torn from clawing to free his nephew. Merit's father was the first man by his side. Jeff's hands and knees were covered in blood from the red snow and his face was streaked with tears. Michael Davenport said nothing. He threw his large frame against the beam and pushed, but its greenery had refrozen into the blood and ice. As he backed up to throw himself against it again Jeff stopped him.

"His back," he sobbed. "It's on his back."

Michael understood. He needed to proceed more cautiously. He reached into his pocket and pulled out a knife, cutting away furiously at the greenery while Jeff, nearly mad with worry, stroked David's hand. Another man, a stranger, came to help. Jeff vaguely recalled seeing him at the concert earlier in the evening, which seemed like a lifetime ago.

Now Sterling Davis was there and more steps were sounding from behind. Then Jeff heard the siren of the ambulance in the distance. "Good girl, Merit," he whispered. The men began to lift the bough from David's back, and Jeff again began to tear furiously at the mound that crushed down upon his nephew and friend. He cleared enough ice and snow to see that David's head was lying facedown to the left with his cheek lying on his left sleeve. Jeff couldn't see his eyes and was momentarily unprepared to face what story that view might tell, so he wiped the snow from David's head, stroking it as he wept, and worked until he found the large gash from which the trail of blood had flowed. It was no longer oozing and Jeff wondered what that meant. *Has he bled to death?*

The paramedics arrived and all the men moved away except Jeff.

"Does he have any family present?" asked a female medic.

"They're all away—" Sterling began shakily.

"You, sir," she posed to Jeff. "Are you a relative?"

"I'm his . . . I'm his . . . friend," he moaned, feeling ashamed and unworthy.

One of the medics grabbed his arm and guided him away from David while three others instantly got to work.

"Is he . . . ?" Jeff choked the words out.

"The cold temperature is on his side," the medic replied. Jeff stumbled away from the working medics, went behind the tree, and fell to his knees. He sobbed and prayed and pled with God. After a minute or so, a calm peace filled his heart, and then there was a gentle hand on his shoulder. He turned, startled, and looked up into Cassidy's terrified eyes. "His pulse is very weak but he's alive," she said softly. He heard the worried tone in her voice but clung to the present knowledge that David was still alive. His head fell into her knees and he whispered hoarsely, "Thank you, Dear God."

Cassidy helped him to his feet. He felt emotionally spent and could hardly bear his own weight, but with her support they returned to the frenzied scene. News teams were waiting at the perimeter, and the police were clearing the area for the medevac helicopter to land. The medic who had comforted Jeff was holding an IV bottle while her partners inserted tubes and needles into David's still, blue body. His bloodstained clothes, now cut away, were scattered on the snow, and his quiet form was wrapped in a special hypothermia blanket. Jeff could see the edge of the rigid board David's body was logrolled onto and upon which he was now resting. Straps now held him securely, and Jeff stared at his blood-mottled face. Cuts and scrapes were framed in dark scabs leaving his face swollen and nearly unrecognizable. His curly dark hair was matted and stiff and Jeff reached toward him, wanting to touch him, in case . . .

Within seconds the gurney was being wheeled toward the waiting helicopter. Jeff followed along mechanically and began to step inside but an officer stopped him. "Family only, sir. I'm sorry. You and the young man's other friends can follow along by car." The words stung Jeff's heart. Cassidy looked nervously at him, wondering how this crisis was affecting Jeff's willingness to see his parents since he refused twice to acknowledge his relationship to David.

Carol Davenport had her arm firmly around Merit, and Michael hovered nearby, now focused completely on his daughter. Merit left her mother's side and ran to Jeff who opened his arms wide to catch her. "I'm so frightened, Jeff. What if he . . . ?"

"I'm frightened too, Merit, but you did a good job tonight. You brought him help and I'm proud of you." He held her for a long time. Two officers approached them to take down their statements. Cassidy and the Davenports sensed that the ordeal these two had shared required time alone and some space, and they went back to the tree to help clean up the debris after the police had taken photos. Carol wandered behind the tree where the police and media stood, snapping photographs. The photographer who had found the opening to the room the day before was giving a statement to the police. "I started to take a few photos of this cavern yesterday but I could see that the limbs were unstable. I was afraid my photos would just make people want to see it for themselves, so I didn't print them. I should have called someone though. I'm so sorry."

Carol smiled and tried to comfort the man. After he had taken his photographs he left, and despite the confusion and debris left behind, she could picture what plan had been laid for her daughter and she called to Cassidy and Michael to come inside and see. The table still stood in the center with the lace tablecloth atop, now sitting slightly askew and littered with icy debris. One of the pieces of stemware stood as a survivor of David's accident as did a plate and the silverware. The candelabra was left lying in the snow with the bottle of sparkling cider and the disposable camera. Michael Davenport picked it up and noticed that no exposures were used. No record of David's efforts had been made.

Carol's eyes teared up as she imagined the effort he had gone to and how his surprise had turned to sorrow. "I don't want Merit to see it this way," Carol said as she began to clear the table and shake the cloth. "And I want David to see it as he planned it." In a few minutes they restored as much as they could, then Michael lit the candles and called to his daughter.

He took Merit's hand and led her to the opening of the ice cavern and said, "This was David's surprise for you. Always remember that he did this for you out of love."

She looked around in awe, then buried her face in her father's chest and walked away.

Jeff called to Cassidy. "I want to get over to the hospital, Cassidy." She came to his side and took his arm as they headed for the cars.

Sterling stood in the parking lot, half in and half out of his truck. "Chet Foster, the sheriff's deputy, offered to sit up at Ben's place to wait for them. I told him I'd keep him posted from the hospital so he'd know what to tell them . . . and if things go . . . well, if things don't look good I'll go and wait myself." Ben's dear friend blew his nose and shook his head sadly. His voice wavered. "I don't think Ben and Natalie can bear to lose another boy . . ." Sterling pulled out and Cassidy could feel Jeff lurch as he reacted to the words of his father's best friend.

Jeff's face had a new expression, even more haunted than on the day Cassidy had found him, and he kept mumbling between shuddering sobs, "Everyone I try to love . . ."

Jeff was filthy, disheveled, and nearly out of his mind, so Cassidy decided to drive. As they walked through the doors of the emergency room's waiting area, a volunteer directed them to the shock trauma suite. It was sterile and cold, filled with people whose expressions were worried and tense. They saw Sterling and his wife seated on a padded bench drinking something hot. Cassidy and Jeff were about to sit when all three Davenports entered. Michael had an overnight bag in his hand and approached Jeff. "These probably won't fit well, but they're clean. There's a shirt and some slacks, and some things to help you wash up." His voice trailed off.

"Thank you," Jeff replied, gratefully accepting the offer to remove David's blood from his body. He headed down the hall to the rest room to change. He shivered as he washed David's blood from his hands. He wet the washcloth and pressed it against his face, enjoying the warmth and freshness of it after breathing the thick scent of sweat and blood for so long. He rewetted the cloth and pressed it to his face again and began to cry. Another life, touched by him, was ebbing. He wondered if this would forever be the course of his life, being the catalyst in the suffering of people he loved. It was almost too unbearable to continue. He hadn't caused David's accident, but what had David told Cassidy? He was trying to "trump Jeff Johnson." Had he blurred the line with David? In his joy of reclaiming his nephew, had he been irresponsible? Had he crossed the boundary between being buddies and being a good example? He slid down on the floor and sobbed, hating himself, and then he thought of Cassidy. She believed

in him. She believed he was a man of worth, a good man, and he had
dared to believe it too. He needed to get to Cassidy. He knew that
whatever happened this night, she would get him through it, and he
clung to that hope.

While Jeff changed, more friends of the Johansons came in. Brian
Hartman came in as well and sat near Merit. "Did you say that you
and David went snowmobiling?" she asked.

"Yeah," he replied. "Yesterday morning. He just came by out of
the blue. I was pretty rough on him though," he laughed sadly. "He
started to get hot, but then he just smiled and took it, and it was like
old times. All the crud just went away between us, you know?"

"Yes," she replied knowingly. "I do know."

A doctor came in through the doors and called to the group.
Sterling, considering himself the closest person to the family, stood up
and fumbled with his hat, anticipating whatever was about to be said.
The doctor addressed him.

"Are you David's uncle?"

"No, sir, a family friend. Can you tell us about the boy's condition?" he asked timidly.

"I can't release that information to anyone but next of kin. I can tell
you that he's critical and that he's lost a lot of blood, but I'm sure most
of you that were at the park tonight already knew that. Hospital policy
invites family and friends to give blood to replenish the supply. That's
about all you can do, and that's really all I can tell you right now."

"His family is away and we don't know how to reach them,"
Sterling added.

"Even his Uncle Jeff?" the doctor pressed.

Sterling looked puzzled and then winced. "The poor lad. His
uncle's been missing for over twenty years. David never even knew
him in fact," he replied. "He must be really bad off."

Cassidy stood now, afraid to acknowledge what she knew, but
curious to understand the nature of the inquiry. "Is David asking for
his uncle, Doctor?"

"Not really asking," he responded cautiously to her question.
"We're performing tests and have been stimulating him to keep him
alert and informed of his situation in order to get permission to treat.
We told him we need to contact his family and he muttered something

about an Uncle Jeff once and then he referred to a TJ." He faced Sterling and asked, "So there is no Uncle TJ either?"

Jeff had been standing, unseen, at the corner near the waiting room. He had heard his name mentioned and leaned against the wall trying to decide what to do when he heard that David had given his name as family. He stepped out from around the corner and caught Cassidy's eye. An entire conversation passed between them and something in the exchange caught the attention of the entire room. Jeff's eyes looked to hers for advice and strength, and she nodded encouragingly. He knew without question what he had to do.

"I am David's uncle, Doctor," he said extending his hand awkwardly. "I'm TJ Johanson."

Sterling and his wife gasped and looked to Cassidy for confirmation. Merit's mouth gaped open and she too looked to Cassidy for answers, but Cassidy saw only Jeff, and her proud smile confirmed his announcement. Sterling rose and walked over to Jeff, his eyes never leaving the younger man's face as the doctor looked on skeptically. Jeff offered the family friend his hand and apologized shakily, "I'm sorry, Mr. Davis. Cassidy and I were waiting to tell my folks on Christmas Eve."

The older gentleman looked at Jeff as if seeing him for the first time. His face was at first a twist of confusion and doubt, but within moments he saw something he missed before in the eyes and in the set of Jeff's bearded chin. His voice, rough and craggy with emotion, spoke. "You're not Ben's son . . . and you're not Natalie's son . . ."

Jeff's jaw tightened and he held his breath, expecting Sterling to deny his familial claim.

" . . . I can see both of them in you." Sterling placed his hands on Jeff's face and then recognition and acceptance, followed by relief and joy, broke across his own face. Jeff finally breathed. "Welcome home, son. Welcome home. You're a dream come true. Your parents' dream." They embraced, then thumped each other on the back.

Cassidy wept as did most of the room except for the doctor who was completely confused and still focused on his critically ill patient. Cassidy explained as briefly as possible, "They haven't seen him in a long time . . ." Then she walked to Jeff and touched his arm. He responded to her touch and pulled her tight against him, completely enveloping her in a swift embrace.

He brushed his lips against her ear and whispered shakily, "I'm welcome here, Cassidy. I'm almost home. Now we just need to pray for David."

Cassidy placed her hands on either side of Jeff's face, and their loving eyes met as she acknowledged what she had tried to assure him of many times but what words alone had not been able to convey.

Aware that Jeff was now ready to assume his place at David's side, she nodded in the direction of the doctor, sending him on to speak with David's physician. The two men walked through the doors to the emergency room, and when Jeff looked back at Cassidy over his shoulder, she smiled at him reassuringly, instantly knowing his concern. She then gathered the friends together and briefly told them the short version of the return of TJ Johanson. They understood Jeff's desire to be the one to reintroduce himself to the family, and they vowed their silence on the matter. The Johansons' had seen too much, faced too much, lost too much during their time on the mountain, and now, on this night when one oft-repeated prayer was being answered, another blow had been dealt.

Chapter Twenty-Six

Jeff followed the doctor past several curtained cubicles housing moaning patients and worried loved ones. Farther along the corridor he saw a group of several nurses and doctors hovering around the cubicle in the corner. Some were scurrying about, ferrying machines and supplies, but many simply stood there and observed. As the doctor led Jeff toward the group, they parted, allowing them access to David's bedside. Even the mangled image of David on the helicopter gurney had left Jeff unprepared for this scene.

The medical personnel had been too busy warming him and getting him stabilized to worry about the blood and minor wounds, so he laid there covered in dried blood. Every visible part of him was bare except for the warm, thermal blankets that covered his trunk and most of his legs. Part of his head had been shaved to accommodate the four inches of stitches used to close the gash to the back of his head. Bottles hung on numerous poles, and tubes ran in and out of his body. There were monitors and machines, each making their own distinctive, eerie sounds. His face was turned to the right and it was swollen and bloodstained, dotted with cuts and abrasions. His eyes were closed, almost buried beneath a bruised and protruding forehead and lids. His lips were puffy and cut and his nose was bulbous. A stream of blood left a trail down his chin and beyond. It was clear he had taken a hard, flat blow to the face.

The right hand that was so blue before was showing signs of pink on top, but Jeff could see that the underside was a dirty gray from its prolonged contact with the ice. He scanned David's covered body and could detect that his right hip and leg seemed misaligned. Jeff's face reflected his shock and disbelief, and the doctor took him by the arm and backed him out of the cubicle again, then told him to wait while he reentered the space and pulled the curtains tight. Jeff could hear muted whispers and strained to catch a phrase or a word, when the curtain again parted and the doctor reappeared.

"David was awake when I came to find you but he keeps fading in and out. The next time the nurse arouses him you'll have a few minutes to speak with him at his request. Do you understand?" The voice was detached.

Jeff nodded silently. It sounded too much like they were giving a dying man his last rites or something. Jeff felt weak and nauseated. "What is his condition?" he asked fearfully.

"He's lucky to have made it this far . . . but it's too early to tell yet," the doctor replied.

"Please, tell me *something*," Jeff pressed firmly.

"Some things we know and some things, the most important things, are still uncertain. We know his right hip is broken. That is serious and will require surgery. He has cuts and abrasions that are more a nuisance to him than a medical threat. The gash in his head has been sutured and should heal fine as well, but here is what we don't know: He's lost a lot of blood. Trauma and blood loss to this extent are very hard on all the body's systems, so we're monitoring him very closely. We're very worried about his right hand. He has signs of frostbite in the fingers, meaning possible nerve damage and perhaps even . . . well, we'll assess the extent of damage to the fingers. We are also very concerned about his head trauma, so we'll run him through some tests to determine whether or not there is any brain injury. It's obvious from the swelling to his face that he suffered at least one, but possibly several severe blows to the head and face, and his inability to remain lucid is a definite concern. I understand a heavy timber fell across his back and legs. That's probably what broke his hip, I'm guessing, since the line of bruising along his back crosses that spot. I am concerned that he's not moving his lower extremities spontaneously, and so he'll be examined further with some X rays and scans to determine if there's any injury to his spine."

"Are you concerned that he may be paralyzed?" Jeff asked in a broken voice.

"We're not comfortable with his responses to stimulation below the waist, and that is a serious worry since it could reflect an injury to his spine. We are also concerned about his kidneys since he has blood in his urine."

The list of his injuries unnerved Jeff. "Is there anything we can do, I mean . . . give blood or something?" Jeff asked, barely holding it together.

"I spoke with your group in the waiting room about giving blood. We are always in short supply at this time of the year. There may be some needs long-term if his kidneys are damaged, but we won't address that while he's here in the ER."

Jeff's head was spinning. *This can't be happening! He was plowing snow and planning a dream date with his sweetheart a few hours ago.*

A nurse came through the curtain and nodded to the doctor who nodded in return. "In the meantime though, David is awake and asking for you. At twenty he would be able to give his consent for whatever procedures we feel are required, but since he is only partially lucid, we may prefer to have the consent of the next of kin. Of course, if his situation deteriorates, we will act regardless of prior authorization. We have explained this to David, and he wants to speak with you." He parted the curtain with one hand, creating an opening, and Jeff reentered the cubicle, a sense of the surreal engulfing him. The doctor walked to David's side and touched his head gently. "David, I'm Doctor Thatcher. I have your Uncle TJ here. Do you understand?"

There was a slightly perceptible nod and then the doctor motioned to Jeff and moved away so he could draw near his nephew. He laid a shaky hand on David's battered shoulder, his fingers gently touching one of the few places not scraped and sore. He drew a deep breath to steady his voice and pulled his chair beside the bed, placing his own face near David's. Then he spoke softly.

"You sure do know how to get a girl's attention, pal." He fought to keep his voice steady. "When we get you out of here I'm going to help you sharpen your dating skills."

David's eyes fluttered slightly and Jeff thought he saw the tug of a smile at the corner of his mouth, then the eyes winced in pain and closed again. Jeff looked nervously at the nurse who was adjusting one of the IVs. She smiled reassuringly and encouraged him to keep speaking. He stroked David's matted head as he continued. "It was a beautiful thing you tried to do for Merit, David. Really. We looked inside and understood what you were planning. It was amazing."

David's eyes remained shut and his breathing was steady, so Jeff just sat by his side stroking his shoulder and staring at the distorted face of the only family he had at the moment. Several minutes went by and he eventually began to pull away to allow David rest.

"David, I'm going to go so you can rest, but I'll just be down the hall . . . I promise, okay?"

David's eyes opened and he moved his right hand to touch Jeff's arm. Then his eyes closed and he shook his head slightly, weakly gesturing for Jeff not to leave. Jeff leaned close to hear the words coming from David's fragile, husky voice.

"They say . . . you saved me." He opened his groggy eyes once more. "Thanks." David's hand attempted to squeeze Jeff's. It was slight, but it meant everything to the man.

"I didn't do it. The paramedics saved you," Jeff replied humbly, through trembling lips.

David's eyes seemed to close each time he spoke as if keeping them open drained his limited reserves. He spoke in short phrases with long pauses between. "But you came looking for me . . . I kept praying, 'Send Uncle TJ.'"

Jeff's heart broke at the words. It had to have been that prayer that kept him checking the clock all evening and sent him searching for David, because right now, Jeff was David's only family too.

"Remember," Jeff whispered in David's ear, "you promised me a rain check for a day of family fun." He leaned down and placed a soft kiss on David's ice-burned hand, still caught in the tender grip of Jeff's own hand. "And I'm holding you to it, got it?"

David again attempted to smile. "A couple things . . ." he said in his fading voice. Jeff remained close to hear. " . . . ask Cassidy to give Merit the tree." Jeff looked confused and David replied, "She'll know. Tell Merit I'm sorry. So much I wanted to tell her tonight . . ."

Jeff swallowed hard and nodded. "Next," David continued, growing more weak. "I love you . . . you're family to me. Tell everyone else I love them too."

Jeff's eyes began to tear and panic tinged his voice. "You tell them yourself, David. Do you understand me?"

David nodded. "Just . . . for now, okay?"

Jeff gripped his hand tighter, willing his fighting spirit into David. "Just for now."

Jeff thought he saw David nod slightly.

"Mom and Dad?"

Does he call Martha's new husband "Dad"? Jeff wondered. "No news yet, but I'm sure they'll be here soon, David."

Jeff considered what kind of man Sam was to win such devotion and affection from David in so short a time. He remembered a portion of their conversation in his office. After he had told David about his birth father, such sadness had filled David's face for a time, that despite the self-recrimination the answers would cause, Jeff pressed David to tell him how the loss of his father had affected him growing up. He was unprepared for the level of sadness expressed by the outwardly confident young man. David had described the shadow that hung over him as he considered why his father had never tried to see him and why his stepfather had walked out, but even more sad were the efforts he had made to keep his sadness hidden from those who could have eased his hurt. His concern had been for Omma, Pap, and his mother, and then Sam came into his life and brought him something that took the hurt away.

"Sam's a good man. Like a dad to you?"

A gentle peace crossed over David's face. "The best." Then a smile crossed his groggy face, and momentarily he became more serious. "I love him."

Dr. Thatcher was evaluating some data coming from one of the monitors and encouraged Jeff to keep David talking, hoping he'd remain lucid a while longer. Jeff's head nodded, signaling his willingness, and he pushed on, though afraid of what lay ahead.

He again rubbed David's matted hair, stimulating his awareness enough to cause him to slightly open his eyes.

"I love you, David. More than you can possibly know." The truth of the words was apparent. "I've thought about you a thousand times, nearly every day since I found out about you. I wondered how you were, what you looked like, if you and your mom were happy. I'm glad you have someone like Sam in your life." Regret mixed with relief hung in his voice.

David began to drift away again and Jeff tried to regain his attention. "Tell me about my new brother-in-law, David. What's he like?"

David's brow furrowed as he tried to understand the request. "Sam?" he asked with confusion, and then that peaceful smile returned to his face. " . . . corny . . . makes us laugh and feel safe . . . he knows God . . . God hears him . . ."

There was security and resolution in David's voice. Sam was David's anchor, and God was Sam's. Jeff wondered what that would be like since he'd had no anchor at all for so long . . . except for the recollections of his childlike faith in his own father. *Was that what Sam had in God?* he wondered.

David's ice-burned hand trembled in Jeff's and a tear trickled down his swollen face. His voice was barely a whispered thought. "I wish he were here . . . to give me a blessing . . . and to pray with me. I always feel everything will be alright when he prays."

Jeff didn't know how to respond to such intimate, spiritual professions. The feelings he felt made him uncomfortable. He was a man at odds with himself, both longing for these feelings and wanting to dismiss them at the same time. He thought about the video David gave him. How he both longed to believe that love and families could be permanent and create such security and, simultaneously, how that level of responsibility frightened him. He wondered what that level of commitment would require of a man. Sam was obviously that kind of man. David would be too . . . But was his father? *And could I be?* A chill ran down his back and he shuddered strongly enough to again cause David to open his eyes and peer into his own, and that look of pure trust and love settled his restless heart so he could comfort his nephew.

"He'll be here soon, David, and until he comes I'll stay close by every minute, okay?"

David squeezed Jeff's hand. "Thanks . . ." he whispered hoarsely, his eyes falling shut again. Jeff looked up into the doctor's face as he continued to pour over the data streaming across the monitor. He walked around the bed close to Jeff to speak to David.

"David, we need to get some more tests run right away. I'm going to send a nurse in with some forms for your uncle to sign giving us permission to treat you. Do you understand?"

"Doctor?" David responded.

Jeff shifted his worried eyes to Doctor Thatcher. "I'm here, David," the doctor said.

David closed his eyes again, summoning his remaining strength to perform his next feat, then opened them wider and used all his energy to lift his head. His eyes moved back and forth between David and Dr. Thatcher as if addressing this comment clearly to them both. "I . . . I'm a fighter . . . I'll do what it takes." It was a statement of fact. " . . . not afraid to die, not afraid to fight either," he said in a voice that was weak but resolute.

His head fell back hard onto the backboard and then he was out cold. Jeff's frantic expression met the doctor's, who was smiling. "He's a fighter. That's good. I don't think we're in a life-or-death struggle anymore, but now we're fighting for quality of life. We need to wait and see. He'll need a fighting spirit. But right now we need to get him down to radiology."

"Can I stay with David until you move him?" he asked.

Doctor Thatcher looked at the nurse and then nodded. "For a few minutes more, and then she'll take you to the lab to donate blood if you'd like."

The nurse pulled the curtain closed and Jeff slowly lowered himself to his knees. He took David's hands in his own and bowed his head. *Dear God . . .* he began silently as he poured his heart out, a willing surrogate for David's beloved Sam. After a few minutes he could hear the sound of feet outside the curtain, and he pulled himself back into the chair. "They're ready to take David to radiology now, and I'll take you down to the lab if you'd like to donate blood."

"Okay, but I'd like a minute to fill everyone in on David's condition first," Jeff said. He turned to leave David and then hesitated. A part of him was afraid to leave his side although he knew he must. He leaned down and whispered in his ear, "I love you, David, and I'll be close by," and then he exited the white curtains.

In a moment he was back in the waiting room and everyone stood in anticipation of some news. Jeff methodically shared some of the information he had been given and they responded with shock at the gravity of David's situation. Jeff pulled Cassidy aside to speak to her privately. "I'm going to the lab to donate blood, but I need to ask you something first. Do you know anything about a tree for Merit?" Jeff asked, remembering David's specific request.

Her first response to the question was a blank stare and then she understood. She reached into her handbag and pulled out a white gift box with silver lettering. She opened the lid then lifted the cotton padding, and showed Jeff the crystal tree she had picked up hours ago, but which now seemed like decades ago. Jeff pulled the tree from the box and stared at it, realizing how much it resembled the ever-green in the park.

"He wants you to give it to Merit and tell her he's sorry. Tell her he had so much he wanted to say to her tonight," Jeff repeated. Then, almost to himself, he whispered, "and pray he still gets the chance."

Cassidy placed the crystal tree back in the box. "I can't believe any of this," she said burying her head into Jeff's chest.

"I know," he replied, the sound of fatigue and discouragement heavy in his voice. He held her close, grateful for the comfort she brought him, and then he pulled away. "I need to go now. You'll talk to Merit?" Cassidy nodded as he turned away down the hall, then she headed toward Merit to give her the gift, hoping it would comfort her young friend and convey all that David had wished.

Chapter Twenty-Seven

Sam and Martha arrived in Raleigh in the afternoon to find her parents half asleep in two of the padded airport chairs. They grabbed their luggage and were on their way north before 3:00 P.M. They had made good time the first hour or so, benefiting from the midday melting, but as they drove on, what was wet became icy and their pace slowed until they were crawling along in four-wheel drive, passing abandoned vehicles that had slid off the road and lodged into the drifts on the sides. The women begged them to pull off and get a motel, and they even obliged once or twice, but every room and restaurant was packed with stranded travelers, so the little company continued.

They had expected to stop for a late supper in Arlington, Virginia, about two hours from home. It was a reasonable expectation considering that in good weather they should have made the trip within six hours, but there they were, just barely north of Richmond, their halfway point, at 8:00 P.M. It was after 3:00 A.M. when Ben Johanson exited the interstate and headed onto the state road that ran past the farm. Sam sat in front with him, having traded off the driver's seat an hour back. Both men were exhausted but had pressed along toward home, making weary conversation to try keeping each other alert. It had been an arduous trip, but the worst leg, as Ben expected, was the ten-mile stretch over South Mountain, but joy seized his heart as he began to see their sign at the end of the road. It was short-lived. As soon as he pulled up the lane he noticed two signs of trouble. A sheriff's car was in the driveway and his Jeep was not. Without even realizing it he gave voice to his thoughts, and Sam repeated the worrisome observation. Martha and Natalie awoke at the same moment, puzzled and fearful.

Ben had not even had a chance to turn the key off before the deputy jumped out of the truck, wrapped in a heavy quilt, and headed for their vehicle.

"Glad you made it home okay, Mr. Johanson. I expected you some time ago, but then the road reports sound terrible. I guess the going was slow."

Ben looked at him nervously. He had bad news. Why else would he be sitting freezing in the driveway? "Where's David and the Jeep, Chet?" Ben asked.

"There's been an accident, Mr. Johanson," he replied cautiously.

"A car accident?" Martha said, panicked.

"No, ma'am," he reassured. "It's a long story, but a heavy branch from the old tree at Veterans' Park fell on David. They took him to shock trauma about nine tonight. Sterling Davis has been updating me on the cell phone. He says you should get right over there."

Martha and Natalie rifled off question after painful question back and forth amongst themselves, while Ben turned the vehicle around and headed in the direction of the hospital.

* * *

Carol had not wanted to impose on her daughter's vigil, but as the waiting room clock hit 2:30 A.M. she tried to talk Merit into going home for a few hours of sleep after which Carol promised to bring Merit straight back to the hospital.

"I can't, Mom," she wailed. "Not until I get a chance to see him, even if it's just for a moment. I don't even care if he knows I'm there. I just need to see him." She buried her head into her mother's shoulder, but there were no more tears. She was exhausted to the point of collapse, and Carol looked to Jeff and Cassidy for help. Cassidy whispered in Jeff's ear and he nodded reluctantly and left. Cassidy looked back toward Carol with a hopeful smile. They had all been through this three times already. Doctor Thatcher had been called away to attend to another case while David was in radiology, and during that time his associate had become the attending physician. Jeff had asked him over and over if he could bring Merit back to see David when he returned from all his tests, but he staunchly refused, saying that only family could be brought back. Finally Jeff had a new idea. It was tricky, maybe even irresponsible, but he thought it might work.

"Is my nephew back yet?" he asked the physician.

A nurse standing nearby overheard the question and replied, "They're bringing him up right now."

"Can I see him when he's settled back in?"

The doctor asked one of the nurses to bring David's chart to him and he asked her a few questions before turning to speak with Jeff.

"He's out of radiology but the radiologist is still reading the results and the reports aren't all in. His vitals look a little better and his body temperature is nearly where we like it. There was a backlog on one of the machines, so while he was waiting the nurses cleaned him up a bit. I think you can see him for a few minutes. We've moved him. He's farther down the corridor and to the left."

As Jeff entered the shock trauma suite again he walked back down the corridor and past the area where David had previously been. When he got to the room, David's eyes were closed, but his face was now washed, making the injuries more identifiable. And even though his face was dreadfully swollen and the bruises were now more apparent than before, there was something in his countenance that allayed some of Jeff's fear and brought him a peaceful sense of optimism. He quietly entered the cubicle and gently drew the curtains closed behind him. The soft rustle of the fabric awakened David. His face soon registered his pleasure at Jeff's return, and he signaled this by extending his shaky, swathed right hand to his uncle.

Jeff took it gently in both of his own hands and drew closer to David. "You look so much better than you did a couple of hours ago," Jeff said with a smile.

"I'm not sure about that, but I feel a little better," David replied weakly.

"You really gave us a scare, pal."

"I know . . . I feel so lame." His eyes closed but his smile hung on and Jeff ruffled his hair, carefully avoiding the stitches.

"So how are you feeling?" Jeff asked more seriously. A broad, darkening line was visible at the top of David's left shoulder and reportedly angled down his back and leg, and he worried about the damage the heavy limb had caused the entire area.

"Warmer," David said, again with a reassuring smile. "Pretty popular too," he joked. "Everybody wants to see me, plastic surgeons, neurologists, orthopedists, therapists, urologists."

"What are they saying?" Jeff prodded.

David was obviously more lucid, but his fatigue was apparent, leaving his speech weak and slow. "The plastic surgeon said I was very lucky my face was resting on my arm so I don't have any frostbite on my cheeks, so that's good . . . but they still seem pretty worried about my hand." He unconsciously moved his wrist slightly. "They've been bathing it, trying to help the circul . . ." He struggled in his fatigue to get the word right.

"Circulation?" Jeff offered.

"Yeah," he said with a weak smile. "My hip has a compound fracture, so I'll be going up to surgery for that at some point. They think the blow damaged one of my kidneys. But, all things considered . . . I think everybody is feeling pretty optimistic about me right now."

"Can you . . . I mean, do you . . . ?" Jeff stammered.

"Does this answer your question?" David asked as he slowly wiggled his toes under the blanket.

"Ahhh," Jeff sighed with relief. "That's the most beautiful thing I've ever seen."

David laughed softly. "Yeah . . . me too." He closed his eyes for a moment, and the two men remained quiet for a while, allowing the joy and relief to wash over them.

"It was going to be so great," David said with regret and then laughed in frustration. "I just wanted to give her one wonderful night that she could remember while I was away . . . so I wouldn't just be a photo, you know?"

"I know," said Jeff, and David knew he did.

"Is she still here?" David asked in alarm. "What time is it?"

"After 3:00 A.M.," Jeff answered. "She's been asking to come back, but the doctors have told her only family is allowed back. But she won't leave until the doctors let her see you," Jeff said, leading David where he hoped he would go. At first David seemed ready to call for her, but then a look of worry crossed his face and he became silent and subdued.

"Maybe they're right to make her wait. I look terrible, and that would probably frighten her. Besides, things are looking better now, but they still aren't sure what the final story is going to be until the reports are all in. What if she thinks I'm fine and then I turn out to have problems? Why put her through that roller-coaster ride?"

"Put yourself in Merit's position. If the places were reversed, how would you feel?"

David considered that. "How can we get her back here?" David asked.

"I don't think they would let just a friend come back." Jeff smiled an I've-got-a-plan smile, then added, "but they would allow your *fiancée* to come back."

David's eyes closed again and he coughed from the exertion of laughing. He took a few deep breaths to calm the spasm, and Jeff tried to mask his worry.

David's coughing spell sent a grandmotherly nurse scrambling in to check on him. "You are about due for pain medication, David, do you need a little something?" she asked.

"I want to stay alert but maybe something just to take the edge off . . ."

Nurse Grace Walker returned with David's pill and as she turned to leave, David seized the opportunity to try to get Merit past the medical guards.

"Nurse, does the hospital consider a fiancée to be a member of the family?" David asked.

"Well, of course they do," she replied curiously.

"Well, tonight was going to be the most wonderful night of my life." His voice was tender but frail as he struggled to make his mouth obey him. "There is a beautiful girl in the waiting room, and I love her. Tonight was supposed to be the night I was going to open a little white box, give her a symbol of my affection, and tell her how I feel . . ." He was weary beyond belief and aching from head to toe, but he continued, " . . . but I never got the chance. It would mean everything to me if I could just hold her hand for a few minutes and say a few words to her myself. Do you think you could help make that happen for me?"

Grace's response could not have been more resolute if Uncle Sam himself pointed his patriotic finger at her and said personally, "Grace Walker, WE NEED YOU!"

Within seconds Grace had a name and was on her way. Jeff
knelt next to David and said, "I concede my title to you, nephew."
David blushed as he considered that his melodrama bordered on
perjury, and then his eyes shut and he became more quiet and said,
"I know I probably went too far but, you were right, Jeff, I really do
need to see her."

Jeff smiled softly back at him. "I know you do. I understand."

It was only a few minutes before the nurse parted the curtains and
returned to David's area. "I have some good news, David. The scan
on your back is in. The spine looks good! That ought to make you
happy." She smiled innocently enough and continued, "I have
another surprise for you." She parted the curtains farther and Merit's
timid face appeared. Her eyes met David's for just a brief moment
before Grace stepped between them, blocking their view.

"Dr. Thatcher knows she's here, but still, she can only stay for a
few minutes, okay?"

Merit slowly approached David, unsure of what to do or how to
be with him. He sensed that her discomfort was equal to his own and
he broke the ice by gently offering his bandaged hand to her. She
took it shakily in both her own hands, and he pulled her softly to
him, drawing her hands near his chest. His eyes were moist as were
hers, and Jeff sensed that it was time for him to make his exit. He
pulled his chair up close behind her and she sat down while her eyes
scanned the totality of David's injuries.

Jeff slipped through the curtained partition, unsure whether to
leave them and return to the waiting area, or to stay close by in case
Merit needed a shoulder to lean on when she left David's side. He
began to walk back up the corridor when he heard the nurse call to
Doctor Thatcher.

"Doctor, David's father and mother have just arrived. Should I
bring them back to his area or do you want to meet with them first?"

Jeff's heart stopped beating for a second. *Martha is here? Is that
what she's saying? My baby sister is here?*

"Just bring them in and I'll meet with them here at the station."

Jeff was torn. He wanted desperately to stay close by and catch a
glimpse of her and her new husband. He needed to see her face, to see
that she was happy, but he knew this was not the time. Martha's only

concern right now would be David, and as selfishly as Jeff wanted to see her, he backed away up the outer corridor, allowing her time to be reassured about her son before he dealt a new surprise to the family.

He walked slowly up the unfamiliar corridor on the far side of the ring of cubicles. He saw the exit door ahead of him and his knees nearly buckled. *If Martha is here, my parents are here too. Right beyond that door . . .* A large button on the wall powered the door. Jeff raised his hand toward it and then paused while his head and heart prepared. The promise of new life lay beyond it, but he had no certainty whether or not it would be a life of healing and acceptance or the belated reckoning for his disappointing past. But one thing he knew for sure, that no matter what, Cassidy would stand with him, and that would be enough if that was all he was to have. He drew in a deep breath and pressed the button and the large, white door swung open.

He hung back against the wall for a moment to assess specifically where this entrance was in relation to the waiting room. He soon recognized it as the hallway he had taken when returning from donating blood. He entered the hallway, walked slowly to the corner, and peered around to where a crowd of people was talking excitedly in the center of the room. There were a few family friends he didn't recognize, and then he saw Cassidy nervously scanning the area around the first entrance, the one Jeff had entered. Jeff knew she was trying frantically to locate him, to prepare him before he walked unaware into this melee. He tried to get her attention but could not, and then the circle shifted and Jeff caught a momentary glimpse of his father.

His feelings were both natural and surreal. His brow furrowed as he considered his dad's appearance. He had caught a few sweet glimpses of him the morning of the breakfast, but he had been dressed as Santa with most of his face hidden behind his beard. Tonight, the years were showing in the deepened creases in his face and the pale color of his skin. *How much of this is his worry over David?* Jeff wondered. It was hard to tell. But in either case, he still looked wonderful. Even from forty yards away there was something about the way he carried himself, and his expressions, filled with strength and caring, that made Jeff remember how safe and secure he'd felt in his father's presence. His father wasn't speaking much. He had asked his questions and now stood rather quietly, absorbing the frantically delivered information being thrown at him. His right hand was on his face. His thumb and fingers framed his chin while his index finger tapped firmly against his tightly pursed lips. His left arm was elevated, and then Jeff saw that it was resting across the shoulders of his worried mother.

She seemed more distracted, listening to the chatter going on around her but leaning heavily against Ben, and Jeff's heart broke as he considered whether this latest family accident would be the straw that would break her spirit. He watched her cautiously, concerned about her darting eyes and the confusion she reflected. *Is she okay?* Then he noticed how frequently she met Cassidy's gaze and how many attempts Cassidy made to avoid it, and then Jeff knew his mother was searching for him and begging for confirmation from Cassidy that he was indeed there.

Again, Jeff tried to get Cassidy's attention, but she was still focusing on the door he had left by, with no idea that he would possibly return from a different direction. He stayed near the corner, trying to catch snippets of the frantic conversation to get a feel for the mood of his parents, and then he saw the Davenports seated alone against the wall. Carol's head was resting on Mike's shoulder, but her eyes were scanning the room as she tried to catch some news about David's condition while trying not to be too apparent. Jeff now tried to get her attention while he monitored Sterling's recounting of David's rescue.

"When we got the call over at the home, it only took seconds before we had twenty men rushing over to the park. You'd have been proud of them, Ben. The people of this town love you and your family. That's for sure."

Sterling went on detailing who the paramedics were and about the helicopter's arrival. Jeff knew he was trying to satisfy his father's need for information without disclosing anything he had recently discovered about Ben's long-lost son. *Poor Sterling,* Jeff thought to himself.

Ben's brow furrowed and his eyes reflected a question forming in his mind. Jeff knew that it would only be moments before someone would slip up and leak out the secret that he had carefully planned to reveal to his family in private. He finally managed to catch Carol's attention, and after he gestured for her secrecy, he mouthed for her to get Cassidy.

Carol walked casually toward the inundated woman and tried to sidle in near enough to her to whisper in her ear. Just as she reached for her arm to get her full attention Ben posed his question and brought the room to a sudden silence.

"Who made the call?" he asked Sterling.

"What . . . ?" Sterling asked, dodging the question.

"You said a call came into Brighton and then twenty men hurried over to the park. Who made the call? Who found David?"

Sterling cast his eyes to the floor, as if hoping some suitable answer would be found there. Natalie picked up on the stall immediately and now bore her eyes into Cassidy.

"I just want to thank whoever it was who saved my grandson," Ben reassured Sterling. "If you don't know who called, then who took the call?" he pressed.

Sterling's eyes instinctively shot an involuntary peek at Cassidy, who finally felt the firm tug on her arm. Delighted for any diversion at that moment she turned to face Carol who whispered her message. Cassidy's eyes also shot involuntarily in Jeff's direction. No one caught it—except for Natalie.

Ben was getting frustrated now as he too could sense that the question was being dodged. "Cassidy, did you take the call?" he asked more directly.

Cassidy conferred with Jeff with a glance from the corner of her eye. She caught a slight but definite nod and a nervous smile granting her his approval to answer. "Yes, Ben," she answered warmly. "I took the call last night. It was from Merit." She looked at Natalie, paused, and smiled a knowing smile. "Merit and my fiancé found David."

Natalie grabbed Cassidy's arms in both of her hands, looked into her eyes for confirmation, and upon finding it, nearly sunk to the floor in relief. Cassidy hugged her tightly and then relaxed her hold as Ben's questions began again. She was so caught up in them that neither she nor anyone else in the group noticed that Natalie had pulled herself away and was walking in the direction of Cassidy's stolen glance.

Jeff saw her coming. He saw every weak-kneed, love-filled step as she approached the darkened corner. He stood there, frozen and immovable with tears streaming down his face. "She's looking for me," he muttered through his quivering lips, and then he was not even aware that his own feet began to propel him toward her in return.

Ben saw Natalie's awkward, almost dumbstruck motion and called to her, but she heard nothing but the pounding in her heart. Alarmed, he too left the group and followed slowly behind her, quizzical about her strange, numbed behavior. Then he realized she wasn't walking away from the group, she was walking toward a man.

When Natalie came within four feet of Jeff she stopped. He looked into the loving eyes of the mother who had cradled and loved him through sickness and sorrow. Her face, firm and resolute a few minutes earlier, melted into peaceful exhaustion. He came within arms' reach of her and touched her face with his hands, his fingers trembling as was his frame. Natalie's hands also reached for his face and, for the first time, she broke into an idyllic smile.

"I recognized you that morning," she cooed to her boy through her tears. Jeff could only nod in response. "Every day for twenty years I've held your image in my memory, searching for you in every young man's face . . ."

Jeff's response was automatic. "That day, at Brighton, I couldn't take my eyes off you, Mom. I wanted . . . but I . . ."

Natalie brought his face close to hers and kissed his forehead. "A mother knows her child . . . a mother always knows."

They fell into a tight embrace. Jeff buried his face in his mother's shoulder and she patted his head as she had done when he was a child. "I'm so sorry, Mama," he cried.

"No sorrows, TJ, and no more regrets. You're home now. That's all we've ever wanted."

Ben had moved within steps of Natalie, wondering about the man in the shadows who now filled his sobbing wife's arms. He had caught a glimpse of his face during the moment between the time he had walked from the hallway and when he'd buried his face in her shoulder. Ben knew that face. He recognized it . . . but why? And then he heard Natalie say it. She spoke the nearly sacred name that had hung in the very air of their home for twenty years—the name that had been in every prayer he'd uttered the past twenty years. *TJ.*

He stalled in his place, and then he spoke his son's name. It came out more like a guttural moan than a name, and the depth of the emotion that pressed it from his lips caught Natalie off guard and brought her back to the present. She lifted Jeff's head from her shoulders, looked into his eyes and smiled, and then backed away, clearing the space between father and son. It was such a simple act, but as she did it she thought how different things might have been if she had simply done that long ago, if she had simply cleared the space between them and allowed them to clearly see each other, instead of hovering around trying to make everything pretty and fine. But what had she said to TJ? *No more sorrows, no more regrets,* she remembered, and she let go of the thought.

Jeff was slow to let go of the complete and nonjudgmental love his mother offered him. He felt her pulling away and fought it. It had been the theme of so many terrible night terrors. He would find her and she would love him, and then she would hear about his past and pull away. But he had heard something behind her and knew someone was there. Yet sensing that her release of him was as hard for her as he found it to be, he relaxed his embrace, coughed to clear the emotion from his throat, and took a deep breath. He wiped a shaky arm across his reddened, wet face and looked up into the face of the man he most revered and feared, who now stood just a few feet away. Ben's tall, proud frame sagged as the recognition hit him.

"TJ?"

It came out softly and guarded. *Could it be?* He doubted. He looked deeply into the eyes of the man before him. "TJ?" The words were filled with desperate wanting. Jeff stood, silently quivering, assessing his father's reaction. Ben searched the eyes some more and recognized them. He felt like he was falling, being pulled through a funnel of time to a place where a handsome, rascally young boy followed adoringly after him through the fields and orchards. He looked past the early lines around the reddened eyes and recognized the soft smile of the adolescent who asked a million questions and wanted to mimic his father's every move and labor. Where had that love gone? Where had that boy gone? Then Ben saw the sadness in those same eyes and knew that the rebellion had passed and had evidently taken his precious young son to a terrible place, where the price extracted for his inner turmoil had been high. Now he simply wanted to hold his boy and recapture some of his terrible loss.

"Son!" Ben fell into the trembling embrace of his relieved boy. "TJ . . . TJ . . ."

The embrace was long and still. They held each other, treasuring the feel of strong arms. There was peace and forgiveness in their embrace, and slowly, as their personal recriminations melted away and mercy filled those places, they relaxed and moved apart to again stare into their loved one's eyes, each one now filled with joy and hope.

"I love you, Pop." Jeff spoke hoarsely.

"I love you, son," Ben replied, smiling through joyful tears. "We prayed for you every day, son. Every day . . . prayed you were all right, prayed you'd walk through the door . . . or call . . ."

Jeff's heart stung at the realization that he had been welcome. He had always been welcome. "I wanted to call. I wanted to come home, Pop. I just messed up so badly I didn't know if you'd still want me." Jeff's voice broke. Ben's heart broke. He began to offer his firm assurance that he and Natalie always wanted the return of their son, but he suddenly halted, his heart painfully considering what he had done to leave such a doubt in the mind of his son.

Ben put his hands on Jeff's shoulders and the two men's heads bent and touched, unable to meet one another's gaze. "I'm sorry for whatever I did or said that would have made you wonder that, TJ. I never stopped loving you, son. And your mother, well, you can imagine the vigil she has kept for you all these years."

Jeff's voice broke and caught. "You don't know, Dad. You don't know what I've done . . . where I've been. What if . . . ?"

Natalie had hung back, acutely aware that their family's future rested heavily on the success of these two men connecting during these early minutes, but this time it was right for her to jump in with a different goal, to rebuild this bridge between these two men she loved so much. She approached quietly and laid her arms softly across the backs of each of the men she loved, then she spoke. "Let's all make a promise right here, right now, okay? No more sorrows, no more regrets for any of us. You're home now, TJ. That's all we've ever wanted. We do want to hear everything about these last twenty-one years, where you've been, what has happened to you all this time . . . but not to question you or to judge you. Just to understand who you are now."

Natalie took a finger and brushed a sweaty wisp of hair from Jeff's brow while the arm that hung around Ben's shoulder gave her grateful husband a reassuring squeeze. He looked at her and nodded, encouraging her to continue on as his voice as well.

" . . . and then, we won't look back anymore. We'll make a fresh start and just enjoy being a family again. Sound good to you?" Her voice broke as the tears ran freely.

Cassidy and the little band of Johanson friends watched from an understanding distance. She saw Natalie rejoin her men and then watched their response as she spoke in soft, steady tones. And then she watched their embrace tighten and their circle close, their bodies shaking once again with emotion. But this time it was intermingled with laughter and kisses.

Jeff's head lifted and he scanned the room to locate Cassidy. He found her, watching the reunion with the others, silently weeping for joy. Ben noticed the shift in Jeff's attention and he looked over his shoulder to see who was capturing Jeff's eye. When he saw Cassidy he immediately broke his embrace, stepped back, and opened the circle to draw her in. There was another round of tears and congratulations and soon the rest of the group was upon the family, shaking hands and thumping their backs. A few moments later Martha, Sam, and Merit emerged from the emergency room door to find that the mood in the room had changed dramatically. Natalie caught Martha's searching expression and began to walk over to her. Before she reached her, Martha sighted TJ, screamed his name, and ran full tilt into his arms.

"Thank you, TJ . . . thank you," she repeated over and over in his ear as she squeezed him close. He was speechless. He could neither reply nor reconcile her response to his presence. *How did she recognize me after all these years?* And then he had his answer. *David . . . David must have told her about me!* With his questions answered and his fears of their first meeting suddenly dispelled, he allowed himself to enjoy this smothering of family love. He whispered in Martha's ear, "I've been so worried about you all these years. I'm so sorry for all the problems I brought into your life."

Martha pulled away from him and looked him firmly in the eye. "Never apologize to me again, brother. I made my own choices. They may not have been the best ones at the time, but they were *mine*. And now I still have my wonderful son, thanks to you. I love you, TJ. I've loved and missed you every day."

She drew him close and hugged him again and the years melted away. He picked her up as he straightened his back until her feet left the ground. Then he swung her, sending her legs splaying like a rag doll until everyone was laughing at the sight of sibling joy. "Martha, Martha, you're still my little pet."

"I'd forgotten how wonderfully annoying it was to be 'big brother's pet,'" she teased as he placed her softly back on solid ground.

"How's David?" he asked more somberly.

She sighed. "The tests came back and David's back is fine. One of his kidneys is badly damaged but they don't know yet to what extent. They're still worried about his hip. He's going to need surgery, but they're waiting to make sure his lungs are clear enough to handle the anesthesia. Isn't that good news?" It was more a call for support than a medical report, and everyone knew it. Natalie and Ben placed rallying arms around her and Sam comforted her.

"How . . . is his hand?" Jeff asked tentatively.

Martha began but her voice wavered, and Sam answered for her. "He has tissue damage from the frostbite. They're not sure if they'll be able to save all the tissue on his fingers. I looked at them. They're pretty bad, but only time will tell. He has a bad cough from a pulmonary contusion—a bruise to the lung—which probably occurred at the same time the hip and kidney were damaged, so that's preventing them from moving ahead with the hip surgery. But if the tests on the kidneys indicate an elevated myoglobin level, they'll probably remove the damaged kidney tonight or early tomorrow morning." A little sob issued from Martha, and Sam came behind her and placed his gentle hands on her shoulders to comfort her. "But all things considered," he reminded everyone, "he's out of the woods and we'll get him home with us soon."

Martha looked back at Jeff and spoke in hushed tones. "It's because of you. If you hadn't gone looking for him . . ." Her voice trailed off and her head fell back against Jeff's chest. As he held her, his eyes met his new brother-in-law's for the first time across Martha's tired head.

"David kept calling for you," he whispered to Sam as he stroked his sister's hair with one hand and extended the other in his brother-in-law's direction. "He calls you 'Dad.' He really loves you."

"I feel like I let him down tonight. I know it wasn't our fault that we weren't here, but to know he needed me and I wasn't there . . ."

"He wanted to . . . uh, pray with you," Jeff said awkwardly. "Did you give him a . . . a blessing? He kept mentioning that."

Sam nodded his head. Martha could sense that he was now the one in need of comfort, so she turned, placing a hand on his arm. "It was a beautiful blessing, Sam."

Jeff marveled at this little family, with their gentle touches, the way they immediately responded to each unspoken need, the comfortable way they spoke of God and godly things. It wasn't pretentious or showy. It was as subtle a part of their communication as a smile or a nod. They had built something special. Something he would have to carefully consider. He thought about Cassidy and knew he wanted that kind of closeness with her and with any children they might have. Yes . . . they would have to carefully consider what this could mean for their future family.

Chapter Twenty-Eight

The family all remained in the waiting area until David could be seen in the recovery room the following removal of his kidney. He had been taken up at 4:30 A.M. and it was almost 9:00 A.M. before they spoke of leaving. Suddenly Martha grabbed Jeff's arm. "You're not going to drive all the way back to Frederick, are you? Come home to the farm. You can have your old room back."

It was the very suggestion Natalie had been dying to make. Jeff looked into the faces of his parents and then looked into Cassidy's eyes. He saw encouragement and accepted the awkward but desirable invitation. Sam drove Ben's Suburban with Natalie and Martha in tow, and Ben followed Jeff to his car. "Mind if I ride with you, son?" he asked.

Jeff tilted his head down to mask his nervous smile. Then, no longer afraid to let the depth of his emotions show, he raised his head and replied, "Climb on in, Pop."

The first few minutes passed silently, and then Ben began making idle small talk, but Jeff heard none of it. He just marveled that he could steal glances at his dad from time to time. He slid a shy hand across the seat to take hold of the work-worn hand of his father. Ben smiled back and squeezed his son's hand in return. It was as if a vacuum had burst and fresh air rushed in. The heavy awkwardness was swept away. No more words. Not right now. None were needed.

Jeff paused the car at the foot of the driveway. Ben squeezed his hand, prompting him on. The car proceeded slowly as Jeff drew in every sight, his mind racing between the images of the past and the present. Not much had changed. It was comfortable and familiar.

"You never took down my old fort," Jeff whispered in wonder. "It looks the same."

Ben's lip quivered. "Thought about it several times," his voice wavered. "Just kept repainting it . . ." He coughed to clear the emotion from his voice and went on. "I've probably spent as much time in there repairing it as I did building it," he laughed.

Jeff understood the message. He was home. The door had always been open and they had always been waiting. When they reached the house it was as if time had stood still. There was a new porch and some obvious signs that they had prospered and improved the property, but it felt like home. He walked up the stairs and rang the dinner bell. He placed his trembling hands on the door handle that he had closed so many years before and paused as that last day ran through his memory. He winced at the pain of it, then pushed the thoughts aside along with the door.

In the kitchen the aroma of bacon and eggs already hung in the air. Natalie turned to face the door as the two men entered the house. She wanted to rush back into the arms of her son but she held back, aware of how fragile his composure was. Jeff scanned the scene, aware of the tension as each family member awaited his reaction to his homecoming. He saw Martha, dear, shy Martha, and Sam, trying to appear "natural," flipping pancakes and scrambling eggs, casting smiles in his direction as if his entrance were an everyday occurrence. He glanced in the family room, which, though silent to everyone else, was filled with the chatter and laughter of every memory he had ever conjured of home. He moved through the open space between the large kitchen and the family room, ghostlike, hovering over everything familiar but touching nothing, as if corporeal intent would shatter the dream and render him lost and alone again.

Finally he could resist no more as he reverently touched his father's chair, which, although replaced several times over, still sat in the same place. And then he moved to the mantel and the photo. He was there, frozen in time, just like his memories. He reached to take it and pulled back again, then finally broke the spell that bound him and reached for it once more. He held it in his hands staring into each and every smiling face, standing before the great, gaudy Christmas tree, and then he drew the photo to his breast, stared at it again, and winced in pain. No one knew what to do. Natalie wanted to run to him and embrace him while Ben seemed to cower. Slowly, so slowly he approached his son, unable to meet his gaze.

"After you . . . after you left, I couldn't bear to see that picture. I guess I was hurt . . . and angry for a time. And then," he paused long while he ordered his thoughts, "I was ashamed . . . Every time I saw the photo I felt so ashamed that I had let you down . . . that I hadn't made you feel loved enough to believe that I would love you no matter what. I failed you, son. I knew that. And every time I looked at that picture, I was reminded of that."

Jeff stood riveted in his place, his eyes never leaving the photo, his ears not missing a word. The pain in his father's voice chilled him. He knew those feelings. They had been his feelings. Guilt, hurt, shame. *How could they have been my father's feelings too?*

" . . . so I tried to hide it. I tried to make your mother put it away so I wouldn't have to face my failure, but she wouldn't hear of it. No, sir . . . not for one minute. Almost destroyed us. Almost tore us apart. Then one day we realized that we were both hurting and missing you separately, and that was what was tearing us apart. So we finally started to miss you together. I've been writing my feelings in my old journals for almost forty-three years, but I never learned to really talk about how I felt, until recently. Forty years of silent suffering and it took me having a near-fatal run-in with an old steer to finally jar your mother and me out of our pride and make us talk." He shook his head in sorrow then turned to face Martha as well. "We realized that mistakes we made when you were both little kept us from being the kind of family we wanted, from being the parents you both deserved, and giving you the support you both needed. Our problems came back to hurt each of you, and the guilt we each felt made us unwilling to forgive or to ask for forgiveness. Finally, after the accident, I asked your mother to read what I had been unable to say. Now I have to live with the knowledge that if she had known those things years ago, things might have gone a lot different around here, and that my pride—"

Natalie spoke up firmly as she came to Ben's side. "Our pride . . ."

Ben clasped his hand over hers and smiled at his wife. " . . . has hurt us all."

Jeff tried twice to speak, but no words would form. Finally he uttered, "I know about pride too, Dad." He replaced the photo and slumped into the sofa, burying his head in his hands. "I always wanted be like you, but the pedestal I placed you on seemed too high, so I quit reaching. I thought I'd set my own standard, but when things started spiraling out of control, I was too proud to ask for help until I was just . . . lost."

A suffocating silence separated father, mother, and son. Sam had been observing this agonizing exchange from across the room until he could no longer refrain from sharing the thought that kept pressing upon his mind. He cleared his throat nervously and spoke. "Back in California, David kept trying to fill me in on the family lore, the stories and the miracle of David's Tree. When I arrived here the reach of that evergreen marvel amazed me, but I think you have an even greater miracle right here, today."

The room remained quiet. Martha looked into Sam's face and smiled a grateful, adoring smile. Watching her two families, and thinking of the home she had finally built, she knew what was different about Sam. He was open and fearless about his heart. Her family loved one another, but they had become masters of tucking away the unpleasantries in closets or behind walls where those forgotten hurts had time to fester and grow until they could no longer be contained. There were no walls or closets in Sam's heart. He loved unconditionally. The good, the bad, the messy parts of life seemed inconsequential to him in the whole scheme of things. Sam didn't work on a standard calendar. He was working on a much broader understanding of time. Love was forever to Sam, and in forever, a crisis was nothing but a glitch in time, worth consideration but promptly passed through on a journey to something better. He had taught this to Martha and to David. He rose from the sofa and passed her, placing a kiss on her head and a wink to excuse himself. He shook Jeff's hand and patted Ben's arm as he passed by, and on Natalie's cheek he placed a soft kiss. "I'm going to take a little nap," he said as he climbed the stairs, leaving the Johansons alone.

It was nearly two hours later when the phone rang, awakening him. Martha was nowhere to be seen and he stumbled sleepily down the steps back to the kitchen to an unbelievable sight. There, gathered around a table laden with cookies and crackers and cheese were the completely sleep-deprived, giddy Johansons. Laughter and joyful ribbing accented a lively board game in progress. When Martha saw Sam she giggled and explained.

"Just as we gave each other final hugs and kisses and headed for naps, Jeff found this old game tucked above his closet and begged us to play like old times, and we've been playing ever since."

"Aren't you all exhausted?" Sam asked incredulously.

"Completely!" they all answered in concert. "We're so tired now that we're beyond sleep. I think we're running on pure adrenalin," Natalie added.

"Have you heard anything about David?" Sam asked sleepily.

Martha fielded this one. "The nurse said we should let him sleep for another couple of hours and then we can go and visit him. He's heavily sedated still but doing well. We're going back to the hospital around two."

"I can see I'll have to be today's designated driver." He turned comically, then declared, "Therefore, I am going back to bed." He laughed and winked again at his bride and climbed the stairs.

* * *

It was nearly eleven when Merit rose from bed to the smell of hot muffins baking. Her mother and father were talking softly across the table, but Merit was able to make out the name "Simon," and she felt sure she knew what they were discussing. That very notion had initially crossed her mind her first day at Brighton when she saw how completely smitten her mother was with him. Then, each time she would stop to pick her up or drop her off, the two always made it a point to steal a smile or a hug. At first she was disturbed by the feelings the pair stirred in her, but she had eventually become resigned to it and was now actually intrigued by it.

"So what's all the talk about Simon?" she asked. "Are you going to try to adopt him?"

Merit's casual reference to the possibility took Carol aback, and momentarily made her reconsider her position, but she looked at Mike and the peaceful confirmation returned.

"We've talked about it. I fell in love with that little character that first day we visited Brighton and then I secretly started volunteering there. Two weeks ago I stole part of Simon's file and almost flew to Chicago to confront his father. Cassidy was very forgiving and didn't press charges, but the important thing is *why* I didn't go, Merit. It was because of you. I . . . we feel we have a lot of ground to make up with each other before we can bring another person into our family. We'd like to spend this year enjoying you before you're off to college."

Merit didn't know what to say. A flood of warmth rushed over her as the meaning of her mother's words hit her—she made their family complete. She smiled and replied, "I'd like that."

"No matter what happens in the future, I don't regret this experience with Simon. I now know I can love children again without feeling like I'm betraying Markie. I needed to learn that."

Mike Davenport put his big arms around his wife and made room for Merit too. She was surprised by how disappointed she felt that Simon would not be coming home to live with them as she had assumed, but this closeness felt good and right, and who knew what was yet to come?

* * *

The Johansons passed the rest of Christmas Eve day at the hospital, maintaining a sleepy vigil in David's room. He'd had a bad day that sobered the otherwise joyful family. At least they now knew what they were facing. One kidney was removed early in the morning, but the doctors assured them David would be fine as long as the other continued to function properly. Once the bruised lung posed no further worry, the surgery on his hip was scheduled in the afternoon. It had gone well although the two traumas had taken their toll on the already weakened David, and only time would tell the residual effects the break would leave behind. Even in his sleep his face contorted from discomfort, and the monitors were again connected and beeping all around him. Nurses came in and out, continually checking the machines, listening to his heart and lungs and monitoring his fluids.

The medical consensus was that there was definite tissue and nerve damage on the pads of the fingers of his right hand. A hand specialist suggested they give the tissue more time since these scenarios usually were resolved through auto-amputation when the body sloughed off the dead tissue on its own. Surgery was an option if circumstances warranted it, but the question that now hovered over David was how much tissue was damaged, and what would be the residual impact.

Merit came by in the afternoon for a few minutes right before he was whisked away again. They had only a few moments to talk, but when she left, David marveled with joy at Merit's increasing desire to learn more about what he'd earlier tried to share with her, and he thanked his Heavenly Father for touching her heart.

Chapter Twenty-Nine

Christmas could have been any other day of the year. To the Johansons and their circle of friends, too much had happened, too much had been restored for them to care much for pretty packages and holiday feasts. Most of the day had centered around room 412 of the hospital where David Johanson had been recuperating. The following week was crammed with adjustments and preparations. Jeff and Cassidy had decided to move their wedding day up, so wedding plans were being hastily thrown together, while mission plans were being postponed. To each person, it was clear that a wondrously miraculous chapter was drawing to a close and new, hopefully equally wondrous chapters were about to be written.

It was decided that Jeff and Cassidy would be wed in a simple New Year's Eve ceremony at Brighton. The guests would be few: Jeff's family, the Davis family, the Brighton children, Mrs. Sherman, the Davenports, and Jeff's friend, Dennis Martin, and his family. The volunteers at Brighton had all been invited, but instead insisted to offer their culinary services for the after-wedding supper, which was to be their gift—although they did promise to peek around the corner during the ceremony. Cassidy had called her brothers, who couldn't get away on such short notice, but even Kevin had wished them both well and promised to see them as soon as possible.

The last detail to arrange was getting David to the ceremony. The doctors had intended to keep him hospitalized for a few more days, but owing to the fact that his parents were both medical professionals, they relented. Finding a vehicle that could move him from the farm to Brighton was a bigger problem. Word of the dilemma reached David's original rescue team, and a plan was devised; their names were added to the guest list and they proudly accepted the invitation, planning to arrive by ambulance with David in tow.

Around five o'clock, about the time Cassidy was beginning to dress, the doorbell rang. She paid little attention to it until she heard the bewildered voice of Mrs. Sherman calling to her. When she came to the last step she found herself standing in front of a very large box, beautifully wrapped in pink and silver paper, with a huge silver bow and dozens of curly, silver tendrils cascading all over the top. The swooning began as the children and Mrs. Sherman forgot all about dressing and begged Cassidy to open the enormous gift.

An embossed card was tucked inside a small, satin-lined envelope dangling from one of the silvery ribbon tendrils. Cassidy's hands trembled as she read the card.

> *My first gift of love on the day I give you all my love.*
> *Yours, soon and forever,*
>
> *Jeff*

She wiped a tear from her eyes as the impatient children begged her to rip into the paper. She tried to open it carefully, patiently, but her excitement soon overwhelmed her. Jagged, ripped pieces of wrapping soon covered the floor revealing a brown corrugated box containing layers of white tissue paper. When the paper was finally pulled back and the box's contents were visible, a strange confusion washed over her face, and the children sighed their disappointment. The treasure that was so exquisitely wrapped turned out to be nothing more than an evergreen log!

Mrs. Sherman looked curiously at Cassidy. "Does this mean anything to you?" she asked.

"No . . ." Cassidy began to reply questioningly, and then she saw another envelope tied to the piece of wood. She opened it and pulled out the card.

> *They were topping the old tree at Veterans' Park and I searched through the sawed wood so you'd see how long I've loved you.*
>
> *Jeff*

As Cassidy looked more carefully at the log she could see the dark, carved image cut deep into the evergreen's bark. It was a heart shape with the inscription, "TJ and CB, 1975." It was the section of the tree where Jeff had confessed his secret love for her twenty-two years ago. She ran her fingers lovingly over each of the marks on the wood, considering how the young girl immortalized there would have felt had she discovered it herself.

Mrs. Sherman caught a glimpse of the inscription and understood her friend's thoughtful mood. She placed her finger to her lips, signaling the children to quietly withdraw and return to their dressing, leaving Miss Cassidy alone to think. In a moment Cassidy finally recognized the feeling of weight remaining in the envelope. She shook the white rectangle and a silver trinket fell into her hand. It was a silver wedding-bell charm with a diamond embedded in the center. It would be added to the tree, the sunburst, and the heart that already dangled from her treasured bracelet. She then realized that the bracelet would be her "something old," and the new wedding bell charm would serve as her "something new" for her wedding day. Cassidy lifted the limb from the box and immediately carried it to the mantel and laid it in its new place of honor. Nearly all the pieces of the past were in place now.

The family began arriving around six. The great room was still decorated for Christmas with David's Tree shining in all its glory, but a few additional candles and some flowers now added a matrimonial touch. The ceremony was simple and sweet. Cassidy wore a long white evening dress she had purchased the day before from a local department store. Into her bouquet of white roses were several small, dried, blue flowers from the vase Jeff had brought to their cliff-top breakfast the day he proposed. *Something blue,* she mused.

Mrs. Sherman served as matron of honor and Jeff asked Dennis to be his best man, while the pastor from one of the community churches performed the brief ceremony. Sam walked her down the aisle between rows of seated guests, and as she reached Jeff she raised her hand and jiggled her wrist so Jeff could see the bracelet she now cherished. It had been a mysterious link between them during all those lost years. He smiled a quivering smile, his eyes dancing with light and love, ready to make his vow.

The vows were simple. They cast off the written "textbook" vows and pledged their love, faithfulness, and charity to one another without notes or cues. Merit then accompanied and led the children as they sang an old love song Natalie used to sing to her babies as she rocked them to sleep. As the last sweet note hung in the air, they were pronounced "man and wife" and shared an ardent kiss and a long, tight embrace. There was no formal exit. Family and friends rushed in upon them until their embrace became the center of a budding flower of laughing, crying, hugging people. The children jumped up and down to get a glimpse of whatever was happening in the middle, and finally a few clever ones carefully climbed on top of the gurney where David sat elevated and propped.

Mrs. Sherman and the volunteer ladies of Brighton had prepared a ham supper, and after that was served, the bride and groom cut the magnificent cake. By nine the dishes were done and the group was sitting around the great room negotiating bedtime with the children. Meghan, the precocious surrogate mother to Simon, drew close to Cassidy and sat upon Jeff's knee.

Her head suddenly popped up excitedly. "Babies!" she squealed.

"What babies, Meghan?" Cassidy asked curiously.

"Well, now that there's a mommy and a daddy we'll get babies, right?" she testified with conviction and understanding.

"Well . . . Meghan . . . it, uh, it doesn't work quite like . . ." Cassidy stammered.

In mock scolding Jeff looked at his new bride. "Sweetheart, don't confuse the children." And to Meghan, in complete seriousness he added, "Of course you're right, Meghan. Now that there is a mommy and a daddy there will be babies . . . plenty of babies."

Cassidy gave him a shocked look of laughter as he added, "Now you children go with Mrs. Sherman and get to bed and dream about good names for babies."

"Boy names or girl names?" they questioned.

"Some of each," he replied to raucous laughter.

One by one the friends said their good-byes and began to leave, followed by the medics who made their exit, promising, like fairy godmothers, to return around midnight to pick David up and transport him home to the farm. As the rest of the group resettled from all the commotion, a quiet joy settled over the room.

After a few seconds of silence Sam broke in with an odd remark. "Speaking of babies . . ." and his voice trailed off as he made a silly attempt to look nonchalant until his gaze fell on Martha. She held a blank expression until a smile tugged at the corners of her mouth and a loud snicker finally broke loose.

"You?!" Natalie squealed. "No!" She could hardly dare to believe the news.

Martha's hands went up instantly to stop the rumor. "Noooo, noooo."

"Not yet anyway," countered Sam, and then to Jeff he added, "but we're planning on giving you a run for your money in that department."

Martha punched him. "We are not going for the title, dear. One, maybe two. That's it."

"So when did this all change?" asked Natalie. "You were so sure you didn't want to start a new family."

Martha looked at Sam. "I've felt that way all along, even after we arrived at Thanksgiving. I just didn't think I was a good mother. David is the result of a Johanson team effort. You know, Mom and Dad, that you had as much of a hand in rearing him as I did. It just overwhelmed me. All I could see were all the opportunities to mess up and fail. I knew Sam would be a wonderful father, and he and David assured me I'd be a great mom, but I needed . . . I don't know, the desire or the confidence. Being here was different this year. You two are different this year. I can't explain it. I guess it sounds corny, but I felt so much love here this trip, it made me hungry to have a child."

"Did you know all of this, David?" Natalie asked, surprised at how good her grandson had been at keeping secrets this holiday.

"I knew they were discussing it, but I didn't know Mom had changed her mind until yesterday. I think it's wonderful." He beamed at his mom and Sam and watched how instinctively Sam's arms wrapped around her and how naturally she responded to his loving gesture.

"Oh," sighed Merit as she sat beside David's gurney. "I was just thinking, if they have a baby while you're on your mission, the baby won't even know you when you come home."

David looked knowingly at his parents. "That's why they included me in the discussions. Mom and Dad wanted me to consider that before I made my final decision."

"So despite all this, you're still determined to go?" she asked.

David heard the confusion in her voice and answered gently, "More than ever. I don't just believe I was lucky, Merit. I know I was spared. The Lord has something He wants me to do and I want to try and do it, whatever 'it' is. I don't know how He can use me now, or where, or even when, but I know He will." He measured her reaction and added, "Can you understand that?"

She nodded her head. Her response wasn't joyful, but it was honest. He understood how each crisis had led her to hope that he would stay, and now again she was facing their separation. Jeff saw the disappointment and turned to Sam to change the conversation.

"So, you're leaving early in the morning?" he asked.

"Yeah. I guess you haven't heard the new itinerary since you've been so preoccupied with the wedding and all. I have to be back at the hospital the day after tomorrow, but Martha is staying here for three more weeks until David can travel comfortably, and then they'll all drive him out together so your folks can visit California. Depending on when he's completely healed and they allow him to leave, they might fly back out again for David's farewell."

"That's wonderful," said Cassidy.

"I'll help out around the farm while you're away," offered Jeff. Ben smiled and nodded. His eyes were moist and Jeff's chest tightened with emotion.

David chimed in, "A few days of mucking stalls and you'll wish we hadn't found you."

"No," he replied, his voice husky again. "There's no chance of that ever happening." His eyes met those of each family member and then he leaned over and kissed his bride soundly. "Never," he promised.

"Well," David said to Merit, "it looks like you'll have three extra weeks to pity and adore me. I guess we'll have to find a new hobby," he said looking at his wounded hands. It was true, there would be no more piano for David, at least for the near future. It was doubtful all the once-frozen tissue could be saved, so there would be no more flirtatious piano duets with Merit. They also warned him that he would have a residual limp from the fractured hip and thigh; but he was alive, and getting stronger every day. He would yet serve his mission, and Merit would write.

"Actually, I already have a new hobby for the next three weeks."

"You do?" he said sadly. "Doing what?"

"The night of the children's program, when I ended up filling in at the piano for a certain no-show . . ." She bumped his arm affectionately. "Well, one of the guests was a friend of the mayor who's a big patron at the Peabody Institute of Music. He arranged an audition for me in front of the director in February! There's no guarantees, but it's a nice opportunity." Her face was lit with excitement, but as she hugged him his face registered joy and sadness. He knew he would be moving forward but he hadn't allowed himself to consider where the next two years might take *her*. "So you, sir, will have to endure hours of listening to me while I rehearse."

David got it now, and the warm, knowing smile that spread across his face registered it completely. She knew that listening to her and watching her play were about his favorite things to do. It would be a glorious three weeks.

"Well," he teased back, "if the diva wants an audience she'll have to suffer through on the old Johanson upright since poor Davy is an invalid. He can't walk or take care of himself because he was trying to do something romantic and wonderful for a heartless entertainer . . ."

"Oh, you!" Merit smacked him.

He leaned forward and whispered, "Watching you play? It's the best medicine I could get."

"I love to play for you. I always see you when I play," she whispered back as tears welled up in her eyes. "I always will."

"Really?" asked David. "Really . . ." he repeated to himself with great thought as a faraway look came over him. "Then we had it!"

"Had what?" Merit asked.

"Our memory, Merit," he spoke seriously now. "Through the accident and the surgery and everything else these past two weeks, the one overwhelming regret I had was that we wouldn't have a 'moment' to hold onto while we are apart. Even when I was lying in the snow, and when I was in the emergency room, my greatest regret was that I didn't leave you with any special moment to remember me by . . . so you'd know that. . . "

"That for this moment . . . we loved each other?" Merit asked.

David looked at her and his still-bruised eyes were now moist. "Yes," he said hoarsely. "That we *love* each other." He took her in his arms. It was all right. They both understood. Soon, he was going to leave and she understood why.

Jeff looked into Cassidy's eyes. She smiled and stole a look at the clock, indicating that it was soon time for them to go.

"Before Cassidy and I leave, David has a gift he wanted to share with you tonight and he asked me to help him out since he can't do it himself."

Jeff left the room, leaving his curious audience looking at David and murmuring their questions. The back door opened and then closed, and then the sound of Jeff's footsteps could be heard approaching. In his arms he carried a log tied with a big red bow. One end was splintered and broken and the other was clean cut. He handed the log to Ben and then nodded to David who began to explain the significance of the log to everyone but Ben. No one needed to tell him what it was. He knew the second he saw the splintered end.

"This is our family Yule log. It's from David's Tree," David explained. "It's the bottom section that was splintered off when the truck ran over it. I couldn't let them toss it out. Somehow, it just didn't seem right. The day I found the tree was the day I met Merit and the day Jeff found Cassidy. It was also the day before the morning I told you all about my decision to be a missionary and shared my testimony with you. I thought, since it's such a part of each of us, we should burn it together tonight. So I'm giving it to you, Pap. You always thought this tree was your sign that God heard your prayers and that one day the family would be gathered back to the farm. Well, it seems as though you were right."

Ben pressed his lips to still their trembling, and nodded. His eyes were shining and his hands shook as he lifted the log from his lap and walked to the fireplace. Jeff had already set a bed of kindling in place, and so when Ben struck the match and touched it to the ribbon, the fire quickly caught. As if drawn like fireflies to the flame, the rest of the family rose and drew a circle around Ben, and Sam wheeled David in to close it. Ben turned toward his grandson and put his arms around his neck and kissed his hair.

"Dear Lord, thank you," he whispered.

A contemplative silence fell over the family. Natalie drew close to Ben and smiled. "Whatever will we do in that big empty house after all this company and commotion?"

Ben gave the question some serious thought and then replied. "Well, for starters . . ." He wrapped his arms around her and looked deeply into her eyes. " . . . I'm going to chase my lovely wife around the house, and when I catch her . . ." He raised his eyebrows and gave a flirtatious wink.

"And when you catch her, you're going to what?" Natalie asked boldly.

Ben framed her face in his hands, pressed his lips to her forehead, and spoke in a husky voice. "I'm going to tell her how much I adore her, always have, from the first time I saw her in the canteen. I'm going to tell her how grateful I am to God for her, and how she made me a better man than I ever could have hoped to be."

"And then . . ." Natalie asked behind moist eyes.

Ben smiled again. "And then . . ." He picked her up in his arms as humor gave way to affection. " . . . I am going to do this." He lifted his elbow to raise her head and he kissed her. She waited, thinking he would pull back from his sweet gentle kiss, but he didn't, and her arms instinctively slid up around his neck and held him tightly in a moment filled with the love they had first known. No, with a love deeper than the love they had first known, because they knew that greater than the passion of discovery was the passion of history.

David looked at these two people who had shaped so much of who he was and for a moment he was afraid to leave for two years. What if either or both of them weren't there when he returned. What would he do? Then the understanding of eternal life that Sam had brought into his life washed over him and filled him with peace. Still, he wondered what his life would be like when they were gone. Could their family continue without Omma and Pap? And then he looked at Sam, good strong Sam and his gentle mother, and felt the same security with them. He would love Omma and Pap every day of his life, but he knew that when their time would come to part, the family would carry on. The legacy was set.

Perhaps it was Jeff who had come to understand his parents' example best. It was simply that they had been there. They had loved him though he'd rejected them and their name—and they loved the man he was now, Jeff Johanson, a son proud to reclaim all he had once treated as dross. No matter what happened now, or how long they would have together, their lessons would last. And though he had not yet spoken to Sam or David about what it meant to be together forever, today he felt he was on his way to comprehending it. He finally understood that love didn't run. Love stood its ground and defended its home. And Jeff was a runner no more. He was rooted, solidly, in his family tree.

ABOUT THE AUTHOR

Laurie Lewis was born in Baltimore, Maryland, in 1957, and is a 1975 graduate of South Carroll High School in Carroll County, Maryland. She attended Brigham Young University and Hagerstown Community College. She was married in 1976 to her high school sweetheart, Tom Lewis, and the couple are the parents of four wonderful children: Tom, Amanda, Adam, and Joshua. They were recently blessed by the birth of their first grandchild when their son, Tom, and daughter-in-law, Krista, had a little boy named Tommy.

Laurie has always loved to write and sing, and has taken every available opportunity to do both whenever possible. Her amateur writing career includes a series of short stories and a collection of Christmas pieces, as well as various motivational works for young people. She has always had a special fondness for working with youth. She spent seven years working in the public school system in the very high school from which she graduated, and she currently teaches early morning seminary in her hometown of Mount Airy, Maryland.

Unspoken is Laurie's first published novel.